Peabody's familiar clump. It didn't surprise her to hear McNab's—her partner's cohab, and e-man—prance along with it.

"Passcoded." Without looking, Eve held up the 'link. "Seal up, fix that."

"Will do," McNab said cheerfully.

"Shit, damn, *jeez*!" Peabody, her red-streaked black hair bouncing with curls, crouched beside Eve. "That's Brant Fitzhugh. McNab, it's Brant Fitzhugh."

"Yeah, it is. That's a major low."

"We love his vids. Man, he's really great-looking. Even dead. Shit, I can smell almonds. Cyanide. Who'd want to cyanide Brant Fitzhugh?"

"You know, I was just wondering the same thing. Strangely, it's our job to figure that out. Big party," Eve continued as she looked at her partner—and the flouncy, low-cut dress with the skinny shoulder straps. "Looks like you had a party."

"Date night, salsa dancing. We're getting less sucky at it."

"Standard five-digit passcode, Dallas." McNab, in shiny red skin pants, collarless polka-dot shirt, held out the 'link.

"Take a quick look, since you're here, then bag it. Big party," she repeated, "so we've got close to two hundred guests, add staff—catering and personal—tucked away. The new widow's upstairs in her bedroom with a friend and a doctor."

"The widow's Eliza Lane. You know, right? Eliza Lane," Peabody repeated. "She's, like, legendary."

"She sure as hell will be if she put the cyanide in her husband's champagne."

"Probably not. I know the spouse is first on the list," Peabody continued, "but their romance, marriage, all of it? Also legendary." Frowning, Peabody studied the body while Eve emptied the other pocket contents into an evidence bag. "No cheating on either side—and you know the gossip media's always sniffing for that. They're both loaded, so it wouldn't be money. He was about to start shooting a major vid—and he's one of the exec producers, too—in, like, I think, New Zealand, and she's heading back to Broadway for a revival of *Upstage*. She played the daughter decades ago, and it made her a star. Now she's playing the mother, who's the actual star."

Eve simply stared. "How do you know all that?"

Peabody just lifted her shoulders. "I like that stuff."

"Okay." Eve stood up. "McNab, you start with the guests—uniforms on that, too. Have one of them sit on the body for now. Some of the guests are media types."

"Crap."

"Yeah. Peabody, bring in the sweepers, the morgue. Considering the dead guy and the spouse, this is going to be high-profile, so we definitely want Morris. Then take the caterers. We'll hit the live-ins and assistants after, but we're going to need to let some of these people go. I'll take the spouse."

She started up the long curve of stairs. She heard voices behind a set of closed doors, thought witnesses, and kept going.

She opened other doors as she went. A slick, masculine home office with posters of the victim in leather, hair flying, sword in hand, on horseback with a flat-brimmed hat and gun belt, another of him holding a martini glass and dressed in a tux.

She'd make use of McNab with the data and communication center on the big black-and-silver desk.

She avoided another door from where she heard numerous voices, found a guest room—more luxury—a powder room, another office. From the decor—feminine elegance, a wall of photos of the widow alone or with other luminaries, a lot of trophies—she assigned it to the widow.

She approached the double doors at the end of the hall, gave one brisk knock, and opened it.

A woman in a red dress lay on a bed with an arm tossed over her eyes. Beside her, a woman with a fall of reddish-brown hair held her free hand. A man—silver hair, dark suit, active physique—paced in front of the terrace doors.

"It's you!" The woman who sat turned red-rimmed green eyes to Eve. "Oh, thank God! You're Dallas."

"That's right."

"Eliza, sweetie, you're in good hands now. You and—and Brant are in good hands. We were just talking about her, remember? She's the best of the best. I think. I hope. Oh, Eliza."

"I can't, Sylvie. I can't. I can't. Brant. My Brant."

"Officer—"

"Lieutenant," Eve said, and turned to the man as he crossed to her.

"Of course, I'm sorry. Lieutenant, I'm James Cyril. Dr. Cyril. I asked the MTs to give Ms. Lane a sedative. Mild, hardly more than a soother."

"You're Ms. Lane's personal physician?"

"Oh, no, no. I came as Roland's plus-one. Roland Adderson. We've been friends for years, and he knew I was a particular admirer of Ms. Lane. He's the assistant director on her new production of *Upstage*, and—I suppose it doesn't matter."

"Let's step outside for a minute."

She went out into the hall. "This is the first time you've met Ms. Lane?"

"Yes, and Mr. Fitzhugh. It was such a lovely, exciting night until . . ."

"Walk me through what you saw, what you did."

"Of course." He looked to the closed doors. "She's just devastated. I was on the terrace. I was having the time of my life, meeting all these people in theater, in vids, and in such a setting. Then I heard Eliza—Ms. Lane—start to sing."

He pressed a hand to his heart. "The opening from 'Is It Your Life or Mine?' I came in, and I stood just feet away from her and the young actress who'll play her daughter. Beyond thrilling. Then I heard glass break. I thought nothing of it at first, but someone shouted, someone screamed, and everyone crowded around. Ms. Lane rushed over, and I heard her scream her husband's name. That's when I went over, and saw him on the floor, gasping for air.

"I moved in to try to assist, shouted for someone to call for the medicals, ordered people to move back, give him air, room, but he started to convulse. Eliza was trying to cradle him in her arms, kept saying his name. I told her I was a doctor, and to let me try to help him."

He shook his head. "She wouldn't let him go, but begged me to help him. Unfortunately it was already too late. Even though the MTs came so quickly, there was nothing that could be done. I smelled almonds. I've told no one that, as Ms. Lane was already inconsolable, and I felt I should tell someone in charge. So I am. I believe Mr. Fitzhugh ingested cyanide."

"What happened next?"

"I asked them to give her something to calm her, mild, as I knew the police would come. The MTs would recognize the signs of poisoning as I did. Then Ms. Bowen and I helped Ms. Lane upstairs."

"You were on the terrace. Did you see where Mr. Fitzhugh got the champagne?"

"No, I'm sorry. I didn't know it was champagne. There was broken glass, a spill." He glanced at the heel of his hand.

"Cut yourself?"

"Just a nick. I used the en suite to clean it after Ms. Lane came out. Just a scratch. I didn't see where he got the glass. And at the point when I came in, to be honest, I was so focused on Eliza I didn't see anyone else until it happened."

Could've been the point, Eve thought. Taking advantage of everyone looking one way, hand the victim the poisoned champagne.

"I appreciate your help and your cooperation, Dr. Cyril. I'll need your contact information in case we have any follow-up questions."

"Of course. Such a tragedy. A horrible thing. Someone they invited into their home did this horrible thing."

People did horrible things every day, she thought as she took his information. It was her job to see they didn't get away with it.

Once again she gave a brisk knock and opened the door.

She had her first good look at Eliza Lane, as the widow sat up in bed now, wrapped in the arms of her friend.

The eyes that had been bright and clear in the portrait were cloudy from the sedative, swollen from weeping. But they looked directly at Eve.

"I'm all right, Sylvie. I'll be all right." She eased back. "You're the policewoman from the Icove vid."

"No, that was an actor. I'm Lieutenant Dallas, NYPSD."

"Lieutenant Dallas, NYPSD, you're going to find out who did this to my husband, to my partner, to the love of my goddamn life. And make them pay. It'll never be enough." She covered her mouth with both hands, stifled sobs while her eyes went fierce. "Never be enough."

"Eliza—"

"No, no, I won't start up again. I won't. Please, Sylvie, get some water, will you? The dressing room friggie. I shouldn't have let them give me the damn sedative." She pushed herself off the bed. "I'm muddled, and I don't want to be muddled. I want to be clear."

She moved to the terrace doors, struggled to push them open.

"I need some air."

Eve moved over, opened them for her.

"I feel a little sick, but I'm not going to be sick. Some air, some water. A minute to get my head clear."

"Ms. Lane, why do you believe someone caused your husband's death?"

"Because I saw him, I saw my Brant. He was . . . he was dying in my arms, and his fingernails were going blue. I smelled the almonds. I know you did, too," she said to Sylvie when her friend came out with glasses of water on a small tray.

"Oh, Eliza, yes. Oh God, I did. But—"

"Cyanide. Just like in *Body of the Crime*."

"The body of what crime?"

"A vid," Sylvie explained while fresh tears leaked. "Eliza and I met making that vid."

"Sylvie and I played sisters, it must be fifteen years ago now. Sylvie's character put cyanide in brandy, to kill a man pursuing me for my fortune. A man she loved, who betrayed her for money and planned to kill me."

Eliza sat, took the water, sipped slowly.

"But none of that was real. Oh, Sylvie, how could this be real? What happens now? Will they take him away? Will they take Brant away? Why would anyone want to hurt him? He never hurt anyone. Why would someone do this?"

"I'm sorry for your loss, Ms. Lane. There are questions I need to ask."

"Should I leave?"

"Oh, no, no." Eliza reached for Sylvie's hand. "Please, can she stay? Please."

"All right. Why don't you sit down, Ms. Bowen? We'll make this as quick as possible."

2

Eve took a seat facing Eliza.

"Do you have any idea who'd want to hurt your husband?"

"God, no! Brant got along with everyone."

"He hadn't received any threats?"

"No. He'd have told me. We shared everything."

"Someone he argued with recently," Eve pressed. "Even if it seemed minor to him, to you."

"I really . . ." She looked blankly at Sylvie. "There's nothing I can think of. Brant didn't like conflict, and found ways to avoid it."

"That's true," Sylvie confirmed. "Brant loved his life, his work. He's very active in Home Front—an organization working to provide safe, affordable housing."

"He was so generous," Eliza murmured. "With his time as well as his money. Professionally, anyone who worked with him would say the same, wouldn't they, Sylvie? He was generous as an actor."

"Were there any problems in your marriage?"

Eliza jerked as if struck. "How could you—"

"It's a question I have to ask, Ms. Lane."

"We *adored* each other. Not a day went by when he didn't show me what I meant to him. We were one, Lieutenant. Lovers, partners, soul mates."

Weeping again, she lurched up, walked to the terrace wall.

Sylvie moved to her, rubbed a hand up and down Eliza's back. "I know it's horrible, I know. But she has to know, sweetie. It's for Brant. You didn't ask me, Lieutenant, but Eliza and I have been friends, the best of friends, for fifteen years. She'd have told me if she and Brant had problems."

"Sorry. I'm sorry." Turning back, Eliza wiped her hands over her face. "Of course you have to ask. And I expect you'll ask if either of us had affairs. We didn't. I've been cheated on, Lieutenant Dallas. I know what it feels like, looks like, hell, smells like. Brant . . . he was an honest and honorable man. Did he have opportunities? Did I? Absolutely. But we loved each other, and just as important, we respected each other."

"All right." She'd come back to that, try another angle on it, but for now, move on. "You were by the piano, performing, when Mr. Fitzhugh collapsed."

"Yes." Now she gripped the water glass in both hands. "The party was a celebration of the revival, so all the cast and crew, the money people, the media. Samantha—that's Samantha Keene—plays my daughter. She's brilliant, but still a bit shy socially. I thought we'd do a duet, from the play."

"And before that? Do you know where your husband was?"

"With me. Sylvie and I were talking, back near the foyer, watching the party, taking a moment, I suppose you'd say. Brant came over to bring me a champagne cocktail. I suppose we chatted for another minute, then I decided—no, Brant asked . . . We needed to mingle?"

As Eliza rubbed a hand at her temple, Sylvie shifted. "I suggested it. I remember. I said it was time for me to mingle, and time for you to give us a song."

"That's right. That's right. So I thought of Samantha, and I handed Brant my glass and went to get her. As I hoped, people circled around. Then someone screamed, and Brant—Brant was on the floor, and he was choking and gasping.

"It doesn't seem real." Panic flew into her eyes again as she clutched at her friend. "How can this be real?"

"You handed him your glass of champagne?" Eve prompted.

"Yes, I wanted to have my hands free. The number, the duet, there's a lot of gesturing and business, so I—"

"Did he have another glass, or just yours?"

She frowned now, eyebrows drawing tight together. "I—I don't know. No, I don't think . . . Sylvie?"

"He didn't. He offered to get me a fresh glass, but I was fine."

"Did you drink it?" Eve pressed. "The champagne?"

"No. We were all talking. You have to be careful not to overdrink at a party or in public. We were talking, then I handed it off, then . . ."

She groped blindly for her friend's hand as she stared at Eve, as awareness crept into her eyes. "Oh my God. Oh my God. I gave him the champagne. I gave him the poison. I killed him!"

"He brought it to you. Where would he have gotten it?"

"I don't know. I don't know. Sylvie, I just pushed it at him. 'Here, hold this while I go sing and dance so everyone watches me.' And now he's gone."

"You stop." Sylvie snapped it out. "And you think, Eliza. You stop and you think. The champagne and what was in it was for you."

"Brant would never—"

"Of course he'd never. He didn't know. You didn't know. Jesus, he'd hardly have drunk it if he knew. He drank it because it was there, in his hand. As, God, you'd have done if I hadn't said to give us a song. The poison was meant for you."

"We won't assume anything at this point," Eve interrupted. "You have bars set up on the main level."

"Yes. Three spread out, and with two servers passing wine and champagne. Brant—Brant most often likes a single malt or a good beer, though he wouldn't drink hard liquor at a party like this. We're careful, and he had early meetings tomorrow before he left for location. I like a champagne cocktail, so that's what he brought to me. He drank it because I handed it to him. He toasted me with it. Oh Christ, I can see him in the crowd, toasting me as we did the duet."

"Who'd know he intended that glass for you and not himself?"

"Anyone might. I couldn't say. He'd often do just that at a party. Bring me a champagne cocktail, twist of lemon. Because it's my favorite. He looked after me in countless little ways."

It changed things, Eve thought, at least potentially. And the potential ranked strongly enough to change her angle.

"Have you received any threats? Or do you know of someone who might wish you harm?"

"No. I mean— God, my head's spinning. I need a minute. Can I have a minute?" She shoved up again, paced around the spacious terrace.

"I don't have Brant's skill with people, with situations. We joked that he got his share of patience and tact and at least half of mine. I like to think I'm a kind and decent person, but not everyone would agree. While I'm absolutely sure there are any number of people who'd be delighted if I retired to a villa in the south of Who Gives a Fuck, I can't think of one who'd murder me. Jesus, Sylvie, even Vera doesn't hate me that much."

"Vera?"

"Vera Harrow. A colleague. Competitor, I suppose, at least in her mind. We did a vid together a decade ago. Brant was the male lead—

it's where we met. At the time he and Vera were involved. Not married," she added. "Not committed, but involved. In any case, Vera and I just rubbed each other the wrong way. Our styles, our worldviews, you could say. Still, we were both professional, and skilled enough it didn't show on-screen. We were both up for a Golden Globe. I won; she didn't. But more to the point, Brant and I fell in love. He broke things off with her, and we were married a short time later."

"She'd be happy to poison Eliza to the media, to the fans, to industry professionals." Sylvie gestured with her water glass. "But she wouldn't go so far as to poison her drink, or Brant's."

"Was she here tonight?"

"Yes. Vera's based in New York now. She's doing a series that wrapped its very successful sophomore year a few months ago," Sylvie supplied. "She's got her Golden Globe now—in fact, three or four of them, and a pair of Emmys, and a frosty young lover—her plus-one tonight. She may hold a grudge like a toddler holds a teddy bear, but she wouldn't risk all to pay Eliza back for Brant, or him back for Eliza."

"Anyone else with a grudge?"

"Probably." Coming back to sit, Eliza dropped her head into her hands. "I'm pushy, I'm exacting, and I don't consider either of those flaws. Onstage, on-screen, I'm going to give you my very best, each time, every time. And I damn well expect anyone on that stage or screen with me, or behind them, to do the same."

"Employees? Anyone unhappy with the exacting push, anyone you've let go?"

"More than one, but not recently. Cela—she handles the professional end of things—media, meetings. She's held that position for four—no, five years now. And Dolby, my personal assistant who handles everything, has only been with me for three, but if I didn't have Brant and Dolby wasn't gay, we'd build ourselves a love nest. He's another soul mate."

"Domestic help?"

"Wayne and Cara Rowan—he's our cook, she runs the house. Seven years now, and they're like family. Then there's Lin, Brant's right hand—much more than a personal assistant. Lin's been with Brant for at least fifteen years—I think more—and travels with him. There's Marta, Lin's assistant for the last—I'm not sure—four or five years, I think."

"All of them here tonight?"

"Dolby and Cela, Wayne and Cara, Lin, all of them, certainly. I believe Marta—she'd have been expected, but I don't know if I saw her. So much is a blur now. No, wait! God!" She covered her face with her hands, breathed through them before she dropped them. "Marta's already in New Zealand. She left yesterday or maybe the day before."

"You'd have had a caterer tonight, and that staff."

"Yes, I've used All Elegance for, God, it must be a dozen years. Georgia—the owner—and I worked on all the details. Food, drink, staffing, serving dishes, and so on, and with In Bloom florists for the flowers."

"You have a guest list?"

"Yes, yes, of course. Dolby can get that for you. Lieutenant, they took Brant away. I know they've taken him, but I need to see him. I need to—to say goodbye."

"I can arrange for that tomorrow, and I'll contact you. Who would benefit from your death, Ms. Lane?"

"Brant. Of course Brant." She pressed a hand to her mouth, closed her eyes briefly. "There are other beneficiaries. If you'd ask Cela to give you the information for my estate handlers. They'd have all of that."

"And Mr. Fitzhugh? Who would benefit?"

"Financially, I would. And the same. Lin would have the information you need. I know he intended to leave a large monetary gift to

Home Front, as we discussed it. In solidarity, I also have them as ben-eficiaries. Lieutenant, both Brant and I have had very long, successful careers. Money wasn't an issue."

Money, Eve thought, was always an issue.

But she rose. "Thank you. I know this is difficult. Is there somewhere you can stay until we clear your apartment?"

"I have to leave?"

"I'm sure that's best, sweetie. We'll pack what you need, and you'll stay with me for a while. My apartment's just two floors down," Sylvie told Eve.

"That's helpful. You can contact me at any time if you think of some-thing, any detail that may help. Again, I'm very sorry for your loss."

"You'll tell me when I can see him? When I can see Brant? Please."

"Yes. Tomorrow. Meanwhile, Dr. Morris will look after him."

"Thank you. Thank you for that. They took him from me, Lieutenant. I know they took him from the world, too, but I don't care about that right now. I don't care if they wanted to take me, because they took him from me. You have to find them, find them so I can look them in the eye and wish them to hell."

Eve started downstairs and met Peabody on her way up.

"Oh, you're finished with her?" Longing eyes scanned over Eve's shoulder. "I was hoping to meet her."

"You'll have that opportunity before we're finished. You got state-ments from the staff?"

"Began with the catering staff." They started down where the sweepers in their white protective gear spread out over the living area, out on the terrace. "The owner always works Lane's parties and was in the catering kitchen—they have a freaking second kitchen just for that—when Fitzhugh collapsed. Five wits in there with her who all confirm she'd never left the kitchen since the party started. Started running through the rest of the catering staff and hit on the one who made the cocktail—but not for Fitzhugh, she claims. He told her, specifically, it was for Lane. Champagne cocktail, twist of lemon."

"That tracks. He brought it to her, then the friend who's up there with her suggested she do a number, so she passed the drink back to Fitzhugh."

"No way he'd have downed it if he'd known."

"Unless he wanted to self-terminate at a party." Eve shrugged. "Can't get her with it, so fuck it, I'm going out. Not likely, but . . . Did you run her?"

"Yeah, Monika Kajinski, age twenty-six. No dings on her record. She's only been with the catering company for about six months. Doubles working as bartender at Du Vin. I think you know that one."

"Shit. Roarke's."

"And she's been on the bar there a couple years. She came right out with the fact she mixed the drink. No bullshit about it. She said Fitzhugh told her exactly how Ms. Lane liked it, complimented her tat—she has a little sunflower on her left thumb—and was chatting with someone he called Lin."

"Personal assistant."

"He thanked her, and he and this Lin walked away together."

"Where was her station?"

"The terrace. She said she noticed they walked inside together, but that was it. She was busy, at least until Lane started singing. Most everyone drifted inside, or at least to the doors. Then she heard the first scream."

"Hold it there. You've still got her?"

"Yeah. I'm using the butler's pantry. They've got one of those, too. I put a couple chairs in there so I could take people one at a time. She's in there now. I figured you'd want to know it looks like Lane was the target. But you already did."

"Lead the way."

"Okay. This place is enormous," Peabody told her. "They actually bought two units, combined them. And one would've been a hell of a lot of space. Formal dining room," Peabody pointed out, and Eve judged it would seat at least thirty. "Then there's another one, I guess for more intimate dinner parties. The cook and housekeeper—a married couple—have their quarters over there, then you've got the main kitchen, which even though I'm getting the kitchen of my dreams, I envy. Not the decor—too lab-like and sleek—but the space."

Eve paused a moment, glanced around. "You could have a freaking rodeo in here."

"Not my first thought, but sure. Catering kitchen through there—and that's where we've got the rest of the staff. Butler's pantry."

Peabody opened a set of white pocket doors.

The woman popped up from a low-backed steel chair between long white counters. She had short black hair with spiky bangs over almond-shaped brown eyes and lips dyed stoplight red that set off creamy light brown skin.

"Monika, Lieutenant Dallas."

"I know, I know. Jesus. I just made the drink. I swear to God. La Fleur champagne, six dashes of bitters, one white sugar cube—real sugar, not fake. Twist of lemon."

"Got it. You also work at Du Vin?"

"Oh God, oh God, I wasn't even there when that gossip reporter was killed. But I'm starting to wonder if I'm bad luck."

"Relax. Sit down."

"I can sit, but I don't know if I'll ever relax again. I made the drink. But it was just a drink."

"Then how do you know it was the drink that killed Mr. Fitzhugh?"

"Because people were buzzing around, talking about poison, and the cops. And oh God, when I came inside, I saw him on the floor, and I saw the broken glass. Am I under arrest?"

"No. Who was talking about poison?"

"I don't know. Wait, um, Jed—one of the servers. He was standing next to me, and he said, like: Holy shit, somebody must've poisoned his drink. Something about his face. He came in with me, Jed, I mean. He was serving the terrace."

"You told Detective Peabody Mr. Fitzhugh was talking to someone while you made the drink."

"He called him Lin. They were really friendly, laughing. Um, something about heading out of summer into winter."

"And they walked back into the living room together."

"That's right."

"Did anyone follow them?"

"Not that I noticed. I was pretty busy. I did see Mr. Fitzhugh stop to talk to a couple people. This woman, she had a killer dress. I don't mean killer!"

"What did she look like?"

"I think she's somebody—she looked like somebody. Tall, a lot of boobs, blond hair. I mostly noticed the dress. Gold and shiny and cut down to her navel, practically, and to her ass crack in the back, with these glittery crisscrosses holding it together. Anyway, I caught him talking to her for a minute and saw them do one of those kiss-kiss deals, and how she jammed those boobs into him. Then I got busy, and I didn't notice where he went after."

"Okay, Monika, we appreciate it. If you think of anything else, please contact us."

"That's it? I can go home? You're not going to arrest me?"

"For mixing a drink and cooperating with the police? I don't think so."

Monika let out a shaky breath, pressed her fingers to her eyes. "Okay. Okay. Thanks." She got up. "I want to say, he was really nice.

Mr. Fitzhugh. He looks at you. I don't mean like coming-on-to-you look. Just that a lot of people don't look at you when you're making a drink or serving. And he did. I'm really sorry about what happened."

When she left, Eve turned to Peabody. "See if the killer dress is still here, Peabody, and send this Lin in."

"Got it."

He got the drink on the terrace, Eve thought, letting herself see it in her head as she wandered the area, opened what turned out to be a liquor cabinet—freaking alphabetized, she noted.

He tells the bartender it's for his wife, and how she likes it. Anyone could overhear, she decided, and found a cabinet filled with glassware— sparkling and arranged by size and use.

Or, according to the wife, many would know it was for her. He's with his assistant. So opportunity there. Stops to talk to Killer Dress, another opportunity. Makes his way through the crowd, and very likely stops here and there to mingle. More opportunities.

She continued to imagine it as she found serving dishes, bar tools.

A hand on his arm. "Hey, Brant, great party." Kiss-kiss, handshake, guy hug. Easy enough to drop a little poison in the glass heading for Eliza Lane.

But she doesn't drink it. The good friend suggests she perform. Coincidence—which is bollocks. Or just twist of fate, bad timing, both of which could happen.

But damn conveniently.

Then again.

Lane hands the glass back and goes to the piano. Fitzhugh moves into the crowd. More, plenty more opportunities to doctor the drink. Not his usual drink, but instead of just holding it, he toasts his wife and seals the toast by drinking.

Did the killer expect that, or not?

Which one was the intended victim?

As she leaned back against one of the long white counters, Peabody stepped in with a man, about five-eight, with a tough, muscular build filling out a suit the color of crushed raspberries. His eyes, lion tawny, showed signs of weeping. He sported a ruler-straight, narrow scruff along his jawline and a thick mane of brown hair.

"Lieutenant, Mr. Linwood Jacoby, Mr. Fitzhugh's personal assistant."

"And friend." He spoke in a voice thick with tears. "Brant was my friend."

"We're sorry for your loss, Mr. Jacoby."

"I lost my brother to addiction five years ago. I thought I'd never know a loss that deep. I was wrong. What the hell happened?"

"That's what we're here to find out. Please, sit down."

"I need to do something. Anything."

"You will be. How long have you known Mr. Fitzhugh?"

"Ah, seventeen years, I guess it is. They hired me to beef him up. I was a personal trainer, and the studio wanted Brant to put on more muscle, and to sharpen up his martial arts skills. I'd worked with other actors, built a good rep there, so I worked with Brant for ten weeks before they started shooting *Warrior King*. We hit it off, and he asked me to work with him through the production."

"And you became his assistant."

"Trainer, assistant, friend. I stood up for him when he married Eliza. When my brother died, he was with me for the memorial."

"You were with him shortly before he collapsed."

"We were on the terrace, at the bar. He wanted to take Eliza a drink. We talked a few minutes, then I walked inside with him. I peeled off to mingle, and Vera cornered him."

"That's Vera Harrow?"

"Yeah, and I don't mean corner like that." He scrubbed his hands over his face. "Vera and I aren't especially friendly."

"But she and Fitzhugh were?"

"They had a history—and I mean history. They had a thing for a few months, but that was a decade ago. Then Brant met Eliza, and, well, stars burst, angels sang." He smiled a little.

"She and Brant get along fine. Brant has a way of getting along. But me? I'm the hired help as she sees it, and she makes sure I know it. So I steer clear if we're in the same space."

"Where were you when Mr. Fitzhugh collapsed?"

"I was in the main dining room, talking to Dolby—that's Eliza's assistant. I was actually getting ready to slip out. Great party, but I had a lot to do tomorrow before we left for location. And then Eliza and Samantha started the duet. I sort of hung back, figuring I'd wait until they finished, then ease my way out. Then . . ."

He closed his eyes. "Okay, then somebody screamed, and people either pushed back or rushed forward. I didn't see Brant at first, but I started to go over, see what was wrong, how I could help. People were shouting and scrambling around, and somebody yelled out to call for a medical team. And that's when I saw him, on the floor."

He paused, looked away as tears swirled into his eyes again. "Eliza was down with him, and a man I heard after was a doctor. And Brant's face was red, and he was shaking—seizing. I shoved my way through. It was all so fast, so insane.

"I watched him die, right there on the floor. I watched the light go out of his eyes. I watched him stop fighting to breathe. He was just gone, and Eliza was pulling him into her arms and rocking and wailing."

He knuckled away tears.

"I had to pull her away from him when the MTs got here. She fought me, but they needed to work on him. If there was a chance—I knew there wasn't, but if I was wrong . . . I held on to her, and Dolby helped, tried to calm her down, but she was crying so hard. And one of the MTs gave her a sedative. Sylvie—Sylvie Bowen and the doctor . . . I'm sorry, I never got his name—took Eliza upstairs. We tried to keep everyone calm until the police got here. Somebody called for the police.

"People were saying heart attack, stroke, but I thought, no, no. He was in perfect shape. He'd had a complete physical just last week— studio policy—since he'd start shooting in New Zealand in a few days. And I heard somebody say poison, say cyanide. I thought, ridiculous, dramatic, but when the police got here, I started to wonder, so I looked it up on my 'link. Was he really poisoned?"

"The medical examiner will determine cause of death. As his assistant, his longtime friend, you'd know if anyone held a grudge against him, if he'd received any threats."

"I can honestly say Brant is—was—one of the best-liked people in the business. He never threw his weight around, and he could have. He took his work seriously, and was always, always prepared. But he also found the fun in it and never took himself too seriously. Now, he would, occasionally, get a letter—the you sucked in whatever vid— and some were on the ugly side, but nothing like a credible threat. Certainly some in the business might have envied him, but he just had a way of defusing resentments and charming people. He avoided conflict and controversy."

"Former employees, former relationships."

"He's had the same agent and the same manager throughout his career. His assistant before me? He helped her land a bit but meaty part in one of his vids—that's what she wanted, and he helped her. She's had a low-key but solid career ever since. His ex-wife? They parted as amicably as you can, and he ended up introducing her to her current husband. They just had their second kid."

Lin shrugged. "That's Brant. Give me something to do, Lieutenant. I need to do something, anything that can help."

"Mr. Fitzhugh had a home office?"

"Yes, second floor."

"Did he have an office outside the home?"

"No, we worked here. Dolby, Cela, Marta, and I have office space on the third floor."

"We're going to need to go through those spaces, and the electronics. Detective Peabody can take you to Detective McNab—he's with EDD. If you can give him any passcodes, provide any personal devices other than what Mr. Fitzhugh had on him at the time of his death."

"Yes, yes, I can do that. I'd be happy to do that. Eliza. Is there anything I can do for her?"

"She'll stay with her friend Ms. Bowen for a few days."

"Oh. That's good. But . . . will I be able to take her, to go with her when . . . She'll want to see Brant. She'll need to."

"We'll contact you. Peabody, take Mr. Jacoby to McNab, and bring in Dolby Kessler."

"If you'd come with me, Mr. Jacoby."

He rose.

"I know this isn't really relevant, but I saw *The Icove Agenda*. Twice. Brant worked with Marlo once—one of her first vids—and he'd worked with Julian. After it came out that Julian was nearly killed, and his personal issues became public, Brant reached out to him."

"Did he?"

"Offered help. Someone for Julian to talk to as he worked his way through those issues. And Brant went to bat for him with the producer, the director putting the Red Horse sequel together. If Julian stays clean and clear, he'll play Roarke again in the sequel. He and Brant didn't run in the same circles, not really, but Brant reached out and stood up. That's Brant. I just wanted you to know."

When he left with Peabody, Eve looked up at the classy, coffered ceiling.

Brant Fitzhugh might've been a solid, stand-up guy, she thought. But he was still very dead.

3

Dolby could've given the colorful McNab a run for it in his scarlet skin pants, the sunburst collarless shirt, the black vest with its silver buckles, and the black high-tops with scarlet laces.

Like McNab, he wore an ear full of tiny hoops, and also sported a fancy wrist unit with a red band. His hair fell to his shoulders in tight black curls offset by a single bright red braid wound from his forehead, over the crown, and down his back.

He had skin like polished oak, so his eyes, clear as blue glass, seemed to pop out of a face with razor-sharp angles.

He carried a glass of wine in a hand that trembled.

"They said it was okay if I had a drink." His voice—baritone, faintly Midwestern—shook, like his hand. "Nobody will let me see Eliza. She'll need me."

"She's with Ms. Bowen."

He took a deep breath. "Okay. Okay, but she still needs me. I need to be strong." He sat, took a long, deep drink of wine. "I need to pull myself together and be strong for her. It wasn't an accident or a stroke or something. People are talking, and saying it wasn't an accident. But that doesn't make any sense. And I don't understand how Brant could be dead."

"You work for Ms. Lane."

"Yeah, yeah, yeah."

He closed those blue-glass eyes, made a little humming sound in his throat as he took three steady breaths.

"Strong," he said, and opened his eyes again. "I was a wardrobe assistant—low rung—when she did *All's Fair* on Broadway. And her personal assistant just couldn't handle it, couldn't keep up, and Eliza expects you to keep up, right? So she said, 'How about working for me, Dolby,' and I'm, like, 'Bet your ass.'"

His lips curved a little, and he put his fingertips to his mouth as if to hold back the quick smile. "I actually said that, and she just laughed. I can keep up, and I tell her straight when she asks for my opinion. 'That color sucks the life out of you,' or, 'Don't mention Gino when you have lunch with Mina because they're over.' And I know when she needs a neck rub or wants some quiet time. I help her rehearse, make sure she has her favorite flowers, know when to tell everyone to clear out so she and Brant can have a romantic dinner at home."

He paused, drank again. "Brant. It had to be an accident or something that just went wrong inside him. He's the sweetest man in the world."

"He and Ms. Lane—did they have any problems?"

"You mean like marriage stuff?" His curls swung when he shook his head. "They were like a fairy tale, I swear. Always doing little things for each other. Big stuff's all that, but it's the little things that count. I don't know how she's going to get through this."

His eyes watered up again. "They loved each other so much! She was like his queen. She'd say how he always made her feel like the center of the world, and he was her knight in the shiniest armor. He was like a dad to me."

He swiped at a tear. "I know that sounds weird, because Eliza's not like a mom, she's my best friend. But Brant's like a dad. He's like: 'Are you still seeing Franco? Is he treating you right?' And if I said, 'We broke up,' Brant would just say Franco wasn't good enough for me, and I'd find the one just like he did with Eliza."

"The former assistant, I assume Ms. Lane fired her."

"Sure, yeah."

"And do you know where this person is now?"

"Um . . ." He swiped at more tears as his brow furrowed. "I think she went back to Kansas or out there. She just wasn't cut out for New York."

"Would you have her name?"

"Sure, sure, give me a second to pull it out." He closed his eyes, hummed to himself. "There it is. Suzannah Clarkson. And not Kansas. Kansas City, but Missouri."

"That's a good memory you've got there."

"I keep it all filed." He wagged a hand beside his head.

"How about you run me through tonight?"

He did, and in detail, providing what people wore, snippets of conversation, who came with whom, who he felt hit the bar or the buffet a little heavy. He hadn't invited a plus-one because he considered it a working party, and besides, he'd just broken things off with the aforementioned Franco.

"Lin and I were in the dining room when Eliza and Samantha started the duet. I wanted to move in, because there's nothing like watching Eliza sell it, but I hung back so other people could. And I had this little skip in my heart when I caught sight of Brant lifting a glass, toasting her, and how they looked at each other. Just for an instant, because she was in character for the duet. It was magic, you know? Those voices, and all the people dressed so fine, New York out the windows. I got lost in it. I'll never take all of it for granted, so I got lost in it. I thought I heard a glass break, and remember I thought: Oops. Just oops. Then screaming, and it was awful, it was all awful."

He stopped to drink, and shuddered with it.

"I didn't know what happened, didn't know it was Brant. I just wanted to get to Eliza, but I couldn't get through all the people. I heard her crying, but I couldn't get to her, not at first."

"When you did?"

"I froze, I think. I just stood there, frozen. I kept thinking this isn't real, can't be. It was like passing out, but standing up. And when Lin pulled her away, I tried to help, but nothing worked right in my head. I heard them say he was gone, but he was right there, on the floor, so I didn't get it."

His voice hitched now, and he pressed his fingers to his mouth again. But this time to hold back a sob.

"The one who said he was a doctor and Sylvie took Eliza away, so I got a rag and I cleaned up the glass. It was like moving in fog. I thought, I better clean up the glass before somebody gets cut. I shouldn't have, but I wasn't thinking straight. I'm sorry."

"It's all right. We got it."

"I knocked on Wayne and Cara's door. They don't stay long at a party if they're not needed. I just started crying. And the police came. Can I go down to Sylvie's and see Eliza?"

"Maybe tomorrow's better. She's probably resting by now. Just a couple more questions, then you can go home."

"Can I go to my mom's? I don't want to go home. Can I go to my mom's instead?"

"That's fine. Just a couple more questions."

When he left, Eve considered. "How about Killer Dress, Peabody?"

"Vera Harrow. McNab reports she's bitched about being held like a prisoner of war."

"Great. Change of pace. Let's have her, and can you see if they've got any coffee in this place?"

"I can attest they do, and some good stuff."

Eve busied herself doing some quick runs until Peabody brought both the witness and the coffee. Vera, obviously undeterred by potential poison, carried a flute of champagne.

She paused—no doubt for effect—with one hand on her hip. "The butler's pantry? Seriously?"

"We take investigations very seriously. Have a seat, Ms. Harrow."

"I want it on the record that I object—also seriously—at being held here like a common thief for well over an hour. Nearly two goddamn hours now."

"So noted."

The dress might've been a killer, Eve thought, but the body inside it was the true perpetrator. Lush and luxurious, and not afraid to show it. Vera swiveled her way to the chair, sat, crossed long, shapely legs.

"I know who you are," she began, in a voice like white satin. "Don't for a moment think your reputation intimidates me."

"Okay. You and the deceased were once involved."

"Brant and I had a blistering, bountiful, brilliant sexual affair." She tossed back her hair and, with a little smile, sipped from the flute. "A weak man, but a Trojan in bed. Then Eliza got her claws in him. She'd recently been tossed aside so naturally wanted what I had."

"You sound bitter."

"Have you ever been cheated on?"

"Irrelevant."

"No, it's not. If you have, and had any pride, you'd understand the bitterness of being cheated on and cast aside, and lied to about the cheating." She flicked a hand in the air so her diamonds flashed in the light. "I don't believe in water under the bridge or over the dam or wherever the fuck it's supposed to go. Eliza stole something from me, and very deliberately."

"Something?"

"A lover I very much enjoyed, and the resulting media was brutal to me. They, the starry-eyed couple, and me, the discard." With eyes somehow smug and feral, she hooked an arm over the back of the chair. "I say when an affair's over, as others have learned. I enjoy the bitterness."

"Enough to poison the man who once discarded you?"

She blinked, and for an instant her eyes reflected shock. Calculation followed swiftly. "If I'd thought of it, I'd have done it years ago. But I'd have been more inclined to poison Eliza. But then I'd have to give up my very tasty bitterness. I prefer standing back, waiting for their we're-so-perfect marriage to implode. Which it would, in time."

A hard-ass, Eve thought. Generally speaking, she admired hard-asses. She found it easy to make an exception for Vera Harrow.

"They were going on ten years."

"In time," she repeated with another flick of her fingers. "Nothing lasts forever. Then I'd lure Brant back, use him, and discard him as publicly and cruelly as possible. Payback doesn't have to be immediate." She smiled, a feral cat's smile that matched her eyes. "It just has to be satisfying."

"Did you come here tonight hoping for that implosion?"

"You never know." She lifted one smooth shoulder, sipped from the flute. "Besides, even I can admit Eliza throws a spectacular party. I'm sorry he's dead. Now I'll never get the chance for that payback, and Eliza snags the role of the grieving widow. The media will lap it up like cream. Add murder, if that's what this was? It layers on shock, drama, titillation."

She raised her glass. "The bitch wins again."

"Having her husband die in her arms doesn't feel like a win," Peabody commented.

Vera laughed. "Oh please."

"You spoke with Mr. Fitzhugh shortly before he died."

"Apparently so. I arrived late with my date and hadn't had the chance to say hello. We spoke, I showed off the delicious young Rico, and like a good doormat, Brant moved on to ferry the champagne cocktail to Eliza. He's always . . ."

She sat up straight. "Oh wait. Wait. Her drink. It was her goddamn drink. He said he needed to take Eliza her drink, and to enjoy the party. Hers. Jesus Christ, the man was such a putz he ended up dying in her place."

Throwing back her head, Vera let out a howl of laughter. "It was meant for Eliza all along. You with your brilliant rep didn't put it together. Eliza was meant to drink the poison."

"Gee, thanks. We never would've figured that out without you."

Vera's eyes narrowed, then she shrugged. "So you had. That's your job, after all, such as it is. We'd only arrived ten or fifteen minutes before I spoke to Brant, and I could hardly know in advance he'd have a drink for Eliza in his hand when I did."

"Being he was such a doormat, I'd think you'd assume he might, at some point in the evening. Or you might take a moment or two to greet the hostess when she had a drink in her hand."

Eve drank coffee, watched her quarry. "Kill the old rival, then follow through with the payback. Offer the grieving husband your comfort. Lure him in—your words. Then discard him. He not only loses his wife, he's cut down in public and humiliated. It's a solid plan."

Vera's lips twisted. Not a grimace, Eve thought. A silent snarl. "I wouldn't give Eliza the satisfaction of killing her and making her into a martyr. Are we done?"

"We can be done for now. I'm sure we'll have more to talk about later."

"You can talk through my lawyers." She rose, tossed back her hair again.

"No problem."

She started out, paused, looked back over her shoulder. "And *The Icove Agenda* was overrated."

Eve looked at Peabody, knocked a fist against her own chest. "Oh. Ouch."

"What a stone-ass bitch."

"I think more gold-plated, but yeah, a bitch. And not in a good way. The first with any kind of clear, if twisted, motive. We'll dig deeper there because she sure as hell deserves it.

"Bring in the other assistant—Cela Ricardo. And get the passcodes for Lane's electronics from her and to McNab. We need to let people go, make sure we have statements and contacts, but we can't get to everyone tonight anyway."

She didn't get anything more from Cela but found the contrast to the other assistants interesting. No tears from this cool-eyed, contained woman, but an efficient, detailed relay of observations.

"I was on the second floor when Ms. Lane began singing." Cela kept her hands neatly folded in her lap as she spoke. "My employer prefers to keep guests out of private areas, so I'm tasked at events such as this to conduct a regular sweep of those areas."

"Anybody up there?"

"I had yet to complete the sweep when I heard the sounds of alarm from the main level. At that time I was at the far end of the second floor, as I always begin the sweep at the master bedroom suite. I chose to postpone the duty to go back down, see if I could lend some assistance. I had no idea, of course, of the severity of the issue until I reached the curve of the stairs."

Shoulders straight in a black dress, Cela shifted slightly in her chair. The only sign, Eve saw, of any distress.

"From that vantage point, I saw Mr. Fitzhugh on the floor and Ms. Lane holding his head and upper body. Dr. Cyril, who attended the party with Mr. Adderson, appeared to be attempting some medical aid. Mr. Jacoby, Mr. Fitzhugh's assistant, was kneeling next to Ms. Lane. I determined Mr. Fitzhugh was in serious physical distress and contacted nine-one-one for assistance. I believe one of the guests or staff had already done so, but I was unaware of that at the time."

She cleared her throat. "Might I get a glass of water?" Cela gestured to a glass-fronted friggie under the counter.

"Sure."

She rose, retrieved a tube of spring water, a glass from a cupboard. "Would you care for one, Lieutenant?"

"I'm good, thanks."

After pouring the glass, rolling the tube, depositing it in the recycler, she sat again. And took three slow sips.

"It was, for several moments, very chaotic."

"Did you come down to the main level?"

"Not at that time, no. I thought it best to stay out of the way. Dolby, Dolby Kessler, Ms. Lane's personal assistant, pushed through the crowd. There was broken glass on the floor. Dr. Cyril cut his hand on a shard. Superficially, I believe. The bell rang—the door. That's when I went down, and I let in the medical technicians. Though I'd already seen, again from my vantage point on the stairs, that Mr. Fitzhugh had died."

She stopped, sipped again. "It was shocking. I couldn't imagine how such a young, fit individual, and one who'd just had a complete physical evaluation, could simply collapse and die within minutes."

When Eve said nothing, Cela shifted again. "I've heard several comments and speculation regarding poison, which I discounted as dramatic. Expected with so many theater people. But I've also been told you specialize in murders."

That was one way to put it, Eve supposed. "I'm with Homicide. The medical examiner will determine cause of death, and for now this apartment will be treated as a crime scene. That's standard."

"Of course."

"That said, are you aware of anyone who might wish either Mr. Fitzhugh or Ms. Lane harm?"

"I couldn't say. There's considerable competition in their chosen field, naturally. And some fans or critics can be harsh in their evaluation of a presentation of a role. Others become, in my opinion, of course, far too enamored of the person they see in that role and take strange flights of fancy. Such as Ms. Lane's stalker."

"Stalker?" Son of a bitch! "What stalker?"

"A young man named Ethan Crommell. I'm sorry, I should have said this was fully three years ago, and he was ultimately arrested."

She paused, cleared her throat, drank more water.

"Ms. Lane was starring in *All's Fair* at the time, and he came to numerous performances. More, after virtually every performance, he would linger outside the stage door for a word, an autograph, or simply to catch a glimpse. He often had a single red rose to give her."

"She interacted with him?"

"Ms. Lane is very generous with her fans. But after a few weeks of it, she limited the contact. Then he wrote letters. Even that seemed harmless enough at first, if obsessive, but it escalated."

"In what way did it escalate?"

"He sent flowers, small gifts, and in his notes he started to insist they were meant to be together. That they had been together in a former life. He began to follow her, and then to approach. In any case, over a period of about three months, his behavior became more delusional, and he more insistent."

"Insistent how?"

"He accosted Mr. Fitzhugh once, claiming he—Mr. Fitzhugh—kept Ms. Lane away from him—Ethan Crommell—by force and intimidation. At one point, he had to be physically removed from a restaurant where Mr. Fitzhugh and Ms. Lane were dining. The police who responded found he had a knife in his possession—one he claimed he intended to use to cut the bonds that tied Ms. Lane, unwillingly, to Mr. Fitzhugh. He was arrested and charged, and is, I believe, currently in a facility for mental disorders."

"No one else mentioned this."

"I suppose because it was years ago, and he certainly wasn't here tonight. Guests and catering staff are checked through security downstairs, and again at the door here. I keep the list of invitees. I gave that list to the other officer."

"Yes, we appreciate that. And thank you for your cooperation. If you think of anything else that might help, please contact me. You're free to go."

"Is there anything I can do for Ms. Lane?"

"I'm sure she'll want your help over the next days, but tonight, she's with her friend."

"Ms. Bowen, a most excellent friend." She rose. "If this was murder, Lieutenant, it was a despicable act."

"Murder tends to be."

"Yes, of course, but . . . While I worked for Ms. Lane, she and her husband were very close. I saw him nearly every day if he wasn't away on a project. I knew him to be a very good man, a kind one, and a loving, considerate husband. Good night."

She left the handful of interviews remaining to Peabody and went upstairs to McNab.

"Hey, Dallas. Nothing smoky on any of the devices so far—and they've got a crapload of them. First-rate, every one." He gestured to the D and C on Eliza's office desk. "I've been through the vic's, and most of the widow's. Nothing that smells like either of them had any side action going on. Nothing that smacks of problems. Have to say the opposite. Found some notes between the two of them, all snugglylike. She does have a sad face emoji on her calendar for tomorrow.

Well, today now, considering the time," he corrected. "It says Brant to NZ, sad face."

"He was starting a vid in New Zealand."

"Gotcha. Both of them have a crowded calendar. Meetings, dress or suit fittings, lunches, dinners, interviews. Lots of party arrangement dates on hers. Not so much on his. But nothing smoky.

"Zipped through his 'link, his tablets," McNab continued, one air-booted foot tapping as he spoke. "He's got one just for scripts, the other for mobile communication, another calendar that mirrors the one on his desk. He was having flowers delivered to her today—sad face day—and every week following."

"You can keep at it while Peabody finishes up, then take off. We'll turn the place over tomorrow. I'm just going to have a look at the bedroom first and do a walk-through."

"I haven't started on the offices upstairs."

"We'll secure the place and get to them tomorrow."

"Today. Because tomorrow's today."

"Right. If necessary, we'll take them in, but I'm doubtful we'll find a handy invoice for cyanide on any of the electronics. How old is that thing?"

"This unit." He stroked it like he might a beloved pet. "This model, and it's sweet, only came out last year."

"Yeah, I figured something like that. Run a search on it anyway for Ethan Crommell. Maybe they transferred files. Any communication from or to him, any data on him. He got kicked for stalking Lane about three years ago."

"I'll get that going, and plug it into the vic's, too."

"Good. If you find anything, copy it to me."

She moved on to the master. Judging the distance, she estimated Cela would have taken a full minute—more if she hadn't hurried—to walk from the master to the stairs.

It tracked, time-wise.

She saw Eliza's dress, a red streak on the bed, and the shoes beside the bed. Either she or Sylvie had closed and locked the terrace doors, but the water glasses remained on the table outside.

She opened a bedside drawer, found a tablet. Since it wasn't passcoded, she opened it, found what she recognized as a script, with some notes added. Eliza's. She found song lyrics, with notes, a list of names with character names or positions. Dir, AD, SM, PM, LD, and so on.

She set the tablet aside to examine the other contents. The stylus for making notes, a jar of hand cream, a hand mirror—who looked at themselves after they went to bed?—a couple of sex toys.

She walked around the bed to the other drawer. No tablet here, so the vic kept his, at least that day, in his office. Likely would've packed them. A single joint of what a sniff told her was Zoner, meticulously rolled and unused, and a couple of sex toys. No condoms, so that wasn't a concern.

She moved to a dressing area, and tried not to be embarrassed her closet portion was nearly as large. Then again, this one opened into a dressing area holding a vanity with drawers loaded with facial enhancements, hair stuff, body creams, and a lighted tri-fold mirror.

Well organized, she noted, like the clothes, the bags, the footwear, the undergarments, the sex-me-up lingerie. A single bottle of scent sat on the vanity. Fancy bottle with a script running across the glass.

Eliza

Signature scent, she thought. One made for her. She'd done that for Charlotte Mira once as a gift. Curious, she gave it a spritz, sniffed.

More floral than fruity, she decided. But not crazy with it. And . . . maybe *mature* was the word. It wasn't like girl-dancing-in-the-meadow floral, but more woman-gliding-through.

She poked around in a few handbags, opened cupboards, but found

nothing of interest other than the expected safe. A big one, fitted behind a tall cabinet.

A woman like Eliza Lane would have plenty of sparkles, she thought.
The safe could wait.

She did the same look-through in the victim's closet. No vanity here,
but what she supposed he'd thought of as a grooming station, and a
large section of athletic and workout gear. Suits, and plenty of them,
three tuxes, sportswear, and another good-size safe.

She wandered to the bathroom. A multi-head and jetted shower big
enough for a dozen close friends, with a soaking tub inside the sparkling glass doors. A long white counter with clear glass vessel sinks
at either end.

Flowers—a trio of slim vases—between. An army of drawers holding more grooming products, hair products, skin gunk, hygiene products, all high-end but nothing surprising.

Vitamins, but over-the-counter type.

No hidden cache of illegals (she didn't count the single joint), no signs
of any dark sexual proclivities or multi-partner games. Just a space shared
by two privileged, successful, and apparently busy people.

She started out and met McNab in the long, wide hall.

"Got your Crommell, and he's a loony squared. Copied everything
on him to your units—home and Central. She's got a lot of fan mail on
file, has an address for that specifically that goes to her assistant, but
gets copied to a file for her. Fitzhugh had the same docs, so he kept the
Crommell stuff. Media report, too. He got three years in, mandatory
psych evals and treatment."

"Three?"

"Yeah, he was released according to the files. I can take a quick pass
at the third-floor e's."

"No, let's get a fresh start in the morning. Clear that with Feeney,
since there's so damn many of them."

As they both heard Peabody's signature clomp, he looked over his shoulder. "There's my girl!"

"We're clear. Nothing new popped, Dallas. The servers backed off when Lane and Keene started to sing. Standard policy for a party here, according to the caterer. Don't get in the way of the performance or the guests. The cook and housekeeper were in their quarters. It's sound-proofed, so they didn't hear anything until Dolby knocked on their door."

"Lane had a stalker a few years ago. McNab will fill you in. I'm going to do a run, make sure he's still inside. We'll meet back here in the morning. Given the size of this place, I'm going to call in Baxter and Trueheart, if they're clear, to help comb through it. Nine hundred—we'll say nine hundred so I can start a board and book at home. I'll lock up and secure the scene. I want a walk-through first."

"Nine hundred. I'll tag Baxter," Peabody offered.

"Yeah, do that."

She listened to their voices, Peabody's quick laugh at something McNab said, then the silence.

She walked back to the bedroom where Cela said she'd been when she heard the scream from downstairs. Yeah, she decided, the noise would have carried up the stairs if the doors had been open.

Probably stood, wondered what the hell, then lots of commotion, so walks down to see what the hell. Takes a minute to get to the stairs, start down. Stop at the curve.

As she did so herself, Eve looked down. Bird's-eye view, she noted. Even with the crowd around, she'd have seen the victim on the floor as she'd stated.

Eve went the rest of the way down, stood where Lane and Bowen stated they'd chatted.

Lots of people milling around, somebody playing the piano, servers winding through. Lots of conversation.

Victim on the terrace, getting the drink, talking to Jacoby, making nice with the bartender. Starts in, gets waylaid by Vera Harrow, Jacoby heads off.

Kiss, hug, opportunity.

Not clear, at this time, how many others Fitzhugh spoke with or had contact with, had opportunity on his way across the large room to where his wife and her friend huddled. Also not absolutely clear how many he mixed with after Lane left the huddle to get Keene and start performing.

And still, he held Lane's signature drink, not his own preference.

Going by probabilities, the poison was for her, not him. He just had bad luck.

But.

She took another long look, walked out to the terrace, then back again. Secured the doors, retrieved her field kit. She checked the block on the private elevator. Sealed it.

She went out, locked the doors, sealed them.

One person out of all they'd interviewed had spoken ill of either of them. And in Vera Harrow's case, of both of them.

And sometimes, Eve thought as she walked to the main elevators, life and death were just that simple.

She'd run Harrow on the way home, she decided, and see what she could dig up.

And she'd run Crommell.

Then she'd start fresh in the morning.

4

Eve drove through the gates well after two A.M. She saw, down the long wind of the drive, lights glimmering. Security lights splashed against the towers and turrets of the castle-like house Roarke built. But it was the gleam against the windows that offered a welcome home she cherished.

Though her body felt the length of the day and the lateness of the hour, her mind refused to turn off, and picked apart the scene, the interviews, the data she'd accessed on the short drive home.

Part of her wanted to keep going, head to her office instead of bed. Start her board, her book. But she told herself to let it settle in, give it and herself a rest so she could pick it up fresh in a few hours.

The warm night air smelled of flowers she'd never identify, of green summer grass, and, she admitted, of peace. The city revved and rumbled along, no matter the hour, but here, the quiet held like a tiny miracle as she walked from her car to the front door.

The foyer light glowed, but quietly, like the air.

She climbed the stairs thinking only a handful of blocks away, another grand and privileged space lay empty and smelling of flowers and sweepers' dust.

He'd left the light on low in the bedroom, and it occurred to her that he never did that for himself when he, routinely, rose before dawn to dress in one of his god-of-the-business-world suits.

The cat lay sprawled, a pudge of gray, where she'd normally be. For a moment, she just took in the picture, the sleeping cat, the sleeping man, a man so ridiculously gorgeous it clutched at her heart.

And they belonged to her.

She didn't make a sound, and still the man's wild blue eyes opened. Even in the dim light she saw them come fully awake in a finger snap. Beside him, Galahad's bicolored eyes opened, lazily, to stare at her.

Yeah, they belonged to her.

"And there she is," Roarke murmured with a hint of Ireland in his voice.

"Sorry. It's really late."

"Later for someone."

"Yeah, there's that. Brant Fitzhugh," she said as she took off her linen jacket, tossed it over the sofa in the sitting area.

"The actor?" With that, Roarke sat up.

"That's the one." She removed her weapon harness, her badge, set them on the dresser. "Cyanide in the champagne. Morris will confirm, but that's how he ended."

"That's a bloody shame. A very talented man, and a well-respected one."

She frowned over at him as she emptied her pockets. "Did you know him?"

"I met him a few times. Lunched with him once a few years ago when he pitched for a major donation for his pet cause."

"Did he get it?"

"He did, yes. His involvement in affordable housing was genuine, and heartfelt, if I'm a judge. Suspects?"

"Since he drank the champagne at the big, splashy party he and his wife threw, plenty of them. And the drink was initially meant for her."

"The inestimable Eliza Lane." Roarke shoved back his mane of black hair. "I'm fascinated."

"He brought her the drink—the bartender who made it's clear. Good thing, as she's one of yours. She works at Du Vin." Eve rubbed at her tired eyes. "Then Fitzhugh schmoozed his way through the party, including a close encounter with a former—Vera Harrow."

"Ah."

"She's on my list," Eve said as she undressed. "She's got motive, and seemed pretty pleased to tell me how much she disliked both of them. Anyway, he takes Lane the drink, and she's with a friend. Sylvie Bowen."

"You had a night with the stars, Lieutenant."

"And one of them could be a murderer. Lane didn't drink it because she decided to perform. Handed Fitzhugh the glass to hold while she got the actress who's playing her daughter in this Broadway deal."

"A revival of *Upstage*."

"That's the one. People crowd in, including the victim, who decides to toast his wife, drinks the champagne cocktail. And what do they call it—took his last curtain call. Why is it a call? Nobody's calling anybody."

"I couldn't say. So then you can't be sure, at this point, if Fitzhugh or Lane was the intended victim."

"No." She pulled on a sleep shirt. "Lane's most likely the target, at least on the surface. That's her particular drink, and he was taking it to her. But there was time and opportunity to slip the poison into the glass after she gave it back to him.

"That's my spot," she told Galahad, then nudged him aside to curl up beside Roarke.

"But he's dead and she isn't, so."

"Would she have any motive for pulling the switch herself?"

With their faces close, she smiled at him. "See, that's what I like about you. You think like a cop."

"Much too late at night for insults, darling Eve."

"Everything points to them having a solid marriage. No side pieces, no money issues—always the top two. But you've gotta look at the spouse, and she handed him the drink. The trick here is the spouse might have been the intended victim. Right now, I'm going to treat them both as victims on one hand, and keep her on the suspect list on the other."

"The media will be all over this."

"Especially since they invited some to the party. Nothing I can do about that, or the fact the crime scene was fucked when I got there. I'm going to start work here tomorrow, then meet Peabody, McNab if Feeney clears it, and Baxter and Trueheart. We have to go through the place. A lot of place in that place."

"Then you need some sleep. Turn that brain off for a bit." He pressed his lips to her forehead.

"Yeah, that's what I'm telling myself. Thanks for leaving the lights on."

"Always. And now? Lights out."

In the dark, he drew her close, and the cat curled against the small of her back.

Home.

She woke with a vague memory of a dream where people in glamorous costumes sang and danced their way around a stage. Until one by one, they all dropped dead.

Then she had to wade through the bodies, trying to figure out who was actually dead and who was acting.

She thought, as she surfaced, she'd found a lot of both.

Roarke sat, already dressed in a pale gray suit, pale gray shirt, and a precisely knotted, striped tie of gray and burgundy.

The financial reports scrolled by on the wall screen while, with the cat across his lap, he worked on a tablet.

She smelled coffee, and yearned.

"Even the financial news headlined Brant Fitzhugh's death," Roarke said conversationally. "I had a meeting with Singapore shortly ago, and it wound its way into the conversation. So did you."

"Me?" Because the idea annoyed, she scowled as she rose to hit the AutoChef for coffee. "Why?"

"'Lieutenant Eve Dallas, who solved the Icove case and starred in the person of Marlo Durn in the Oscar-winning vid *The Icove Agenda*, has taken charge of the investigation of Brant Fitzhugh's murder.'"

"You don't solve a damn case, you close it."

"Take that up with the reporter." He smiled at her. "When a star of Fitzhugh's magnitude dies in his wife's arms—which was captured on camera—the media will run with it. For days if not weeks. Add you and two of your high-profile cases as the thrust for two bestselling books—"

"Damn it, Nadine."

"Well then, Lieutenant, there's a cargo hold of juice to squeeze. Lamentations and tributes are pouring in. From Hollywood, Broadway, across the globe. He was an important man, and as I said, a well-respected one."

"Someone disrespected him, big-time."

"Or meant to disrespect Eliza Lane, who is another important actor, and well-respected. You should grab your shower and get some breakfast into you. I expect you'll be getting tags, and very soon, from your commander, from Kyung." He held up a hand as if to ward off a curse. "Kyung, as you're fond of saying, isn't an asshole. And he knows you'll have to do a media conference."

"And say what? I haven't even started the murder board or book. I haven't consulted with Morris. The media can just bite me."

"Be sure to mention that to Nadine. I've no doubt she'll be tagging you, and might even beat Whitney there."

"Christ." She took her coffee and her foul mood into the shower.

"It's a heavy burden for our Eve, isn't it?" He gave Galahad a long stroke. "We can paraphrase in that some are born in the limelight, some achieve the limelight, and some, like the Lieutenant, have the limelight thrust upon them.

"Let's set her up with a full Irish. She'll need the fuel."

When she came out in a short white robe, he sat, scrolling through his tablet. She stared at him, this man of hers in his perfect power suit. The black silk hair glorious around a face kissed by clever angels.

And she damn well knew he enjoyed what she considered a monumental ass pain. Notoriety was a bitch.

"Nadine Furst is absolutely not writing a book about this bullshit."

"Hmm. I believe she's already at work on one highlighting the murderous cult you broke. And," he said before Eve could speak, "you'll have to agree it will, particularly in her skilled hands, bring that particular evil into the public consciousness."

"Damn it."

"Come now, sit and eat." He patted the seat beside him. "You'll need it."

"You're riding on all this."

"Not the murder, no. I admired Brant Fitzhugh, as an actor, an activist, and a person. But I will ride on watching you hunt his killer, and have no doubt you'll bring them to ground. And the rest, it's not just fluff, Eve."

She sat, muttering, "Seems pretty damn fluffy to me."

"Not altogether. He deserves you and your team—every victim does, but he was an admirable sort of man, at least from what I know of him. The interest in his death, and the way he died, is a natural thing. And the reality is, you won't be able to brush it aside, so best prepare for it."

He lifted the covers off the plates and gained the cat's attention. Galahad sauntered toward them, stopping only when Roarke aimed a long, cool look.

"If the killer had waited a couple weeks, we'd have been in Greece."

He gave her knee a quick rub. "We'll get there. Why don't you tell me how you see it while we eat?"

"I'm not sure how I see it. Clearly, someone came planning to kill, and knew enough about their habits to know what kind of drink Lane goes for—or just used that moment as an opening."

"They couldn't know she wouldn't drink it, and he would, so you'd be leaning toward Lane as the target."

"Unless the killer slipped the poison into the glass when Fitzhugh moved across the room with the glass to watch her perform. People crowded in, and at that time, he didn't have a drink of his own, just hers."

"There's that. Could it be it didn't matter which one drank? Kill one, devastate the other?"

"Maybe." She crunched into bacon. "You'd have to look at Vera there, and I will, as she held a grudge toward both of them. Seems stupid to kill that way, and she didn't strike me as stupid. But wouldn't it be satisfying to exact your revenge in that sort of a public way? Party time, and Lane's up there in the spotlight. Devoted husband—the guy who tossed you for her, looking on devotedly. He's about to head off to a major project, and she's about to star in a major project."

She ate, considered. "The same one that launched her long career, right? And there was a death there, too. Something about the actress cast in the role of the daughter back then overdosing. I have to look at that."

"I couldn't say, as I'd've been running the streets of Dublin at that time and more concerned with survival than Broadway musicals."

"I need to look at it. There could be a connection. Somebody holding a really long grudge." She shoveled in eggs as she thought it through. "Lane gets the spotlight because somebody dies. In a way, poisons themselves," she said as Roarke topped off her coffee. "And here she is, using that same show to get all this media, the applause, maybe another whatever it is you get for plays. The statue thing."

"A Tony."

"Whatever. She got one all those years ago in the daughter role, I got that much. Now she's going to try for another in the mother role."

"A quarter century," he commented. "A long time to wait."

"It makes a circle. Maybe somebody connected to the original show, or more, to the original actor." Eve shrugged. "It's shaky, but worth some digging. Just like we'll dig deeper in case one or both of them were smart about screwing around. Or if, say, Lane had some money issues we don't know about. She'll be raking it in from his estate. Other beneficiaries we'll look at. She cleared us for a copy of his will."

She frowned over a bite of egg. "Every single person we interviewed last night cooperated. Vera bitched, but she cooperated."

"Any chance someone crashed the party?"

"I've thought about it. The security was tight, but it happens. Nobody used the private elevator. But you had a lot of those plus-one deals, so we'll dig there. A couple hundred people in one space, a big space, but still one space. A lot of opportunity to poison a drink.

"I need to get started. Setting up a board should give me a clearer picture."

She rose, went into her closet.

"I've an hour or so this morning. I could look into the financials, the victim and the widow."

She poked her head back out. "You're just looking to have more fun."

"Always. I do know Fitzhugh formed his own production company a couple years ago, and they've done a few projects. One was up against the Icove vid for best picture. And, I believe, the one he was about to start, as lead, is the first he'd have been in as well as producing."

"Maybe that pissed somebody off," she called out as she stared blankly at the forest of clothes surrounding her. "Maybe one or both of them nixed some other actor from getting a part in these big deals they're doing. Actors are weird, right?"

"Are they?" Roarke said from her open closet doors.

"They've got to be. They make their living pretending to be somebody else doing and saying the stuff that fake person says and does. Then somebody's always whining they didn't do it well enough."

"That's one way to look at it. You can go with black. You'll be speaking to the widow again today, I imagine. But not severe, so a pastel shirt to soften it. Professional, but not funereal, as you'll have that media conference as well."

"Fine. Great." She grabbed clothes at random. "I can maybe wheedle out of the media thing."

He kissed her cheek, like a father to a naive child. "Good luck with that."

She dragged on trousers, a pale blue tee, and came out for her weapon harness. "I can't feed them what I don't have."

"Darling, you have quite a lot. And the fact is, you're better at dealing with the media than you care to admit."

"Yeah, but—" Her 'link signaled. Snatching it up, she frowned. "Nadine. I can ignore that."

"And I repeat myself. Good luck with that, as she'll just keep tagging until you answer. Or show up at Central with brownies."

"Brownies make it go down easier," she muttered, but knowing he had it right, she answered. "I got nothing but a dead guy and a couple hundred potential suspects. Don't hound me."

"What kind of poison? The word is cyanide, but it's not confirmed."

"Because it's not confirmed."

Nadine Furst, crime reporter, writer, friend, gave Eve a long look out of shrewd green eyes. She'd styled her blond hair, streakier than usual, in a sleek bob. A new look that framed her foxy face. She simply said:

"Dallas."

"Morris has him, and Morris will confirm."

"Cyanide in a champagne cocktail."

Damn public crime scenes, Eve thought.

"I'm not prepared to confirm or deny."

"I met them. Brant Fitzhugh and Eliza Lane."

Eve shrugged into her jacket. "Why weren't you at the party? Media types there."

"Entertainment media types," Nadine pointed out. "And I met them. We weren't friends, not even really acquaintances. I met them at one of the after parties at the Oscars. They were both very gracious— very," she repeated, "considering we beat them out on three of the major awards they were also nominated for. I liked them," she added. "It wasn't just the dazzle of the moment."

Because she knew Nadine had an exceptional gauge, Eve decided to pump the source as she walked out of the bedroom. "How did they strike you as a couple? A married couple."

"Happy, and in tune. While we were chatting, he slipped away, and came back with a drink for her. Champagne cocktail, twist of lemon. I've had time since I got word on this to look, and that's her signature drink. How come he drank it?"

"Circumstances." Then she decided what the hell. "He brought it to her, but she decided to do a number, and he ended up drinking it."

"So she was the intended victim—some of the reports are hinting pretty strongly there."

"That's not what I said. I'd be careful there, Nadine." Here she warned both reporter and friend. "We still have witnesses to interview, data to accumulate, and Morris has yet to confirm COD."

"Give me something, any little thing."

"The bartender who made the drink is clear. The victim stood there telling her just how to make it to his wife's preferences. She couldn't have slipped anything into the glass."

"Okay, that's a good little thing. What's her name?"

"I bet a hotshot reporter like you can find that out. Shit, shit, I've got another tag. It's Whitney. I have to go."

"Wait—"

She didn't, simply broke the transmission with Nadine and answered her commander as she walked into her office. "Sir."

"I need a full report on the Fitzhugh investigation asap."

"Yes, sir. I'm working from home right now. I'll have the report to you within the hour."

"Bring it with you. One hour, my office. We'll have Kyung set up the media briefing at ten hundred hours."

"Sir. I have a team meeting at the crime scene at nine hundred, to execute a full search. At that time I plan to follow up with Ms. Lane. She's staying in the building with a friend. I have a man on the door. I would also like to consult with Morris, ascertain the official COD, and any other information he can provide."

"The media's already gone wild, Lieutenant."

"I understand that, Commander, but I can't possibly begin to tame that without some solid facts. And without determining which of those facts can and should be released to the public."

He said nothing for a moment as his wide, dark face filled the screen. "Noon. We can hold it off until noon. This is going to be a media shit show, Dallas, so prepare for that. You'll be giving updates regularly, even if it's just repeating the same damn thing."

"Yes, sir."

"Get me that report."

"Within the hour."

When he clicked off, she scrubbed her hands over her face. "Don't say it."

"Now then, Eve, when have you known me to say I told you so?"

She shot him a stony stare. "How about now?"

He laughed. "I did sneak that in, didn't I then? I'll get started on those financials."

She programmed more coffee and started on the board. As she printed out data and photos, she sat to write up the report. She'd rather have the book in place, the board set up so she could study it, but when Whitney said asap, he damn well meant it.

By the time she'd written the report, opened the murder book, Roarke came back in.

"You can't have dug down that deep already." She paused after adding another photo to the catering section of the board.

"I gave you the hour, and a bit more," he began.

"It hasn't been—hell, it has been that long. Damn it. Can you give me what you've got while I finish this?"

"I can, as I found nothing that hints at hidden accounts or shady practices. They have excellent business managers and share the same excellent financial advisers. They invest well, if conservatively, and are each very wealthy in their own right. He died worth about eight-point-six million. His production company is in the black—barely at this point, but it's solid enough. She has a bit more, at about nine-point-two.

"They live well," he continued. "Expenses are what you might expect given their financial status, their lifestyle and careers. And nothing indicates outlays that would support secret lovers."

"Secret lovers are secret for a reason."

"So they are," he agreed. "But secrets cost to keep. He's been more generous than she—particularly to Home Front—but she hasn't been stingy about it. They pay their staff well, maintain their various residences—which is, at this point, the bulk of their debt. But it's not a debt out of line with their income."

He picked up her coffee from her command center, drank a little. "I can dig a bit more later, but my sense is there's nothing there for your motive. Not from her to him, and not to anyone else. I suppose his will may tell a different story, but she certainly didn't need his money to live her life as she's used to living it."

"Okay. So if that pans out and we can eliminate money and cheating as motives, we're left with secrets, envy, and whack jobs as top of the lists. Thanks."

"Anytime at all."

"She had a whack job awhile back."

"Did she?"

"A stalker. Ended up doing time in a whack job facility. He's out, two months ago. I ran him on the way home. He lives in Queens. So we'll pay him a visit, try his court-appointed therapist, too. I don't see him getting through their security, but it's possible."

She tapped a photo, stepped back.

Ethan Crommell had shaggy brown hair, and the eyes of a puppy who might decide to take a quick bite at any moment. At thirty-eight, he had the look of a Zoner-head college student. Scruffy, soft, vaguely pretty.

"That's his most recent ID shot, but you can see he hasn't changed much from the one from his stalker days. She'd have recognized him, and so, I imagine, would Fitzhugh. Unless he's become a master of disguise and got his hands on some swank clothes. Since he's working as a stock boy at a market in Queens, I don't think his income runs there."

"He looks harmless at first glance," Roarke remarked. "Then he doesn't and not at all."

"Yeah, not harmless, so a trip to Queens. If he's still obsessed with Lane, that's motive. Opportunity's another thing. And where would someone like him get his hands on cyanide?"

"I'm sure you'll work it out. I have to go."

"Yeah, me, too, in a couple minutes."

"I'll wish you luck, Lieutenant." He pulled her in for a kiss. "And see you take care of my cop."

"If I have a lot of luck, I'll be taking care of a killer."

When he left, she looked back at her board. Vera Harrow and Ethan Crommell. Her two top suspects, such as they were, couldn't have been more different.

"But . . . maybe one of you will give me a buzz today."

Crime scene, she thought, Lane, Morris, and she really wanted to jam the lawyer in there and get a sense of Fitzhugh's will before she met with Whitney.

And then the damn stupid annoying media conference.

"Better get started," she murmured, but gave herself five minutes to sit there and just study the board.

5

Eve got to the scene early, unsealed the door. Inside the foyer, she stood, scanned the space, the distance from where she'd examined the body and the piano, the terrace doors.

The sweepers had examined the portable bars and cleared them, as well as the catering equipment in the kitchen, the dishes and serving platters.

At some point she'd need to let the caterer know they could take it all away.

Meanwhile, she crossed to the terrace doors, unlocked and opened them. The party debris remained, empty glasses, half-full glasses, plates, napkins, candles that had guttered out. The sweepers had done their job there, too, but she took the time to go over everything, search under cushions, inside pots of flowers and greenery.

From there, she moved into the main living area and did the same. Cushions, drawers, cabinets, behind paintings, closets.

When she heard someone mastering in, she laid a hand on her

weapon. Then dropped it as Peabody came in first, followed by Mc-Nab.

Baxter, in one of his slick suits, and the earnest-eyed Trueheart came in behind them.

"Swank digs." Baxter looked around, nodding in approval. "Superior swank digs. Shame about Fitzhugh," he added. "I liked his work."

"My mother has a major crush on him," Trueheart said. "She tagged me this morning to ask if it was true about him being murdered."

"Seal up. I've finished the terrace on this level, and nearly with this living space. McNab, you can hit the rest of the electronics. Master bedroom, second level's also cleared. Peabody and I can take this level, Baxter and Trueheart the second floor. Oh, McNab, there are safes in the master bedroom closets, his and hers. Let's open those up. And if we find more, the same."

She hooked her thumbs in her front pockets and looked around again. "There's a third floor—assistants' offices, two sitting rooms, bathrooms, a small kitchen, and a couple bedrooms. Clear what you can today, record everything."

She blew out a breath. "I can give it another hour, two, tops, before talking to Morris. I have to meet Whitney and Kyung in Whitney's office by noon."

"Media's whacked on this, Dallas," McNab told her. "Scrolling through social media was wild. Photos and vids from last night already making the rounds."

"Can't change that, so we'll deal with it. No fucking respect," she muttered. "Let's get started. Peabody, take the kitchens, both of them on this level."

They spread out. She'd barely begun her sections when her 'link signaled. "Lane," she called to Peabody, and answered.

"Dallas."

"Lieutenant. Please, do you have anything more on Brant's death?"

The woman looked like death herself, pale, hollow-eyed, lines of strains around those hollow eyes.

"I'm in your apartment now with four detectives. I can't promise we'll complete the search and be able to clear the scene today, but—"

"Search? You're searching our home, our things?"

"It's a crime scene, Ms. Lane. It's procedure. Whoever did this to your husband may have left something behind."

"Of course, of course. It just gets worse and worse."

"Ms. Lane, it would be helpful if you gave us the combination to the safes in your bedroom."

"My jewelry safe? Why—"

"We can clear those areas. The search will be fully recorded and documented. Also any other combinations would save time, allow us to complete the work and allow you back in your home more quickly."

"It doesn't feel like home without Brant. I—all right. My jewelry safe's combination is Brant's birthday, and his bedroom safe is our anniversary."

She rattled off the numbers. "There's a safe—for important papers and so on—in Lin's office. I'm not sure I remember the combination."

"We'll get that."

"The media—we've blocked reporters and anyone we don't know personally, but . . . And Sylvie ordered me not to turn on the screen. I know much of it's a tribute to Brant, and genuine grieving, but . . ."

"Listen to your friend on this. Please don't speak to reporters at this time, as it could impede the investigation. You should have your people prepare a statement, a brief one, asking for privacy. I'd like you to run that statement by me before you issue it."

"Yes, yes, that's best." She looked vaguely around as if searching for something. "I'm not thinking sensibly, I know that. I'm trying. I need to see Brant. If I could—"

"I'm going to consult with the medical examiner when I leave here.

Either he or I will contact you later this morning and arrange for you to go in."

She squeezed her eyes shut. "Thank you. I—I need to make arrangements. Could I have Dolby, at least Dolby?"

"Sure."

"I don't know where to begin. I think when I do, when I begin, I'll know what to do next. The statement. I'll do that right away. I'll begin with that. Thank you. Please, please contact me as soon as you can."

"I will. If you think of anything else, any small detail, let me know."

"I will."

Eve continued her part of the search, and formed a clearer picture of the victim and his wife. They both enjoyed fine things, polished spaces. And each had what reflected their personal spaces, but they very much lived together.

Luxury in every inch, but a lack of fuss with it. Clean and organized so the remains of the party, the confusion murder brought with it, stood out.

She gave it an hour before deciding to call it.

"It's a serious kitchen," Peabody told her when Eve stepped in. "As up-to-date as it gets, and really well supplied and organized. I'm going to say the guy they have doing the cooking knew what he was doing. A lot of recipes on the kitchen tablet, dietary needs—Lane's allergic to shellfish—marketing lists regularly updated, an inventory of supplies."

Peabody stood back, looked around the vastness of stainless steel, clean white lines, sparkling glass.

"You can keep at it. I'm going to hit the morgue. When you finish the kitchens, leave the rest to Baxter and Trueheart. I think we keep this whole space secured for at least another day. You can go down, check on the widow before you leave. Get a sense of what she's planning, how she's coping. The longer we can keep her from talking to the media, the better."

"Got it. You don't really expect to find anything linking the murder here."

"Not really. But people have secrets. Everybody does. So we see if we can uncover any the victim, the widow, the staff had tucked away."

She circled the room. "It was slick, the way this went down. Quick and done—immediate confusion and chaos, especially since you had a crowd, including media. Somebody's pretty damn smart, even if we can't be sure they hit the intended target.

"If you can make it to Whitney's office by noon, be there."

Before she left, she jogged up to the third floor to find McNab deep into tech.

"Anything?"

"Lin Jacoby likes to play the horses."

Her gaze narrowed. "Really?"

"Yeah, but kind of the way I'd play them if I made bigger bucks and wanted the fun. Not big-time, right? And wins more than he loses. Got some losses that would sting some, but not too many. No sign so far he dipped into the boss's pockets. And he had a pretty serious relationship that ended, like, eight months ago."

McNab pushed back, shrugged his skinny shoulders. "He's got all the vic's data on here—calendar, expenses, income—but it comes off clean. Personal correspondence is separate from the work stuff, with some overlap. And that comes off clean, too, Dallas. His financials are on here, and he copped a nice salary, benefits. He's got investments, and he lives within his really solid means. Bought his parents a house four years ago."

"Keep at it. There's another safe in here." She walked to a storage closet and found it. "Lane isn't sure of the combo. Contact Jacoby, get it. See how he reacts. I've got the combos for the bedroom safes."

"Saves time."

She gave them to him, left him to his work. Then stopped briefly on the second floor.

"Not just swank digs, but massive." Baxter paused in his search of yet another closet.

"What are we looking for, Dallas?"

"A bottle with a skull on it and *poison* in big red letters would be dandy. Otherwise anything that doesn't fit." She looked around the guest room he searched. "Everything really fits. Is that normal?"

"I like to think everything fits in my place. Big party, right? So they'd want everything just right. Especially since they had media."

"Yeah. That fits, too."

She chewed on that on the drive downtown.

The ad blimps were out in full force, hyping summer sales. People swarmed the sidewalks—the tourists obvious in their colorful shorts, their I ♥ NEW YORK caps, their loaded shopping bags as they, most likely, hunted for some of those sales.

Traffic bumped its way along, so she drove with her windows open to the summer air. She smelled the truly terrible glide cart coffee, grilling soy dogs, the occasional whiff of flowers from outdoor stalls or the concrete troughs planted by the city that competed with an overstuffed and out of order recycler.

When she stopped at a light, she heard a sidewalk vendor with a Bronx accent she couldn't have cut with an axe tell a customer to "Fock off if yous don't like it, bud."

And the customer focked off in a huff down the sidewalk.

Christ, she loved New York.

At the morgue, she made her way down the long white tunnel. The smells here, as always, carried the scent of death under chemical lemons and bleach.

She opened the doors of Morris's arena to the music of Broadway.

Even she recognized Broadway as a woman's voice belted it to the back rows.

Morris stood over Brant Fitzhugh, carefully completing the stitches on the Y-cut. The ME wore a blue linen suit under his protective cape, with a crisp white shirt and deep blue tie.

His hair, braided and wound into a coil at the back of his neck, left his sharply boned face unframed.

He called for the music to lower as he looked up at Eve.

"I thought he'd enjoy hearing his wife sing, as they had a fairy-tale sort of romance, from all the reports and interviews. A strong talent cut down in his prime. And one in superior physical shape."

"Yeah, he kept in tune. COD?"

"Exactly what you discerned. Potassium cyanide, ingested via a good champagne, sugar, and bitters. A painful death, but a quick one. No signs of violence on the body other than the contusions where he fell. No signs of substance abuse. And remarkably, given his physique, no signs of work on the body. A bit here and there on the face, and understandable given his line of work. Nothing obsessive."

Stitching complete, Morris walked over to rinse his hands of blood and sealant. As Eve walked to the body, he got two tubes of Pepsi from his cold box.

"Thanks. Did he tell you anything?"

"That he took his health and physique seriously. His muscle tone is admirable. He had good nutrition, and I would surmise good medical care. He's had a broken bone or two in his time, but well healed. Prime," Morris repeated as he broke open his tube. "I liked his work, and his activism for the homeless."

"Yeah, I'm hearing that a lot. We don't know if the poison was meant for him or for Lane. It was her drink," she added. "But he ended up drinking it while she . . ." Eve pointed up and the voice rang. "Performed."

"So a mystery within the mystery."

"Crowded party, he schmoozed and mingled with the glass in his hand. No way to know when the poison went in. So . . . His widow wants to see him."

"I can have him ready for her at her convenience."

"Okay, I'll tell her to contact you and set it up. I'll have some officers bring her in. Media's got her building staked out, so we'll send an unmarked car. Pain in the ass."

"Price of fame."

"Can't see it'd be worth it. I appreciate the quick work."

"All in a day's. And I'll wish you the same—quick work on finding his killer."

"If I can pinpoint the target, I'd have better luck with that."

Delegating gave her a solid thirty minutes to spare when she walked into Homicide. Detectives Jenkinson and Reineke huddled together at Jenkinson's desk. She marveled that Reineke willingly stood so close to his partner's nuclear reactor of a tie.

This one sported madly purple and pink dots over a piss-yellow field. A glance at the bullpen board told her Detectives Carmichael and Santiago had just caught one, a floater.

Since Jenkinson and Reineke were three days into an investigation of a stabbing in Alphabet City, she left them to it and veered into her office.

She snagged coffee and downed it while she set up her board, dealt with the murder book, adding what she'd gotten from Morris.

Then, finally still and with a few minutes to spare, she sat and studied the board.

Lots of pretty people, she thought, all polished and smooth. She needed time to study what lived under all the polished and smooth.

Not a crime of passion or a murder of the moment, but one planned, timed, and executed with some skill. Even at a crowded party, someone could notice another person slipping something into a drink.

Willing to take the risk.

Women went for poison more than men, she considered, though that wasn't a hard-and-fast rule by any stretch. But it did speak to a lack of violence, or the need to use force, to spill blood.

Her vic, a man in his prime. A well-muscled, healthy man. Strong. Poison didn't require physical strength.

She might even say the method, the vehicle used presented a kind of elegance. And that, too, fit with many of the images on the board.

She rose and, pulling out her 'link, contacted the estate lawyer as she took the glides up. And found herself pleasantly surprised to learn Eliza Lane had already cleared the way there.

Whitney's admin glanced over as she came through. Nodded.

"They're waiting for you."

Even so, she gave one brisk knock before she opened the door.

Whitney sat at his desk, a big man whose shoulders carried the weight of command. His dark, close-cropped hair was salted with gray, and the dignity of it suited him.

Behind him, the city he stood for spread.

Kyung, who she'd designate as polished and smooth, stood by the wall of glass, tall and lean in his excellent charcoal suit. It baffled her anyone would happily steer the public relations ship, but as she knew he respected the work above the media, he ranked as not an asshole.

"Lieutenant." Whitney merely spread his hands.

"Sir. Morris has confirmed the COD as cyanide poisoning. The victim shows no signs of violence, was in good health and excellent physical shape. I've contacted the estate lawyer, and his office is sending a copy of Fitzhugh's will. They'll also provide a copy of Lane's. This was requested and cleared by Eliza Lane. Morris is arranging for her to view the body early this afternoon. I've arranged an unmarked car to transport her and her party to and from the morgue."

"Yes, that's best. The media frenzy's barely begun."

"At this time," she continued, "Detectives Baxter and Trueheart are continuing the search of the crime scene, and Detective McNab is working on the electronics. Thus far we've found nothing that points to motive or a suspect. However, Vera Harrow, in her own statement, admitted to grudges held against both Lane and Fitzhugh."

"The actress?"

"Yes, sir."

Whitney sent a steely glance at Kyung. "Just what we need. Another celebrity as a suspect."

"The bulk of the party consisted of actors or those attached to the entertainment business," Eve said.

"I'm aware," Whitney responded. "All too well aware."

"Detective Peabody and I will interview the individual convicted of stalking Ms. Lane three years ago, and recently released on parole from the MD facility."

She paused a moment.

"I realize most of this information was included in my report this morning, but the investigation is in its very early stages, with a great deal of work to do. We haven't formally interviewed all of the guests present at the time of the murder."

"Understood. Make a list of those you feel, at this time, require you and your partner to interview. You can delegate the rest, and request additional manpower to cover it, if necessary."

"Yes, sir. I'd prefer to do at least a standard run on those individuals before making that list. The killer obtained the poison and brought it to the event. A connection to Fitzhugh and/or Lane would be key. Cross-referencing the guests, staff with the beneficiaries of the victim's will, and Lane's will, as she may have been the intended victim, will also give us some direction."

"I can authorize more eyes on the cross-referencing." He sat back when she said nothing. "Problem, Lieutenant?"

"Sir, we've barely begun the investigation, but are making considerable progress in the initial processes. I've already pulled three additional detectives into that process and assigned uniforms for Ms. Lane's security. I don't feel the need, at this point, for additional officers to take up routine procedures."

Whitney nodded, tapped his fingertips together. "What you're not saying is within hours of this murder, the NYPSD will add considerable manpower and budget to this single investigation. Because the victim is famous."

He hadn't reached the position of command without knowing how to interpret even a carefully worded statement. So she laid it out plainly.

"I have two detectives working the stabbing death of a waiter. A mixed-raced male, age thirty, sliced up on his way home from work. This is day three of that investigation. There's been no demand for a media conference, no additional manpower or budgetary increase. He had a six-month-old son, but he wasn't famous."

"Your point, Lieutenant, carries the weight of morality and the heft of equality. But it doesn't account for politics or the voraciousness of the media—which carries its own weight. I have no doubt your detectives will pursue this victim's killer as dedicatedly as you will Fitzhugh's."

"Yes, sir. No question."

"But the Fitzhugh investigation will lead every media vehicle today, tomorrow, and very likely until you identify and apprehend his killer. After that, there will be more—the follow-ups, the profiles. He was—is—a household name," Whitney continued as he rose. "The president of the United States has already issued a statement of condolence and a call for justice. Other heads of state will do the same. You're in the crosshairs on this, Dallas, and I intend to give you every tool available."

"Yes, sir."

"And to that end . . ." Whitney turned to Kyung.

"The mayor will give a statement to the media in approximately thirty minutes," Kyung began. "It will be made clear—I've seen the draft of the statement—that the mayor's office has every confidence in the NYPSD, and in you and your team to conduct this investigation. To the conclusion, the apprehension of whoever took Fitzhugh's life. The mayor will take questions for about five minutes."

Kyung paused, gave her a quiet look of sympathy. "You can expect that to expand to at least ten, if not more."

"Got it."

"It's a bit more than politics, Lieutenant, though I understand your feelings on it. The mayor serves the city as well, and all in it. Whether a waiter or a vid star. But the vid star, and the ways and means of his murder, bring the drama, the scope, the fascination. You want to get on with your work, but this is part of that. You will reassure."

"Reassure who? And how? I don't have anything yet."

"Your presence brings reassurance. And, though it annoys you, drama and scope." He smiled at her then. "There's no need for me to tell you what to say or how to say it. You dislike that part of your job, but you know that part of your job. And if I tried to guide you, it would just piss you off."

"Got that one."

He smiled again. "I will ask that you also take questions. There will be a deluge, and many will annoy you, but I'll end that part of things as soon as I can. It won't be as soon as you like."

"You're cleared to give them TOD and COD," Whitney told her. "Much of the rest is, well, theater. But it's necessary."

"Lane is, at my request, working on a statement of her own. I also requested she run it by me before issuing it. I think running it by Kyung makes more sense."

"I'll see to that," Kyung agreed. "If you, and Detective Peabody, if available, will meet me in the media room in forty minutes."

"I'll attend. I won't speak." Whitney sat again. "I'm window dressing—and reassurance and support, as is Chief Tibble, who will also attend. Theater," he said again, "and when the show's over, you'll get back to work."

He paused a moment. "I'd like an update on the investigation into the stabbing case when you have it."

Before she could speak, Peabody knocked and stepped in. "I'm sorry, I was delayed. I spent a little more time with Ms. Lane, helping her and her assistant with her statement."

"You have it?"

"I have a copy," she told Eve. "I promised we'd clear it asap."

"If you'd send it to me, Detective, I'll see to that," Kyung said.

"Did you get anything else out of Lane?" Eve demanded.

"Not really. She's holding up reasonably well. Her assistant, that's Dolby, broke down a couple times, and she did better when she focused on him. She has a lot of questions, and I gave her the standard. Media's camped out, and security's run a few pushier types out of the building."

She let out a breath. "I checked in with the team on the crime scene before I left. Nothing that pops on the electronics so far, and there's still a lot to go through in the residence, but nothing that pertains as yet."

"Keep me informed." Whitney tapped his wrist unit. "Forty minutes, Lieutenant."

"Yes, sir. Peabody, with me." She strode out, decided not to even attempt the elevators, so headed back to the glides. "Media bullshit in forty, and that's after the mayor does a song and dance. COD and TOD confirmed, and Fitzhugh died healthy and fit. I need you to go through the guest list, start doing some runs on the plus-ones. The brass is going to overwhelm us with help on that kind of thing, but you get going on it. I'll do the same with the invited types."

"Okay." Peabody slipped her PPC back in her pocket. "Statement to Kyung—it's a good one, I think. She's not an idiot, and kept it brief, with a plea for privacy she knows she won't get."

"We're heading to Queens to shake down her former stalker after the media circus. We should have both wills by then, so you can go through them on the way. We'll flag any beneficiary who was at the party, or connected to someone who was, take a harder look. I want us—you, me, our division if necessary, EDD—to handle as much of this as possible before they send in officers to assist in the investigation. If we need to, we'll pass on some of the drone work, but that's it unless we stall."

"Jeez, we haven't had time to stall."

"Fucking A," she said, and swung into Homicide. "Plus-ones—wrap it up in thirty."

She headed straight to her office, sat down, and ordered the guest list on-screen. A long list, she thought, but she'd had longer. And damn it, she didn't give a rat's ass about politics, could've cared less about scope and theater and whatever the fuck.

She cared about murder, the victim, and hunting the killer.

She'd do the damn media briefing—no choice anyway, but she'd do it because Kyung wasn't wrong. It was part of the job—a tiny sliver of an ass-pain part, but part.

But she'd avoid the "help" coming her way for as long as possible. If you scattered the work into too many other hands, in her opinion, you risked having something slip through the fingers.

On the thirty-minute mark, she broke away, allowed herself a full minute of creative mental cursing. Then walked into the bullpen.

Peabody rode solo in the detective area.

"Jenkinson and Reineke lured their prime suspect on the Dobson case into Interview. They think they've got him."

"Good. Let's go get this bullshit over with. I've got three soft connections that we'll dig into," Eve added as they started out.

"I've got one, but it's almost squishy soft."

"We'll work them and keep eliminating. Stalker Guy's the most promising right now, if we can place him at the party—which heads into the squishy—or find a cohort. Catering staff or a plus-one's most likely there."

"You'd need somebody who'd kill for him."

"Yeah, either because hey, that'll be fun, or profitable if he's got any ready cash, or through blackmail or other pressures. It's worth a trip to Queens, even if it's just another elimination."

Eve suffered the elevator because, as far as she was concerned, this entire deal was suffering.

"Say Lane was the target," Peabody speculated. "It could come down to competition. She snags a lot of major parts—stage and screen. Major vids, guest spots, important interviews, endorsements. Maybe we look to see somebody who was up for a big part, and she got it instead."

"Same goes for him, right? But yeah, we look there, too. Roarke told me Fitzhugh's newish, I guess it's 'ish,' production company's doing some solid stuff. Looking at him as the target again, somebody whose project didn't get picked up, or again, somebody who didn't get a part, or a job."

She rolled it over, again and again, then ultimately pushed off the elevator as more pushed on. Enough suffering.

"It feels personal. Not the method, as poison creates a distance. But the choice of when and where. The party, the celebration, and just before Lane goes into rehearsals, and Fitzhugh leaves to start a big shoot. That's a deliberate choice."

On the glide, she turned to face Peabody. "I've looked at their calendars and appointment books. Busy. Lots of events, parties, galas, red carpet crap. Lots of opportunity, right, for just exactly what went down. But you pick this time, this place. Their home. That's personal."

Hopping off the glide, Eve walked toward the media room.

Kyung waited, signaled to her.

"You're prompt. Appreciated. The mayor's just finishing up. Detective Peabody, if you'd stand to the lieutenant's right, and be prepared if any questions are addressed to you. Chief Tibble and Commander Whitney will be on the left, and also prepared to take the podium if necessary. Lieutenant, Ms. Lane's statement is on the podium screen. She's asked that you read it. Well done, Detective. It's brief, clear, and just emotional enough.

"Excuse me."

Kyung walked out where questions still flew like manic butterflies. In his smooth way, he stepped beside the mayor, took charge.

"Thank you. Lieutenant Dallas and Detective Peabody will give an update from the investigative area. Chief Tibble and Commander Whitney remain available to answer any relevant questions. Thank you, Mayor, for your time and information."

With that, he effectively shifted the focus from politics to cop work.

"Lieutenant. Detective."

Eve stepped out, and Peabody took her place. She knew cameras whirled, and in studios some talking head blathered.

She spotted Nadine, front row—no flies on her—in the packed seats.

"I'll begin by reading, at her request, a statement from Mr. Fitzhugh's widow, Eliza Lane.

"'My heart is broken from the sudden, inexplicable death of my husband, my partner, my life mate. Brant Fitzhugh was a man filled with love and talent and kindness, and the world is a darker place without his light shining. It is my deepest hope that the authorities identify and apprehend the person or persons responsible for this despicable act. And it is my heartfelt plea to be granted the privacy to mourn my loss as I know the world mourns with me.'"

She scanned the room, thinking what Roarke had said to her earlier: Good luck with that.

The media hounds would hunt and howl relentlessly, just as Whitney had said.

"The chief medical examiner of New York has confirmed Brant Fitzhugh died of cyanide poisoning. And shut the hell up," she added as a handful began to shout questions. "I'm standing here instead of working this case in order to inform you of what I can inform you. My partner, Detective Peabody, and I are leading the investigation into Mr. Fitzhugh's death. I arrived at the residence he shares with Ms. Lane last night at shortly after twenty-three hundred hours. The medical team who responded to the nine-one-one pronounced Brant Fitzhugh dead on the scene. The uniformed officers responding to the nine-one-one call had secured the scene prior to my arrival."

6

It wasn't sexy, and it wasn't dramatic, but she went over the salient details that could be made public. The hounds, she could clearly see, were restless. They wanted to pop up, shout out, get their faces on-screen. And, though every one of them should know better, to try to squeeze out some shocking detail, some slippery bit they could finesse for their particular audience.

"We are in the very earliest stages of this investigation and will pursue same with the full force of the NYPSD until Mr. Fitzhugh's killer is identified. We will follow any and all leads, compile any and all evidence, and continue to do the work necessary to bring the person or persons responsible for Mr. Fitzhugh's death to justice."

She paused a moment, then held up a hand to hold off the questions that started shooting out.

"There's no point in any of you asking if we have a suspect or suspects. If we did, I wouldn't tell you and risk compromising the investigation. There's no point in asking if we have any leads, as we are, as

I've said, following any and all leads. There's no point in asking me or anyone up here for more information on the investigation, as we've given you all we're free to give at this time. So anybody who wastes my time will be ignored."

Hands shot up, questions flew. She deliberately didn't call on Nadine—not first. It would look like bias—when, in fact, it would've been logical. Nadine wouldn't waste her time.

She pointed to a camera-ready man with shining blond hair in a dark suit.

"Gregg Ortz with GNN. Lieutenant, it's been more than twelve hours since Brant Fitzhugh's murder, a public murder, as there were, by accounts, about two hundred people present. Have you, in these twelve hours, eliminated any of those present as suspects?"

"That's pretty much the long way around of asking if we have any suspects. So that part's ignored. Twelve hours? To respond to a dispatch, secure a crime scene, examine a body, bring in crime scene investigators for forensics, begin to interview and vet a couple hundred witnesses, gather evidence, process evidence.

"And for all of that, starting the clock on that over twelve hours at twenty-two-forty-three and the first nine-one-one call. That's ten-forty-three P.M."

She let that hang a moment. "We're working on it, Gregg Ortz with GNN. You," she said, pointing to another.

"Abbie Korick with *Entertainment Daily*. Can you confirm the name of the catering company the Fitzhugh-Lanes engaged for the event last night?"

"No." She tried another.

"Lowell Tucker, *Blogasphere*. Some of the guests attending have granted interviews. As statements and recollections differ somewhat, can you tell us what Fitzhugh drank that killed him?"

"Cyanide."

"Sorry, I meant what drink the poison was added to?"

"Champagne."

She took two more that earned ignore status, two others to which she answered with information she'd already given, then acknowledged Nadine.

"Nadine Furst, Channel Seventy-Five. My information is the guest list included the cast and crew of Eliza Lane's upcoming revival of *Upstage*, as well as other friends, acquaintances, plus-ones, and members of the media. Can you confirm that?"

"Yes."

"Follow-up, please. My information is security was two-leveled. A name check in the lobby of their building before giving access to their apartment, and again at the door. If you can confirm this, would you say, in your professional opinion, the chances of someone slipping through security, not on the list, would be slim?"

"That's two questions in one. However, security was two-leveled. In my professional opinion, it's never impossible for someone to slip through solid security, if they're motivated enough."

"What was the motive!" someone shouted out.

"To kill." She barely glanced at Kyung, but he stepped out.

"That's all, ladies and gentlemen."

It didn't stop the barrage of questions, but she walked away.

Peabody said nothing until they were well out of earshot. "You don't actually believe somebody snuck in and poisoned Fitzhugh."

"No, but I answered the question accurately, and it's done. A plus-one has reasonable probability," she continued. "But managing that means somehow making a connection, or already having one, with an invited guest. Enough of one to get that tagalong to a fancy party."

"With enough time in there to access some cyanide. The invitations went out ten days before the event."

"True, but word went out prior. Planning started nearly three weeks before. And that expands the time."

She shoved out of the elevator, with gratitude, on her level of the garage.

"Some people came stag," Peabody began, "but—"

"What does that mean? 'Stag'? It's a kind of deer, right, with the horn things? How does that translate to somebody going to a party alone?"

"I . . . Um." Peabody got into the passenger seat. "Maybe stags are loners?"

"Are they? Are they really? How do they get other deer? They've got to hook up sometime."

"I could look it up." At Eve's slow stare, Peabody shrugged. "Or not." Maybe later, she thought. "Some came alone, some were invited as a couple, but a lot of people had a plus-one. I get that because fancy party, bring your spouse or cohab, show it off to a date, or bring a pal to treat them. And some sort of came as a group."

"We'll eliminate the stalker—or get lucky and find out he managed to hit the low probability of slipping in, past security, went unrecognized, and dumped some poison in his rival's drink. Or meant it for Lane. 'I can't have you, nobody can.'"

She streamed out into traffic. "Check out the wills, give me beneficiaries if they've come through."

While Peabody pulled out her PPC, Eve programmed coffee for both of them from the in-dash AC.

"Okay, lots of legal mumbo, but Lane gets it all—but for specifics. A lot of their stuff, from the last decade, is joint anyhow, but he had a property in California prior to the marriage, and she gets it. He leaves a good chunk to his parents, a smaller chunk and a classic roadster to his brother."

"None of whom were at the party, or in New York at the time."

"No. He leaves a cool million to Lin Jacoby, along with some personal items. A wrist unit, cuff links, and so on. He leaves a half mil to the cook and housekeeper. Another classic car, wrist unit to his agent. He designated two million to the homeless organization, and there are some smaller bequests to other charities."

"How about hers?"

"Let me switch over. And blah blah, wherefore, bullshit blah. Okay, much the same. He gets the bulk, including the property she owned prior to marriage on the Italian Riviera. Dolby Kessler gets a million, a pair of diamond stud earrings—Cartier—a framed caricature of Lane—an original by Jorje Talbet. Famous for them," Peabody added, "so that's probably worth something. Cela Ricardo gets fifty thousand a year for every year of employment. Sylvie Bowen—no cash bequest but several pieces of jewelry, a collection of perfume bottles, and other odds and ends. The house domestics get half a mil, her dance instructor her toe shoes, tap shoes, and the costume she wore in the 'Swing Around' number in the original production of *Upstage*."

Peabody shrugged again, shifted toward Eve. "Some small stuff, some charities."

"So, motive—monetarily—the spouses each benefit most, with the personal assistants raking it in. There's Bowen—the jewelry's probably worth considerable. And Lin likes to play the horses. A million places a lot of bets. A half million either way for the house crew, so it wouldn't matter much which one of them downed the poison—but statements indicate they were in their quarters at the time."

She stopped at a light, tapped her fingers on the wheel. "The domestics. They draw a good salary, with benefits, have exceptional living quarters. Kill off one of the employers for the quick payoff? You risk losing all that. Doesn't play for me, especially since both come off squeaky clean."

"I'd say the same for Ricardo. If you're going to get fifty large for every year you work, you'd be inclined to want to keep the job a long time."

"Unless you hate the job, or the boss. Alternately, you aim for Fitzhugh because you calculate Lane will need you more as a widow. That's stretching it," Eve admitted, "but I'd put her above the domestics."

"You could say that about Kessler, too. She'd be more emotionally dependent on him now, at least in the short term. Maybe it's not so much the money but the dependence. With him gone, she'll lean on me, need me. And maybe Fitzhugh handled the money areas, or more of them. Kill him, and possibly dig into the till without getting caught."

"They have a business manager, financial guys, but yeah, easier to dip if the person with the till isn't paying as much attention. Or maybe somebody already did."

Roarke would have seen it, she thought. But . . .

"They've all got free access to the big fancy place with all the fancy stuff. Maybe one of them lifted a couple things they figure wouldn't be noticed, pawned them. But Fitzhugh noticed. Mr. Nice Guy gave them a second chance, but you're worried he'll change his mind. Or you're just greedy."

She hissed out a breath as she drove. "And all that's just weak. If money is motive, the surviving spouse benefits most. But both of them were loaded on their own, so it doesn't stick well. The homeless deal. It's solid, but there might be somebody who works there who's just sick greedy and weirdly driven. And still, Fitzhugh was likely worth more than the eight-plus mil alive by bringing the cause into the public consciousness, drumming up big-ticket donations."

"I'm with you on that. He hyped it on social media all the time. Did PSAs, attended benefits, hosted them, and gave them money annually. But say Lane was the intended victim."

"How does that change any of the above?"

"From what I know—that's going from media, and statements, interviews—she's not as soft a touch as he was. If she noticed something went missing, I think she'd start kicking ass. And there's the production company."

"His. But hers now." Eve nodded. "She'll have something to say about that now, or at least her lawyers will have a look there."

"And maybe there's been some hanky in the panky Fitzhugh didn't know about, or was handling in a soft-touch way. That's big money, right? All those millions that go into producing a feature or a series, and just running the day-to-day expenses."

"That's a good thought." And yet another area to look at, Eve decided. "That was his baby, not hers. If it's not doing as well as it looks on the surface, if money's sliding away somewhere, you don't want her nosing in. And you don't want to kill him—he's the name, he's the draw. Kill her, get her out of the picture, distract him. Either you figure to recoup the losses before he notices, or wring it all dry and blow. Could play."

In Queens, she hunted for parking on a narrow street and opted for a squat, two-decker parking garage.

"Twenty bucks an hour." Disgusted, she aimed her 'link at the device on the gate to record her time in and pay the required hour minimum. "Shouldn't be legal."

Despite the cost, she had to wind to the second level and take one of three empty slots left.

"We'll check his work first." From the open second level, she pointed down. "He stocks shelves at that Mini-Super. I don't get the 'mini' and 'super' when it should be one or the other."

"You really almost always have to go to the 'burbs for a super-super. Rent's as pricy as parking around here."

For a moment Eve watched bumper-to-bumper traffic inch along the skinny street.

"It's like nobody's heard of public transportation here."

They took the stairs down, boots clanging on metal treads.

People shuffled along the sidewalk with the same lethargy as the vehicular traffic. A kid popped out of a salon and sauntered his jaywalking way across the street through the creeping cars.

A woman popped her head out the salon door. The hair came first, a swirl of pink and blue like an ice cream cone served on Pluto. "Julio! Get me an iced coffee and a cruller!" she shouted in a voice thick with Queens before she slammed the door again.

Music banged out of cars; voices rang out of windows. A man in baggy shorts and a tight white tee with every inch of his muscular arms tatted led a dog the size of a well-fed rat on a pink leash.

A pair of women who looked as if they'd recently visited Ice Cream Cone's salon stood outside a shop with little portable fans whirling at their faces as they dished about someone named Ernestine and her recent weight loss.

"Paid to have it sculpted off, take my word."

"Don't I know it! All that talk about diet and exercise? As if! She paid good money for that new ass."

"Why would they care?" Eve wondered while they waited at the crosswalk. "It's Ernestine's ass, and her money either way."

"They're checking out your ass now and deciding you paid for it."

"Yeah?" Eve tipped down her sunshades—ones she'd managed not to lose in the short time she'd had them—and aimed a long, cool look. It had the women turning away casually, much like Galahad did after Roarke aimed a look at him.

They crossed the street, hiked up to the Mini-Super.

Inside, the air blasted cool to the point of cold. Business ran as brisk as the air at all five checkout stations. One offered a human element to ring up and bag. The rest ran on auto and self-serve.

Eve headed toward the human.

"We're looking for Ethan Crommell."

"Don't know. Haven't seen 'im." Her fingers—nails tipped with sky blue—flew as they rang up a carton of egg substitute, a sack of fake coffee. "Ask the manager."

"Where's the manager?"

She sighed audibly, then tapped her lapel mic. "Carmine to Checkout One!"

She finished with a carton of ice pops and a jumbo carton of soy milk. "Your total's ninety-eight-fifty-six today, Ms. Mussy."

"Lord, lord, lord." Ms. Mussy ran her 'link over the scanner while Blue Nails began to bag.

A man built like an overweight fireplug with slicked-down ink-black hair and a mustache that actually curled at the edges waddled up.

"Help you?"

Eve shifted, palmed her badge. "We need to speak with Ethan Crommell."

"That boy in trouble again?" Carmine fisted his hands on his husky hips. "Try to do a public service, try to give somebody a second chance, and what do you get?"

"We just need to speak with him."

"Well, he ain't here. Called in sick this morning—texted it, middle of the damn night. Gave him a chance 'cause his parole officer's my second cousin once removed. He's been reliable, I'll say that. Does his job and doesn't screw off too much."

"Does he call or text in sick much?"

"First time for it. And here the cops show up. If he's in trouble with the law, I don't want him back here."

"We just want to talk to him. Did he work yesterday?"

"Eight to three." The mustache quivered as if alive and outraged. "Didn't look sick, either."

"Seemed like a good one to me," Ms. Mussy put in. "Didn't he help me take my groceries home once when he was on his break? Then you hear axe murderers can seem like good ones until they chop your head off your shoulders. Hack the rest of you up into little pieces to feed to the dogs."

"We don't want to talk to him about decapitation," Eve assured her. "It's just routine."

Ms. Mussy nodded wisely. "They say that a lot, then—" She made a chopping motion with her hand before wheeling her cart away.

"How many axe murders have we investigated since you came to Homicide, Peabody?" Eve asked when they walked back outside and into the heat.

"I believe that number is zero."

"Exactly. But people sure like to talk about them like they happen every day. Crommell lives just down the block."

"We had that decapitation," Peabody recalled. "But that was a sword, so it doesn't count as an axe murder. Anyway. It's funny he'd call in sick the first time on the night Fitzhugh dies."

"Yeah, that's funny all right. It'd be funnier to me if he'd called in the day of the murder, then had that time to get to the Upper West, execute whatever plan he had for getting into the building, much less the party, poison Fitzhugh, and get out again. But it's still funny."

She stopped outside the building—four stories of graffiti-etched pitted block with barred windows as the only visible security.

Since the single door didn't require a buzz in, she didn't need the master to step into the closet of a lobby. With no elevator to reject, they took the stairs.

She heard music, voices, a baby screaming as if that axe murderer got busy chopping it up for the dogs. She smelled old piss, more recent Zoner smoke, and somebody's takeout that had gone bad at least a day before.

On the third floor, a cat howled behind one of the closed doors, and the tinny laughter of a comedy on-screen sounded behind another.

She heard Eliza Lane speak clearly behind Crommell's door. Even as her eyes narrowed, Peabody spoke up.

"That's from a vid. He's watching one of her vids."

Eve banged the side of her fist against the door.

From inside, sound of the vid shut off. Eve heard footsteps, hurried ones, heard another door close.

Whatcha hiding, Ethan? Eve wondered.

It took a couple of minutes before she saw the shadow cross the Judas hole.

"Whaddaya want?"

"Police, Mr. Crommell." Eve held up her badge. "We need to speak to you."

"I haven't done anything! I'm sick. I'm taking a sick day. I called in and everything. I didn't break parole."

"Yes, sir. We were informed of that. We just need to speak with you."

She heard a lock click, another thump, then the rattle of a security chain.

No, Crommell didn't look sick, Eve thought when he opened the door. In fact he looked better, healthier, than in his mug shots or ID shot.

He hit about five-ten in his bare feet. He wore cotton pajama pants with blue-and-white checks and a baggy white tee that could've used a good wash. He had a headful of curling dark hair, a full, well-shaped mouth, slim blade of a nose. The light scruff on his face helped disguise a weak jaw.

He might have been deemed almost handsome—if you ignored the eyes. Though an inoffensive pale blue, they carried a look in them that said clearly to Eve:

I'm not quite right.

"I'm allowed to take a day off work when I'm sick. Nobody wants you coming in sick and spreading germs all over. I got a stomach bug."

"I'm sorry to hear that. If we could come in to speak to you and avoid contacting your parole officer? We could also report back to your manager that you are, indeed, not feeling well today."

"It's not fair a man can't take a day off when he's sick."

"We'll make this as quick as possible."

"It's not fair," he repeated, but backed away to let them in.

She smelled candle wax, something very fragrant, very sweet, but saw no candles in the room. A room, she noted, very spare and very clean, but for the pullout bed where he'd obviously nested with a huge bowl of popcorn, a smaller bowl of gummy-type candy, a bag of chips, and a dish of white gunk he'd used for dip.

The pullout and all the snacks sat across from the wall screen.

The table beside the pullout held a quart bottle of Coke, half full.

"You're probably not doing that stomach bug much good with the junk food," Peabody commented.

"I can eat what I want. It's not illegal. I was just lying down, taking it easy."

"Watching some screen," Eve added. "Eliza Lane."

"I'm allowed to watch vids. I made a mistake, and I had treatment and therapy. I'm allowed to watch vids. Ms. Lane is a talented actress, and her vids are very entertaining."

"Uh-huh." Eve wandered a bit, noted Crommell's eyes tracking her. No increased nerves when she stepped closer to the kitchen alcove. "Just watching vids while you're recovering? No news media today?"

Those eyes cut away. "Not today. News isn't happy. I wanted happy because I'm sick."

"I get that," Peabody said as Eve wandered.

"What's this about anyway? I want to go back to bed. I gotta get better so I don't miss more work."

"I guess you got sick last night. That's when you texted your manager."

"Yeah, woke up puking, if you have to know."

"Where'd you go after work yesterday? You got off at three."

"Home, right here. I wasn't feeling all that good." His fingers scratched at the sides of his thighs, and his feet couldn't stand quite still. "Had this stomach bug coming on so I went to bed, tried to sleep it off."

"See anybody, talk to anybody from the time you got home, right after three, until you texted your manager?"

"No. I said I wasn't feeling good, didn't I?"

"You sure did." She watched the nerves light in his eyes as she stepped toward the pullout, and the closed door beside it. "I guess that takes care of it. We appreciate the time, and sure hope you feel better soon. Hey, we've got a long ride back. Mind if I use your bathroom?"

"I guess."

"Thanks." As she turned the knob on the closed door, he jumped.

"Not there, not there. It's over there."

But she'd already opened the door.

And found the shrine to Eliza Lane inside.

7

Photos of Eliza Lane covered the walls of the narrow space. Some struck as paparazzi-style shots, others he'd obviously printed out from articles or interviews.

Vid posters she imagined he'd bought from some fan-based online site crowded in.

A shelf ran across the closet and held more photos—framed—along with flowers and the candles she'd smelled. On a higher shelf he'd arranged signed playbills, also framed.

Eve took it all in at a glance.

"Well, Ethan, I wonder what your therapist would say about this."

"That's my personal property!" His voice hiked up two or three registers, and his face burned red. "You get out! You get out now."

"I think we'll all get out, head into Central for a nice chat. We'll see if your parole officer wants to join in."

"I'm not going back in that place. I'm not going back! You can't make me."

He dropped to the floor. Like a toddler, Eve thought, and wondered if he'd start banging his fists and kicking his feet.

Instead, he swiped a hand under the pullout and came out with scissors.

She said, "Seriously?"

"I'll cut you to pieces!"

"Okay. Hey, don't look now, but my partner has a stunner aimed at you." His head swiveled to where Peabody stood, stunner in hand. "Told you not to look. Now I've got a stunner aimed at you, too. Let's do the math here, Ethan," she said as his eyes wheeled back and forth. "Two police-issue stunners in the hands of trained officers. One pair of scissors in the hand of a delusional fuckwit. What do you figure that equals?"

She gave Peabody the barest head shake to signal her to hold fire. "Put those down."

Instead, he lunged toward her. When she blocked his arm, brought her elbow up to tap his chin, the scissors clattered away. He dropped to the floor again. Though he didn't bang his fists, kick his feet, he did cry like a baby.

"I'm not going back there. You can't keep me from her, you can't keep us apart, she needs me!"

"Who needs you?"

"Eliza!"

"How do you know she needs you?"

"She told me!"

"Yeah? Did she tag you on your 'link, maybe come by to pay a visit?"

"She speaks to me." He lifted his tear-drenched face and his crazy eyes. "We're connected. Our minds and hearts are one. He had to die, you see. He was keeping her prisoner, keeping us apart. She's so brave! She's waiting for me to go to her, to find the way. And we'll go away together."

"Okay, Ethan, you need to put some shoes on." Eve hauled him to his feet. When he shoved against her, she ignored it, swung him around to cuff his hands behind his back. "Find him some shoes, Peabody, and get those scissors. Ethan Crommell, you're under arrest for violation of conditions of parole, for assaulting an officer with a deadly weapon. You have the right to remain silent," she began, and read off the Revised Miranda.

"Got shoes under the bed, and a scrapbook. Lots of Eliza Lane in here."

She held up the book so Eve could see it.

He'd drawn a big heart on the cover, and inside had merged a headshot of himself, one of Lane, so they appeared to smile out, cheek to cheek.

He'd titled the book E&E 4 EVER.

She debated: Pathetic or pathological? And concluded it could be both.

"Bring it."

When Peabody brought out a pair of what Eve thought of as institutional shower slides, she ordered Ethan to slip them on.

"Peabody, make sure we've got an open Interview room, and check to see if Mira's free to observe."

"You won't keep us apart!"

Pretty sure we will, Eve thought.

He wept all the way to Central.

He blubbered on the elevator. Since he'd exhibited violent behavior, she didn't feel justified in yanking him out and onto the glides. She let him blubber and wail as cops shuffled on, shuffled off.

"What's his problem?" one asked her.

"Love," she said. "Mad, mad love."

"It'll get you every time."

When they reached Homicide, he was down to snorting sniffles.

"Set him up, Peabody. Let's give him a few to compose himself. I'll contact his parole officer."

That set off another round of wailing. "I'm not going back! You can't keep us apart!"

"Christ," Eve muttered, and escaped to her office.

She contacted the parole officer, who looked weary, frazzled, and unsurprised. She grabbed coffee as she reviewed Ethan's file.

And rolled her eyes at the conclusions and recommendations of his facility shrink.

"Conquered his obsession with Eliza Lane, my ass," she muttered. "Cooperative, productive, nonviolent. Oh yeah? Try saying that after he stabs you in the throat with his scrapbook scissors. Parole recommended with conditions of continued weekly talk therapy, gainful employment. No contact with Ms. Lane, blah blah blah."

Peabody tapped the doorjamb.

"Interview B. I got him some ginger ale and a bunch of tissues. Mira's on her way."

"Great. I think we'll have her in the interview instead of observing it."

"Can I?" When Peabody pointed at the AutoChef, Eve waved an affirmative. "It's hard for me to see the crybaby we just hauled in having the skill and smarts to pull off Fitzhugh's murder."

"The crybaby who tried to punch a hole in me?"

"Yeah, he's got a violent streak, but poison's not. Not physical violence."

"You've got a point there. And while it may be hard to imagine him having the skill and means to pull this off, crazy can fool you. He managed to convince his shrink and the parole board he was okay to resume his place in society. Had freaking conquered his Eliza Lane obsession."

She pushed up. "And what do we find? A shrine, a scrapbook in progress, and unless I'm very much mistaken about the contents of the basket beside his bed, a guy spending his day jacking off in his socks to her vids."

"Eeww."

"You can repeat that when we go back after the interview and toss his place."

"I'll just repeat it now. Eeww. But . . . the commander said we'd have any extra manpower we needed. He could authorize another team to do that."

Eve debated handling it personally, which would include handling what she knew damn well would be several cum-soaked socks, or delegating. And pointed.

"Yeah. Oh yeah, that's a fine idea. Set that up. He had a tablet, his 'link. Unless he has other electronics tucked away, that's it. The search team should bring those in. And contact the locals, give them the rundown. They can have uniforms do the knock-on-doors. Let's see if anyone saw him go out or come in last night, early this morning. Also check if he had a locker at work and search that. If he had any kind of bank box, storage unit."

Then she shrugged. "If he did it, or knows who did, we'll get it out of him. He'll be proud of it. He already said Fitzhugh had to die. Let's see if he's stopped crying."

When she walked to the bullpen, Jenkinson and his tie hailed her.

"Closed the Dobson case, LT. The vic's brother-in-law. The vic's good at his job, see. Pulls in solid tips waiting tables. The sister's husband keeps hitting him up for loans on the sly. Twenty, fifty, a hundred, until the vic cuts him off. Can't keep shelling it out."

"Gambling, illegals, or sex issues?"

"Sex. A lot of virtual sex at fifty a pop. So the sex freak son of a bitch goes after him after his shift, says he's gotta have some cash, says how he knows he's got plenty on him. Vic says he's got his own bills to pay, his own wife and kid. Says to stop hounding him or he'll tell his sister. So the fucker pulls a sticker. To scare him, he claims, and things just got out of hand."

Jenkinson bared his teeth. "Got out of hand so he had to stab his wife's brother fifteen times before he took the hundred and twelve dollars the vic pulled in cash tips that night. Took his 'link, his wrist unit, his damn wedding ring."

"Comes off as a mugging."

"So he figured. Greedy bastard couldn't toss the 'link and such. Thought he'd be smart and pawned them up in the Bronx. Got a lousy hundred for them."

"So he killed his wife's brother for four rounds with a virtual pro. Good work."

"Thanks. Anyway, we're clear if you need any help on the Fitzhugh case."

"We've got a suspect in Interview now. We'll see how it goes."

She found Peabody with Mira outside Interview B.

The department's top shrink and profiler's mink-tipped-in-sunlight hair framed her calm and lovely face. Her eyes, a soft and quiet blue, met Eve's. Her lips curved—lips tinted a rose the exact shade of her suit. The suit had the sheen of silk and showed off good, shapely legs.

Eve supposed the shoes showed off the legs, too, but she'd never get voluntarily working all day on skinny stilts.

"Peabody's catching me up. I'm still stunned by Brant Fitzhugh's death."

"Did you know him?"

"Not personally, but Dennis and I enjoyed his vids. I remember reading about Eliza Lane's troubles with a stalker. I refreshed myself a little on the way here. Delusional, projecting an intimate relationship with her. One that has spanned numerous past lives. An eternal connection. You found a kind of shrine to her in his apartment?"

Eve pulled out her 'link to download the feed from her recorder. Held it out.

"Ah, yes. Classic."

"Do you know Dr. Ivan Horowitz?"

"Yes, somewhat. Is he Crommell's therapist?"

"He is, and pushed for the parole. He states Crommell had overcome his obsession with Lane—which, obviously, not even close—was nonviolent. Since he tried to stab me with a pair of scissors, I'm forced to disagree there, too."

"I see." Mira's soft blue eyes could go to frosty ice. And did. "After the interview, I'll contact Dr. Horowitz and give him my thoughts."

"If it turns out he let Fitzhugh's killer out of a cage, I'm going to have a few thoughts of my own to give him."

Eve opened the door.

"Record on. Mira, Dr. Charlotte; Dallas, Lieutenant Eve; and Peabody, Detective Delia; entering Interview with Crommell, Ethan, on the matters of parole violation, assaulting an officer with a deadly weapon, and resisting arrest."

"You opened my closet and didn't have permission."

"Thought it was the bathroom, for which you did give permission. You were read your rights, on record. Do you want me to go over them again, or do you understand your rights and obligations?"

"I understand fine, just fine. I was protecting my personal property."

"You were protecting a closet lined with photographs of Eliza Lane, candles, flowers, and so forth by threatening to stab an officer with a pair of scissors?"

"That's right. They're my property."

"You were recently released on parole from incarceration in a facility for the mentally and/or emotionally ill. You were, three years ago, convicted of stalking Eliza Lane, the actress, of harassing her, accosting her and her husband, Brant Fitzhugh, actor."

"He was keeping us apart."

"Fitzhugh kept you and Lane apart?" Eve spoke in pleasant, conversational tones. "How did he do that?"

"He blurred her memory of me. Sorcery." He said the word in a horror-vid whisper. "Dark magic. He's obsessed with her."

"He's obsessed. Okay, why did she file charges against you, and testify against you in court?"

Ethan rolled his crazy eyes. "Sorcery. Black magic. I've had to break the spell time and again, over our lifetimes."

"How do you break the spell?" Mira asked him.

"Love, deep and true. Or white magic against the dark. Or in battle. We face this in different ways in every life. But Eliza and I share mind and heart, a bond that can never really be broken. Fitzhugh—as he calls himself in this life—will always fail, always fall. By my hand or hers."

"His death, you believe, breaks the spell he has over her so her memory returns?"

He nodded at Mira. "Inevitably, until it all begins again. It can take years before we recognize each other, but the heart sees. She's waiting for me now."

"If she's waiting for you," Eve put in, "why didn't you go to her? Why were you watching her vids in your apartment?"

"I had to finish the spell—the white magic. You interrupted me."

Apparently, Eve thought, his white magic included masturbation.

"And he has minions guarding her."

"Minions."

"Oh yes." Crommell nodded enthusiastically. "Those loyal to him. They surround her, and me. We have to carefully plan our escape. I know you're one of them."

"I'm a minion?"

He leaned toward her, crazy eyes, shaking finger. "I see you for what you are, but nothing you do will stop me."

"Ethan, did you kill Brant Fitzhugh?"

He smiled slyly. "Which time?"

"This time. Last night."

"I wasn't given that privilege in this life. But I knew, I felt her break the chains. And I saw and heard, on-screen, that he'd fallen at last. Poison, they said. She'd used it before."

"Eliza poisoned him?"

"She's brave and strong, but he's stronger. She can't beat him with sword or fists. Though once she was able to slit his throat, and twice she ended him with a bullet. But poison and wiles are her usual weapon."

"I thought he had her under a spell."

"White magic." Crommell hissed out an impatient breath. "I weakened his hold."

"The altar to her," Peabody supplied. "The candles, photos, flowers. White magic."

"That's right, that's right, that's right. The white, and our love, will always defeat the dark."

"And what's the plan now?" Eve wondered.

"We'll wait until the time is right, and when it is, I'll go to her, take her away where we can live the rest of this life together. And when the cycle of life ends for one, the other will take theirs so we begin again."

"Have you been in Eliza's apartment? In this lifetime," Eve added.

"He keeps it guarded. Well guarded. Once I scaled her tower over the cliffs and we sailed out to sea to an island of our own. But the walls of her prison now are sheer."

"Maybe you could get in wearing a disguise," Peabody suggested.

"I tried, but the spell was so strong. They chased me away. I would die for her, but if I die, she dies. It's our bond."

"Maybe killing her this time around, you'd start the cycle over, have a better chance."

His eyes widened at Eve. "I could never harm her!"

"There was a big party last night, a lot of people. You could've slipped in, broken the spell."

"If I'd known, I could've tried. Fought my way through the guards and minions, beaten him in battle, and swept her away to safety. I would have tried. But this is better. You understand now. She broke the spell, and we'll find our way back to each other."

"It seems to me slipping in, going unnoticed, then getting close enough to add poison to his drink's a better way. Slip out again and wait until it all simmers down to sweep her away."

Now he looked insulted. "I'm a *man*! A man faces his enemy head-on. She's only a woman, so has to use wile and subterfuge. I would have spared her that if I could have gotten through."

"How will you communicate with her?" Mira asked.

"Mind to mind, heart to heart. She can speak to me now. I hear her song." Closing his eyes, he laid a hand on his temple and smiled. "She sings for me. Only for me now."

Enough, Eve thought. Just enough.

"Okay. Ethan, you broke your parole and threatened a police officer with a weapon. You're going to be taken down and booked, and wait until you can be transferred back to your facility, reevaluated."

"You can chain me as before, lock me away, but love will rise, love will triumph."

"Okay. Interview end. Peabody."

"I'll take him down."

Eve went out with Mira, rubbing her eyes as they walked away from Interview. "He's crazy as a box of rabid monkeys, but he didn't kill Fitzhugh."

"I suspect learning of Fitzhugh's death caused yet another breakdown. I also believe he was misdiagnosed and should never have been released. I'll write a report, and trust me, share my considerable thoughts with Dr. Horowitz. Crommell shouldn't go back under his care, and I'll throw my weight on that."

She glanced back as Peabody led Crommell away. "Poor man."

"I'm having his place tossed in case he was bullshitting us in there. And no, I don't think he was. But it's possible somebody could have used him and his delusions to work the murder. The timing," she added. "He hasn't been out long, and Fitzhugh's dead. We'd have to look at him for it."

Eve paused at the entrance to Homicide. "He'd have gone after Lane, sooner or later."

"Absolutely."

"Thanks for taking the time to sit in."

Eve went to her office, sat, looked at her board and Crommell's ID shot. "Crazy as fuck, and pathetic with it."

Turning away, she wrote her report.

Once done, rather than go back to doing runs on guests, she walked out to Peabody.

"Rico Estaban, that's Vera Harrow's plus-one, is shooting some deal in the West Village. Let's go talk to him."

"He's a small-screen guy," Peabody informed her as they started out. "Mostly one-off parts in series. Did some daytime dramas, and those holiday romance deals I can't help watching during the season."

The thought put a dreamy look on her face.

"Like gorgeous, cranky guy hates Christmas, gets stuck in a small town for a couple of weeks during the season, finds love with small-town girl—maybe the local vet with a sweet, frisky puppy—and the true meaning of Christmas. Or he's the gorgeous, Christmas-loving guy who owns the local diner in another small town where the gorgeous, high-powered ad exec gets stuck, and she falls for him, his adorable niece, and Christmas."

"I love those damn movies."

Eve glanced back at the burly uniform wedged into the elevator with them. "Seriously?"

"And I ain't ashamed. Did you see the one where the big-shot developer comes into town? He's going to tear down this old Christmassy inn to build a fancy resort."

"And he falls for the daughter of the family who's run the inn for three generations," Peabody continued. "With Christmas renewed in his heart, he buys the inn, but to restore it, and the whole town comes to sing carols on Christmas Eve. Made me cry."

"Me, too."

"Jesus" was all Eve could say. She pushed off the elevator to clang down the last two flights of steps to her garage level.

"I especially like to watch them when I'm baking during the holidays."

"It's summer," Eve reminded her. "I refuse to discuss Christmas and think of all the stupid presents I have to come up with when it's eighty and sunny."

"Maybe you need to get stuck in a small town and find Christmas in your heart."

"That'll be the day."

She zipped out of the garage.

"I want to pump him about Vera Harrow. He's small-time, she's not. What's she doing bringing him to the party?"

"Did you get a look at him? Absolute frosty supreme. I did the brief on-scene interview with him, and he piled on the charm. He looks you right in the eyes." She two-fingered her own, tapped them out. "Sexy."

"Might be that simple. Might be, 'Hey, sexy B-lister, how about I take you to this bash, you dump a little of this into my ex-lover's drink, and I make you a big star.'"

"Well . . ."

"Yeah, probably not, especially since she struck me as a woman who takes care of her own business. But we'll get a sense. We know Fitzhugh had the glass when he stopped to talk to them."

"The more I think about it, the more I think Lane was the target."

"Expand."

"Her drink of choice. He took it to her, and according to witnesses said just that as he moved through. The only reason she didn't drink it is because Bowen nudged her to perform first. And the only reason he drank it instead was to toast her performance. I'm leaning toward she got lucky, and he didn't."

"Agreed."

"You think she was the target?"

"Probability and logic point there." Stopping at a light, watching the pedestrian river flow, Eve tapped her fingers on the wheel. "The other possibility is it didn't matter to the killer which one of them drank it."

"Vera Harrow."

"She had it in for both of them. Women opt for poison more often than men. A violent death—and cyanide's not bloody, but it's sure as hell violent—at a big, splashy, media-attended party gets a lot of attention. Attendees are already getting that attention. Seems to me attention is vital to people in this line of work."

"Publicity as motive?"

"Or a handy by-product."

The production shut down a block, with plenty of lookie-loos neck-craning outside the barricades. Rather than hunt for parking, Eve pulled up behind them, flipped on her On Duty light.

"Estaban's got a guest shot in *City Living*," Peabody read off her PPC as she got out of the car. "It's a new series about three roommates—struggling actor, chef, blogger—looking for love and their big break."

Eve signaled a bored cop posted at the barricade.

"What's up, Lieutenant?"

"We need to speak with Rico Estaban."

"They're doing a scene. See, right down there?" He gestured about halfway down the block where cameras and crew converged outside a coffee shop. "They'll start people walking by in a second, then these two come out, stand there talking. They'll walk this way, stop, talk. She walks off, he stands looking after her. Then they'll go back and do it all over again. And a-freaking-gain."

"Let whoever needs to know we need Estaban."

"You got it. Hold on once. Here they go again."

She watched people begin to walk, then the door to the coffee shop opened. It ran as the cop had told her. With the couple—a woman and Estaban—pausing to talk as people streamed around them. The woman shook her head, laughing as her long blond ponytail swayed. They walked again, stopped again. This time she gave him a playful smack on the arm before walking on alone with him watching her.

She heard the call for cut, and the officer tapped his earbud. "Hey, this is Officer Rye. I've got a Lieutenant Dallas, NYPSD, needs to talk to Mr. Estaban."

Eve nodded to him and started down the block.

"She's coming through now."

A woman, stick thin, with a skullcap of orange hair and lime-green high-tops, hotfooted it in their direction.

"We've got the block for another forty-eight minutes," she began.

"Great, congratulations. I need Rico Estaban, and hopefully it won't take that long."

"If you could just wait until—"

Eve held up her badge again. "Does this look like I'm inclined to wait? The sooner we talk to him, the sooner you'll have him back."

"Hold on."

She ran back, talked to another woman with an explosion of dark curls under a ball cap. The second woman turned, stared, snarled, then called out:

"Rico, visitors on set. Linny, let's get your close-ups and reaction shots."

Estaban sauntered over. He wore jeans, a black tee—both showed off his excellent build. He aimed a killer smile.

"Detective, I love your boots. Ride 'em, cowgirl. And you must be Lieutenant Dallas." He offered a hand. "We didn't meet at the unfortunate event last night."

"No, we didn't. We have some questions."

"I'll do my best to answer them. Do you mind if we walk over there? Craft services has the world's best lemonade, and some shade."

Taking their assent for granted, he started toward a trio of carts, several picnic-style tables, all under a big awning.

"We lost a legend last night," he began. "It was my first time meeting Brant in person."

"You came with Ms. Harrow."

"With Vera, yes. Three lemonades, Dru darling. You'll thank me," he said to Eve and Peabody.

"You spoke to Mr. Fitzhugh shortly before his death."

"I did, and it was a thrill. I've been a fan since I was a boy, and my years in the business haven't jaded me. In fact, the opposite. To have maintained that career, that level of professional and creative excellence?" Estaban shook his head as he passed Peabody, then Eve, a cup of lemonade. "A legend."

He took his own, gestured to an empty table. "Here, I'm playing a new love interest for our aspiring actress, who works at the Café Olé. It won't work out, but it'll be fun while it lasts. I'm a major league pitcher," he explained, "and I can't count the hours of training I've done for the handful of minutes I'll be on the mound. And there's Brant, decades of work—the riding, the swordplay, the fight scenes." He shook his head again.

"How would you describe your relationship with Vera Harrow?"

"Oh. Gloriously sexual," he said, and beamed that killer smile.

8

"Okay. That's it?"

Estaban laughed. "I failed to shock you. Vera is a beautiful woman, an energetic one. We enjoy a robust physical relationship. It won't last, of course, any more than my ballplayer and the wannabe actress, but we enjoy the moment. I enjoy her. She has a biting wit, a towering talent. And she's generous."

"How long have you been involved?"

"Who keeps track?" He drank some lemonade. "A month or two, I think. Yes, a couple of months now. We met at a party, hit it off. So we ditched our dates, went back to her place, and had glorious sex."

He drank again. "She likes that I'm younger and not nearly on the same level as she is professionally. I like that she's older. More mature women are so interesting—they've lived, they understand who they are and what they want."

With a smile, he gave an elegant shrug. "And, without shame, I like that at her level she may help boost my career. We're media hounds,

Vera and I. If the paparazzi want to snap pictures of us naked on her rooftop terrace, it's press. And fortunately, we both look very good naked."

"Being a guest at a party where a major celebrity's murdered generates press."

"It certainly does." He agreed with ease. "I've already done an in-person interview in studio this morning, conducted three others via 'link, and I'm booked on *Screen Talk* tonight. Brant Fitzhugh's dead, and I can't change that."

He spread his fingers, and as Peabody said, looked directly in Eve's eyes. "I wasn't blowing smoke about being a fan. I can't count the number of times, as a boy, as a man, I've seen *The Sorcerer's Quest* or *Hunt the Dark*. But I can't change what happened, and I have to work at my own career."

"How does Vera feel about his death?"

"She's shaken more than she'll let show, if I'm a judge. A shitheel—that's how she described him before this happened. You don't end things with Vera, you see. She ends it."

He shrugged again. "So Brant would forever be the Shitheel, and Eliza the Whorehound. But last night, she was shaken. Physically as well as emotionally. I took her out to the terrace for air, she was so pale, got her a brandy from the bar there to help steady her. It's the first time I've seen her vulnerable.

"Some part of her loved the Shitheel." He polished off his lemonade. "It may be in the way you love what you lose, but it's still a kind of love, isn't it?"

"Some people hurt what they love," Eve countered. "Especially if they've lost it."

"I guess that's true. But I'd say, again if I'm a judge, Vera's more the kick-you-in-the-balls type than the cyanide-in-the-champagne sort."

"Eliza Lane might have drunk the champagne, and she doesn't have balls to kick."

"Hmm." He sat back, and those deep, dream-god eyes went to calculating. "Now, that's a thought, isn't it? We were standing fairly close to Brant when he stepped through to watch Eliza sing. It seems to me, if Vera had gone crazy, decided to poison Eliza, she could have easily stopped Brant from drinking. Just knocked the glass out of his hand, for instance. Oops!"

"How close?"

"Ah, let me think. I was on Vera's right. Yes, on her right. There was someone—another woman—thirty-something, redhead, attractive—on Vera's other side. And someone just behind her and Brant, just to his right. I can't tell you who else. We were all sort of massed together in the moment."

The woman with orange hair came bounding back. "Rico, we really need you for the long shot."

"Right there. Is there anything else?" he asked Eve.

"Not right now. We appreciate your time and cooperation."

"It was my first murder." He rose. "I really hope I live the rest of my life without an encore. And I really hope you catch whoever killed him. I was, sincerely, a fan."

Eve signaled Peabody to walk back to the barricade.

"Let's see if we can talk to Samantha Keene. See if you can find out where she is. We'll take her, and another shot at Vera Harrow."

While Peabody set it up, Eve checked in with the search team.

"We've cleared the second and third floors," Baxter told her. "There's a lot of stuff, a lot of space, boss, but so far nothing hinky. I'm going to say these people know how to live. Or he did until he didn't."

"What's McNab's status?"

"He's still up there. When we broke for eats, he'd finished with the vic's assistant's e's and was into the first of Lane's assistants. No hinky there, either, so far. If any of these people killed Fitzhugh, they were damn careful about sweeping up bread crumbs."

"Yeah, they would be. Anything otherwise?"

"We did have one guy get to the door here—main level. Pulled the flower delivery shtick. Reporter, bribed one of the tenants to pass him up to their floor, used the stairs to get up here. Building security spotted him."

One way to crash a party—maybe. "He made it all the way to the main level door?"

"They alerted us when they spotted him coming up the stairwell. Quick response on their end, boss. They got up here when he's hitting the buzzer on the door. Escorted him down and out."

Then he grinned. "Dropped the flowers when security nabbed him. Trueheart's taking them to his mom." Anticipating an objection, he shrugged. "They were just going to lie there and die otherwise."

"Right." Flowers were the least of her concerns. "Let me know your status at end of shift. If you can't clear it all, pick it up in the morning. Tell McNab the same."

"Got that. You know, Dallas, I started out thinking this was my dream house, but there's just too damn much of it. You'd have to have the domestics or droids—they don't have any droids—the assistants and whatever the fuck poking around all the damn time. The whole third floor's basically laid out for assistants, and the domestics have a space about the size of my apartment down here."

He shook his head. "How's a guy supposed to walk around naked with all these people around?"

"That's one benchmark for city living. Dallas out."

"I'm trying not to imagine Baxter walking around naked in his apartment, and failing." Peabody scrubbed at her eyes. "Samantha

Keene's just out of dance class. She wants us to meet her at Footlights. It's a café off Broadway. She's heading there now."

"Plug in the address."

As she did, Eve's 'link signaled. When she saw Nadine on the read-out, she took it on her wrist unit.

"Dallas."

"You made an arrest."

"Did I?"

"Ethan Crommell, convicted of stalking Eliza Lane, assaulting Brant Fitzhugh, trespassing, harassment, and so on."

"Oh yeah, that arrest."

"My sources say he'll be returned to the Gordon Institution to serve out his sentence, and face additional charges of assault with a deadly on a police officer—betting that's you—and resisting arrest. He's not currently being charged with Fitzhugh's murder."

"The investigation is active and ongoing."

"Uh-huh. Since notified of Crommell's release on parole, Lane's building security, the security in the building where *Upstage* was in workshops, the Crystal Gardens Theater where they'll move into re-hearsals, the security in the building housing the offices for the New York base of Fitzhugh's production company all have Crommell's description, his photo, and instructions to detain him for the police should he attempt to enter."

Nadine held up a finger before Eve could get a word in.

"Building security at Lane's residence maintains, firmly, Crommell didn't attempt to enter last night, and hasn't attempted to enter at any time since his release."

"You've been busy."

"A girl keeps her hand in." And Nadine polished the fingernails of that hand on her shoulder. "I've researched him, Dallas. He's an obsessed fan with serious issues and delusions, in mandatory lockup and therapy for nearly three years. Supposedly rehabilitated enough to meet the standards for parole."

"Not nearly enough, but not a suspect in the murder of Brant Fitzhugh."

"Not nearly enough why, and why not a suspect?"

She could blow Nadine off, but calculated. If she had to do another media briefing—and odds were—she'd address all this anyway. And beyond friendship, it never hurt to have a skilled crime reporter with integrity on your side.

"During a routine interview with Crommell at his residence, as he had taken a sick day from his place of employment, the investigators found what could be called a shrine to Eliza Lane, a small area papered with her photographs and other memorabilia. When confronted with this discovery, as his probationary release was precluded on his controlling his obsession with Ms. Lane, Crommell attempted to stab the primary investigator with scissors it appeared he used to create a scrapbook containing more photos and memorabilia pertaining to Ms. Lane."

"Did he cut you?"

"I said 'attempted,' but thanks for asking."

Concern turned to amusement. "Need to get any and all facts."

"Right. Crommell was restrained and transported to formal interview, at Cop Central, with Dr. Charlotte Mira in attendance for psychiatric observation and evaluation. During the course of the interview, the investigators and Dr. Mira concluded that while it was extremely unlikely Crommell had any part in the death of Brant Fitzhugh, his mental and emotional state, his delusions and intentions made him a danger to himself and others. In addition to his violation of the conditions of his parole, he was charged with assaulting an officer with a deadly weapon and resisting arrest."

"Nice report, Lieutenant, but it doesn't actually answer the questions."

"Off the record."

"Shit." Nadine puffed out air, frustrated air. "Damn it. Fine. We're off."

"He's batshit, Nadine, and thinks Lane talks to him, is begging him to save her. They've done this dance throughout time, right? Past-life crap. He's just not capable of planning something like Fitzhugh's death and carrying it out—even if he could've gotten in the building, had known about the party, been able to access cyanide. And if he had? He'd have said so. It's his mission in this life and all his delusionary lives to reunite with Lane and live with her under rainbows while they ride unicorns or whatever.

"He didn't kill Fitzhugh," she concluded. "So the investigation is active and ongoing."

"Give me a nugget."

"All that wasn't a nugget? Wasn't that a nugget?" Eve asked Peabody, who just shrugged to stay neutral.

"Try this. Who's the last person you talked to—regarding the murder?"

When Peabody shrugged again, Eve decided why not. "Rico Estaban."

"Ah, the Holiday Hunk. It wouldn't be Christmas without seeing Estaban, bare-chested, near a Christmas tree. He's Vera Harrow's latest boy toy. They came together?"

"That's right. He isn't a suspect at this time and was cooperative."

Smiling, Nadine tapped a finger on her temple. "Hmmmm. 'At this time' makes me wonder if I should tag him up, get an interview."

"I can tell you he'd jump at it. He may be able to serve you up some dish, but other than bouncing on Harrow, he's not connected."

"The dish could do. About Harrow—"

"Gee, this was fun. We really have to do it more often."

And Eve cut her off. Peabody had to laugh.

"I'm surprised you didn't do that sooner."

"It passed the time and helped me lay it out again in my own head."

She veered into a loading zone, flipped her On Duty.

"Crommell has motive but no skill, no brains for it, and no opportunity. Estaban's going to have skill, brains, had opportunity, but no motive. Add Estaban's focused on himself, his career, and his own pleasures."

Gauging the traffic lumbering down the side street, Eve waited, waited, then pushed out to skirt around the hood of the car to the sidewalk.

"You could project Harrow saying, 'Drop this cyanide in the Shitheel's glass, and I'll make you the star he was.' But I don't see him trusting her enough to kill for her. It puts him on the hook. Now, say she said, 'Look the other way, give me a little cover while I drop this poison in the Shitheel's glass—or the Whorehound's'? Yeah, maybe."

"And if we busted her for it?" Peabody put on her shocked face. "'Oh my God, I can't believe she did it! I was standing right there.' And get lots and lots of media attention if she went down for it."

As they walked the half block to the café, Peabody sighed. "If it turns out that way, or close to it, I'm never going to be able to watch him catch the Christmas-loving heroine when she slips off the stepladder while hanging the shining star on the top of the tree, then go in for the long, slow kiss. I resent that."

"Your loss would be, of course, the major downside."

"It's a personal downside."

Footlights hummed with voices. Its fake brick walls displayed dozens of photos of what she assumed were Broadway stars, troupes, productions. Couples and groups filled tables and booths, most of which had backpacks or duffel bags crammed beneath. Waitstaff chattered with them while they served fizzy water, iced coffee or tea, oddly colored protein drinks, and smoothies.

A few sat on stools at the bar where a blender whirled, making those smoothies.

She spotted Samantha alone at a booth, frowning into a smoothie.

Given its army-green color, Eve would have frowned, too.

The pretty young blonde had her hair twisted into a single braid and wore a short-sleeved black sweater over a pink tank and a minuscule black skirt.

No makeup, Eve observed—or none that showed. No jewelry but for the trio of tiny studs curving up both ears.

She looked up as Eve approached, and her bright blue eyes lost the frown. "Eve Dallas. Wow. Detective Peabody, we talked a little last night. Please, sit down. I appreciate you meeting me here. I didn't want to talk about this at my apartment. My roommate's at an audition, but I'm not sure when she'd come back."

"No problem."

She had a voice as clear as church bells, and tired eyes.

"I was sitting here wondering why I ordered a kale and berry smoothie when what I really want is a double espresso."

She shrugged, downed a gulp of the smoothie. "I didn't sleep very well last night."

"Understandable."

A waitress glided up. "What can I get you today?"

"Got Pepsi?"

"We do."

"Diet version for me," Peabody told her.

"Coming right up. How's the smoothie, Sam?"

"You make the best." She smiled, then sighed again when the waitress moved on. "They're horrible. Or, they're not if you like kale and berry smoothies. But sometimes I ask myself does anyone, does anyone really? And I'm making small talk, my way of procrastinating."

"Last night was a shock." Peabody spoke gently, all sympathy.

"God, yes. I've played it over and over in my head—who can sleep?—and it still doesn't seem real."

"How well did you know Brant Fitzhugh?" Eve asked her.

"Well enough to know he was a sweetheart. He dropped in on workshops a few times. After I got the part, they had me over for dinner. Eliza and I worked at their place a few times. He was just so nice—not that I-have-to-be-nice-or-she'll-bitch-about-me, but real."

Tears swirled into her eyes as the waitress brought the drinks.

"Just shout out if you need anything." The waitress rubbed a hand on Samantha's shoulder before she left them.

"I really liked him. I liked watching them together. They're good together, and witty and fun. My parents divorced when I was nine, so it felt good to see a couple who genuinely liked each other."

"How about Eliza? Do you like her? Please be honest."

"Absolutely. I won't say she's a sweetheart, not like Brant. If you screw up a number or miss a line too many times, she'll sure as hell let you know it. But she'll work with you until you get it right. And she'll let you know you got it right. She's exacting, and I'm learning a lot. She's, obviously, old enough to be my mother, and there are times I can barely keep up."

She drank more smoothie. "If I'm honest, I'll say I wondered how it would be to work with her. I wanted this part, so much, and when I got it, I immediately started worrying about that, about her."

"Why?"

"I'm playing the part she played when she was my age, and how was that going to work? Then she took me out for coffee, and she told me she wanted me to shine. She was going to make sure I did, because

Marcie, my character, was part of her. She makes me work harder and be better than I might have without her.

"In the play—it's called *Upstage* because while the mother is always pushing the daughter, the mother is constantly trying to upstage her, to take the spotlight. She's never been the star she wanted to be. She loves her kid, but she can be selfish and oblivious to what her daughter needs and wants. That's Eliza, in the role."

Pausing, Samantha drew half circles around the base of the smoothie.

"But the woman, the actress?" she continued. "The opposite. She's generous. Last night for instance—she didn't have to bring me up with her. She shared that with me. 'Let's knock 'em dead, Sam.'"

Instantly, Samantha's eyes widened. "She didn't mean it like that. It's an expression."

"Yeah, I've heard it."

"Have you spoken with Eliza since last night?" Peabody asked.

"No. I don't know what I should do. I thought about texting her or leaving a straight to v-mail. I don't know what I should say, or if even just saying I'm sorry is intrusive. I've never been close to anyone who's died before. And this is worse than that. Somebody killed him. I can't get my head around it. Why anyone would."

"When you were with Eliza, performing by the piano, what did you see?"

Samantha frowned at Eve. "See?"

"Did you see Brant?"

"Oh." She breathed out. "Yeah. Okay. We sort of play off each other in that number, that duet. I'm pushing back, she's pushing back, and it builds, so we're basically singing to each other. But you always play to the audience, and we'd already worked on some staging, small bits of choreography in workshops, so there's that. I saw Brant ease through people to watch. I saw him lift that glass. I didn't actually see him drink because I'd turned toward Eliza."

"When you saw him, who else did you see? Near him."

"Oh, oh, okay. Minx."

"Minx."

"Choreographer. Minerva Novak—everyone calls her Minx. She was standing next to Brant, and her husband was just behind her with a hand on her shoulder. Um. Next to her, Vera Harrow. I met her that night." Samantha rolled her eyes. "Diva-time, and she's with the iced smoothie, Rico Estaban."

She shifted, rubbed her eyes. "Let's see. Pretty sure Carla—she plays Angie, my bestie—was just in front of Brant, and her date—I can't remember her name—was beside her, sort of. So kind of beside Brant but in front. Tessa—that's our director—was in there. Honest, the rest is kind of a blur."

"Tell us what you remember happening from there."

"I saw, for just a second, Brant stepping back. Just caught a glimpse, the movement really. And honestly I wouldn't have thought of it except for what happened to him. I think I heard glass break, but you learn to block out noises, so I'm not sure if I actually heard it or somebody said it so I think I heard it. But somebody screamed, I know I heard that. We kept singing for a couple seconds. We were face-to-face, then people were shouting and scrambling around. I didn't see him at first—so many people. Eliza stepped over."

"She wouldn't have seen him, either, from where the two of you stood."

"I don't think so. She just started over, like what the hell, then she called out his name, and people made way for her, and I saw him on the floor."

She looked away. "It was horrible. Like he was choking. And Dr. Cyril—I met him earlier—he was on the floor trying to help, saying to call nine-one-one, and Eliza was crying and pulling Brant into her arms. I just froze there. It was like everything froze, but it all happened so fast, too. He was standing there one minute, smiling, and the next . . ."

"Did you notice anything else, anyone else's reaction?"

"I don't think so. It was a lot of confusion, and Eliza was sobbing. I started to cry. A lot of people did. Oh, Vera Harrow brushed by me. Rico was leading her out to the terrace. She shoulder-bumped me, and that sort of brought me out of it for a minute. That's when I started to cry."

She shoved her half-full glass away. "Can't stomach any more of that."

"Here." Eve pushed her glass across the table. "I haven't touched it."

"Really?" Samantha knuckled a tear away, sipped. "God, so much better. I really liked him. I never, honestly never, heard anyone in the company say anything bad about him. Some of us are meeting up later, to talk. We don't know what's going to happen. Will Eliza come back? Will they cancel the production, or recast her part? It wouldn't be the same if they did. Most of us really need this job. I know how that sounds—"

"Human?" Peabody suggested.

Gratitude showed in her damp eyes.

"It's just—we've really worked hard, and . . . But I'm sitting here, and I'm alive. I can drink a lousy kale smoothie and chase it with a Pepsi. I can walk home and maybe buy some flowers on the way to cheer myself up. I can do whatever I want because I'm alive. If this production ends, I'll still be alive, and I'll get another part, get another chance. Brant's dead. He'll never get another chance."

She let out a long breath. "You both deal with this sort of thing all the time, so can I ask if you think I should contact Eliza? I don't want to push in, but I . . ."

"Send a text or straight to v-mail," Eve told her. "It lets her know you're there, and gives her the choice of getting back to you when she's ready."

"Okay, thanks. That's what I'll do."

They left her there, staring at her 'link, working out what to say.

"She comes off sincere," Peabody commented as they walked back to the car.

"She does. Add Fitzhugh's death puts her big break on the line, she's got no motive. What she did was give us a clearer picture of who, during the performance, had reasonable opportunity. We're going to find out more about Minerva Novak. We've got time to take another swing at Vera Harrow."

"I'll do a run on Novak, but can I have two minutes on the Great House Project? I've been good, I've been really good about not talking about it, and everything's so awesome mag. Stuff's happening every day now so every time we go over it's like: Wow! Look at this, and—"

"You're eating into your two minutes."

"Right. Okay. Go. I'm starting with our side because you didn't get over there last time. Our kitchen's finished! You saw Mavis's, and it's so her, all that color. Ours is, well, quieter, I love my cabinets, and I have so much counter space. I'm going to bake my ass off! And last weekend when we were clear, I worked on the water feature. August, the nanny, pitched in. He's great, handy, and it's going to be completely uptown."

She sucked in air. "The main-level powder room's done. We have a main-level powder room! It's so pretty. I can't decide on the colors for my craft room. I'm going to have my very own craft room! One minute I think I want to go really bold, and the next maybe I should go soft so all the yarns and fabrics put on the show. But I found this terrific old curvy divan in a thrift shop. I need to reupholster it, but it'd be perfect once I decide on bold or soft. Next day off, we're going to spatter-paint our home office."

"With McNab's blood?"

"Ha! No, you just take all kinds of paint, dip the brush in, then flick the paint at the walls. Crazy, fun patterns. Lots of energy. We figured we wanted lots of energy in our office. My dad's building us a partner's desk. Can you believe it?"

"He's building a desk?"

"A partner's desk. You sit on opposite sides of it. It's perfect for us, and it's so sweet of him. My mom's making us the light for the dining area."

"You can make lights?"

"If you're my mom, you can. Blown-glass pendants. I'll have pieces of them in my home. McNab's parents shipped us some rocks from Scotland."

"Rocks?" On this Eve turned her head, genuinely stunned. "They shipped rocks? Don't you already have rocks?"

"Not from Scotland—or we didn't. I'm incorporating them into the water feature, so we have pieces of McNab's family in our home, too. I know it sounds silly."

It should have, Eve thought, but somehow it didn't sound silly at all.

"It's weird, but in a nice sort of way."

"His uncle carved our names into them. All of our names. Mine, McNab's, Mavis's, Leonardo's, Bella's. And they're going to send another when Mavis has Number Two. And, man, you should see Leonardo's attic work space. It's crazy artistic, but efficient. I'm stealing some of his concept for my craft room. I think I'm going soft."

"I'll say."

"For the color. I'm going to have a whole wall—maybe two walls—of cubbies and open shelves for the yarn, the fabrics, the trim. That would really pop against the soft, then I could go bold or fun on the divan. There's a lot left to do, and so many decisions. Like do I want to keep the old bathroom vanity in the guest bath. It's outdated and funky, but if I painted it and changed out the hardware, it could be fun and retro."

"These are the choices that define our lives."

Peabody just smiled. "You let me go over two minutes."

"Maybe I'm going soft. But time's up. Run the choreographer."

"Minerva Novak." Peabody pulled out her PPC. "Age thirty-six, lives on West Forty-sixth. Married, six years, to Malcomb Furrier, age thirty-six, one offspring, female, age two. He's a composer. Born in Columbia, Maryland, parents Roger Novak and Alyson Crupke, divorced— she'd have been six. Both remarried, subsequent divorce for Alyson. Three half-sibs, two from the father and one from the mother. She studied dance at Juilliard, worked as a professional dancer—has a list of credits—then moved into choreography about eight years ago. More credits. She's worked with Tessa Long—that's the *Upstage* director—on two other shows. The best I can tell this is her first time working with Lane. No connection to Fitzhugh shows here."

"We'll look closer. Do you have her statement from last night?"

"Yeah, McNab talked to her and her husband. They were, they both believe, standing next to the victim for a few moments. But he was behind them when he collapsed. They have their arrival time as about eight-fifty, both spoke with Lane and Fitzhugh—separately— and spent time with others from the show. Spoke with Long and her wife for a longer period, out on the terrace. They were actually about to say their goodbyes—had told the babysitter they'd be home before eleven—when Lane and Keene started the number. So they watched. McNab's notes say she was visibly upset, kept a grip on her husband's hand throughout the short interview, but they were both cooperative."

"Okay, I'll poke around there tonight."

Vera Harrow had her own penthouse on the Upper East Side. Eve took advantage of their guest parking, on-site, using her badge to clear the way.

She termed the building Old New York. Dignified elegance, edging toward Deco, with solid security, including a doorman, and a lush lobby centered with an intricate tile rug and ripe with flowers in clear glass tubes suspended from the west wall.

The suit manning the lobby counter gave them a polite, uptown smile. "Good afternoon, how may I help you?"

"We're here to see Ms. Harrow."

"I'm sorry, Ms. Harrow has issued a Do Not Disturb. If you'd like to leave a card or a message, I'll be sure she gets it when she's available."

Pleased to erase the snooty smile, Eve pulled out her badge. "I think she should be available now. Why don't you check?"

"Officer—"

"Lieutenant." Eve tapped the badge, where her rank was clearly posted. "Lieutenant Dallas and Detective Peabody, Homicide, NYPSD."

"If I may verify your identification?"

"Have at it." Eve held it out for the scanner.

"Thank you. Lieutenant," she said, very deliberately. "If you'll give me a moment, I'll check with Ms. Harrow's domestic and see if she's available."

"Great, do that. When you do, you might mention that Ms. Harrow can be available here, or available later—at Cop Central."

"Excuse me." All dignity, like the building she served, the suit stepped back from the counter to put some distance between them, then murmured into her headset.

She didn't bother with the smile when she stepped back.

"You're cleared. Please take elevator three to the thirty-sixth floor. Ms. Harrow is available for your visit in Penthouse C."

"Great."

She moved to the silvered elevator doors with Peabody.

"Why do people like that, working a lobby desk, figure they're so superior to the rest of the world?"

"Brushes with the rich and/or famous, I guess. And the little secrets they know about them. Who visited Ms. Rich when Ms. Rich's spouse was away? How many times a month does Mr. Famous hire an LC? How about that time Mr. and Ms. R and F's minor kid stumbled in drunk and/or stoned?"

Peabody shrugged as they got in the elevator. "I bet it gives some a real sense of power."

"Cops know lots better secrets than that. So . . . Harrow's got a DND on her place. Didn't you say she does some screen series? Shouldn't it be a workday for her, like it is for Estaban?"

"I don't know. Maybe they're on summer hiatus."

"We'll find out. You've seen it?"

"Sure. I've caught some episodes. It's good. Pretty solid."

"Let her know that. She'll play to that."

The dignified elegance continued on the thirty-sixth. More flowers, but in standard vertical vases here. Matte black doors—each with cams—to contrast against snow-white walls.

Penthouse C had two of those doors. The left opened seconds after she pressed the buzzer.

The droid replicated a young, fit male of mixed race with deep brown eyes and flowing brown hair highlighted with blond. It wore a dark suit with a white shirt open at the collar.

"Good afternoon, Lieutenant, Detective." It spoke with a cultured British accent. "I'm James. May I see your identification?"

The dark eyes scanned their badges with a thin red light.

"Very good. Please come in."

9

The droid ushered them into a living area done in what Eve supposed Peabody would call soft colors. Lots of curvy furniture, she noted, and silky fabrics. A many-tiered crystal chandelier spilled from the high ceiling, and art in ornate gold frames crowded the walls.

The triple glass on the east wall invited the river view in. Beyond the glass, verdant ornamental trees in dark blue pots stood in the sunlight.

"Please sit. Ms. Harrow will be down momentarily to join you. She was resting when you requested the visitation. Perhaps you'd enjoy a cool drink while you wait."

"We're good, thanks. Is Ms. Harrow home alone?"

"She is. Please sit," it invited again. "If you'll excuse me, I have duties. You've only to press the button on the house intercom if you require anything."

"A hunked-up house droid," Eve observed when it left them. "Droids know secrets, too, but all you have to do is wipe them or reprogram."

Rather than sit, she wandered. A more intimate sitting room to the right, and double pocket doors closing off the area where the droid had gone to the left.

Stairs wound up to an open second-floor balcony. More little conversation areas there and, she assumed, bedrooms. Likely another terrace off the master and that same killer view, as the glass rose to the lofty ceiling.

She continued to look up when she heard a door open and close, so watched Vera glide along the balcony.

She wore wide-legged white lounging pants and a flowing top. Also, Eve noted, full makeup, diamond studs, a ruby ring that could've put someone's eye out, and a ruby pendant in the shape of a heart.

She cast her eyes down. It surprised Eve they didn't stay that way given the heft of the false eyelashes.

"I don't appreciate being disturbed this way."

"I'm betting Brant Fitzhugh doesn't appreciate getting dead. We have some follow-up questions regarding same."

"I'm aware you've interrogated Rico, again."

"Did he call it that? Gee, I thought we had a nice chat. Didn't you, Peabody?"

"It was really interesting seeing them shoot that scene, too. I really enjoy your work on *The Matriarch*, Ms. Harrow. Your Nita is so layered and fascinating."

"Why, thank you." She sent Peabody a winning smile as she sat on one of the sofas. "I do find her challenging and rewarding to explore. Ah, James, just what I needed."

He brought her a glass of pale gold wine.

"Is there anything else I can do for you?"

"If you'd tidy up the bed. I don't think I'll be able to rest after this."

"Of course."

She sipped the wine as he started up the stairs.

"Despite the unfortunate incident in our history," Vera began, "Brant and I had a history. The shock of his death, the suddenness and permanence of it, hit a kind of delayed reaction, I suppose. I had a key scene this morning for our first episode of the new season. I got up, started to get dressed, and simply couldn't. It's the first time I've ever canceled, but I couldn't face it. Not today."

"You were very open about holding a grudge regarding that unfortunate incident last night."

"It didn't seem altogether real. And I did hold a grudge. Do," she added after another sip of wine. "People say 'Forgive and forget.' I say 'Pay back and remember.' But death . . . How do I needle Eliza now? She's the widow. She, even more than Brant, will be the tragic figure in this, and if I point out she lured Brant out of my bed into hers, I'm the bitch. It means I'll have to say sweet things about her, and that galls."

She took a slug of wine and repeated, "That galls."

"That's your take on all this?" Eve wondered. "You'll have to say sweet things about a woman you dislike so you don't look bad?"

"That's the reality of my position, and the blueprint for my public statements and behavior." She curled up her legs. "I didn't wish him dead. I could wish his career dead, wish him caught with his pants around his ankles and his cock in some ingenue. That won't happen now. I didn't want him, if that's what you're wondering. Good God, look at Rico. Half Brant's talent, yes, but that body, that face. And the glory of youth. I didn't want him," she repeated, "but I hated she did. And the son of a bitch loved her."

"And she him?"

"Eliza discards what she doesn't want, and why not? Why keep what doesn't work? The bitch loved him. She may have snagged him to slap at me—I'll never know for certain—but she'd have used him up, tossed him back if she didn't want him. I'm not an idiot, Lieutenant. And

I observe. Good actors do, just as I imagine good cops do. They loved each other. It burned my ass, but they loved each other."

"You were standing beside him when he drank the poison. You had an incident in your history you held on to like a lifeline. That's motive and opportunity."

"I didn't want him dead," she said flatly. "I'll cut you, or anyone, to bloody ribbons with my tongue given the motive and opportunity. I'll feed the gossip sheets nasty tidbits to humiliate you. They have to be true—I don't lie because lies come back to bite you. And I once punched a director who thought I wanted a part bad enough to let him grope under my skirt. He threatened to have me fired and arrested for assault. I threatened to rip my shirt and scream rape."

She smiled, thinly, at the memory.

"I kept the part; he didn't try anything again. And a year later, when the opportunity arose, I tossed out some nasty tidbits. I hadn't been the first, or the last, you see. It ruined him, made him a pariah. That's how I pay back."

She hissed out a breath. "But for his lapse in preferring Eliza, Brant was a decent man. I didn't want him dead. In fact, my agent just started negotiations with Brant's production company. They sent us a script a couple weeks ago. A rom-com, with teeth, and a damn good part. My agent was smart enough to send me the script without telling me where it came from. Or I'd have said fuck no without reading it—a mistake."

"You were considering playing opposite Brant in a vid?"

"No, but God, that would've been delicious!" Her face actually lit up at the idea of it. "No, he'd produce. They'd already cast the male lead."

"Did Eliza know?"

"I'm sure she did. Or if not, he'd have told her when I contracted."

"How does she feel about you?"

"Smug." This time she guzzled wine. "Bitch. Look, as of tomorrow, I'm going to have to say nothing but lovely things about both of them. My assistant's already sent out a statement doing just that, and I'll have to come up with those sweet things. No more subtle little jabs— and I'm so damn good at them. And the hell of it is, I'm sorry, deeply sorry, on a personal level he's dead. I'm angry, deeply, someone took his life. Believe it or don't, and you can tangle with my lawyers if you keep pushing."

"You were standing next to him." Eve held up a hand when Vera snarled. "And you were close to him—an embrace close—after he came from the terrace with the drink. Who else was? You observe," Eve reminded her. "Tell me what you observed. Start with Brant coming in from the terrace with the drink."

"Oh." Shifting, Vera sipped more wine and looked, for the first time, engaged. "All right. I saw him with Lin at the terrace bar. Rico and I were chatting with Tessa, Tessa's wife, and . . . Kurtis Walter—he's with *Stage and Screen*. I saw Brant was directing, as he does, how the bartender should make what was clearly a champagne cocktail. Eliza's drink."

She ran a hand over her hair as if it would help her think.

"As I recall, I'd seen Eliza and Sylvie back near the foyer. I suppose Eliza was taking a break from mingling, or they may have had something to discuss. Obviously, Brant would have to cross the entire room to take her the drink, so wanting a moment, I drew Rico away a bit as Brant and Lin came inside."

"Positioned yourself," Eve commented.

"Yes, exactly. So I greeted Brant with an embrace. Long enough for photos if any of the entertainment media around grabbed the shot. And close enough to remind him why he used to call me the Bod."

She smiled a little. "I keep in shape, Lieutenant. And these?" She gave her breasts a light tap. "One hundred percent real. He told me

I looked amazing, as always—which was true. I said something about a lovely party, introduced him to Rico. Rico's a serious fan, and actually said so. Brant told us to enjoy the party, said he'd find us again, but wanted to take Eliza her drink."

"He said that—'her drink'?"

"Yes. He moved on. I was careful not to watch. Others observe, too, and if I'd watched him move on, that would be remarked on. Rico got us both fresh drinks as one of the servers passed. We mingled a bit, there was Dirk Russell. He directed the pilot for my series, and directed Brant's Oscar-nominated vid—the one your vid won."

"It's not my vid."

"Now, now, credit where it's due. They could hardly have made it without you. In any case, we talked to him and his date—who turned out to be his daughter—and with Cosmo, Cosmo Wise."

"I really like his vids," Peabody commented.

Vera smiled, genuinely. "He's charming—and I don't say that unless it's true. He and Brant have been friends for years. He played my love interest in—"

"*Do Over*," Peabody supplied. "It was so much fun."

"And nearly as much to make." She shifted again, obviously pleased. "He played Eliza's in . . ."

Peabody laughed. "*Can't Dance*. But he can!"

"He can. I introduced him and his almost as charming wife of twenty years or more to Rico. Then he called over another couple. Ah, yes, Malcomb and . . . something. Sable, Foxy . . ."

"Minx."

"Yes! Malcomb Furrier, often of Caine and Furrier. He's a lyricist. And the woman—Minx—is choreographer on Eliza's revival. And it turned out she worked with Cosmo on *Class Reunion* on Broadway a couple of years ago, so we all chatted away. I genuinely enjoyed myself. Then Eliza drags the girl—Samantha—to the piano. Now I'm stuck, basically front row center, because if I'd tried to slip away—"

"It would've been remarked upon," Eve finished.

"You bet your ass it would. Eliza's introducing the girl. 'For those of you who don't know Samantha Keene, my stage daughter, believe me, you will. And we're going to give everyone a taste of what they expect this fall in the twenty-five-year—where did the time go?—revival of *Upstage*.'

"Applause, applause. They started a duet, and I'll say the girl has strong pipes and presence. Brant made his way forward—and the crowd made way for him. Then—"

"Who stood where?"

"Ah . . . God. Rico, myself . . . I think Minx beside me with Malcomb just behind her. He's a tall one, Malcomb, and she's petite. Then Brant. I think, yes, another girl—young, sort of slid in—two of them. I don't know them. But Tessa was on Brant's other side, and Cosmo—another tall one—shifted back so the young girls could see, and—I'm not sure, honestly. I know the group of us who'd been chatting more or less spread out, like an audience in a theater."

She shrugged, polished off the wine. "Most came in from the terrace to stand to the back and side of the piano, more crowded in from the dining area. I couldn't say who was behind us. Then."

She looked down at her empty glass. "Brant lifted the flute—Eliza's drink—like a toast. His right hand lifted, his left on his heart. Then he drank it. I know he stepped back, which surprised me. Glass shattered, somebody screamed. I looked behind me, but I didn't see Brant at first. There were too many people crowded in, and more screams, shouts. The one who said he was a doctor pushed through, and then I saw Brant on the floor."

She touched fingertips to her mouth, briefly.

"Eliza shoved past me and dropped down with him. He seemed to be choking, then convulsing. Then he was dead. It was so fast."

Lifting her hand, she rubbed the center of her forehead. "I suppose you've seen someone die before."

"Yes."

"I hadn't. We act death scenes. Rehearse them, stage them, do countless takes of them. But it's nothing like reality. I know that now."

"What else did you observe? Did you notice anyone around him who seemed off?"

"My powers of observation dimmed considerably. I saw Brant, and the doctor—he had blood on his hand. Shattered glass. Eliza holding Brant. It was chaotic. I think . . . the doctor tried to do CPR. Eliza wouldn't let go of Brant, but he did that . . ."

He pumped downward with her hands.

"It was Lin, I think, who finally pulled her away when the medical team got there. And the police soon after. I didn't see that, actually, but heard it. Rico pulled me out onto the terrace. Made me sit down, got me something from the bar. Brandy. Yes, brandy. He stayed with me. He's a hound, that's part of his appeal, but he stayed with me and held my hand."

She let her head fall back against the cushions, closed her eyes. "So. Am I under arrest?"

"Not at this time."

Vera opened her eyes, smiled. "You're a hard case."

"It takes one, they say."

"They do. I don't like Eliza. And I resent not being able to stop myself from feeling sorry for her. I hope to get over that very soon."

"Thanks for your time." Eve stood. "Would you consider Eliza a colleague or a competitor?"

"That's a clever question, so here's a clever answer. We're competitive colleagues. She has her Tonys and Grammys—I don't. We each have an Oscar. But I have two Emmys—so far—and she doesn't. She's nipped me by one on Golden Globes to date, but I intend to fix that."

"We'll see ourselves out."

Peabody glanced back as they walked to the elevator. "She's a hell of an actress, but I don't think she killed Fitzhugh."

"Neither do I."

"You don't. Okay, you go first."

"The motive's not enough for her to risk getting caught, and she strikes me as a risk/reward type. Plus, she liked him. Despite the grudge, she just liked him. And with him dead she loses any chance to get him back into bed and wreck his marriage, and instead puts Eliza front and center."

"I do think she liked him," Peabody agreed as they rode down, bypassing the lobby for the garage. "And I think the whole grudge/ competition thing is more like a game to her."

"Some games are deadly. Now, ask if I think she could try to kill Eliza Lane."

"You do?"

"She knows he's getting the drink for Lane, something he did routinely according to several statements. She positions herself, by her own admission. There's opportunity. And she's smart," Eve added as they walked into the garage. "Smart enough to stand back, chat away while he delivers the drink, one she expects Eliza to drink. But it doesn't work that way. Now she sees him with it. She's close, but not really close enough to stop him from drinking it without making a move. Still, she could have, but then he's toasting her enemy, with a hand over his heart."

Eve got behind the wheel. "So she thinks: The Shitheel, just that instant of resentment, and he drinks. Too late now, play it through. She has the chops for it."

"I guess she does—if Lane was the target."

"Factor this. It's not unusual for people to say positive things about a victim, but it is less usual to not hear a few digs here and there. People liked this guy. We could consider a demented fan, or again a competitor, but it's more unlikely than not. And we go back. He got the drink for her, and he ended up drinking it as a tribute."

"Killing Lane . . . It puts Harrow in a better position to get him back in bed, then boot him, so there's that."

"There's that. And it's time to start digging up anybody who has a motive for Lane."

"Statements have been pretty positive there, too."

"She's fired assistants," Eve reminded her. "Keene was positive, but she also mentioned Lane lets you know if you don't meet her standards. She had no problem going after a man who was involved with another woman at the time. Maybe she invited Harrow—they're not pals—because she likes rubbing her nose in it."

Eve glanced at the time. "Shit. I'm dropping you at the subway. Go play with paint or whatever, but cull through gossip stories, find us anything bitching about Lane."

"Those are both fun things. It's like a reward! What are you doing?"

"I'm going to talk to Lane again, then go work this at home. I need to lay it out, start putting people in places." She veered to the curb. "We'll set up interviews—let's go to them—with the composer and choreographer. And the director and her wife. I want to put those people in those places first, so that's for tomorrow."

"Paint and gossip tonight, more celeb types tomorrow. I love my life!"

Eve pulled away to head across town. Close to home, she thought, and followed impulse to tag Roarke.

"Lieutenant. In the car, I see."

"Yeah, you, too. Where are you?"

"Actually nearly home. I had a meeting canceled so I'm taking advantage of it. And you?"

"I'm going to talk to Eliza Lane again. You said you know her."

"Met her, which isn't at all the same."

"Point. I sprang Peabody. I could use another set of eyes and ears if you're up for it."

"I'll have the car drop me at her building, wait for you outside unless you beat me there." She waited while he gave his driver the new address.

"I'm heading over from the East Side, so you're closer. Who cancels on the emperor of the business universe?"

"I could say some impressive head of state, but an engineer whose fiancée went into labor."

"Okay then. See you in a few."

When she did, the emperor of the business universe stood outside, chatting companionably with the doorman. Because he had, said doorman gave her no guff about leaving her car at the entrance.

"Lieutenant Dallas, ma'am."

He beamed so cheerfully she swallowed the *ma'am*.

"You're already cleared up to Ms. Bowen's apartment. We're all real sorry about Mr. Fitzhugh. A hell of a guy."

"So I'm told."

Reporters—she counted six—raced up or down or across the street, already shouting questions.

"Hey!" The doorman went from cheerful to tiger snarl in two seconds flat. "What'd I tell you? You back off or I call the cops again. You don't get to harass residents or visitors."

Since they'd obviously gone this round before, not one of them came within ten feet of the entrance.

It didn't stop them from shouting questions or recording, but Eve ignored that.

"A hell of a guy," the doorman repeated. "Always took a minute to say hello. Never puffed himself up."

"How about her, Ms. Lane?"

"Oh, maybe she doesn't always say hello, but no snoot there." He pushed up the tip of his nose. "Remembers your name. Got me house seats once when she heard my wife wanted to see a show."

"Do you know if my men are still in the building?"

"I couldn't say, but I can sure find out for you."

"It's okay, I'll take care of it."

He beat her to the door, opened it for her and Roarke.

"Maybe you could tell Ms. Lane condolences from Henry on the door."

"All right. How much did you give him?" she muttered to Roarke.

"Now, that would be telling. And speaking of your men."

She watched Baxter, Trueheart, and McNab pile off an elevator. Baxter in his slick, tailored suit, Trueheart in his off-the-rack navy, and McNab in his EDD circus gear of bright baggies, brighter T-shirt, and neon-orange air sneaks.

"Dallas, fancy meeting you here. Hey, Roarke."

"Status, Baxter."

"Cleared. We decided to stick it out—only about thirty past shift. Nothing there, boss."

"Party clutter," Trueheart added, and tucked a florist box under his arm. "And the sweeper dust, but under it, the whole place is really clean. Everything has a place, no secret stashes."

"The catering kitchen recyclers were run twice yesterday. From the timing, I'd say during food prep, and again about an hour in. Sweepers took the contents anyway. All recycler contents. Saved us, right, pal?"

Trueheart just smiled at Baxter. "They have a lot of really nice things."

"Any more trouble with reporters?"

"There's a couple camped in a unit in the building across the street."

Trueheart nodded. "We saw them hanging out the windows with cams. We've had the privacy shades down all day, but they got some shots when we went out to process the terraces."

"A bunch of them outside. Anyway, your go, McNab."

"Nothing funny on the e's. These people liked order. Makes my own system look like chaos, and it's just not. But everything's in place, just like the stuff. Personal stuff separate, and nothing weird or off about it. Assistant Ricardo's been seeing some guy for about a month, but I ran him, and nothing popped. Assistant Kessler had a bad breakup— bad for him because heartbreak and all that—about four months back. He's dipped his toe back in, but nothing serious. He's got a tight circle of friends, mostly theater people, two of them roommates. They come off clean. Little bumps here and there, but nothing violent, nothing major."

He rubbed the back of his neck. "I ran Assistant Jacoby by you already, and that's it for him. Nothing squirrelly on Jacoby's assistant— she's been in New Zealand for a few days already.

"Cara Rowan, the housekeeper, she's into crosswords and word jumbles and scrabble—plays online with a group. Lots of correspondence with her sister, a niece, a nephew, her mother, her mother-in-law, some pals. He's into food, cooking, baking, and a little soft porn. Really soft. They're planning a vacation, like a family reunion deal, next Thanksgiving."

He shrugged. "There's no vibe there, Dallas. If their bosses come up in personal correspondence, their response is pretty much everything's frosty. They don't gossip, at least not over the e's."

"Okay. I'll let Lane know the scene's cleared. Peabody's on the way home, or probably to the house."

"I'll tag her up. Need to rain-check it, guys. Cha!"

"We're heading out for a brew," Baxter said as McNab pranced off.

"Maybe some eats. There's a nice tavern down the block if you finish up and want to join."

"Can't. I've got a pile left to work on."

"Aren't we glad we're not the boss?" Baxter slapped Trueheart on the shoulder. "Let's go drink, eat, and be men, my young apprentice."

"Reporters outside," Eve called. "Avoid."

"You didn't warn McNab," Roarke pointed out as they walked to the elevator.

"Did you see his getup? Maybe they make him as a cop, but they're third- or fourth-string, since they're stuck out there hoping for a mark, so I doubt it."

In the elevator, she called for Bowen's floor. "Here's what I think."

He trailed a fingertip down the dent in her chin. "I always want to know."

"Lane or Fitzhugh or both, probably both, were extremely careful with who they hired who'd have access to their home. They probably have custodian staff in their other properties, and we'll find the same. And those they hired, if they want to keep the job, know the rules of the road and keep to them."

"Sounds sensible to me. I'd think those in the public eye would value their privacy even more than most. When the door closes, those eyes are shut out."

"And you let out only what you want—that's control. Handpicked media at the party. I'll bet not one of them has written a nasty feature or review pertaining to either of them."

"You find that odd, or suspicious?"

"No," she admitted. "Just interesting and telling. I'm going to find it interesting to hear what you think after we talk to the widow and her best friend."

10

When they stepped on the elevator, Eve turned to Roarke. "I think Lane was the target."

"Do you?"

"Yeah, here's why. Her drink—that's the most obvious. He clearly had it made for her. Anyone at the party—and undoubtedly the killer—knew it was her drink. That's basic observation and research. The killer's not stupid. Multiple opportunities to slip something into the drink as the victim worked his way through the party. Multiple statements verify that."

"But she didn't drink it."

"That's the glitch in the plan. She decides to perform, hands the drink back for Fitzhugh to hold."

"And as you pointed out before, there were also multiple opportunities to slip the poison into the drink when he worked his way back through the party to watch the duet."

"Yeah, and he's the dead guy, but—" When the elevator doors

opened, she pressed hold. "Sure, there's the possibility he drinks it, because he did. But it was just as likely he'd hold it for her, give it back to her after she took her bow. What I'm hearing, and seeing, is he drank it on impulse. 'Here's to you, Eliza.' Drink, choke, die."

"Harsh, but true."

"Another factor, motive. I'm not getting any sense he had genuine enemies. People liked him. I'm not getting any subtle digs. You know, 'How I loved that bastard, he was a fucking prince among men. Even when he was a dick, he was a prince.'"

"A prince of a dick."

"That's how it goes a lot of times. 'Dead Jack? Sweet guy. Sure, he had a temper, but mostly when he was drunk.' Or, 'Dead Bob? He'd give you the shirt off his back—when he wanted it laundered.'"

"You know such interesting dead people."

"I got files of them. But with Fitzhugh, there's none of that. It may be bullshit, because everybody's a dick sometimes, but it comes off sincere. Even with Harrow, who calls him the Shitheel."

"I'm going to agree about Brant," Roarke decided. "As no one who mentioned him to me today did so with the *dick* or *drunk* qualifiers."

"It's different with Lane."

"In what way?"

"Nobody's calling her a dick, but I'm getting 'She's tough, she's a perfectionist, she'll let you know when you don't meet her standards,' that kind of thing. All respectful, even admiring—not counting Harrow—but it's a different sensibility."

"Are you going to tell her you're leaning, and hard it seems, toward her as the target?"

"She's already got that in her head. I'm looking three ways. The killer didn't care which one of them died—you could look at Harrow on that. Lane was the target, and there I look at a lot of people. Harrow again, and former employees, somebody who didn't get a part because they didn't meet her standards, ex-lovers, and so on. Or it was Fitzhugh all along, and there you look at Harrow, or somebody who just wanted him gone for reasons we haven't found yet. Or you look at Lane."

"As the killer? Because?"

"She didn't drink it, she gave it back to him. She's the spouse, and the spouse is always a contender."

"Ah. Is that part of the Marriage Rules?"

"It's in the—what do you call it?—forward. The Pros and Cons of Marriage."

He had to laugh. "You have a list of pros and cons?"

"Sure." She released the hold and stepped out.

"Is it a general list, or specific to us?"

"Oh, you've got your own separate list, pal. The coffee and the sex weigh heavy on the pro side. But in general, pros are companionship, accessibility to free sex, like minds—or close enough—if you're lucky, somebody who tolerates your flaws, and so on. Cons are potential cheating, assholeyness—"

"Is that a word?"

"In my book, yeah. Boredom, which leads to both of the above, someone who ends up griping about all your flaws because now they're living with them, meddling in-laws, divorce. And the big? Somebody who decides to kill you dead."

"Is that it?"

"No, plenty more on both sides. So I'll look at Lane, as target, as suspect. Add her best pal Sylvie as possible suspect, and/or her faithful assistants."

"Then it appears your investigation got wider rather than more narrow over the course of your day."

"We'll squeeze it down. Be your usual," she added as they approached Sylvie's door.

He skimmed a hand over her hair. "Which is?"

"Do the sympathetic charm thing."

"Ah, and is that a pro or con on the list?"

"It goes back and forth, depending."

Charmed himself, he ran a hand down her back, then patted her ass. "I adore you."

"That doesn't hurt." She paused to look at him. "Mutual," she said, and pressed the buzzer.

Sylvie answered the door herself. She'd dressed casually, cropped pants, a simple shirt. She'd done minimal makeup and yanked her hair back in a tail.

And Eve saw, instantly, the minute Sylvie's eyes landed on Roarke, she wished she'd groomed more.

"Oh, Lieutenant Dallas, please come in. And Roarke. I recognized you."

"And I you, Ms. Bowen. I very much admire your work."

"Thank you so much, and it's Sylvie. Eliza's out on the terrace. I'd just come in to get us some wine. Please, go right out. I hope you'll join us in a glass."

"Thanks, but I'm on duty."

"I'm not," Roarke said, "and would love one. The lieutenant's for black coffee if you have it. Can I help you with that?"

"No, no, please, go out and sit with Eliza. She's had a very difficult day. Dolby was here for most of it. He's such a comfort to her."

"As I'm sure you are."

She smiled at Roarke. "I'm trying. Go right out. I'll only be a moment."

She gestured toward the open terrace doors across the living area. Not as spacious as Lane's penthouse, and, to Eve's eye, homier with its beachy wall art and faded colors.

Sylvie turned off into a dining area where a glossy gray table held a colorful arrangement of summer flowers and a breakfront displaying framed photos and the shiny whatnots people seemed hell-bent on collecting.

Eliza reclined on a lounge chair under the shade of a candy-pink umbrella. She wore black skin pants, her feet bare and her toes painted tropical blue, with a sleeveless white shirt. She'd done her makeup more carefully than her friend, but not well enough to cover the circles under her eyes.

She stared out at New York while twisting her wedding set, a thick white gold band paired with a square-cut pink diamond, around and around her finger.

"Ms. Lane."

She jolted, blinked at Eve, then at Roarke. "I'm sorry, I was . . ." She started to get up, but Roarke touched a hand to her shoulder.

"I'm so sorry, Eliza. I didn't know Brant well, but liked and ad-mired him very much. I hope you'll call on me if there's anything I can do."

"Thank you. He admired you, and was grateful for your generosity to Home Front. Please, sit. The desk said you were coming up, but I got lost in my thoughts. I went—we went, Sylvie, Lin, and Dolby went with me—to see Brant. Dr. Morris is very kind. Still, it doesn't seem real."

"I'm sorry I have to intrude at such a difficult time," Eve began.

Eliza shook her head. "It's not an intrusion. You're going to find who did this to Brant. I'm holding on to that. Sylvie." She smiled a little when her friend came out with the drinks. "My rock."

"You're your own rock, Eliza." She set the tray down, passed Eliza her wine, Eve her coffee, handed a glass to Roarke. "Should I leave you alone?"

"That's not necessary," Eve told her. "First, I can tell you we've cleared your apartment. You're free to go back at any time."

"Oh."

"Stay," Sylvie said immediately. "At least tonight, Eliza. If you're ready to go back tomorrow, I'll go with you."

"My rock. Yes, I'll stay tonight. But you have your table read in the morning. No," she said before Sylvie could object. "You're not going to put it off. I have to face it sometime, and I'll ask Dolby to be there. I need to start making arrangements. Brant deserves a memorial as wonderful and loving as he was."

"I'll help you. So will Dolby and Lin. Cela, too."

"We joked about it, Brant and I, the way you do. 'When it's my time, Eliza, I want my best clips run on the biggest screen you can find, and you singing "My Always."'"

"Oh, honey."

"I sang it—by his request—at our wedding. And I'm going to do it, Sylvie." Her eyes filled, but the tears didn't fall. "I'm going to find it in myself to give him that. Because he is. He's my always."

Sylvie sat on the edge of the lounger, took her hand.

"I know some of this is repetitive, but it's part of the process." Eve waited a beat. "Can you take me through last night? You could start when the caterers arrived."

"All right. I dressed early. That's my habit so I can be ready early and supervise the setup."

"You've used this caterer in the past?"

"Years, but . . ."

"Eliza's fussy," Sylvie supplied, and earned a weak laugh from Eliza.

"*Controlling* is the word she's too polite to use. I want things a certain way—and that's my way. Brant came in just as I was finishing, and we had our usual 'plenty of time' from him, 'don't take too long' from me. And he said he'd be dressed and down for our pre-party good-luck drink. It's our tradition, and this was supposed to be a big night, a celebration."

"You invited media."

"Yes, carefully handpicked. I wanted . . . want," she corrected, "a lot of positive buzz for the revival. It owns a big part of my heart, and playing the role of Lily is a kind of milestone for me."

"You said 'want,'" Sylvie interrupted. "You've decided to go on with it."

"Yes. The cast and crew have put in so much time, so much work. I won't say it can't go on without me, but frankly, it wouldn't have the same punch. And, if I'm honest, I need it. I need to get out of my own head.

"They're family," she told Eve. "When you put your heart and soul, your art into forming a company, putting a play together that you hope will run and run and run, six days a week, eight performances a week, you're family. I need them, every bit as much as they need me."

"It doesn't concern you one of them might have killed your husband?"

"I don't believe that. I can't believe that," she said, her voice firm and steady. "I simply can't. Maybe that's naive and foolish, but I can't and don't believe that."

"What did you do when you came downstairs, while your husband was dressing?"

"I talked with Dolby. He was here to take the floral delivery. Then, of course, I fussed with that." She sent a sidelong look to Sylvie. "The caterers arrived, and I went over the menu, the setup, the timing—which, of course, wasn't necessary to anyone but me. I took a walk through the entire apartment to make sure everything was in place. Spoke with Cela when she arrived about doing the sweeps on the second and third floors.

"We prefer guests stay on the main level," she added, "but some will wander. We once found a guest asleep in a guest room tub. He'd had a little too much to drink and wandered up, decided it was a fine place to take a nap."

She shifted to draw her legs up, sit beside Sylvie.

"I think that's about the time Brant came down. He made the drinks. We went out on the terrace. It was just perfect weather. He was leaving the next evening for New Zealand, and I told him how much I'd miss him. It's the longest we'd be apart since we married. We've usually been able to mesh our schedules so it would never be more than a week, two at the very most, but we both had these major projects hit at the same time."

She looked at Roarke. "I suppose you have to travel quite a bit with all your interests."

"Now and then."

"And of course your work keeps you here," she said to Eve. "It takes sacrifice and balance to make it work. In any case, guests began to arrive. We had security in the lobby, and on the door here as well. We've been very careful since Ethan Crommell."

"The man who stalked you. You didn't mention he'd been released recently."

"I didn't? I'm sorry. God! So much is confused in my head after . . . But he couldn't have gotten in! I would have seen him, surely, and that would only happen if he got through security. They have his name, his photo. I—"

"No, he didn't get in. But you should know he's been sent back to serve out his full sentence. By his own admission, he still believes you want and need him to save you."

"From Brant," she murmured. "Oh my God, if he somehow— You need to check the security feed! Sylvie, if he hurt Brant—"

"We have checked. Crommell isn't a suspect, Ms. Lane, and he's no danger to you now."

"How do you know for certain he didn't kill Brant? He's crazy. I was upset when I learned they were giving him parole, but Brant said he had three years of treatment, and deserved a chance. But—"

"I'm not going to say the treatment worked, but I will say he didn't gain access to your apartment. We brought him in, and I had our top profiler and psychiatrist in the interview with us. She concurs. He heard about your husband's death after the fact."

One hand clutched at her throat. "You're absolutely sure?"

"Our investigation is ongoing. If we turn up any evidence that implicates Crommell, we'll act on it. But at this time, evidence points away from him. Take me through the rest, from when guests started to arrive."

"Oh, well, we started with drinks. Passed champagne and wine. Mixed drinks at the bars. Then passed food. Oh, sorry, Grant—Grant Pfiffer, the pianist. He'd arrived before the guests—but after the caterers. We went over a playlist, though he'd take requests and so on. And I had him get some food before the guests arrived, as he'd play throughout the evening. He began shortly after the first guests got there. I've worked with Grant a number of times before. He's marvelous."

"All right."

"Once we had, say, twenty people or so and more arriving, Brant and I mingled separately. But we try to keep an eye on each other, if you know what I mean. Sometimes you can get cornered, need an escape hatch."

"Did that happen?"

"Actually, it did. One of the plus-ones latched on a bit longer than she should, but before I could catch Brant's eye, Sylvie rescued me."

Eliza tipped her head toward her friend's shoulder.

"I know the signals, too," Sylvie said, "so I wandered over, made some excuse, and drew Eliza back toward the foyer so she could have a break. Everyone was there by that time, and the party was in full swing, so we took a few minutes."

"What did you talk about?"

"Oh, the party, my cheating ex—gone now. Then Brant came over with Eliza's drink."

"We stole a minute more," Eliza continued. "The three of us have been friends a long time. And I said something stupid." She tipped her head toward Sylvie's again. "As soon as it was out of my mouth . . ."

"Don't be silly." Sylvie gave her a pat on the knee.

"What did you say?"

Eliza glanced at Eve, then laid a hand over Sylvie's. "Something about cheating, and it was tactless considering Sylvie's situation."

"The cheating ex," Sylvie explained, "who decided he wanted a younger, sleeker model."

"As I can't decide if that's his loss or his stupidity, I'll assume it's both."

Sylvie let out a quick laugh as she sparkled at Roarke. "Thank you, kind sir."

"It's not kind to speak truth."

"It's a struggle not to envy you," she said to Eve, "so I'm giving it up. Eliza worries I'm still in love with him, which I was up until the moment I discovered he'd booked a flight for two and a villa on the French Riviera using my account."

"What!" Eliza shot up straight. "You didn't tell me."

"I found out right before the party, and didn't want to talk about it there. After . . . it didn't seem very important. I handled it." She patted Eliza's knee again. "It only took contacting my lawyer. In any case, Eliza thought she'd hurt my feelings, which she hadn't. But it upset her, so I pointed out it was time she gave the party some entertainment. Others had, and the room was full of talent. But—"

She wrapped her arm around Eliza in a hug. "There's only one Eliza Lane."

"We're going to talk about this other thing later, in detail."

"You handed your husband your drink," Eve prompted.

"Yes, sorry. My mind's all over the place. I'd already planned to bring Sam up at some point, do that particular duet, so I handed Brant the drink and went to get her."

"You and Brant stayed where you were?"

"For another minute," Sylvie agreed. "He kissed my cheek, said Mikhail—that's the ex—was a fool. I wished him a safe, smooth flight to New Zealand, and promised I'd look after Eliza. Then Grant played a quick run on the piano, and Eliza introduced Samantha. We moved forward. I stayed back a bit—it was crowded—but Brant made his way to the front. He'd have known Eliza wanted to see him."

"He would," Eliza murmured. "He knew how much it meant to me to know he was there."

"What else did you see?"

Eliza sent Eve a puzzled look. "I'm not sure what you mean."

"Did you see anyone watching your husband more than you, for instance?"

"Oh. No . . . No, I didn't. I saw him. He toasted us, Sam and me. I saw that, but honestly, for the most part the duet demands you play to your partner. Do I have to go through the rest again? The glass breaking, the scream?"

"No. Only if you remember anything more, or anything differently."

"I don't. I just don't. Everything after the scream is a blur. And now I keep thinking I gave him a hard time."

"About what?"

"Oh, leaving. The shoot. Just that morning I whined about it, asked him who'd rub my aching feet when I got home from rehearsal. And he said, 'Dolby, of course,' and made me laugh. He always made me laugh. He was a good man, that's something you need to know. I can't imagine anyone who'd want to hurt him."

"What about you?"

"Me?" Shock ran across her face. "Hurt Brant?"

"No, who might want to hurt you? It was your drink, and it's just a matter of timing that you didn't drink it."

"I know you asked before, but . . . I'm never going to claim I'm as kind or generous as Brant, but—"

"That's not true." Sylvie interrupted with a firm shake of her head. "You are kind, and generous. Brant's more—was more—easygoing, no question. You didn't have to include Samantha, do a duet last night. You did that to showcase her."

"And for the revival," Eliza added.

"You considered pulling out of that. If you did, who'd take your place? You'd have an understudy."

"This far out, no. If I decided I couldn't do it, they'd get another name, someone who'd create some buzz, excitement."

"Anyone like that on your guest list?"

"Well . . . there's Sylvie," she said, and now Sylvie laughed.

"In my dreams. I don't have Eliza's pipes—her range. That's just fact. I'm a better dancer."

"Bitch. She is. And you could absolutely handle it. In fact, when I was wavering, I thought about asking you if you'd step in. Even knowing you have other commitments, which goes back to me not being as selfless as Brant. I'd have leaned on her some there. But moot, because I will do it."

"You've fired assistants."

"Yes." She rubbed her eyes now. "I'm demanding and insist on loyalty and efficiency. But there's been no one I've let go in the last three years or so. And again, no one like that would have been here. Do you really think someone wanted to poison me, and Brant . . ."

"We have to look at that possibility. Why did you invite Vera Harrow? You're not especially friendly."

"Include her, there's talk. Exclude her, there's talk." With a shrug, Eliza drank more wine. "As Brant would say, take the high road. And she's a draw. My goal was to have today's entertainment media loaded with reports on the party, the guests, the shine, the, well, swank of it all."

She looked down into her wine. "That was the plan," she murmured.

"Is there anyone else who might hold hard feelings, resentments, someone you've had conflicts with?"

"Oh, Lieutenant! I'm in show business. It's drama, conflict, *feelings*, egos, tears, and tantrums. It's also work, respect, shared joys and sorrows. Ah, Bristol, the director, and I locked horns countless times on my last vid. There were days I hated him, and I know it was mutual. Yet we pushed each other to do our best work, and when we came out the other side of it, we had nothing but respect for each other. Even Tessa and I—whom I adore—have butted heads.

"I've been in the business since I was fifteen. I don't have Brant's temperament, the easygoing, but I honestly can't think of anyone I've tangled with who'd want to kill me. Maybe I just don't want to think of anyone."

"I can think for you," Sylvie put in. "And no. Now, can I think of plenty who might, at one time or another, want to give you a good shot?" She tapped her fist gently on Eliza's chin. "I sure can, and that's me included. But, Lieutenant, killing someone's a long, long way from that."

Not as far as you think, Eve mused, but left it unsaid.

"And you and Brant. Conflicts?"

"We were married almost ten years, so we had conflicts. Disagreements, annoyances. And I'll admit I'm more easily annoyed. Things tended to roll off Brant. And he made it difficult to stay mad or annoyed. I'm sure the two of you have the occasional spat."

"I married a bright, beaming ray of sunshine." Roarke took Eve's hand, kissed it. And earned a stony glare. "And one who's often armed."

Eliza let out a sighing laugh. "You know each other, love each other, so you understand. There are times feelings get hurt or tempers flare. It's just part of it. We were always, always there for each other.

"We were lucky. We both loved our work and were successful with it. Successful enough we could, and did, live our lives as we chose. Beautiful homes, a lovely circle of friends. Fame, and we both enjoyed fame. We fell in love, and stayed there, and both felt the bumps we had on that road before we met were a kind of training ground, a rehearsal if you like, for the marriage we made together."

"Both of you are in a business with considerable temptation."

"Very true. But why take a bite out of the apple when you can come home to the whole pie? I've been in Sylvie's position, and it's humiliating and painful. Brant? He never cheated on his first wife, and she'll tell you the same. He didn't cheat on Vera—I might have, but that's not who he was. When he realized he had feelings for me, he went to her, broke it off. There's been no one for either of us since."

A breeze kicked up, fluttered at the pink umbrella and at Eliza's hair. She lifted her face up to it a moment, eyes closed.

"You have to ask," she continued. "I suppose you have to wonder. It's part of how you find out who and why. But being without Brant? I don't know how to be without him. Who do I talk to first thing in the morning or the last thing at night? Who knows me like no one else when the curtain's down or the camera's off? I don't think you get another once you find the love of your life. When someone or something takes that away from you, you're alone. You have friends, you have work, but first thing in the morning, the last thing at night, and at odd times between, you're alone."

"Let me ask this. Is there anyone who didn't want you to take this part, to do this revival? Someone who might have wanted to see the entire show go down?"

"Well, Maeve Spindal had a few choice things to say about it. She played Lily, was nominated for a Tony for it, in the original production. She was brilliant—and she didn't particularly care for me. I was nominated, too—my first starring role. I won; she didn't. Add I got a lot of attention, and she was the headliner, and I the understudy, as she's fond of reminding people, who got lucky."

"Lucky?"

"Leah, Leah Rose, was cast in the part. God, what a talent. I was cast as her best friend—as Angie—and her understudy. The morning of opening night . . . Leah had a problem with pills, pills and alcohol. And that morning, the stage manager found her in her dressing room. She'd overdosed."

"There was an investigation?"

"Oh yes. It was all horrible, heartbreaking, terrifying. We'd had the out-of-town shows, and a performance in New York, the VIP production, and she was just stunning."

She looked up at the sky again. "God, it takes me right back. Leah had words with her mother—her mother was a royal pain—before curtain."

"About?"

"I couldn't tell you, just that it threw Leah off a bit. But the show goes on, of course. She flubbed a line or two in the first scene, nearly missed her mark, but nothing anyone who wasn't in the company would notice. And she found her groove again quickly. But . . ."

She shook her head, took another sip of her wine. "After the show she had a fight with Gary, Gary Proctor. He played Charlie, her love interest. They'd been seeing each other, but they had a spat after the show. She'd been drinking in her dressing room, and she'd promised him she'd stop. Whether the thing with her mother or the fight with Gary, or both, had her reaching for the pills and the bottle, we'll never know. Eighteen years old," she murmured. Shook her head again.

"The rest of us went over to Act Two—that was a theater hangout in those days—to unwind, celebrate, but she stayed back. I suppose I thought she'd just gone home, nearly tagged her, as we were friends—theater family—but I didn't. And she stayed in her dressing room, drinking Grey Goose and swallowing pills. They ruled it an accidental overdose. She couldn't have meant to kill herself, not over a couple of missed lines and a fight with a boyfriend. She got a standing ovation that night."

Eliza shuddered. "Jesus, the memories. I went on opening night, and Maeve reminded me I was only there because Leah was in the morgue."

"It was cruel of her," Sylvie murmured.

"It was. True, but cruel. She's had a few barbed things to say in the press about me trying to step into her shoes now, the way I did Leah's. And how at least she's still wearing hers.

"Well. God. I think I need more wine."

"Why don't I get that for you?" Roarke rose.

"Oh." Sylvie gestured vaguely as she put an arm around Eliza. "On the counter in the kitchen."

"I'll find it."

"Was she at the party?" Eve asked as Roarke went inside. "Maeve Spindal?"

"Oh, good God, no." Eliza shuddered again, but theatrically. "I might have felt obliged if she'd been in New York, but fortunately, she's in London, getting raves—and I'm forced to say probably well deserved—onstage in *Lady Miss Diva*. And there's a title she also well deserves.

"Thank you," she added when Roarke brought out the wine bottle. "I dedicated my first Tony to Leah, but I can't, and haven't, lived my life constantly questioning why and how I got the chance to earn it. She made a terrible choice. Maeve's a viper, and I say that with some respect. But it's been twenty-five years, and she wasn't here."

"Okay. I appreciate your time." Eve rose. "You should know everyone we spoke with today in the course of the investigation offers condolences. Your doorman asked me to offer his."

"Thank you. That matters. It just shows how loved Brant was. Please find who did this to him."

"She won't stop until she does," Roarke said, and reached down for Eliza's hand. "Please don't hesitate to contact me if there's anything I can do."

"People say that, but I see you mean it."

"Let me show you out."

"No, that's fine," Eve told Sylvie. "We'll show ourselves."

11

"The wheels are turning." Roarke tapped Eve's head as they walked to the elevator.

"It weighs more she was the target."

"I'm going to agree. By her own admission, she's a controlling sort, one who micromanages. All the rest points to him as easygoing, friendly. She butts heads, he smooths feathers. And, yes, the drink was hers."

They stepped into the elevator.

"Taking that route," Eve continued, "we have Vera Harrow still on the list—on it either way, really. We have the director of her last vid, so I'll follow up there. Maybe he wasn't so much bygones as she seems to be. We have her ex-assistants, and I'm going to track them down. She has an ex-husband—in California, but. Fitzhugh's got an ex, too, but she's remarried and in Europe. Now there's this Maeve Spindal, and the whole deal about the dead actress."

She shot him a look. "How come you didn't know about that?"

"I've failed in my duty to know all about all, even what happened in New York when I was roughly twelve and in Dublin."

"Well, yeah. It's got juice, and you usually have the juice. Anyway, something to look at. And this Gary—I'll get that going, make sure the investigation didn't miss anything back then. Maybe Feeney knows something."

"Why don't I drive?" They crossed the lobby. "And you can ask him."

Henry had the door open for them. "You have a good evening now, Lieutenant, sir."

As Eve got into the passenger seat, she shot Roarke another look.

"You slipped him another tip, didn't you?"

Roarke just settled behind the wheel. "Is it home then?"

"Yeah, yeah. I need to talk to the director, the choreographer, some others, but I need to put this together." She pulled out her 'link, tagged Feeney.

His rumpled face topped with his explosion of ginger hair filled the screen. He said, "Yo."

"Yo back. Twenty-five years ago, Leah Rose, about eighteen years old, ruled accidental OD, found in her dressing room in the Crystal Gardens Theater before the opening of the Broadway musical *Up-stage*."

"Huh. Not my case, but yeah, I remember some of that. It's how Eliza Lane got her big break, right? The wife's a big fan. You caught Brant Fitzhugh. Damn shame. He made the kind of vids a guy could sit back with, crack a brew, and relax."

"Do you remember the primary?"

Feeney blew his lips, rubbed the back of his neck. "It's gonna be Holister, yeah, Holister and—shit—Wimbly. Holister put in his papers a few years back, moved to, I think, Florida. Wimbly, she may still be on the job, but—you know what, she moved to Bumfuck, Somewhere. Took a chief of police slot. I can find out."

"I'll find her. I'm going to dig up the files, have a look through."

"You figure a connection with Fitzhugh?"

"Don't know until I look."

"I can get them faster. I'll send them to you. Pills, wasn't it? Pills and . . . vodka."

"That's the information I have. Take enough pills, mix with liquor, it's like poison."

Cop's eyes met cop's eyes as Feeney nodded.

"I see where you're going. I'll dig up the files for you."

"Appreciate it."

"Poisonings, so to speak," Roarke said when she clicked off, "twenty-five years apart?"

Eve shrugged. "Maybe we'll find more in between. But it's the same play, going into the same theater, twenty-five years apart. So that connects again."

"She loved him. No question she could act the part onstage, on-screen, but what I saw face-to-face? She loved him."

"I won't say no. But I'll say I've put more than one person behind bars who loved the one they killed. 'He cheated.' 'She was going to leave me.' 'He forgot my birthday.' Whatever."

"Any indication of any of those whatevers here?"

"Not yet. What do you know about Maeve Spindal?"

"A formidable stage actor. Musicals primarily. Her screen work wasn't as well received, as she overplays. She sticks with the stage, where it is very well received."

"And here's Lane, well received in both, and now taking a part Spindal initially created. Could be a pisser."

"Hard to poison someone from across an ocean."

"Let's make sure she didn't take a side trip. Or there's murder for hire—always a popular option. In any case, I'd like a conversation.

She was there when Rose OD'd, and she's not fond of Lane, so if there's any dirt, she'd shovel it right up."

She sat back as the gates opened. "A lot to chew on."

"We'll have a meal, and you can chew on that as well."

The mention of a meal reminded her stomach she hadn't eaten since breakfast. Calculating, she decided not to mention it.

"I could eat," she said instead. "After I get the updates done."

"Fair enough." He took her hand when they got out of the car. "That should give me time to have a quick look at Sylvie Bowen's financials. If you're considering Lane a suspect or a target, you'll want more on her closest friend."

"Why do you get insulted when I say you think like a cop when you think like a cop?"

"The reasons should be clear to a trained observer. I'll accept that, situationally, I'm able to think like my cop."

When they walked in, Summerset stood, scarecrow thin in funereal black, with the pudge of a cat at his feet.

"Together, no visible bloodstains or bruises, and barely an hour late. A red-letter day."

"We had drinks with two luminaries of stage and screen," Roarke told him, effectively cutting off Eve's snark du jour. "Eliza Lane and Sylvie Bowen."

"Ah. The media's been ripe all day on Brant Fitzhugh's murder. I enjoyed your media conference, Lieutenant."

"That makes one of us." She sidestepped the cat, currently ribboning his way through her legs, and started for the stairs.

"Is there pie?" Roarke asked. "Pie came up earlier and now I've a yen."

"Lemon meringue."

"Well now, that's perfect, isn't it? Enjoy your evening."

"I'm nearly out the door. Ivanna's goddaughter is performing in a string quartet."

"Give her my best."

When he caught up to Eve on the stairs, she looked at him. "Why is it a red-letter day? Why isn't it ever a blue-letter day, or a green-number day?"

"There's something to ponder on. Absolutely never."

"I bet you know anyway."

In her office, he walked over, opened the terrace doors. "Something to do with calendars and marking the dates of festivals in red."

She went straight to her command center, opened operations. "Then why isn't it a red-number day? Calendars have numbers, not letters."

He crossed to the wine cabinet, uncorked a bottle. After he set a glass beside her, he bent down to kiss the top of her head. "We'll take it up with the management."

She looked up at him. "Things should make sense, and half the time they don't. Stuff that shouldn't make sense, half the time does."

"Then it all evens out, doesn't it? Half an hour," he added, then went into his own office.

"It's chaos!" she called out. "How is that even?"

"Someone once said chaos is a ladder—but then he died a brutal death."

"Ha." She started her update, then paused. "Chaos is a ladder . . . maybe."

Witnesses described the scene after Fitzhugh's collapse as chaos, as confusion. Wouldn't that be a handy ladder for the killer?

She tucked it away, let it brew while she updated her book, wrote a report for Whitney. Roarke came back as she began to update her board.

"Who said that thing about chaos and the ladder?"

"A character in a screen series. One you'd enjoy now that I think of it." He answered from the kitchen, where Galahad had followed hopefully. "And, as I think of it, tailor-made for Brant Fitzhugh. Swords and battles, dragons and political intrigue.

"You've been fed already," he said to the cat.

And Eve knew without needing to see that Roarke caved and set out some of the much-loved cat treats.

She worked on the board as he carried out two domed plates.

"You can climb out of a hole or into a window with a ladder, and if there's chaos, nobody notices."

"True enough." He went back for the wine, then stopped by her board to study it with her. "So many well-known faces."

"And the ones behind them. A party's a kind of chaos."

That made him smile. "For you they are."

"No, really. A lot of people wandering around, clutched into groups, music, food, drinks. Say, controlled chaos. Still, some people, at least some, are paying attention. Servers, for instance, or people who like to watch people, judge what they're wearing—that's a big one. Listen to what they're saying in other groups."

Absently, she took the glass of wine he offered her. "They've got a big space." She gestured to various photos of the crime scene. "Limited to the main level for the party, though they wouldn't do regular sweeps of the two other floors if people didn't get through—like the drunk in the tub."

He nudged her toward the table. "And with people mingling, moving, the conversation, the music, the space, it's not hard to tip a bit of poison into a glass."

"He wasn't going to drink it," she pointed out. "Like the glass you just handed me. That was for me, so you didn't hold it up here." She brought the glass up. "We're talking, drinking, blah blah, I'm more likely to hold the glass up. But you're taking it across the room, so you're more likely to hold it down, not really paying attention to it, especially if you're closing in, having a quick conversation, getting the dumbass kiss-kiss greeting.

"Controlled chaos is still a ladder."

When she sat, he removed the domes, set them aside. She saw fat hunks of pork smothered in sauce, a cold pasta salad, and a bunch of colorful vegetables she didn't bother to identify.

"But after," she continued, and cut into the pork, "chaotic chaos. Shock, panic, people scrambling back or rushing toward. In those first seconds, people react that way—panic—a what the fuck. Except for the killer because the killer knows what the fuck. You could climb that ladder to conceal whatever held the cyanide. If the target's Lane, you would've already done that during controlled chaos. Hell, it's going to be small, has to fit in your pocket and be easily palmed. You could flush it on a quick trip to the john.

"I've asked myself why that night—all those wits—but the fact is, that night was perfect because of all the wits. Jesus, this is really good. What is it?"

"Boneless barbecued ribs. You're sure about the bartender being clear?"

"Fitzhugh directed her step-by-step. That's not only her statement, but Vera Harrow's. And she's clean, no connection we've found to either the victim or Lane, no motive."

"I'm going to tell you, so far, the same applies to Sylvie Bowen, at least as far as her finances go. She was very generous with her ex, which to my eye, he took regular advantage of while he worked on re-jected screenplays. I'll wager she never had to piss him off to convince him to take some cash for his pocket."

She shot a finger at him, then shrugged. "I earn a paycheck," she reminded him.

"And he didn't, or only sporadically. His finances—I couldn't resist— are shaky at best. And since she—wisely—transferred her funds out of the account he grabbed from, put a block on him, and had her lawyers contact him using the word *embezzlement*, I suspect they'll be shakier."

Now he shrugged. "Otherwise? Nothing sends up a flag. She actually lives rather conservatively for someone in her position. She has the flat here, a place in the Hollywood Hills, as she often works there, but her parents, both alive and well, live there year-round. She's given generously to Fitzhugh's cause."

"We'll cross that off. It wouldn't be about money if she's involved. It would be about loyalty. If Lane wanted Fitzhugh dead, and Bowen helped, it's loyalty and friendship."

"And why would Lane want him dead?"

"Yeah, that's the stickler." She stabbed into the pasta. "I've got to lean toward Lane being the target, and the killer not having the opportunity to stop him—or maybe not especially caring—when Fitzhugh drank the poison."

"And that winds you back to Vera Harrow, doesn't it?"

"She stays high on the list. What I don't get? Ten years ago, the guy says, 'Hey, it's been swell, but I'm going to start banging somebody else.' Or worse—because wouldn't it be worse?—'I'm in love with somebody else.' But she doesn't stab his ass with a steak knife or bash his brains in with a doorstop in the heat of the moment. Or, alternatively, do either to Lane. Instead, they keep working together until the project that brought Lane into the mix is finished."

"That's entertainment."

"Is it? You'd think she'd at least have punched him in his perfect face. I'd sure as hell put some bruises on you before I injected you with a paralytic, shaved your head, and tied your dick in a knot."

"How? That particular appendage doesn't lend itself to knots."

"I'd find a way. But instead of finding a way, she waits a freaking decade for payback? I just can't make it play. Something happened now, in the now, I mean. Something more recent triggered the murder."

"Lane's going to get global buzz with this revival," Roarke pointed out. "Not only talking about that, but how she got her start in the same play. And assuming it's a hit—and it certainly should be—she stands to make a great deal of money not only as the headliner but as one of the producers. For his part, Fitzhugh's young production company already has considerable success, financially and critically, and he was off to star in one of his own productions, one with a very big budget.

"I was curious there," he added. "I checked. Everything points to them having a solid, happy marriage, solid, successful careers. And these last ventures? More fame, more fortune."

"Money and jealousy. Maybe. Maybe. I need to look at the cast and crew again, but every one of them benefits from Lane doing this show, so why kill her—or, alternatively, him?"

"I imagine they held a lot of auditions, and that would mean a great many walked away disappointed."

"I didn't get the part, so die, bitch?" She sat back, sipped some wine. "Yeah, I can see that. Then you have to wheedle yourself into the party. A plus-one, a server. A plus-one's more likely. The caterer's fierce about screening. But still, a lot of actor types work in food services to pay the rent. I'll take another look."

"I could do that for you while you dig down on the cast and crew. You may find it's not the person who didn't get the part, but a friend—as you were looking at Sylvie—a relative, a lover. Someone who'd do the deed for someone else."

Smiling at him, she ate more pork.

And seeing the trap he'd walked straight into, he drank more wine.

"Don't say it," he warned. "It's redundant, as I can bloody hear you thinking it."

"You can qualify it as thinking like *your* cop, but any solid cop's going to go down the same road. There's also murder for hire, don't forget that one."

"Most who audition aren't going to have the means to hire a killer."

"They would if the killer's in the same basic tax bracket, or under. Scrape up a couple of grand. Alternatively, offer sex, or hold something over their heads. Blackmail's always good for motivation. Or maybe they come from a wealthy family, but only want the limelight.

"What the hell does that mean?" she demanded. "Limes don't put off light. I hate when I use an expression that's bone-ass stupid. Anyway, it's an angle. Struggling actor breaks, decides if I didn't get the part, nobody does. Maybe it's more logical to poison whoever got the part instead, but you take out Lane, the whole deal goes down. Plus, she's a producer, so she probably had input into who got what. I bet she would anyway. Controlling, she said so herself."

"This is good."

"The food or the angles?"

"Both. The killer doesn't even have to get close to Lane to kill her, and if that had worked, I'd be looking hard, really hard, at Fitzhugh."

She wagged her fork, then ate more. "Which is a solid side motive. Pay them both back."

"And that circles you back to Vera Harrow."

"She fits. I don't like the ten-year gap, but otherwise. She came off believable, but that's what she does, right? Actors have to come off believable."

She put her fork down. "I can't eat pie."

"Later."

"Do you really have time to run a bunch of actor types who didn't get a part in this deal?"

"I do, actually. I went back and did a bit of work last night when you were called in. And I expect you'll show your gratitude for my time and effort."

"Always a catch. I guess we got interrupted in that area last night."

"We did. Aren't we lucky it's far from our last chance?"

On impulse, she reached over, gripped his hand. "Yeah, we are. The cop in me looks at Lane, sees spouse, suspect. A spouse can always have a motive that doesn't show on the outside. She had opportunity. And means? I have to figure she has the means to get the means. But the me in me? I know love when I see it now. She loved him. And all the statements, all the indications, all the evidence points to him loving her. They made a unit, and I know what that is now."

"As do I. As I know there's a hole in her heart that will never fill again."

"The dead aren't the only victims. Your part of the unit got the meal. My part's got the dishes. You gave Galahad some of that cat candy, didn't you?"

"Guilty."

"Thought so." As she rose, she glanced back to where the cat sprawled over her sleep chair. "You won't get any out of me, tubby."

She dealt with the dishes, then went back to her command center. Programmed coffee. Then took ten minutes to just sit, boots up, coffee in hand, to study the board.

The failed audition was a good angle, she thought. It had to sting to be told: No, not good enough. If it happened over and over, did you give up, or keep working that food service job and trying? Some obviously did one or the other, but a certain type could crack, strike out.

Then there was Vera Harrow. Came off believable, but she made her very good living doing just that. Did she finally exact payback?

Eliza Lane. Eve could feel deeply sorry for her and still suspect her.

Sylvie Bowen, longtime loyal friend. Whose lover had just ditched her and stole from her to do it in style. It could put a person in the frame of mind to help a pal kill an errant spouse.

The trouble there? No evidence he was, in any way, errant.

But maybe she just hadn't found it yet.

And that didn't consider the loyal assistants. It would pay to dig deeper there.

Cast and crew. On the surface, the opposite of motive. But . . . What if someone took the job for the express purpose of killing Lane? Someone, or someone connected to someone, she'd fired, rejected, hurt in some way.

She dropped her feet on the floor, swiveled around.

She started with Tessa Long, the director. Though she'd gone through it before, she read the background again.

Mixed race, age fifty-four, native New Yorker. Mother a pediatric surgeon, father a neurologist. Married fifty-six years.

That got a wow.

One sib, male, age forty-two, orthopedic surgeon. Married nineteen years, wife, general surgery. Two offspring, male, sixteen; male, thirteen.

Bucked family tradition, didn't you, Tessa?

Married to Mai Li, professional mother status, eighteen years. Two offspring—female twins, age sixteen.

No criminal.

Residence, Chelsea; secondary residence, Oyster Bay.

Solid education, theater major, financially stable. With a steady boost from a trust fund.

Eve skimmed through her employment history. Started young, summer theater work, interning, assistanting, gofering from the looks of it. Worked her way up. No connection to Fitzhugh that showed, except through Lane, whom she'd worked with prior to the current project.

The first, twenty years before, Broadway, Lane headlining, Long assistant stage manager. Then three years later, as assistant director, five years more, director, then as Lane's director on a screen special four years after that—one that included Sylvie Bowen—and as director on a major vid two years after that. Now this production.

She'd leave it to Peabody's gossip search to see if there was any juice or scandal or rifts, but from their work history, she'd say no.

She couldn't see Lane working with someone that often if there was friction.

Add gay and long-term married, so probability very low for any really well-kept affair with the victim. And as Long was listed as one of the producers, money didn't gel as a motive.

She moved on, ran through the assistant director, the lyricist and composer. The woman who'd written the original book had been dead for eight years—private shuttle crash.

At some point, Roarke glided in, set a piece of pie by her elbow, glided out again.

At some point, she ate it because holy crap it was good.

She programmed more coffee, gave a hard look at the other backers.

Nothing there, nothing popped.

So she moved on again to the choreographer.

Minerva Novak, Caucasian, age thirty-six. Parents Roger Novak, Alyson Crupke, divorced, no sibs from that marriage. Half-sib, male, age twenty-nine, half-sib, female, age twenty-seven, from Novak's marriage to Heaven (seriously) Colby Novak. One stepsib, female, deceased, from Crupke's marriage to Lloyd Bernstein—divorced. One stepsib, age forty-four, one half-sib, age twenty-two, from Crupke's marriage to Benson Pickett. Divorced.

"Jesus, lady, give it up."

But no, she read on. Try, try again with Edwin White-Mitchell, one stepsib, male, age fifty-three.

"Went for an old guy on the fourth try." Eve took a quick look at White-Mitchell. "Old really rich guy, and you're his number four. Let's see how long that lasts."

Minerva Novak, born in Chicago, relocated to New York at age sixteen to attend Juilliard, father and stepmother as custodial parents, and under the guardianship of an aunt—father's side—with New York residency. Father and stepmother remained custodial parents.

Small wonder the mother didn't get custodial rights, Eve thought.

Novak married Malcomb Furrier, four years, one offspring, daughter, age two.

No criminal—though Malcomb had a drunk and disorderly in his college days. She didn't hold that against him.

Financials . . . not rolling in it, but very solid.

No prior work with Lane or Fitzhugh. Plenty of work, though, dancing professionally until an injury sidelined that and turned her to choreography.

Eve sat back, rubbed her eyes, drank more coffee.

A lot of siblings of one sort or another. "We're this far in. Let's have a look."

She worked her way down, starting with the father and stepmother. Both the half-sibs lived in the Chicago area, the half brother an architect, the sister a personal shopper for a major department store. She pushed a little deeper but couldn't find any recent travel to New York. It appeared both of them, the father, the stepmother, had come to New York for Novak's kid's birth.

The mother hadn't, she noted, but both the half- and stepsib from the mother's third marriage had. No visits from the stepsib old enough to be her father.

So some family ties, she thought, enough to bring them in to see their half niece, step-niece within a few days or weeks of her birth.

But none of them lived in New York, or had any obvious connection to either Lane or Fitzhugh.

"Okay, what happened to the dead one? Rose Bernstein."

She ran it, skimmed the birth and birthplace, the paternity, maternity. Narrowed in on the date and cause of death.

"Died in '36, death ruled accidental overdose. Well, Jesus! Age eighteen? New York City, stage name Leah Rose. Son of bitch. Bang!"

12

Roarke strolled in.

"I heard the bang."

"Damn right! Try this. The choreographer's mother's second husband's daughter, stage name Leah Rose. That's the one who OD'd on opening night of the original *Upstage*."

"Convoluted," Roarke considered. "And yet a worthy bang. And I'll add an aha."

"Minerva Novak's mother's on husband number four."

"An optimist."

"That's one way of looking at it. Thanks to optimism, Novak's accumulated a bunch of siblings—the halfs, the steps—and every one of them came to New York when she had a kid a couple years ago—except the last husband's son. That indicates a certain closeness, right? Odds are she was close with the stepsib who died and opened the door for Lane's breakout."

He edged a hip onto her command center, glanced at her screen. "I'd have to agree there. It's certainly a connection to Lane, and through her to Fitzhugh, that can't be ignored. Were they aware of that connection?"

"I'm going with no, as nobody bothered to mention it. But I'm sure as hell going to ask. I mean, Jesus, you'd have to think it's worth mentioning. Oh yeah, by the way, the dead girl whose dance shoes I inherited? She was the sister of the person who decided how many pirouettes we do."

The idea of it pushed Eve to her feet, had her throwing out her arms. "And Novak. Did she think we wouldn't find the connection? It's right there!"

"Different surnames, a many-married mother, and twenty-five years. She might very well have assumed it stayed buried. Or taken that risk."

"If there hadn't been so many people at that party—and what looks like the wrong person on a slab—I'd've dug it up inside an hour with a . . ." She dug shallowly at the air with her hand.

"Garden spade?"

"That. I need to talk to her, but I need to read the file on Rose Bernstein aka Leah Rose. Feeney came through with that. I'm going to put Peabody on that, too. I want to know everything there is to know before we interview her."

She turned to him. "You could do me a solid and do a run on her financials. Her husband's, too. And since they're maybe a tight family, at least those directly connected to Rose Bernstein."

"You want me to poke around in the financial business of complete strangers? No wonder I adore you."

"You don't pick up a vial of cyanide at the local twenty-four/seven, so an odd payment or cash withdrawal, likely within the last two or three weeks. Or—"

"I believe I know what to look for."

"Yeah, right. Yeah." She stared at the board. "All that mixed-up family. There could be a chemist, someone connected to a chemist. Or a chemi-head who cooks. And there are legit uses for cyanide— photography chemicals, right? And textiles. You have to go through some hoops to get it, document its use and all that, so maybe a paper trail there."

"And if you find a link there, it adds weight to what you already found."

"Another bang wouldn't hurt." She sat again. "It's not a damn co-incidence."

"I'll see if I can find you more weight."

"Thanks."

She opened the file Feeney sent, copied it to Peabody along with the data on Minerva Novak.

It didn't surprise her as she began to read the case file to receive a quick response from Peabody.

It said: Bang!

"With a bing and a boom," she muttered.

She read to gather facts, information, and to look for any holes in the investigation. And more connections. She studied the facts and evidence, compiled information. Though she didn't find any holes, at least not on the first pass, she found more connections.

She expanded her board to create a section for the Bernstein case.

Then she read it all again before looking over the various inter-views Peabody sent her from articles on Leah Rose's death, the reactions of cast, crew, friends, compared them to the statements given the police, the interviews conducted by the investigators.

She went back to the pathology report. He'd listed signs of an eating disorder, chronic drug and alcohol abuse, and a terminated pregnancy. Which jibed with her medical history—treatment for anorexia, emergency treatment for an overdose of sleeping pills, and a medically induced abortion.

And all before she'd hit seventeen.

Since the investigation into her death unsealed her juvenile records, Eve found the busts for possession, underage drinking, the court-ordered rehab.

A short, fucked-up life, Eve thought.

She programmed more coffee as Roarke came back in.

"I'm for a whiskey. You know," he began as he got himself one, "when you do that poking about, finding law-abiding, tax-paying citizens takes all the fun out of it."

After toasting her, he sat at her auxiliary station and drank. "I'm running more on auto, but I can tell you Novak and Furrier have no dark secrets or murky shadows in that area. He's fairly successful and draws in a steady income from royalties as well as his fees for current work."

"He's the one who makes up the words that go with the tune, right?"

"Yes. Her income took a hit when she injured her knee, but revived when she focused on choreography. She supplemented that, initially, by teaching dance, and will still teach occasionally."

He paused to sip whiskey while Eve considered the data.

"They bought a nice property about a year ago, Lower East, and they're investing quite a bit in remodeling same. She also has a share in a vacation home—with her father, stepmother, and half-siblings—on Hilton Head. They opened an education account for their daughter shortly after her birth."

He studied the new section of her board as he spoke. "She has a cousin of some sort—the family is very convoluted—who's a tax lawyer. He takes advantage of any option or opening, but keeps them within the law."

"Is that it?"

"Not altogether. She has a sibling from her mother's . . . Ah Christ, which? Third, yes, third marriage who's a photographer. One who does film—and his own darkroom work—as well as digital. You'll want to check yourself, but my initial research shows some of the chemicals he uses may contain some cyanide, but he'd have to find a way to extract that, wouldn't he, so none of the rest showed in autopsy. And there's no indication I found he purchased any separately."

"It's worth a look."

"As I assumed." He sipped more whiskey. "Another sibling's spouse is an office manager for a pharmaceutical company. They have their own chemists."

"That's good. Another worth a look." Eve gestured toward the board. "Rose Bernstein, started dance and voice lessons at two. She started picking up work—ads, local vids, some stage stuff—before she was three. Bit parts, lots of ad work, did the tutor thing to get her high school diploma. Daddy has some money. Mommy—that's Debra Bernstein—wanted her baby to be a star. I got that out of the case file. Also it looks like she had a pretty solid addiction to amphetamines—to keep off the weight, keep up the energy—and barbs—to come down and get some sleep—by the time she hit puberty."

Like Eve, Roarke studied the photo of the bright, pretty young woman on the board. "There's a tragedy already made."

"She relocated to New York with her mother at fifteen. Bernstein would've been married to Novak's mother for a couple of years—and that was about to end. But Novak and Rose had to spend some time together, especially since Novak also took dance classes."

"Common interest."

"Exactly. Anyway, Rose hits all the—they call them cattle calls, which is creepy on every level. She gets busted for possession—that was back in Chicago, age thirteen. In New York she has a close call with the pills, ends up in the hospital. Rehab, treatment. She gets treat-ment for her eating disorder, but the medical examiner cited recent abuse there at TOD. She gets pregnant and terminates same at fifteen, about six months after she gets to New York."

"A child still. Where was her mother, as her mother was in charge?"

"A good question. But Rose is getting work, getting good reviews on that work. Then she gets one with what do you call it—billing. She's six-teen, runs with it for nearly two years—got one of those nominations—the Tony thing."

She rose, paced.

"The day, and I mean day, she turns eighteen, she boots the mother, gets her own place. A few months after, she auditions for *Upstage*. She gets the part, and six months later, she's dead, full of barbs and vodka."

"A short, sad life. Do you have any reason to think it wasn't acci-dental?"

"Looking at the case files, her history, the pathology and tox re-ports, it plays that way. But I want to talk to the investigator, maybe the ME at the time. Just cross those off. Novak would've been about eleven when it happened."

She tapped Minx's photo on the board. "Big sister—if she thought of her that way—about to take a major leap in her career. Instead, she's dead, and Lane gets to make the leap, right into the big, shiny spot-light."

While Roarke drank his whiskey and watched her, Eve circled the board. "So, try this. You're sad about that, maybe even resentful, but you're a kid. Nothing you can do. You push on with your own dream of that spotlight. You even do big sis one better and get accepted into Juilliard. You stay clean, at least as far as it shows re drugs and alco-hol, and you're on the rise.

"Then boom, bad spill, bad knee, dream dashed. Now you're teaching instead, showing other people how to do what you've wanted since you were a kid. You're choreographing those big-ass shows instead of taking the bows."

Hooking her thumbs in her pockets, she nodded toward Minx Novak's photo.

"You get married, have a kid, sucking it all up, living a life. But then, it all comes around, it comes around and shoves it all in your face. There's Eliza Lane again, making the big splash, riding on the break she got all those years ago because your sister died. Your sister's dead, and Lane is going to sing and dance right over her dead body, again."

Eve walked back, picked up her coffee. "All those memories come flooding back. So it's fuck that, and fuck her. This one's for Rose."

She drank some coffee. "It's a theory, and it smells like motive. Now potentially two lines of means, with two other sibs. And opportunity, no question on that."

"An opposing view? Even a loving sister—assuming she is—would have a difficult time blaming anyone but Rose herself for her death."

"Novak's eleven, and her mother's on marriage number three. Scars," Eve said. "Sometimes scars rip right open and bleed again. It doesn't have to be Lane's fault Rose died. But it's her fault for profiting—fame and fortune–wise—from it. She plans to do it again. And there's the whole payback is a salad thing."

He looked, as he rarely did, baffled. "All right, there you've lost me. How is payback like a salad?"

"It doesn't have to be hot, right? You eat it cold, a salad."

"Ah, I think we've gone around this one before, so I should've gotten it. Revenge, darling Eve, is a dish best served cold."

"What I said, basically. And I don't know about best anyway, because a lot of people like it served up all hot and bubbly. But a connection like this isn't bollocks."

"I wouldn't argue with that, only tell you her finances are above-board. Her father's and stepmother's as well. Solid citizens there. I didn't see anything to flag on the two—the photographer and the office manager—that may be your cyanide source. The photographer has financial ups and downs, but nothing murky. And the officer manager is clever financially, but straight with it. If either of them accessed the poison, it doesn't show there."

"If either did, it'll show somewhere else."

"All right then, we'll each take one, do the run, and see if something pops up."

"I can toss one to Peabody."

"I'm sitting right here," he pointed out, "and may as well keep myself busy until this part's done and we can go back to where we were interrupted last night."

"Will do cop work for sex?"

"It's become my daily mantra."

He gave her one name, took the other.

She pushed, and hard. An hour later, even after the cat had deserted them, after reviewing her own results, Roarke's, running probabilities from every angle she could think of, she had nothing more to hang her theory on.

"Could be one of the in-laws; she's got plenty. Or she found another way to access it."

"All true." Roarke took her hand, hauled her to her feet. "You'll confront her about all of this in the morning and get more answers."

"I can buy nobody making the connection. Novak to Bernstein to Rose. Plus, nobody, after all this time, would remember Bernstein if it wasn't for Lane. But Novak not telling anybody? I want the why."

"I've no doubt you'll get it. I have to admit, looking at her, her husband, the family I've poked through? She doesn't strike as the murderous type. And before you remind me," he added as she walked into the bedroom, "I'm aware of how many murderous types hide under the gloss of innocence.

"Their last big purchase? Furniture for their daughter's bedroom."

"Killers have kids."

"So they do. Did you know Malcomb Furrier wrote the lyrics for 'Only One'?" At her blank look, he smiled, turned her into his arms. "We danced to it at our wedding. Entertainment unit, play 'Only One.'"

As the music slid into the room, she had a picture, a vivid one, of dancing with him under summer skies, the scent of flowers everywhere.

"I remember," she said as she moved with him now. "I remember feeling weird I didn't feel weird dancing with you while everyone stood around watching."

"Almost three years now."

"I had a shiner. Fucking Casto."

He kissed her under the eye that had been blackened. "It didn't show, thanks to Trina."

"Don't say the name." She put her head on his shoulder. "I like dancing with you better when no one's watching, but that was good. I dumped all the plans on you."

"Fucking Casto."

She laughed, tipped back her head. "It probably came off smoother without me. It was a really good day." Then she laid a hand on his cheek. "I love you more now."

"Eve."

"Because I know more now. It was all such a rush, wasn't it? And I know more now. What it takes, who you are, what we have. Even when I piss you off, you're going to be there. Like I'm going to be there even when you piss me off. So there's more."

"Loving you changed everything for me. Being loved by you opened everything for me. Every day is more," he said, and lowered his mouth to hers.

She remembered the first time he'd kissed her, all that wild urgency and need. And remembered the stunned joy of the kiss on their wedding day, under an arbor of flowers.

Now this, soft, strong, sweet, while music played, after a long, hard day, this gift of knowing, of being home again.

He circled her around, a slow dance, then eased her weapon harness away to set it aside. She tugged the leather tie out of his hair and did the same.

The end of work mode for both of them.

"Replay," she ordered as the music faded off. She began to unbutton his shirt. "We had a really big party after that dance."

"We did."

"It was pretty late when people finally went away, but then we came up here. Like this." She ran her hands up his chest, then linked her arms around his neck.

"The wardrobe was considerably different," he pointed out as he emptied her pockets—the badge, the 'link, the communicator. "But otherwise . . ."

With the memory in mind, he picked her up to carry her to the bed. The cat sprawled over it, stretched out as far as felinely possible.

Eve said, "Scram."

Galahad opened one eye, aimed a baleful look with it before he rolled, leaped down, and stalked away.

"We're going to need the room," she finished as Roarke laid her down. With her arms still linked around him, she drew him down with her.

He simply sank into her, into the kiss, into the moment.

She could wipe the world away for him, and had owned that power almost from the first instant. Those eyes, the color so like the whiskey he'd sipped, looked, saw him, loved him anyway.

Was there a more precious gift?

His fingers skimmed through her careless cap of hair, with tones like a deer moving through sun and shadow. He knew the angles of her face, her body, and the fierce, vulnerable, courageous spirit inside it all.

He'd wanted her, somehow recognized something . . . something in her, of her, almost from that first instant. And the wanting had only deepened with the having.

Even as he let his hands roam over her, he knew he'd fall deeper yet.

She slid his shirt away; he tugged hers up and off. When they were skin to skin, she rolled, a lazy move to change the angle of the kiss, to draw it out and out. Hands gliding over him, kindling already glowing sparks. Fingers kneading into muscle, tongues sliding.

He rolled, unhooking her belt as he did. His teeth grazed her shoulder, her collarbone, her breast. Everything in her went soft. He could melt her, seduce her so she craved the yielding, arouse her so her world contracted down to the two of them, only the two of them, mating in the dark.

Already her heartbeat thickened, her pulse quickened. She could float and float and float on the clouds of pleasure he conjured like a sorcerer. Before she lost herself—so easy, nearly there—she pushed away.

"Gotta get these damn clothes off." Breathless, she dragged at her boots.

When they thudded to the floor along with his shoes, he pulled her to him again.

"I'll handle the rest."

He could, and would, she knew, again like that sorcerer—or the nimble-fingered thief he'd been. She shifted her weight, overbalanced him so her body stretched over his.

"I'll start," she said, and unhooked his belt.

She'd float, and she'd fly, but she'd make certain he did the same.

She loved the feel of him under her, the warm skin, the taut muscle. She loved feeling him yield to her, though she found him granite hard, heard the drum of his heart against her mouth before she traveled down.

She destroyed him, stretched his control to a thin, vibrating wire. Slowly, relentlessly, she took that wire to the edge of snapping before easing back just enough, barely enough for him to maintain a slippery grip.

"*A ghrá.*" He murmured it, and other words in the language of his heart as the air grew so thick he could barely draw it in.

"*Tá grá agam duit.*" She mangled the Irish, and touched his speeding heart as she slid slowly, so slowly up his body. "Tell me. Say it to me."

"*Tá grá agam duit.* I love you."

She pressed her lips to his as if to taste the words.

He rolled her onto her back, then lowered his forehead to hers. To steady himself for a moment, just a moment.

"I'll finish."

She cupped his face. "I want you inside me."

"I know." He pressed his lips to her throat. "I know."

Her pulse beat against his lips, her heart thudded against them as he took her breast. Her hips arched as he stripped away the last barrier.

He pressed his hand to the heat of her, the core of her. "Let go," he said, then his clever fingers gave her no choice.

When her gasp of pleasure wasn't enough, he drove her up and over again until she shuddered, until she went to candlewax in the sun.

"Take me now. *A ghrá, mo chroí.*"

At last, he slipped inside her, full, deep. Again she shuddered, and thought: This. This.

With the world gone and time stopped, she took him. They took each other, rising, falling, falling, rising, until they flew.

When they slept, wrapped close, the cat jumped back on the bed.

She woke with dawn breaking, shedding pinks through the sky window over the bed. Roarke sat—fully dressed, of course—in the sitting area, tablet in hand, cat across his lap, wall screen muted.

She wondered if she'd wake this way when she hit, oh, maybe a hundred and ten. Would they have slept through the night, sated from sex, or . . .

A sudden thought struck and shot her straight up in bed.

Roarke glanced over. "Well then, good morning to you."

"We had all that sex, and while we were having it, clothes got tossed around."

"Something that happens with happy regularity, thank the gods."

"Yeah, yeah, but it just hit me. The clothes aren't all tossed around in the morning. You pick them up, right? Right? Summerset doesn't come slinking in here while I'm conked and do that."

"Summerset doesn't slink." Roarke reached for his coffee. "Or, I suppose he does, now and then. But no, he doesn't come in while you're asleep."

"Okay. Good, really good. Listen, I help toss them around. I can take turns or whatever scooping them up."

"It's not a problem."

"Well, if you ever have to skip it to go buy Canada, I'll take care of it."

"If I ever get a tip Canada's for sale, I'll leave the rest to you."

"Deal. Jesus, that sudden thought was almost like a jolt of coffee. Almost," she repeated, and got up to get the real thing.

"I had a bunch of dreams. Not bad ones," she added quickly when those eyes lasered on her. "Just weird ones all jumbled up. Like I have this lineup, but it's like an audition, and all the suspects are in there singing and dancing around."

She gulped coffee, shaking her head as she headed to the bathroom. "Just weird."

"Not especially for her, is it?" Roarke asked the cat.

When she came out, he had two domed plates and a pot of coffee waiting. He'd banished the cat, who sat in front of the fireplace staring at the plates as if the power of his mind could transport them.

"Novak was there."

"In the lineup audition?"

"Yeah, that. She's more telling the others what to do. Like 'Kick! Plié! Jump!' What the hell is step ball change?"

"A dance step."

"I know that. I've heard it or she wouldn't have been telling people to do it. What the hell is it? You step while you juggle balls?"

"No, darling. It's the balls of your feet." He tapped his fingers on the table to illustrate.

"Okay, that makes more sense. How do you know that?"

He smiled charmingly. "I've known a few dancers."

"As in banged a few dancers."

"There's no one I'd rather dance with than you."

"Decent save." And when he removed the domes to uncover waffles, she sat beside him. "An even better save." She immediately soaked them in syrup.

"So, the choreographer's the one telling everybody to change their balls. And all the rest," she continued over Roarke's burst of laughter. "That's key when you've got a musical deal with the singing and dancing. You've got a big bunch of people to coordinate. It's like . . . artistic crowd control."

"That's an interesting take on it." He poured her more coffee.

"You could have a dozen people onstage during one of those big numbers, and you've got to figure out what each one of them does, the steps, the timing, the placement, and how it comes together, how it's going to look from the audience."

"And that makes you think?"

"Somebody knows how to plan, how to refine the small details while envisioning the big picture. Plus, you'd have to know the individuals—strengths, weaknesses. You know movement."

"So you could say the party was a big stage."

She swallowed a bite of waffle, stabbed another. "Damn right. She'd know the bulk of the people, too—the cast and crew. She can't control the movements, but she can follow them, anticipate. It's an angle to push when we talk to her this morning."

"Your dreams never fail to fascinate."

"Might as well use them. I want to get her in the box, but we'll start on her turf, throw her off with the dead sister connection, see how she handles it."

She snagged some bacon and noticed his tablet.

"You weren't working on buying Canada."

"Sadly, no. Actually, I was reviewing some progress on the house project."

He was into it, she knew. Deeply. She doubted he'd be more into it if it were his own. But then, considering who'd live there, it sort of was his own.

Sort of hers, too, really.

"I gave Peabody a couple minutes to bubble away on her kitchen yesterday on the way to Queens."

"It's lovely. Would you like to see?"

"I guess. Sure."

He picked up the tablet, scrolled, then turned the screen toward Eve.

"Oh."

She'd known it would be ace work, because Roarke, and Peabody had already practically drawn her a picture. But . . . nice.

She saw soft, warm colors, what looked like miles of counter space, some glass doors on cabinets, some open shelves, shiny appliances that looked like they meant business.

When he scrolled through from different angles, she saw a breakfast nook deal with bench seating and a view of the gardens, a big sink, a gleaming wood floor.

"It looks good. Just a little girly, but really, really efficient. Bigger than it looked before. What's that?"

"Her living wall."

"The wall's alive?"

"She's doing herbs and other plants in those pots you see. She worked with one of her grandmothers on the design, and her sister made the pots."

"Her sister made the pots."

"They just arrived yesterday. Peabody hasn't seen them up yet, as Mavis asked one of the crew to put them up last night. Mavis sent that picture."

"So I shouldn't mention the wall being alive."

"It'll be a surprise."

"She'll go batshit over it. How come that counter there's shorter than the others?"

"There's that sharp eye. It's for rolling pie dough, kneading bread dough, that sort of thing. It's custom to her height. McNab's idea."

"So he pays attention, doesn't just stuff his face with the pies." Major points for him, she decided. Paying attention mattered. "It looks like her. Soft but not bland, girlie but not frilly, efficient but not cold."

"We'll make time to go by together before we leave for Europe. It matters to them."

"I got that. Hell, it matters to me. Just not every detail about door-knobs, but it matters."

He leaned over to kiss her cheek. "I know."

"You like details like doorknobs." She kissed him back. "I've got to get moving." She polished off the waffles. "Need to talk to a suspect about ball changes."

13

In her closet, she steered away from the knee-jerk black only because she figured Roarke would say something about going with it two days running.

She grabbed brown trousers—not Feeney-dung brown but a color that made her think of the candy bar hidden in her office.

Which made her think of the Candy Thief, and that put a scowl on her face as she pulled out a white T-shirt, nearly pulled out a brown jacket before she settled on khaki. She dressed in the closet to avoid comments.

And should've known better.

"A navy belt's a better choice," he said as she reached for a black one.

In his perfect pin-striped suit, he leaned against the doorjamb. "You look altogether fresh and professional, Lieutenant."

"Whatever." She grabbed a navy blue belt.

"I'll send you the results of the overnight runs. You can access them from your car if you need to."

"I appreciate it."

"If you have a minute, let me know if you arrest the choreographer. I'm curious."

"I can do that." After she'd looped on the belt, she scooped a hand through her hair and deemed grooming done.

She moved past him to the bedroom, where the cat shoved a paw against the domes Roarke had replaced on the plates.

"You're just asking for it," she commented.

"But won't get it," Roarke said with a single hard stare.

The cat sat, shot up a leg, and began an intense grooming of his own.

Eve put on her weapon harness, filled her pockets. "Either way, I just know they're going to drag me in front of a bunch of reporters again."

"You'll handle them, as you always do." After she'd shrugged on her jacket, he laid his hands on her shoulders. "And look fresh and professional while you grind them up."

He kissed her. "I'll watch if I can manage it, as it never fails to entertain. Kick the asses you need to kick, and take care of my cop."

"Doing the first hooks right into the second. I'll let you know if we dance Novak into a cell. He's at it again," she added as over Roarke's shoulder she watched Galahad stretch up on his hind legs to nudge at a dome.

"I know. I'll deal with him."

As she walked out, she heard Roarke.

"It appears you and I have to have another serious conversation."

She wondered how many of the scores Roarke could intimidate with a flick of the eye knew he talked to his cat.

The car waited, and as she got behind the wheel, Eve considered her route and texted Peabody.

> Leaving now. Will pick you up, then head to Novak's. Read
> the updates and the auto-runs from overnight.

As she drove through the gates, Peabody's response came through.

> Copy that. Will dig for any comment or statement from Novak
> re Rose Bernstein's death.

Good, Eve thought, and pushed her way downtown. The snarling traffic gave her time to review Roarke's runs.

She had a passing thought about why so many people who lived in New Jersey insisted on commuting to New York, and why so many who lived in New York decided to clog up the tunnels inching their way to New Jersey.

Then the ad blimps came out to play, and she wondered how people who worked the night shifts and were just trying to get some damn sleep felt about that.

People hustled down the sidewalk—too early for shuffling tourists— with their go-cups and earbuds. And most, she noted, made better time on foot than those on wheels.

A few skimmed along in their business suits on airboards, urban surfers bobbing and weaving through human waves.

She saw a couple of funky-junkies in their thick black sunshades, half-blind from their addiction, shambling home to sleep off the night.

It reminded her to grab her own.

A sidewalk sleeper with a harmonica and a pointy-eared dog settled down for a day of musical begging.

A street LC in a skinny top and crotch-skimming skirt that showed off the tattooed snake coiled over her midriff hailed a cab—which told Eve she'd had a successful night.

A couple of street artists chatted away as they set up their easels and canvases. On the next block a sidewalk vendor yawned hugely as she unfolded her table.

Zero-seven-thirty, she thought, and already the city hummed.

She tagged Peabody with a two-minute warning, then braked at a light.

A Black guy, skin shining with sweat, stopped running in place to dash across the intersection. He had legs like a giraffe and wore tiny, red, ball-hugging shorts and bright white running shoes.

By the time Eve made the turn, he'd streaked down the entire crosstown block.

"Fast," she murmured. "Fast feet."

As she pulled up in front of her old apartment building, opera poured out of an open window. Peabody came out the main door. Pink cowboy boots and jacket, khakis, white tee, and her red-streaked hair in bouncy waves.

It occurred to Eve that when Peabody had moved into the apartment, she'd worn a uniform, shiny black cop shoes, and a non-streaked bowl cut.

She climbed into the car.

"What the hell," Eve said, and pointed out and up.

"Oh, that's Ms. Gambini. She's visiting from Italy—her son. Do you remember Mr. Gambini?"

"Yeah, little guy, big mustache. A tailor."

"That's him. This is his mom, staying with him for the summer. She does this every morning. You could set your wrist unit by it. She's a hundred and six, so we're letting it go. Plus, she cooks like a god, and shares. So basically the whole building's letting it go.

"Thanks for the lift," she added. "It was a holy shit moment when you sent the connection to Leah Rose. Coffee, please? I held off because I knew you'd have the good stuff."

"Go. Anything on Novak re Bernstein's death?"

"No statements. She'd've been about eleven, so not surprising." She programmed black for Eve, coffee regular for herself. "Most articles didn't list all the sibs, but I found an obit from Chicago that did. And a lot of dirt dished up on Bernstein's priors, her rehabs, her struggle with addiction. Her mother—Bernstein's—gave a crapload of interviews, but that mostly dried up after a couple months."

She inhaled the scent of the coffee, then drank as Eve drove.

"More interviews after Lane's Tony win, and her dedicating it to Bernstein—well, Leah Rose. They didn't use her legal name, which she was—I dug up—in the process of changing legally anyway."

"Novak has connections to a sib who works for a chemist, a sib who's a photographer, and from the overnights, a sib who's cohabbing with a metal artist. Cyanide plays into all of those professions. Or can."

"Yeah, which equals potential means. Hey, there's Speedo."

Eve spotted the mostly naked runner eating up the sidewalk.

"You know that guy?"

"He runs most mornings. Word is marathon training. We call him Speedo for the tiny, tiny shorts, and because he's, you know, speedo."

"I'll give him that."

She continued crosstown—Speedo outpaced her—then zipped around a corner while she hunted for parking.

She found a space she calculated she could just squeeze into, so went vertical, jigged, jogged, then dropped down between an aging Mini and a shiny sedan.

"There can't be a full inch to spare."

"I got us in, didn't I?" And pleased, Eve stepped out to the sidewalk. "Corner building down the block." Eve pointed when Peabody joined her.

"Nice neighborhood. You can smell the bakery. I wish I couldn't smell the bakery. Oh, oh! Home decor! Look at that lamp. That lamp would really work in my craft room, by the divan I'm doing."

"Stop it."

"They're not even open, so it's not like I'm going to . . ." But she yanked out her 'link, took a quick picture. "It probably costs too much anyway, considering. I'm still walking," she pointed out.

"I want to hit her with the dead sister. Routine follow-up interview. Blah blah, bang! I want her reaction. Not one wit statement mentioned the connection, and that's bogus. That she didn't tell anyone. You're working with the woman who replaced your dead sister, and you don't say anything? She doesn't come out with it when we took her statement that night? Bogus."

"She'd've been smarter to come out with it, right up front."

"Not if she's counting on twenty-five years, that gap, and the multiple marriages involved."

She stopped outside the building. A snooty-looking wine bar and a snootier-looking boutique took street level. Above, generous white-trimmed windows broke up the rosy brick for two stories.

"No apartment number listed. It must be all theirs."

Eve considered, then mastered through the street-level door, one with a cam, an intercom, and good security.

"Let's surprise them."

"The husband's got to know, right? It's possible she didn't tell him, but really unlikely."

"Cela Ricardo's statement—from her view from the steps. He's standing behind her, a hand on her shoulder. Sounds like support to me."

On the second floor, double doors stood open on the right to a large space with mirrored walls.

"Dance studio." Peabody nodded toward a ballet bar.

"And his place." Eve studied the space directly across, the piano, the sound system. "Work quarters here, living quarters upstairs."

She continued up to a wide landing and double doors painted cheerfully blue. A domed skylight overhead must have fed the flowers flanking the doors enough sun to keep them thriving.

Eve pressed the buzzer.

She heard locks click and a male voice. "Kacie, thank God you're early. We—"

He broke off when he pulled the door open, and stood in cotton pants, a baggy tee, and a toddler on one bony hip.

"Oh, I thought— Sorry, can I . . ." He blinked at the badge Eve held up.

"Lieutenant Dallas, Detective Peabody. May we come in, Mr. Furrier?"

"Yes, of course. Sorry. I'm scattered. Didn't recognize you right off. I thought it was the nanny. I'm a little desperate."

He jiggled the toddler, who grinned while she wrapped a hunk of his tousled mane of brown hair around her hand.

She said, "Hi!" and with great enthusiasm launched herself at Eve, who caught her in self-defense. And ended up in the next thing to an embrace with Malcomb, as the kid still clutched her father's hair.

"Sorry!" He tried to pull her back, but she'd gotten a fistful of Eve's hair. "Really sorry. Come on, Ari. Please. It's like she dug up ten pounds of chocolate and ate it."

He managed to free Eve's hair, stepped back. "I'm so sorry. Ariella decided three-thirteen this morning was the perfect time to party. Minx—my wife—dealt with that and finally got her back down a little after five. And about six, she's up and going again. My turn. I have coffee," he added. "I have lots and lots of coffee if you'd like."

He stood, obviously sleep-deprived and frazzled, a tall man with a skinny build, long arms, long legs. He had a night's scruff on his face and exhausted, deep-set blue eyes.

"We're good for now. We have some follow-up questions regarding Brant Fitzhugh's murder. It would be very helpful if we could also speak to Ms. Novak."

"Of course. I—"

"Down," Ariella said, very firmly, and wiggled out of Malcomb's arms.

"Thank God." He rubbed his biceps, rolled his shoulders. "I'm surprised my arms aren't a foot longer. Please, sit down. Minx and I are still reeling over Brant."

The kid strutted—it really was a strut—to a big white chest, pulled out a big pink truck. She strutted back, shoved it at Eve.

"Pay!"

"I'm not buying."

"Play, she means play. Ari, go sit down now. Daddy's going to get you some juice."

Instead, she put on lost puppy eyes and managed to hold on to the truck while she held her arms up.

"Oh God. Okay."

Peabody stepped in. "Is that your truck? I love pink trucks."

Instantly Ariella turned her attention to Peabody and, obviously satisfied by what she saw, took her hand to pull her across the room.

"It's fine," Peabody said. "More trucks!"

"Her current obsession. Please excuse . . . everything," he decided. "In addition to the party animal, we're not quite finished with the rehab, remodeling, whatever it is at this stage."

He dropped down into a chair in the living area, where the walls held several big swaths of paint and the ceiling was stripped down to rafters.

It opened into a dining area with half the table cluttered with what

Eve knew from the Great House Project were sample books. A wide peninsula separated the dining area from the kitchen.

"We thought it best to do our work areas first—the place needed a lot of work. Then we wanted Ari's room, ours, the master bath done before we—and I'm sorry again." He scrubbed at his face. "You don't care about any of that. My brain's still fogged."

"I'm in the middle of a major rehab," Peabody told him as she played trucks. "I know how it is."

"Really? It's exhausting and thrilling all at once. Do you have kids?"

"No. I have a friend with a little girl about a year and a half, and I've got a really big family."

"Only child here, but my wife? Huge family. I wonder if I can answer any questions, at least to start. I'd really like Minx to grab a little more sleep."

"How well did you know Brant Fitzhugh?"

"I'd say I got to know him fairly well over the last few months. The four of us went out to dinner a couple times, and we went to dinner parties at their home."

He gestured toward the dining area. "We're not exactly equipped right now to reciprocate. I'd run into Brant now and then if we happened to drop by the workshops at the same time."

He sat back, one eye on the truck games. "He asked me to write the lyrics for a song for Eliza."

"I didn't see that in the notes."

"I didn't think of it that night. Hard to think at all that night. He played a little piano." Malcomb smiled. "Very little, but he'd composed a sweet little melody, and asked if I could write the lyrics. He wanted to give it to her as part of an anniversary present next fall. He arranged to take a few days off from the shoot so he could be in New York—a surprise for her, and he was going to record the song. He had a good singing voice."

"A surprise?"

"Yeah. He came over—my studio's downstairs—a few times to work on it. I helped him refine the melody some, and I did the lyrics. Recorded him so he'd have it before he left. He was going to make it into a music vid. He'd have everything he needed for it during the shoot in New Zealand, so . . ."

He looked off into space. "I don't know if I should tell her, give her the recording we did downstairs. Or just not. Would it comfort or break her heart all over again? Minx thinks maybe wait until after the memorial. It may be too raw right now."

"Do you know anyone who had a reason to want to hurt him, or Ms. Lane?"

"I've gone over and over it, and I don't. I think some crazy person must have gotten in, crashed somehow or slipped in with the catering staff. People, at least those I know, really, genuinely liked Brant."

"And Eliza?"

"She could be tough—and that's part of her work ethic. She expects everyone to put in the time to shine. And I can admit to being irritated now and then at the long hours she demanded of Minx. But that's part of it, especially with a show like *Upstage*, with a headliner like Eliza."

"Did you and Eliza ever have words over it?"

"Oh, hell no!" He laughed, managed to stifle a yawn that came with it. "One thing, I'm not that brave—and I'm pretty sure she could've eaten me alive. That's whatever was left of me after Minx got done with me. Second thing? It's not my business. This is Minx's career, her work, her talent."

"Maybe someone else in the cast or crew has a family member who decided it was their business."

"I'd have heard, I think, if so. Minx and I tend to vent to each other, or just entertain each other with the stories, the personalities. Sure, some would bitch or whine—and who can blame them? It's long and hard."

He turned his head, smiled again. "Hey, babe."

The woman looked exhausted, Eve noted. And there was some shock in the shadowed eyes, some strain around them. Her short hair managed to go everywhere at once, and took new directions as she hastily ran a hand through it.

She wore cotton shorts and a tank—long legs and arms for her, too, but on a petite, compact body.

"This is Lieutenant Dallas, and Ari's new friend, Detective Peabody. Let me get you some coffee."

"Mama!" With a squeal, Ariella deserted Peabody to run to her mother. Minx picked her up, closed her eyes, nuzzled.

"I didn't realize anyone was here."

She had a throaty voice, one a bit hoarse from spotty sleep now, and maybe that strain.

"We're investigating Brant Fitzhugh's murder, Ms. Novak, and have some follow-up questions."

"All right. We're— We didn't get much sleep last night. Ariella . . ." She went very pale. "Mal!" He came running, and she pushed the kid on him before she ran back to the bedroom.

"Right on schedule," he murmured. "Mama's fine. Morning sickness," he told Eve. "We found out we were expecting another the day before the party. She's only a few weeks in. With Ari it only lasted a couple months, but every morning. Fortunately, it's usually once and done. Which is easy for me to say."

He glanced toward the bedroom. "Let me just get her some ginger ale. That usually helps."

"Juice, Daddy! Please and thank you."

"Yeah, Daddy'll get your juice. Just give us a minute."

He carted the kid into the kitchen, where he held a one-sided conversation about juice, Mama, breakfast.

It struck Eve like Roarke talking to the cat.

"Is it like this at Mavis's in the morning?" she wondered.

"Probably sometimes, sure."

"And yet, they do it again on purpose."

Malcomb came back, and the kid on his hip sucked on a tiny straw stuck in a tiny, bright purple tube. She wore a look of dazed joy.

"I'm sorry we're so scattered this morning. I know how important this is, and how valuable your time. It's just . . ."

He offered a quick smile as he jiggled his daughter. "Our life right now."

Minx walked back in. She'd tossed a long shirt over the tank and looked completely washed-out. Her hand shook slightly as she reached for the glass Malcomb held out.

"Thanks. All done, I hope."

"You sit. Kacie's going to be here soon. Ari needs a change. I'll take care of it, then how about Kacie takes her out for breakfast, then a romp in the park? You could grab some more sleep."

"That'd be great."

"It'll only take me a few minutes. Oh, please don't bother with that," he added when Peabody began to load the trucks back into the toy chest.

"No trouble."

"Thanks. Big thanks. If you have any more for me, I'll just be five minutes."

"He's the best daddy." Taking a seat, Minx sipped cautiously at the ginger ale. "I'm sorry about all the confusion. I guess Mal told you we had a big night. All Ari needed was a damn disco ball and a light show. I'm a few weeks pregnant and dealing with morning sickness. I want to say we're usually more civilized, but not right now."

"Choreographing a major production like *Upstage* must add a lot of pressure."

"The good kind. I'm fine after I toss it, or shortly after, and Mal will take mornings until this stage passes. And we have Kacie. The nanny. She's wonderful. A lot of juggling, but it works for us. In any case." She took another cautious sip.

"I haven't spoken with Eliza since . . . We thought we should wait. But I heard from Tessa—our director—last night. Eliza wants to go forward, and we'll be in rehearsal starting tomorrow."

"How well did you know Brant Fitzhugh?"

"Enough to like him, a lot. I was standing right next to him." Her eyes teared up as she sipped. "Right next to him."

"Up front."

"Yes. Mal and I were standing there, talking to Tessa and Mai, when Eliza brought Sam up. Then Brant moved up. They were just nailing it, Eliza and Sam, even with the early staging we'd played with. The turns, the gestures. They had the room, you could feel it."

She rubbed at those damp eyes.

"I know Brant lifted the glass up because it was in the corner of my eyeline, and after, Mal told me he saw him toast her, drink. I know he stepped back—but that I felt more than saw. I heard the glass shatter, the scream. I couldn't see, but Mal could. He's tall. People were rushing around, and Mal pulled me to him. He said he was afraid I'd get knocked down."

Malcomb brought Ari back. She wore a shirt covered with flowers. Flowers with bright, smiling faces, Eve noted. A little creepy. He'd paired it with pink shorts and sneakers. He'd even put a pink bow in her hair.

What was it with pink? Eve wondered.

He had a big bag over one shoulder, went to a closet, pulled out a collapsed stroller-thing, set both by the door.

"She's set." Even as he spoke, the buzzer sounded. He pulled open the door like a man opening the door to sanity.

"Kacie!"

The kid squealed, launched, and got scooped into the arms of a laughing woman, early twenties, mixed Black and Asian, with impressive biceps.

"There's that girl!"

"I'm going to ask if you'll take that girl out for breakfast and to the park. She had one of her Let's Party nights."

"She's a party animal. How about some pancakes, my scrumptious? You go kiss Mama bye first. How's this morning, Mama?"

"Booted. Better." She gathered up her daughter, kissed her all over the face. "You be good for Kacie, and have fun."

"Bye! Bye! Bye!" As Ariella kissed her mother all over the face, Kacie glanced at Eve, then at Peabody, then back at Eve.

"Oh my God! Dallas and Peabody! Wow, this is . . ." The delighted switched off. "Oh, this is about what happened. I'm sorry. I met him once when he was in Malcomb's studio. He was really nice. I'm sorry for what happened. I really liked the vid, the whole clones among us stuff. I'm going to read the book first chance. We'll get out of your way."

She plucked the kid from her mother's lap. "Kiss Daddy bye-bye."

When Ariella had, Kacie hauled up the bag, tucked the stroller under her arm, and scooted out.

"And peace falls across the land." Mal dropped into a chair. "I'm repeating myself, but sorry again for all the chaos."

"No problem." Eve waited while Peabody took a seat. "So, Ms. Novak, why haven't you mentioned your family connection to Rose Bernstein?"

14

She froze, the glass held a few inches from her lips. The color that had started to come back into her cheeks died away again.

"I— Oh God."

Malcomb popped up, sat on the arm of her chair. "It's okay, babe. Take it easy. Minx, it was bound to come out."

"I know. I know." She handed the glass to him, pressed both hands to her pale face. "I didn't want anyone to know—especially Eliza. I still don't, but I guess that's done now."

"Why?"

"I wanted the job." She dropped her hands. "I really wanted this job, this play, this chance. It's special to me, for obvious reasons. And those same reasons are why I never brought it up. I wasn't sure Eliza would take me on if she knew."

"Again, why?"

"Why? Rose died, in the theater. In *that* theater. My sister. We don't use *step*s and *half*s in our family because we're just family. She was my sister, and she died—stupidly, tragically. Eliza took her place, and the rest is history."

She lifted her hands, a helpless kind of gesture, then let them fall.

"If she knew the connection? Theater people are superstitious. You don't say good luck before a performance, you don't say Macbeth inside a theater, you don't whistle backstage. There's a lot you don't and you do, because luck—good and bad—because superstition and tradition. I wouldn't have blamed her for crossing me off the list of potential choreographers."

"I agreed with her," Malcomb said. "We talked about it, went back and forth on it. It was a big opportunity. You deserve it," he added to Minx. "Why bring up something that happened twenty-five years ago and risk that opportunity?"

"Still, it must be hard for you." Peabody kept it gentle. "Working on the show, thinking of your sister and what happened."

"No, no, honestly, it's just the opposite for me. It— I know it sounds strange, maybe self-serving with it—but it feels, in some ways, like I'm helping finish something Rose couldn't. Didn't."

"Were you close?" Peabody prompted. "She was, what, seven years older?"

"I was six when my mother and her father got together. She was already a teenager. But she was sweet to me. We had common interests and dreams—dance, the theater. I looked up to her. She was so talented, so driven. Even then, so driven, and that was part of the problem."

"In what way?" Eve asked.

"We'd go out for ice cream, and she'd binge on a sundae, then stick her fingers down her throat. She advised me to do the same. I pretended to, but I couldn't do it."

With a wan smile, she tipped her face toward her husband's. "Always did hate to puke."

He bent down, brushed a kiss on her hair.

"Rose took pills," Minx continued. "Her mother knew, and I imagine got them for her. To keep her energy up, her weight down. Take more to sleep. She'd sneak out at night."

Minx put her fingers to her lips when they trembled. "'Cover for me, Minx. Hot date. Tell you all about it.' She was fourteen, fifteen. She got caught with pills, caught drinking, did some rehab, or pretended to. I didn't tell anyone, not even my dad, my mom. Not my mother, my mom. Heaven. She was Mom to me once she came into our life. I should have told them. Told someone."

"You were a child," Peabody pointed out.

"So was she, really. About the time my mother's marriage to her father was hitting the skids, her mother took her to New York. But she kept in touch with me. She'd call, text, do screen time. We were close. I realized, much later, that part of that was she had a built-in audience with me. I loved hearing about New York, her auditions, her performances. I was getting parts, too, and she listened."

Minx let out a sigh. "Rose always listened. I had a baby brother, and I adored him, then a baby sister, same thing. My mother married again, so more siblings there, and we're close, too. We're good. But Rose? Nobody ever understood what I wanted, what I was working for, what was inside me like Rose. Because she wanted it, worked for it, had it inside her."

"Then she died."

"Yes. We were there that night, opening night. Our grandparents—Heaven's parents—kept the little guys, and they surprised me with a trip to New York. They knew how much it meant to me. Rose got us seats—orchestra seats."

Her eyes filled, spilled over. "I was so excited. I had a bouquet for her. She'd gotten us backstage passes, but when we went back, somebody pulled my father aside. They told him what happened. They took me outside, Mom and Dad, by the stage door, and he had to tell me."

"No one notified you prior?"

"We weren't next of kin. Her father wouldn't have thought of me, and her mother? Well, she looked at me more as competition than Rose's sister. The play ran for years. I didn't see it that night, but when I went to New York to attend Juilliard, I went to a Sunday matinee, by myself. It was brilliant. Eliza wasn't Marcie Bright, as she'd left long before, but it was brilliant. And I cried while I watched it because I could see Rose as Marcie. She'd have been perfect."

"Eliza Lane stepped right in, and got everything Rose wanted. You must resent that."

As she swiped a tear away, Minx stared at Eve. "No. Why would I? Rose did this to herself. I hate that, I resent that, but she did it to herself. Eliza stepped in, stepped up because that's what she was supposed to do. The cast and crew depended on that. The audience depended on that. Rose . . ."

She reached up to pat the hand Malcomb had on her shoulder. "I loved her. My beautiful, exciting, wild big sister. But something was broken in her. She wasn't suicidal, but in the end isn't that what happened? She risked her life, her health, her dreams every time she took those pills, washed them down with vodka. Eliza wasn't responsible for Rose's choices."

Malcomb kept his hand on Minx's shoulder, but his eyes were on Eve's now. Hard on Eve's. "You think Minx—you think she might have killed Brant to punish Eliza."

"No." Minx's quick protest faded off. "Oh God, that's crazy." Her free hand pressed on her belly. "I couldn't kill anyone. And Brant—how could I . . . He wasn't even . . ."

"Maybe the wrong person drank the poison. It was Eliza's drink."

"Why would I want to hurt Eliza for something my sister did to herself? Why would I risk the livelihoods of the cast and crew? My own, too? I have a child, and I'm going to have another. I couldn't take a life. Rose has been gone twenty-five years. What kind of person would strike out at someone over a part in a play?"

"People strike out for all kinds of reasons. You've been in these workshops day after day. Pressure builds up."

"That's bullshit." Malcomb shot to his feet. "You're not going to sit there accusing my wife of murder, for God's sake. You need to leave."

"Malcomb, wait, just wait."

"I'm not going to have you upset this way."

"You can do a lot of things." She reached up for his hands. "But you can't make this go away. There is pressure, and I had some moments when we got started. Not resentment, Lieutenant. Some sorrow for what might have been. The idea if Rose hadn't fallen to her addiction, I might be choreographing her in this revival. What might've been. But I never blamed Eliza. I didn't blame my partner for missing a step and dropping me. We were exhausted, sweaty. He fumbled a step, his hands slipped, and I went down, down hard."

Absently, she rubbed her knee.

"I wanted the stage, and I had it. I had it. I was good, really, really good, and that moment, that mistake, that accident ended it. I could have danced, sure, after the surgery, the recovery, but I'd never have been as good. It wasn't his fault, or the choreographer's fault, or the director's fault. But I lost what I'd wanted all my life.

"I went to a dark place for a while, and wouldn't have come out of it without my family. And Rose."

"Rose?" Eve repeated. "She died long before your injury."

"Because Mom sat me down one night. The upshot of what she said was I was alive, healthy, talented, young. But most of all alive. And life meant choices and new chances, new paths. Rose chose poorly.

It was time for me to choose well. It wasn't like a light switch, but I chose, and I chose damn well."

She tugged Malcomb so he sat back on the arm of the chair.

"If I hadn't had that fall, had to pick myself up and choose another way, another dream, I might not have met Malcomb. I might not have Ariella, or whoever this is going to be."

Malcomb leaned down, folded himself so he could kiss her.

"Rose chose poorly," Minx continued. "Who knows who and what she might have been, but she chose. That's not on Eliza, and it sure as hell isn't on Brant. If I were to blame anyone besides Rose herself, it would be her mother."

"Why is that?"

"Because she knew. Now that I'm a mother I understand being one means the most important thing in the world is keeping your child safe, well, happy. The most important thing, when I look back, to Debra, was making Rose a star, and feeding off that light. Her father . . . he was more wrapped up in himself. He was never unkind, but whenever Rose stayed with him, with us, during that period, she did whatever she wanted—as long as it didn't inconvenience him and my mother. And my mother? Rose was a mild annoyance at best. Debra ruled, and she knew."

"How can you be sure?"

"'I can see those cookies you stuffed in your face on your ass, Rose.' Comments like that. And Rose told me her mother scored the pills, at least some of them. And the drinking? Debra had to know. Rose would drunk text or tag me, and more than once on a tag, Debra would come in and cut it off, warn me to mind my own. As I said, she didn't really like me. I know Rose moved out when she turned eighteen, just like I know Debra pushed in whenever she could. Because Rose told me."

"Did you know she'd terminated a pregnancy?"

"No." Minx closed her eyes. "No, she never told me that. I'm sorry. It must've been hard for her."

"Do you know who the father might have been?"

"I don't. She was serious about boys, about men, but not anyone in particular. At least she never told me. Debra might, I don't know. I couldn't tell you where she is, what she's doing. I haven't seen her since Rose's funeral."

Minx blew out a breath, hugged herself. "I was eleven, devastated, and Debra went at me."

"At the funeral?"

"Yes. Shrieked at me. How I'd tried to use Rose, tried to exploit her. I was trying to lay a rose on my sister's casket, and she—Debra—shoved me back. My dad charged forward, but my mom beat him to it. Heaven, I mean. She stared Debra down—I'll never forget how Mom put an arm around me, and just sliced that woman open with a look. She never said a word. She didn't have to."

Minx swiped at tears. "Anyway, I put the rose on the casket, and we went home."

"I'm sorry I lost my temper, but the idea of you accusing Minx of murder . . ." Malcomb gripped his wife's hand. "Jesus Christ. And we were together the whole time we were at the damn party, so you'll have to look at me as an accomplice."

"Malcomb, you throttle back now."

"It's true. We didn't get there until almost nine. I was running late—and you can check on that. We told Kacie we'd be home by eleven. She was sleeping over, but Minx tires out by eleven these days. And I stuck with her because, well, we'd just really found out she was pregnant. I get . . ."

"Protective," Minx finished. "Look, maybe, in hindsight, I should've told Eliza, Eliza and Tessa at least. But secrets get around in theater, and I didn't want to put anybody on edge or go through what I just went through with you, or have people I'm working with sending me those quick looks.

"I don't know what else I can say. I wouldn't even know how to get the poison."

"Let's try this. Did Rose ever talk about Eliza?"

"Oh, sure. She talked about a lot of the cast. She liked her—they liked each other. Debra didn't like her—Rose joked about that, and Rose was contrary enough to like Eliza for that reason alone. Jerry, Gary? Jerry or Gary, maybe. I think he was in the cast and they were sleeping together. Maybe."

She shook her head. "I'm not sure. Lieutenant, I was eleven, already working professionally, taking classes, trying to get through school, imagining myself like Rose, on Broadway. We talked and texted pretty regularly, but I just can't remember all of it.

"She took advantage of her father's self-involvement, had a love-hate relationship with her mother, much like the part she would've played in *Upstage*. Except Lily's not downright mean. Rose sometimes used me as a sounding board, but she also listened. She was talented, troubled, difficult, surprisingly generous, and selfish depending on her mood. That's hindsight, but at the time she was just Rose, my big sister."

"Okay. I can get a warrant to have a team search your residence and studios, to have someone from EDD go through your electronics. Or you can waive that."

"Look at whatever you want."

"Minx, you need to sleep."

"Sweetie, not a chance of that now. Let's just get this done. There's nothing here. We'll get dressed and go meet Ari at the park. I think we could both use the fresh air."

"Should we get a lawyer?"

"That's up to you," Eve told him. "You're not being charged. We'll complete the search as quickly as possible, and your cooperation's noted."

"I'm scared, I admit it. Not of you finding anything, because there's nothing. But that this will be enough to get me fired." Minx rose. "Is it possible for you to wait to tell Eliza? I'd like to tell her myself. I could tag her and Tessa when we get to the park, explain all this. I'd like to get that done, too."

"That's fine. I can have a team here very shortly, and notify you when they're finished."

"All right." Hands clasped, they walked into the bedroom together, shut the door.

"That was a lot." Peabody pushed up to wander the living area. "Maybe I'm naive, but I bought it."

"Everything sounded reasonable and sincere. We'll see if it holds up. Tag McNab. I'll see who we can get to search. We'll get a jump on that when they leave."

"No warrant, do it now? If they're big fat liars and had something here, they've already gotten rid of it."

"Unless it's something they overlooked, aren't thinking about. Tag McNab," she repeated. "Let's get this going."

Since Baxter and Trueheart had caught one, she pulled in Jenkinson and Reineke. By the time she'd set it up, the couple came out. Both wore khakis and T-shirts. Minx had on a cross-body bag.

"We'll get this done as quickly as possible," Eve repeated. "Again, you can refuse, but if I could look into your bag, Ms. Novak?"

"My bag? Oh." She opened it, held it out. "This feels horrible."

Before Eve could ask, Malcomb pulled out his wallet, then turned out his otherwise empty pockets. "I was pissed," he said. "Then it struck me—I saw the vid, too—that to find who killed Brant, and more important to me now, to prove without a shadow Minx had no part in it, you need someone smart and thorough. Somebody who doesn't let the little things slide by. So I've decided not to be pissed at you. As much."

"You get used to it. People being pissed at you."

"I guess you have to. Come on, babe, a walk, fresh air, and our wild child. Just what we need."

When the door closed, Eve turned to Peabody. "You take the kid's room to start."

"We're doing the right thing, for the right reasons. I can't see them in this, Dallas, just can't. But we have to be smart, we have to be thorough before we can cross them off."

"So let's be both. Be both, Peabody. Where's the last place you'd expect to find any evidence of a crime?"

"The baby's room."

"And you're more likely to spot something off in there right away than I am. I'll take the master."

They'd made the bed, she noted, and if any clothes had been tossed around, they'd picked them up. But the room looked lived-in, with kid items scattered around, like the monitor thing so they could spy on the kid.

She started on the closets, finished the room, and had moved into the master bath when the buzzer sounded.

"I've got it," Peabody called out. "Kid's room, bathroom clear."

Eve worked through the room, one she found a calm, updated space. Minx had a solid collection of skin gunk, hair gunk, face gunk, but nothing approaching what Eve had found in Eliza's space.

When she came out, Jenkinson worked through the first of the guest rooms. She tried not to focus on his tie—one covered with multicolored magnifying glasses over midnight black.

"Reineke's doing the living area with Peabody. I'll go through the other rooms after this. Looks like they're remodeling or something. Other room's full of supplies. Got a storage room, too. McNab's in there 'cause it's got the house system e's. Got another john, but that's stripped down—more supplies in there."

"I'll check with McNab and Reineke, then Peabody and I are heading out. Let me know when you're done so I can inform the residents."

"Will do."

She tracked down McNab in what looked like an organized storage and house system room.

"Nice system," he said. "Got your monitor for the door cam, full house—that covers the two floors—audio—entertainment and intercom—temp, and light controls."

"Check the feed, see when the residents left the building and returned, night in question. Do a face rec on anyone who came in. There's a nanny, mixed race, early twenties. She must have a swipe and code for street level, since she buzzed in from up here. Run her just for form, and any other visitors in the last week."

She slipped her hands into her pockets. "You've got two tablets in the master. There's a mini D and C in the dance studio downstairs—the mirrored one—and a full-sized and some other components in the other studio."

"We'll get 'em."

She walked through before heading into the living area, scanned the spaces Jenkinson mentioned, found another room—empty and shabby, another stripped-down bath attached, a large closet holding cold-weather gear—and tubs, she discovered, of baby clothes, maybe maternity clothes, winter clothes.

She found Reineke and Peabody talking home improvement while they searched under cushions, in drawers, behind wall art.

"With me, Peabody. Over to you, Reineke."

"Nice space," he commented. "They must pull in some solid scratch to afford a space like this."

"Apparently they do. Roarke cleared their finances."

"Roarke cleared them, they're clear. I'm going to get over there, Peabody."

"Anytime. Reineke's great-grandfather died a couple months ago."

"Okay, sorry."

"A hundred and eighteen, so that's a life. Anyway, he wasn't rolling it in, but he left Reineke one of his life insurance policies and this house on the Jersey Shore. It needs a lot of work, and he figures a good chunk of the insurance money to fix it up."

"What's he going to do with a house on the Jersey Shore?"

"Vacation place, and he could rent it out all but the couple weeks they'd use it. He's going to try to do some of the work himself."

Eve paused to do another scan of the studios. "He can do that?"

"Maybe. He said his dad's handy, and he's got an uncle who works in construction, so maybe."

"Well, good luck and all that. Run Rose Bernstein's mother. Let's find out where she is and what she's up to."

Peabody pulled out her PPC as they walked down the last flight of stairs. "Where are we headed now?"

"Back to Central. I want another look at the files on Bernstein, and see if I can connect with the investigator."

"A quarter of a century's a long time to remember details."

"Feeney remembered, and it wasn't his case."

"Yeah, but Feeney's Feeney," Peabody pointed out, and Eve couldn't disagree.

"Debra Rose—figures—Bernstein, age sixty-six, no current permanent address. Last employment listed with StarLight Traveling Players—of which she was the owner and main attraction under the name Debbie Starr. That went under—and looks like she filed bank-ruptcy to skip out on civil suits alleging lack of payment. For per-formers, vendors, venues. Close to three years ago."

"So she's broke, possibly homeless."

"Looks like it." Peabody kept reading as she got into the car. "Prior to that, she ran Madam Rose's Dance School, under the name Delilah Rose. Closed that down after five years, and before that. Jesus, Dallas, she's been around. Before that, she ran Bernstein's Talent Agency— that one out of the Bronx, four-year run there. There's independent vocal coach, acting lessons. She worked as a showgirl in Vegas for a few years, and hey, traveled the carny circuit for a year."

"Busy."

"Yeah, busy enough she's got busts for fraud, for petty theft, for oper-ating a business without a license, nonpayment of taxes, nonpayment of rent. She's got a handful of outstanding warrants—out of Kansas, Ne-vada, Ohio, Tennessee, Florida. Nickel-and-dime stuff, but a handful."

"Has she done any time?"

"Just time served when she didn't make bail. Skimmed off with fines and/or probation. She's got one semi-violent bust here, but charges dropped. It looks like she and another dancer got into it. Hair pulling, tit smacking. Both arrested, both released, charges dropped. But the dates match with the end of her Vegas showgirl stint."

"Go back. What was she doing when her daughter died?"

"Second . . . Okay, she's listed as agent/manager, with her daughter the only client."

"According to the files, Rose Bernstein had someone named Fred Aaron as her theatrical agent—no manager—at TOD. I want to look again, but I think she'd had him for six or seven months when she OD'd."

"Wouldn't surprise me that she lied on an official doc at worst, as-sumed she'd talk her daughter into coming back at best."

"Run the agent," Eve ordered. "Fred Aaron. Maybe he's worth talking to."

Peabody found him as they pulled into the garage. "Retired in '56, relocated to Costa Rica that same year. He's still there."

"Contact him," Eve said as they walked to the elevator. "Get his thoughts on the mother, on Rose Bernstein, on the whole deal."

"They've got all these monkeys running around, and parrots and exotic birds and like that in Costa Rica."

"Yet another reason to stay the hell in New York. I want to find the mother. She's a grifter, an opportunist, and Rose was her meal ticket for a long time. She didn't like Lane, and here's Lane about to hit the stage again in the same play."

"She wouldn't have been invited."

"An experienced grifter could find a way in."

Working it through in her mind, Eve shuffled back when the doors opened and cops poured on.

"She's played a lot of roles. How hard would it be to wrangle herself into a plus-one? You can bet she pays attention to who the hell's who in New York theater. Now she's broke, got nothing and no one, and why? Because Eliza Lane got the big, juicy part before she could talk her daughter back into feeding her—ego, finances, dreams."

"She's worth a look," Eve decided.

The doors opened again. Two uniforms flanked a pair of women. One wailed, high enough to shatter glass.

"He stole my purse. I had everything in my purse. What kind of a place is it where somebody can just grab your purse right out of your hand?"

Eve thought: New York, as she pushed her way off.

She heard the second woman's unmistakably excited reply. "It's going to be okay, Winnie."

Eve aimed for the glides. "How much do you want to bet Winnie had her purse dangling off her arm while she goggled up at a building over ten stories or at a pair of shoes in a shop window?"

"Since it's a sure thing, a million dollars. Can I borrow a million dollars?"

"Or they're strolling around Times Square like it's a meadow in the spring. 'Oooh, Mabel.'" Eve did some jazz hands. "'Look at all the billboards! Oh my goodness'—gawk-gawk—'look at those blimps!'"

"Her friend's name is Mabel?"

"Probably. Now, after she files all the paperwork—which'll never get her property back—she'll go back to the hotel and tag Hank."

"Hank's her husband, right?"

"Probably. And she'll cry about it until Hank says, 'Well, Winnie, you were hell-bent on visiting that godforsaken city, weren't you? Things like that don't happen in Nobody Goes There, Idaho.'"

"They're potato farmers. Idaho," Peabody said at Eve's blank look. "Potatoes."

"Probably."

She swung into Homicide. "Contact the agent." Then headed into her office.

She printed out Debra Bernstein's ID shot—eight months overdue for renewal—pinned it to the board. After snagging some coffee, she sat down, studied it.

"Had some work done here and there, didn't you, Debra? A little nip, a little tuck, and one hell of a lot of makeup. Fancy hair, maybe a wig. What I'm wondering is, did you think of her as your kid first or your meal ticket first?"

She opened the file again, found the investigators' notes on Debra, and her statements.

She claimed she hadn't seen Rose for two days before her death, then retracted that after two witnesses placed her in the theater the evening of her daughter's death.

She'd meant she hadn't spoken to Rose, or only for a minute, as Rose was so busy. And the investigators verified she'd spent most of the day in a salon—hair, facial, makeup artist, nails.

To look her very best for her daughter's opening night.

The theater manager stated he'd initially turned Debra away on the evening of Rose's death when she'd demanded entrance. He'd offered to take the flowers she claimed to have brought for her daughter, but she refused.

Argumentative, the notes read. Angry.

That would be a pisser, Eve thought.

But she'd found a way in, according to statements. And since she got in, got into her daughter's dressing room . . . Potential reason the daughter hit the booze and pills harder than usual.

"And who would someone like that blame?" Eve mused. "Not herself, that's for sure."

She read on until Peabody tapped on the doorjamb.

"I had a good conversation with Fred. He's an interesting guy. He remembers Rose fondly. A bright light with dark places, and the light wasn't enough to win over the dark. He claims he didn't know about the pills until after, but knew about her affection for vodka. He talked to her about AA.

"He blames the mother."

"Does he?"

"Fred says in his fifty-odd years of agenting, he's dealt with a lot of stage mothers—fathers, too—but Debra was the worst of the breed. Pushy, bitchy, demanding, even after Rose fired her and signed with him. Debra came to his office, threatened him."

"How?"

"She said she'd ruin him, say he molested her daughter. Raped her unless he cut professional ties."

"That's a step over bitchy," Eve decided.

"Oh yeah. And he told her to go right ahead and try it, and they'd see who got ruined. That's when, he says, she turned on the waterworks. Cried, begged, went on about how she'd dedicated her whole life to Rose. He suggested she try living her own life for a while.

"I liked him," Peabody added. "He said Rose was seeing one of the guys in the company. That's Gary Proctor, and that young Gary—his words—was a good influence. After, he heard they'd had an argument that evening, and Gary went off to the cast party thing without her."

"He's still in New York theater—I've got him on the list to talk to. Just to tie all the ends."

"Well, Fred says Gary talked to him a week or two after she OD'd, said he hadn't said anything to the cops, but that Debra offered to have sex with him if he'd convince Rose to fire Fred. He said he didn't tell Rose, either, because he was embarrassed."

"It's in the file that they fought that night because when he went to get her to take her to the party, she was already into the vodka. She'd promised to lay off it, and he saw the bottle and the vial of pills, and she was already into them."

"Yeah, I read that. We'll talk to him anyway unless we track down Debra first."

"One more? It turns out, back then, Fred was Lane's agent, too. They parted ways a few months after *Upstage* hit, and she hit. She wanted bigger guns, you know? He didn't hold it against her. She invited him to the party, but you know, Costa Rica, but he tagged her up to thank her, and they talked old times. He hasn't seen Debra since Rose's memorial."

"He went to that?"

"Yeah, and he says Debra threw herself on the coffin, wailed about her precious baby. He also saw her go after Minx, just like she said happened."

"Good to know. Why don't you contact the old boyfriend, see if you can shake anything else out of the memory banks. There might be something else he didn't tell the cops at the time."

"Got it. I'm going to grab something from Vending. You want?"

"No, all good. I want to finish this, try to reach the primary."

She went back to the files, got up, got more coffee, paced, studied the board. Then decided maybe she could use a boost after all.

She shut her door, locked it.

She got down on the floor, took out her penknife to work the thin line of tape from the bottom of her visitor's chair. Under the lining of the ass-biting cushion, she'd slid in a candy bar, then carefully taped the frayed lining back in place.

But when she reached in for the chocolate, all she got was the empty wrapper.

She sat there, staring at it. And said, "Son of a bitch!"

15

Deprived of chocolate, thanks to the nefarious Candy Thief, Eve tracked down the primary on Rose Bernstein's OD and prodded at old memories.

"Yeah, I got it. Booze and pills, history of issues with both, and hardly more than a kid. Damn shame. What's up? You got a reason to open that one again?"

"Possibly related case, involving some individuals who were connected to your investigation. Eliza Lane was Bernstein's understudy at that time."

"Yeah, yeah, I got that, too." Former Detective Wimbly of the NYPSD, now Chief Wimbly of Shoresurf, South Carolina, nodded. "You caught the Fitzhugh murder. Talk about a damn shame."

"That's right."

"Well, he sure as hell wasn't around back then. We talked to Lane a couple times, that's in the file. Just a kid herself back then, but she was the one who'd benefit most, so you gotta look. Wits placed her at the bar from . . . before midnight, if I remember right, until closing. Seems to me TOD was in that window."

"Zero-one-twenty," Eve provided.

"Sounds right. We looked at the boyfriend, too, since they'd had a tiff, but had to clear him for the same reason. Fact was, Bernstein had a history, no signs of violence or force. Prescription uppers, downers, both bottles in her name. She mixed the downers with the vodka. She bought the vodka with fake ID the day before she died. Can't see how it connects to Fitzhugh."

"We believe Lane was the target, not Fitzhugh, and we're looking at payback for Bernstein as a possible motive."

Wimbly, a cool-eyed Black woman, shifted, straightened. "Ain't that a kick in the head? You ask me—and I guess you are—the only one from back then I can see looking for payback is Bernstein's pain-in-the-ass mother."

"We're looking at and for her."

"We looked at her. Not just because pain in the ass, but the kid had kicked her old lady to the curb, right? And—what the hell was her name—"

"Debra."

"That's it. Ass-pain Debra wouldn't take no. Kept going around the kid's apartment, trying to get to her at the theater, even went after the boyfriend a couple times. And Lane, some of the others in the play. And this was before Bernstein died."

"And after?"

"Went hysterical on notification. I mean off the charts. Jumped me like an alley cat, scratching, pounding. We had to call the paramedics. Turns out she did get into the theater, and into the dressing room, before the performance that night. Some special performance for VIPs and family. The boyfriend stated he found Bernstein with the bottle after the show, already half-lit, and they had their tiff. Ask me, the kid hit the bottle because of the visit from Mommy."

Wimbly shrugged. "Couldn't arrest her for that, and she went from the theater to a restaurant, had drinks and an overnight with the guy she was leeching off of. Got wits there, too, from the restaurant, then from the night man at the swank place where the guy lived who saw them come in around midnight if I remember right."

"You do."

"Plus, the kid was her meal ticket. She claimed she and the kid kissed and made up, and that was bogus 'cause we got wits from the bar heard her boo-hooing to her date about her ungrateful daughter. Then she spent a few hours the next day—before we managed to no- tify her—getting all buffed up in a salon for opening night.

"Piece of work," Wimbly muttered.

"That's coming through loud and clear."

"Anyways, she went after Lane, the boyfriend, the director, kept at me and Holister, my partner, after we closed it as accidental.

"I can tell you she cleared out her dead girl's apartment, but she was next of kin."

"How did she go after Lane?"

"The boyfriend reported it."

"Gary Proctor?"

"That's it! That would've driven me crazy. Anyway, he told us—and this is after she'd cleaned out the apartment, taken the body back to Chicago—so she came back, see. Rent was paid up in the daughter's place for three months, so she moved on it. Leech. She came to a per- formance. The woman playing the mother got her a house seat. And Debra, she knows her way around the theater. She gets backstage, into Lane's dressing room.

"When Lane comes in, she starts at her. Accusing her of killing her daughter. The boyfriend hears the commotion, comes in, and she pops him one, says how he and Lane killed her daughter."

Now Eve shifted. "That's not in the file."

"We'd closed the case. We'd have charged Debra with assault, but he wouldn't press charges. He asked if Lane could file a restraining order on her, on the quiet, so there wouldn't be any publicity, see?"

"Did she?"

"Didn't have to. Debra wrangled back two months' rent in cash from the landlord and took off. I'd hear how she popped up now and then, giving interviews on her daughter, but I never heard she bothered Lane or the boyfriend again."

"Were they involved? Lane and Proctor?"

"No indication of it, before or after, though Mommy Dearest claimed otherwise. You ask me—I'm not saying the mother drove the kid to pills and booze, but she sure didn't help."

"You mentioned Maeve Spindal arranged a ticket for Debra Bernstein. Were they friendly?"

"Looked that way. Not what you'd call besties, but they got along."

"Okay, Chief, I appreciate it."

"No problem. Old dogs still like to hunt. Good luck finding her, Lieutenant. She struck me as slippery."

"You're not wrong."

Eve got more coffee, put up her boots, and studied the board. Crosses and connections, she thought. Intersecting and diverging lives and fortunes.

She sat up again, then began the frustrating process of winding through channels to speak to Maeve Spindal.

The lady wasn't pleased. She had her face thickly coated with some pale green gunk, her hair slicked back and coated with something that looked uncomfortably like sperm.

"I don't appreciate being hounded by a police officer. I have a performance in three hours. You have five minutes of my time."

"Then let's not waste it. Do you know Debra Bernstein's whereabouts?"

"No. Nor do I believe I know anyone by that name. If that's all—"

"I don't think my five minutes are up. Debra Bernstein, Rose Bernstein's mother. Leah Rose's mother."

"Leah. Rose Bernstein was the cocoon, and Leah the butterfly who took wing. All too briefly."

"You're acquainted with her mother, Debra."

"Of course. I was to play Leah's mother, and in fact did on our out-of-town performances, our VIP performances. We connected, Leah and I, on a visceral level. She was a bright star who shone too briefly. It was a shame her replacement couldn't reach such brilliance."

"You provided her with a house seat for a performance after Leah's death."

"She asked; I accommodated. She was Leah's mother, after all."

"She and Leah didn't get along."

"As with Lily and Marcie Bright, Debra and Leah had a passionate connection, and passionate conflicts. I have no doubt, as with Lily and Marcie, Debra and Leah would have reconciled in time."

"When did you last see or speak with Debra?"

"Why should that matter?"

"Is it a hard question?"

"Don't be snippy. Perhaps two weeks ago."

"You keep in touch?"

"She occasionally contacts me, as she did a week or two ago. She's had a difficult life. I will, occasionally again, send her some funds. As I said, I felt a very deep bond with Leah, so I assist Leah's mother now and again in her memory."

"That's generous of you. Where did you send the funds two weeks ago?"

Spindal let out a huge sigh. "How would I know? My business manager handles such matters. I know she was in New York, as she was completely bereft about *Upstage* going into rehearsals. I wasn't pleased myself to know Eliza Lane will step into the role of a character I created and made famous."

"Are you aware Brant Fitzhugh, Ms. Lane's husband, was murdered?"

"Of course I'm aware. I'm in London, not in some off-planet colony. What does that have to do with anything?"

"I'd like the address where you sent the funds, Ms. Spindal."

"Then talk to my business manager and stop harassing me! Do you know who I am? I have a great deal of influence in New York. It will only take a word to your superiors, to the mayor, for you to be disciplined for this badgering."

An avalanche of bile wanted to spew, but she needed clearance to the business manager. "Ms. Spindal, my superiors, and the mayor, want me to investigate Mr. Fitzhugh's death, and in order to do my job, I need to speak with Debra Bernstein."

"You're an idiot if you think Debra had anything to do with that. Police officers shouldn't be idiots."

Neither should civilians, Eve thought, but more than plenty were.

"It's a process, it's routine. Any information you can give me on Ms. Bernstein's whereabouts would be helpful in that process. I can, if you'd feel more inclined to cooperate, connect you to my commanding officer."

"Is that a threat? You dare!"

"No, ma'am, it's an offer to connect you to my superior."

"Arlo!" The name boomed out of her. "Arlo, get in here! Deal with this person."

She obviously lobbed the 'link, as Eve watched the room blur by before the screen bobbled, then steadied.

"And see that I'm not disturbed again. Get out! Get out!"

The screen bounced a few seconds before Arlo's face—mid-twenties, sharp bones, ruddy—filled it.

"How may I help you?"

"Arlo, this is Lieutenant Dallas, NYPSD. I need the location where your employer sent funds to Debra Bernstein in New York sometime within the past two weeks. Can you connect me with her business manager, or whoever has that information?"

"I have that information if you'll give me one moment. Yes, here it is. Ms. Spindal wired five thousand USD to Ms. Bernstein at the West End Financial Center ten days ago."

"Thanks. Do you have Ms. Bernstein's 'link number?"

"Of course, and her current residence in New York, or where she was staying ten days ago. Would you like that information?"

"I would very much like that information."

"Ms. Bernstein was in residence at the West End Hotel. Shall I get that address for you?"

"No, I've got it. Her 'link?"

He read off the code.

"Great. Can I ask how long you've worked for Ms. Spindal?"

"Three and a half years."

Something passed over his stoic face that Eve interpreted as: It seems longer.

"In that time, has she wired other funds to Ms. Bernstein?"

"Once before, to my knowledge."

"Have you met Ms. Bernstein?"

"I haven't had the pleasure."

"Thanks for your help, Arlo."

"Not at all, Lieutenant."

The minute she clicked off, she pushed up and strode into the bullpen.

"Peabody, with me."

"I just got off the link with Gary Proctor, and— Where are we going?"

"To talk to Debra Bernstein."

"You found her? She's in New York?" Peabody jogged to keep up. "How the hell did you find her?"

"She squeezed some dough now and then from Maeve Spindal, who's an asshole. She's at the West End Hotel, or was ten days ago. My take is she's one of the few people on this or any planet Spindal likes, which tells me assholes attract assholes."

"She drunk tagged Gary Proctor three days ago."

"She what?" Eve thought the hell with the elevators and aimed for the glides.

"He says she managed to get his number, tagged him the other day. He was on his way home from a performance, and said she was drunk and abusive. He cut her off, blocked her number. But he had hers, and I was just going to come in and tell you. But you found her."

"What did she say to him?"

"The usual, he said. Every few years she gets through. He'll block her. And he's changed his number, but she manages. It's all how it's his fault her daughter's dead, how his cheating and conniving drove her to suicide. Or sometimes, he told me, she just points the finger at him. 'You killed her, you bastard, you and that no-talent whore.'"

"Lane."

"Yeah. He swears, and I believe him, he and Lane were never in-volved that way. He and Rose were sleeping together, and he was about half in love with her. But mostly, he wanted to save her."

"From what?"

"From what eventually happened. He thought he'd convinced her to go to Addicts Anonymous and try for a healthier lifestyle, then he found her already stoned and drinking that night, and they had a round about it. She told him to fuck off, he said he was done. It all jibes with the file."

A lot was starting to jibe, Eve thought.

"She's in New York, begging her daughter's onetime stage mother for money, drunk tagging her daughter's old boyfriend. Sounds like somebody who hasn't moved on."

"I got another interesting tidbit," Peabody added. "He said after Rose moved into her own place, Debra got into the building once, and into the theater once, with a kind of disguise. A wig, glasses. She had a hand with makeup and voices, so she got through a couple times he knows of."

Eve felt that hum through her brain. "That is an interesting tidbit."

"I'm thinking—want to know what I'm thinking?"

"I'm breathless with anticipation."

"Okay, so we're coming up on twenty-five years." They shifted from the glides to the garage steps. "That's one of those numbers. People don't pay so much attention to twenty-four years, but twenty-five gets the confetti. This grates on her. More, Lane's taking advantage of the big number, putting on a revival, getting all the buzz. Maybe Debra actually believes Lane and Proctor are to blame for what happened back then. Or she's convinced herself of it. She comes back to New York, stewing on it."

They crossed the garage to Eve's car.

"Now we know she got some money, enough to get the poison. Maybe she can't get her hands on Lane's number, but she drunk tags the old boyfriend. She's drinking, stewing, plotting, planning. Time to avenge her daughter."

"How does she get into the party?"

"I think you got it with the plus-one. That's more likely than the catering staff. Maybe she uses some old acquaintance or vamps up a new one."

"Vamps."

"She's an attractive woman, so vamps. A wig, makeup, she slides in. Fitzhugh, as far as we know, never met her. And Lane, as far as we know, hasn't seen her in twenty-five years. She's after Lane, but she can't do anything about Fitzhugh downing the poison. We've got statements, but maybe she'd already left by the time the first responders got there. We still have a handful to interview."

As Eve pulled out, she said: "Or."

"Or?"

"She gets through lobby security," Eve said. "Yeah, it was pretty tight, but it happens. She can't get to the penthouse by elevator, but she can access other floors. The woman's grifted her entire life. Access the penthouse level by the stairs—the second or third level. She just came into five large, so she gets a master."

"McNab checked for that, all levels."

"Yeah, won't hurt to check again. If she looked like catering staff, or a guest—either way—she makes her way down, dumps the poison. Now, if she's smart—and she has to have some level of street smarts to talk people out of money, into favors—she walks out right after she does that. Takes the stairs down again, at least a few levels, rides down to the lobby, walks out."

"We'll check the feeds again."

"Yeah, we will. Baxter reported a quick response with the flower-delivery reporter, but that's after the murder. So we look again. She probably knows costuming, too. If it's me, I walk in, street clothes, something I can turn into party wear with whatever's in my big-ass purse. I can walk out in the party wear, nobody's going to check on somebody leaving, especially before the nine-one-one."

"That would make her pretty smart and prepared."

"It would." And Eve figured the killer had been both. "Let's see how smart and prepared she is when the cops come knocking."

"From grifting to murder's a pretty big jump."

"Murder's always a big jump. Here's what's not. She's in New York, she has some funds—maybe more than the five, because she could've hit up some others for more. The woman who replaced her dead daughter and became a big fucking deal because of it is about to fill the part of the mother in the same play, in the same fricking theater where her kid OD'd."

She made a sharp turn and pushed it. "I'm going to talk to Mira, but I'm betting she'll say that's a damn good hammer to bring on a psychic break. It's sure as hell a bright, shiny motive."

"Can't argue with that."

"We've got a hell of a lot of overlaps here, Peabody. A fricking time warp with a cast of too damn many." She tapped the wheel.

Since the West End Hotel, which narrowly avoided flop status, didn't run to parking, she hunted for a space before hitting a second-level street spot a block and a half away.

As they clanged their way down to the sidewalk, her 'link signaled. She saw Kyung on the display.

"Oh, fuck me sideways! Dallas."

"Lieutenant, apologies for the interruption to your busy day."

"I'm in the field, Kyung."

"Yes, I can clearly hear that. We feel it's necessary to once again impose on your time and hold a media briefing for an update on the Brant Fitzhugh investigation."

"In the field, Kyung, working on bringing in a suspect for questioning."

"Which would provide an update. Would the end of the day work better for you?"

"The end of time works better for me."

He smiled at her. "Understood. However."

"Let me deal with what I'm dealing with and get back to you."

"That works. Good luck."

Eve shoved the 'link back in her pocket. "Hell."

"If the luck is good, you can go up there and tell them we made an arrest."

"Then they're going to want to know what, when, where, **how**, and what the suspect was wearing, what she said, what we said, what some guy who sold her a slice at a twenty-four/seven thought about it."

"Only the desperate buy a slice at a twenty-four/seven."

"You could be feeling desperate after killing the wrong person. All that time and trouble, and oops. The cardboard slices at a twenty-four/seven might have to do."

She stopped in front of the stubby concrete tower. No, not a flop, Eve thought, but it barely lifted its grimy self over a dump. Obviously, Debra wasn't spending her found money on housing.

Eve pulled open the door and stepped into a sad-looking lobby with a couple of dumpy shit-brown chairs. The single overhead light had three dead bulbs and one on death row as it flicked on and off.

She crossed the threadbare carpet to the counter manned by a bored woman lazily filing her nails.

"Need a room?"

Eve pulled out her badge.

"What's the beef? Look, I'm just filling in for a couple hours because my sister's kid fell off his airboard and busted up his face. Kid's a moron at the best of times, and she had to run to the ER. You want Craig, the manager? He's around somewhere."

"We're looking for this woman."

She stopped filing her nails long enough to give the ID shot a glance. "How'm I supposed to know? I'm just filling in."

"Her name's right here. You could check the register."

"Yeah, yeah, lemme see. My day off, right, and here I am stuck in this shithole with a couple cops. Don't see a Bernstein on this thing."

"Try Starr, two *r*'s."

"Yeah, yeah, what she do? Kill somebody? Okay, yeah, got a Starr here, 301—that's long-term rate, like you're here for two weeks or better."

"Is she up there now?"

"How'm I supposed to know? I'm—"

"Just filling in. When did she register?"

"Um . . . About two weeks ago."

The door behind Eve opened. When she turned, her eyes met Debra's. She wore a short black wig with thick fringe, a flowy summer dress that showed off a curvy body. She carried two shopping bags.

And, Eve noted, made her and Peabody as cops in a single heart-beat.

She spun, hit the door, and ran like a gazelle.

Eve said, "Damn it," and sprinted after her.

Debra had some speed, and would've had more if she hadn't been hampered by the skinny-heeled sandals.

"Police," Eve shouted. "Stop!"

In response, Debra heaved one of the bags. She had a damn good arm, but Eve dodged the bag and gained ground.

She considered a tackle, reconsidered, pumped up a little more speed. When she grabbed Debra's arm, Debra swung the other bag. It thudded against Eve's shoulder.

"Help!" She shrieked it. "Help, help! Police!"

Peabody pounded up, yanked out her badge. "We are the police."

People who'd been curious enough to stop continued on their way.

And Debra elbowed Eve in the gut before trying to wiggle around to rake pink-tinted nails down her face.

"Well, Debra, that's assault on a police officer. You get a free trip downtown."

She slumped against Eve as if in a faint when Eve snapped on restraints.

"Peabody, let's get a couple of uniforms to escort Debra down to Central, book her on the assault to start."

Debra suddenly revived, began to weep, began to struggle. "How could I know you're police?"

"Maybe because I identified myself as such. Debra Bernstein, you're under arrest for attempting to evade a police officer, for assault on a police officer. I could add littering, but—"

She glanced back, noted not only were the contents of the first shopping bag that had spilled over the sidewalk gone, so was the bag.

"My things! Someone's stolen my things! This is your fault! I'm going to sue. This is a terrible miscarriage of justice."

"Yeah? We'll talk about that. Right now? You have the right to remain silent."

By the time she'd finished reading Debra her rights, two uniforms pulled up. She ordered them to log the remaining shopping bag and Debra's handbag into evidence.

"Pretty good luck," Eve decided.

"She ran fast in those heels. You have to admire that."

"If she'd have worn sane shoes, it would've taken me another block to catch her. Let's go check out her room."

Craig, the manager, came out from wherever and took them straight up. The swiftness of his cooperation led Eve to believe it wasn't the first time, by far, he'd opened a guest's door for the cops.

The single room was decent size, separated into distinct areas. Bedroom, tiny sitting room, minuscule kitchenette with a pay-as-you-use AC and a mini-cooler.

Debra had a carton of raspberry yogurt and a bottle of vodka in the cooler.

The single window faced the street and offered a thin privacy screen.

Debra had a few candles set around and some flowers in an empty wine bottle.

Eve opened the creaky bifold doors of the closet.

"Jesus, this is packed. We've got a cocktail dress in here. And check this, a gray maid's uniform. Find out if Lane's cleaning service runs to uniforms like this. A lot of cases in here."

She reached onto the shelf, hauled one down to take it to the counter separating the kitchenette.

When she opened it, it expanded up into tiers. Tiers filled with makeup, brushes, boxes of spidery lashes, vials of iris-coloring drops.

"Oh my God, I have makeup envy!" Peabody gripped her hands together. "Deep, dark makeup envy."

"Uniforms, Peabody, before I bust you down so you're wearing one again."

Eve hauled down another case, found several wigs and the products to care for and style them.

The third case held face putty of varying shades, a folding triple mirror, lighted, a collection of sunshades and jewelry.

And under it all, a hidden compartment with several fake IDs and licenses. And a master swipe that looked well used and very professional.

"Oh, Debra, you're in so much trouble."

"Gray uniforms, pants and tunics," Peabody reported. "And they brought in two temps the day of the party to do a deep clean. One matches Debra's height, weight. They claim she was bonded, had references that checked out during the screening. She had ID under Debra Rose."

"Got that here." Eve held it up. "Let's see what else we can find before we chat with her."

Eve hunkered down to look under the bed. "Suitcases—two," she said as she pulled them out. And glancing over, hissed at Peabody. "Stop playing with the damn makeup."

"I'm not. I mean I might have, a little, but see, she's got all her brushes arranged in the slots, so I wondered what was in this roll down here.

She showed Eve.

"Burglar's tools. Excellent find."

"I don't see a uniform in my future."

"Not so far. Burglar's tools, fake IDs, a master swipe, the uniform." She paced a moment.

"New picture. She talks herself into the cleaning service. That's how she gets in. She's got the tools to break in, but why would you? Could she find a way to smuggle that cocktail dress in there, and whatever else she needed?"

"Maid cart maybe."

"Maybe, maybe. Maybe she finds a way to stay behind, finds a bolt-hole. It's a big place, and most of the activity's on the main floor and in the master bedroom. Tuck yourself into one of the guest rooms, wait it out. Get your party on, slip downstairs once it's going pretty strong."

"She wouldn't be on a guest list, not even as a plus-one. No record of her."

"Act like you belong there," Eve went on. "She probably recognized people, just act like they should know her. Poison the drink, then get the hell out so you're already gone when it hits."

"Why didn't she poof? She should've poofed."

"Yeah," Eve agreed. "But she didn't hit the target. Could be she wanted another shot, or wanted to hang around to see some reactions."

She opened one of the suitcases. "More clothes. Okay, got a PPC—passcoded. We'll get EDD to open it. Something heavy wrapped up here."

She pulled out a bundle, unrolled a length of black velvet.

"Do I hear a fucking aha?"

"That looks like a Tony award."

"And it has Eliza Lane's name on it, for Best Supporting Actress in a Musical. *Upstage.*"

16

She called in more uniforms to transfer everything from the hotel room and into evidence.

Then she took one last scan of the room, because with all they'd found, there was one thing they hadn't.

Any evidence of the possession or acquisition of cyanide.

"Maybe something on her PPC or 'link," Eve muttered.

"Are you going to pull in Reo or another APA?" Peabody asked.

"Read her in, let her know we'll have the suspect in the box within the hour. And you can start talking to the rest of the cleaning crew, get statements. Did she leave with them? If not, why?"

In the hallway, Eve sealed the door. "Let's check with the bank, see if she got any more funds wired there. No cams on the doors, the lobby, the shitpile elevator. Doubtful anybody paid attention if she had visitors, but we'll ask."

The woman currently manning the desk shared a strong family re-semblance with the bored nail-filer. Since the odds favored the regular clerk, Peabody paved the way with a sympathetic smile. "How's your boy?"

"Busted his nose, rattled his teeth, scared the crap out of me. When they hit thirteen, they know everything. Is Ms. Starr coming back?"

"That's hard to say," Peabody continued. "For now, we've sealed off the room. We'll let you know."

The woman leaned over, whispered, "Can you tell me what she did? Something awful?"

"We need to ask her some questions."

"Luce, my sister, she said she ran like a rabbit. She was pretty excited. Luce, I mean."

"I bet. Did Ms. Starr have any visitors you know of?"

"I never saw anybody. For sure this ain't the Roarke Palace, and we got dick-all for security, but I mostly notice who's what on my shift, and nobody ever asked about her. Chance has short shift, the four-to ten. We don't have a night man on the desk, just Bower or Clark bunking in the bank for emergencies and the like."

"Can you give us their contact information so we can check?"

"Sure thing. Craig and I were just talking— Here's Craig now. I'm saying we were just talking about how that Ms. Starr didn't have much to say, but what she did was snooty. Like she was too good to be here."

"Doing us a favor by it," Craig pitched in. The manager—skinny, mixed-race, late twenties—leaned companionably on the check-in counter. "Paid extra—and complained about it—to have her sheets changed twice a week."

"Do you know if anybody shared those sheets?" Eve asked.

"Not that I know of, nope. Paid cash for the first week, right, Adele?"

"That's right. If you want the long-term rate, you pay the first week up front."

"Did you ever see her wearing a uniform? A gray uniform, like a cleaning person might?"

"No, but . . . You know, it's funny you ask that." Adele pointed at Eve. "Not yesterday . . . No, the day before that, just as I was walking down to come in for my shift, I saw this woman coming out—tall like Ms. Starr, but blond, and wearing what I'd call a classy maid service uniform. All pressed up. I thought how somebody must've checked in after I clocked out, and made up a story in my head."

"She does that all the time," Craig commented, and gave Adele a friendly poke in the arm.

"It passes the time. I figure, okay, she checked in last night because she finally left that asshole she's married to, and now she's going off to work cleaning somebody's fancy house."

She flushed a little. "So I checked the register to see who checked in, but there wasn't anybody. Then I decided, okay, she left that asshole and she stayed here with somebody who treats her good, and now she's heading to work."

She shrugged. "I didn't see her face because she was heading the other way, but she was blond—had her hair in a braid and all—so it wasn't Ms. Snooty—I mean, Ms. Starr. I called her the other in my head. Plus, she always dressed fancy, not in something like a cleaning person would."

"Was she carrying anything?"

"Um, had a big handbag." She held her hands out about two feet apart.

"About what time was that?"

"Oh, just before eight. I'm on at eight on Mondays. Nobody's on the desk until eight when I get here."

"Thanks, that's helpful. We'll be in touch."

"Blond wig in the wig case," Peabody commented.

"Yeah, and long enough to braid. So she leaves before anyone's on the desk, gets uptown, and when she connects with the rest of the crew, walks right in the penthouse. I'll take the bank, it's right across the street there. Start on the other cleaners."

Eve jogged across the street. In the bank—a space smaller than the take-out-only joint she'd often used pre-Roarke—she badged the security droid. And waited while he scanned her ID.

Both tellers were human, as was the man sitting at a desk behind a half wall scowling into his comp.

Since she didn't have a warrant—she could get one reasonably fast—she decided to skip the scowl guy and aimed toward the young, perky-looking female behind the shockproof shield.

"Lieutenant Dallas," Eve began, holding up her badge.

"I *knew* it! I knew it when you were talking to Mike over there. I said that's Dallas from the Icove vid. Didn't I say, Jerry? Didn't I?"

"Yeah." The other teller paused in his work to eye Eve carefully.

"I saw the vid three times already. My neighbor was one of the clones—didn't I say, Jerry? I know it! And didn't she move out as soon as the vid hit? She did! She said how she was moving to Atlanta, but come on! Totally one of those clones. You're looking for her, right? That's why you're here."

"Actually, I'm here on another matter. This woman?" Eve held up her 'link with Debra's ID shot on-screen.

"Is she a clone? I should've known! I've got an eye for them. She's been in here three times, hasn't she, Jerry? No, I lie, four! She came in and opened an account, then she came in three more times. Had people—clones, I bet!—wiring her money. Five thousand each time. I know because I handled two of them. Jerry had the other, isn't that right, Jerry?"

"I guess, sure." He hunched on his stool as if trying to make himself invisible.

"It would be very helpful to have that information. The dates of the transactions, the names of the individuals who wired her money."

"So you can trace the clones!"

Eve decided to let that ride. "She may have opened the account with false identification. If you'd check Debra Bernstein first."

"That's it! That's it! I remember now."

"Ah, Dory, maybe you should talk to Mr. Jabbot before you—"

But Dory was already busy accessing the account. "Jerry, this is *Dallas*! Get a grip. Okay, she opened the account on June nineteenth with a hundred dollars. That's the minimum. And the next day, a Maeve Spindal wired her five thousand, and she took all but another hundred out in cash. Then two days later, another five thousand from Steven K. Lewis, and she took all but the hundred in cash. Then! Last Friday, another five from David Quaid, and she took it all in cash."

"That's very helpful." Since, in Eve's mind, you respected the streak, she pushed it. "Could I get a copy of the account information for my files?"

"Absolutely!"

"Dory, you can't just—"

"Stuff it, Jerry. This isn't just police business. It's humanity's business. Humanity, Jerry!"

She printed out a copy, slid it to Eve through the slot. "The other clone who used to live across the hall? She went by Nessa Bowie."

"Very helpful," Eve repeated. "Thank you."

"I heard they're making a sequel to the vid, but it's not about clones. You should really think about making another one about clones."

"Yeah, I'll do that."

Weird, Eve thought as she got the hell out. But if the damn vid cut through some bullshit, who would she be if she didn't take advantage?

Across the street, Peabody leaned against the car, still talking on her 'link. Eve jogged up the clanging steps to join her.

"Yes, thank you, Ms. Gretzy. Best of luck to your grandson at the Academy."

She beamed at Eve as she pocketed her 'link. "Aileen Gretzy's grandson's going into the Police Academy. She's worked for the cleaning service for eighteen years, and, as their most experienced employee, worked with Bernstein on Monday. She was very informative."

"Great. I also hit a very informative. You go first," she added as they got in the car.

"I spoke with the owner first, and she confirmed they'd checked all Ms. Rose's—Debra Rose's—credentials, references, work history. So I'd say she had some help on that end. She assigned her to the Lane-Fitzhugh job, under Ms. Gretzy's supervision, because she had such solid references and so on, had a pleasant, dignified manner and appearance. Plus, timing. She needed additional help for that job, and Debra popped at just the right time."

"Bet she did."

"However, Debra was assigned to another job today, and was a no-show, and her contact number has been closed."

"See my shock and surprise."

"Gretzy said Debra worked hard and well—no complaints. Not especially chatty, but friendly enough, and said she was starting over in New York to be closer to her own mother, and her daughter, an actress."

"When they were leaving, Debra remembered she'd left her bag behind in the third-floor storage room where the cleaning crew stowed their personal items. Gretzy offered to wait, but Debra insisted she go on, and since the others were anxious to call it a day, they all left."

"And she didn't. Found that bolt-hole, waited it out. This is good information."

"It ranks. What did you get?"

Eve braked at a light, watched the tidal wave of pedestrians roll by. "A teller who'd seen the vid three times. Her former neighbor's a clone. She's sure of it."

"Oh."

"In this case, it opened the gates. I'm pretty sure she'd have given me the codes to the vault if I'd asked, because humanity."

On the green, Eve pushed south.

"Bernstein opened an account with the minimum deposit the same day she checked into the hotel. In the last ten days, she's gotten three five-thousand-dollar payments wired to that account. I've got a print-out of all the transactions in my back pocket."

"She gave you a printout?"

"It's humanity's business, Peabody."

Peabody shifted in her seat. "Did you tell her Debra was a clone?"

"No, I did not. She may have jumped to that conclusion, and as I have no conclusive data at this time one way or the other, I felt it inappropriate to confirm or deny."

"Sneaky."

Eve shrugged. "Dory the teller claims to have an eye for them. Clones. I suspect that eye may fall on her coworker Jerry at any time. Regardless, I got the data. Of the fifteen thousand one hundred dollars, Debra left three hundred in said account. I imagine she intended to close said account before she took off."

"We didn't find any cash in the room."

"If she has any left, it's probably in Evidence now." She pulled into Central's garage. "I'm going to see if I can get a quick consult with Mira. You head up, write this up, copy Whitney."

She tugged the printout from her pocket as they crossed the garage. "We'll run these other two idiots who sent her money, determine if they're marks or accomplices."

"David Quaid," Peabody read. "I know that name, I know it."

When they reached the elevator, she started to pull out her PPC and check. A couple of detectives Eve recognized from Fraud hotfooted over.

"Hold the door! Hold it. LT, Peabody."

"Detectives Stringer, Nalley."

"Fitzhugh murder, right? Damn shame."

"I'm hearing that a lot."

"My first ex-wife's cousin had parts in two of his vids. Got lines and everything in the second one," Stringer added.

"What was he doing Monday night between twenty-one hundred and twenty-three hundred hours?"

Stringer barked out a laugh. "He's doing a western in Montana or somewhere out there. Good guy. We keep in touch."

"David Quaid," Peabody said again, as she started the search.

"Pretty good character actor in his day," Stringer commented. "Gotta be past the century mark by now."

"Quaid or your first ex-wife's cousin?"

"Quaid. Jesse hasn't hit forty."

Everyone shuffled back or to the side as more cops piled on.

"That's it! I knew I knew that name. David Quaid—he's a hundred and eleven. Career spanned seventy-five years, and yeah, he's got a filmography a mile long. Retired now, living in County Mayo, where he played Doc Justice, the irascible uncle to Willa Rogan's amateur sleuth, Honor Muldoon, in the long-running series *Honor and Justice*. I've seen that show in reruns, like a million times. It's comfort food, and really pretty."

"Find the tie to Bernstein," Eve ordered, and shoved off on Mira's level.

She expected to get grief from the dragon at Mira's gates, and got a steely stare from same when she walked into the outer office.

"I need five minutes."

"Many do. Is this regarding the Brant Fitzhugh investigation?"

"It is."

She tapped her earpiece. "Dr. Mira, Lieutenant Dallas would like five minutes, if possible. Of course." She tapped again.

"You can go right in."

Torn between suspicion and shock, Eve sent the admin a long look. "A fan? Of Fitzhugh's?"

"He was my hall pass."

"Oh. Okay." She sort of wished she'd skipped that information as she walked into Mira's office.

"Your timing's good. I just finished a consult. Let me get us some tea."

"Honestly, it'll only take a few minutes. We brought in a suspect. Rose Bernstein's mother."

"Well." Mira stayed behind her desk, but swiveled her chair, crossed her legs. She wore a sleeveless sheath the color, Eve imagined, you got when you added just the right amount of melted butter to cream. "That's quick work. You established she was on scene?"

"We've established she faked her way into the apartment with the cleaning crew who worked that morning. She didn't leave with them. I'm going to check the security feed to confirm her time in, to establish her time out of the building. We found Eliza Lane's Tony for the original *Upstage* in Bernstein's luggage in her hotel room. Also a collection of wigs—she wore a blond one when she posed as a cleaner—a large collection of makeup, face putty, and so on. A master swipe, burglary tools, several fake IDs under various names, her maid's uniform that was provided by the company who hired her."

"Nothing on the poison itself?"

"Not yet, but she had fifteen thousand in cash, that we know of. Five thousand each wired to her here in New York in the last ten days from three sources.

"Let me run by you what we know about her from research and statements."

She outlined the background, the observations on her relationship with her daughter, Peabody's conversation with the agent, the boyfriend, the behavior toward her daughter's stepsister at Rose's funeral, and the observations of the primary on Rose Bernstein's murder.

Mira listened in her calm way as she gently swiveled back and forth behind the desk.

"You're wondering if, in my opinion, the revival of *Upstage* pushed Debra Bernstein from a life of, by all accounts, doggedly pursuing fame and fortune—and the spotlight—of assuming other identities to potentially cheat, steal, or con her way into some fame, some fortune, into murder."

"Could it?"

"Her daughter's talent opened the doors to what Debra wanted. It must have been shocking and infuriating to have her own child, one I'm sure she believed then, believes now, she sacrificed everything for, shut those doors."

"And with the OD, shut them permanently."

"Yes. Their last conversation, argument, encounter, may very well have caused Rose—under professional stress, struggling with addiction—to reach for the crutch she'd used before. There may be part of the mother that knows that, fears that, and can't face that."

"Maybe."

"Admitting it would mean accepting some responsibility and blame, something she isn't equipped to do. Others must be blamed. The boyfriend, the understudy, even the younger sister who mourned. She's a narcissist, and though I'd need to do a deeper evaluation to confirm, I suspect borderline personality. She must be the center—and while she could bask in the reflected glory of her daughter's talent, she needed to be the center of her daughter's life.

"A boyfriend, a sister who had talent of her own?" Mira shook her head. "Competition for Debra as she'd see it. 'You can't give them what's mine.' With Rose gone, Debra could reestablish herself, rewrite their relationship, become the center of the daughter who was taken from her."

"And twenty-five years later?"

Idly, Mira hooked a finger around the gold chain she wore with its circles of pale multicolored stones.

"To go through so many ruses to get into Lane's home, to actually spend time cleaning it? It certainly wasn't whim or impulse. Nor was taking that award, that specific thing. Not Eliza Lane's Tony in her mind, not even so much her daughter's by this time."

"Hers."

"Her reward for all the years of sacrifice. As for murder? There's a reason a certain type chooses poison. It has the illusion of being non-violent. It's bloodless. It requires no direct physical contact. It calls on cunning rather than brute strength. From your statements, background, observations, I'd say her conscience is very flexible."

"Yeah, *flexible*'s a word," Eve said, and made Mira smile.

"Killing Eliza Lane, and doing it in a way, on a stage, before an audience, and taking the award, it's very consistent with that flexibility, and pathology."

"She missed with Lane."

"Which may be a reason she didn't leave New York."

"Try, try again," Eve agreed. "Okay, I appreciate it."

"You'll have her in Interview soon."

"Next step."

"I have another consult shortly. I'll see if you're still talking to her when I'm done, and come up to Observation."

"Thanks for that."

She headed out, tagging APA Reo on the way.

"I've got a suspect in the Fitzhugh case, bringing her into Interview."

"So I hear."

"Debra Bernstein, Rose Bernstein–slash–Leah Rose's mother. Rose Bernstein was the actress Eliza Lane replaced when she—Rose—OD'd."

"So she killed Fitzhugh to punish Lane?"

"Ninety-three-plus probability Lane was the target. We can place Bernstein in the penthouse earlier in the day, and she had Lane's award for the play—the dead daughter's play—in her possession."

"That gives me a tingle." Reo did a quick shoulder wiggle. "But theft isn't murder."

"I've got more, will get more yet. Just giving you a heads-up on it."

"I'll let the boss know, and if I can clear things up here, I'll come in."

"We'll copy you the report from the arrest and search."

When she went into Homicide, Peabody was on her 'link. Eve went into her office, got coffee, sat, and read over the report Peabody had written.

Thorough and concise.

And copied Reo.

Peabody hustled in.

"I actually talked to David Quaid—what a sweetie. He's on the frail side physically, but still pretty damn sharp. I also spoke with his great-granddaughter. She and her son live with him. He has a medical aide in addition."

"And?"

"What I got? Debra was an extra on a vid he did twenty-couple years ago—his last project before he retired. They hit it off; she cried on his shoulder about her daughter. He'd lost a grandson to addiction, so was sympathetic. They've kept in touch off and on. Mostly, according to the great-granddaughter, when she's after a handout. But, she said, it's his money, and it's never been more than a few thousand every few years. Plus, Debra always sends him a card on his birthday. As for the other one, Steven K. Lewis, he was a high roller when she was in Vegas, they had a thing. She's only hit him up a few times since."

"Let's get her stuff out of Evidence."

"Anticipating that, I asked McNab to log it out for us. He disabled the passcodes on her PPC and 'link. She had a fail-safe installed on both, so it took awhile."

She gestured to the AC. "Can I?"

"Top mine off while you're at it." Eve opened the file, brought up the security feed for Lane's building. Started at zero-eight hundred on Monday, pushed the speed until she saw the cleaning crew enter.

"There she is—blond wig, gray uniform, and carrying the big-ass bag we found in her room."

"Two of the crew with rolly carts," Peabody observed over Eve's shoulder. "Cleaning supplies."

"Check in, IDs verified, and up they go."

She followed them by the elevator cam to Lane's main level. Hallway cam, door cam.

"That's Gretzy talking into the intercom."

"And Debra keeping her head down. In they go. We didn't go back this far before. Didn't see four went in, three came out. What time did they leave?"

"Gretzy said they left at two-thirty—they took about forty-five minutes for lunch. Wayne Rowan made them lunch, and they ate in the kitchen."

She skimmed until the fourteen hundred mark, slowed until fourteen-twenty. "There they are, the three of them, coming out, main floor again, fourteen-twenty-three, down the elevator, across the lobby."

Eve ran it, increased speed, until fifteen hundred.

"I'd say forty minutes is plenty of time to get your forgotten bag and leave. Let's try an hour before TOD."

They hit at eighteen minutes before TOD.

"She kept the blond wig." Eve froze the screen when the woman stepped into the hall from the main door. "Fancied it up, but that's the same color."

"And that's the black cocktail dress from her closet."

"Yeah, it is. She's keeping her head down—doesn't want her face on camera. Carrying the same giant bag as she did when she went in as a cleaner. She's gone before he took the drink to his wife, down and out and gone while the victim's mingling his way across the room, goes over, talks to his wife and Bowen."

"And then Lane gives it back to him, goes and gets Samantha, they go to the piano."

Seeing it in her head, Eve nodded. "Fitzhugh makes his way up, listens, toasts, drinks. Under twenty minutes, yeah, that plays well enough."

She shoved back. "I didn't see it this way, goddamn it. Didn't see the killer dumping the poison, then taking off before they made sure it worked. Didn't see the lying in wait, right in the damn apartment. She slipped right through."

"No, she didn't. She's in a holding cell."

Eve scrubbed her hands over her face. "You're right. Let's bring her up, let her sweat in the box while we check out her PPC and 'link. She'll slip through nothing after this."

17

After Peabody went out, McNab came in carting an evidence box. "Peabody gave me a list of what you'd want. If I missed anything, I can go back, check it out."

"Let's have a look."

When he put it on her desk, she opened it.

"Blond wig, maid uniform, cocktail dress. Good, we've got her on the security feed with these." Eve took out the PPC. "Did you go through this?"

"Quick skim." He sent a longing glance toward her AutoChef, added a winsome smile that went big when she jerked her head in permission.

She watched him, the very clever e-man with his shiny tail of hair, the baggies in screaming red, the black, yellow, red circus-striped shirt over his skinny frame.

"Might as well have my coffee to wash down the chocolate."

He looked back as he programmed his coffee. "You got chocolate up for grabs?"

"Apparently, I did."

She imagined hauling his bony ass into the box and grilling him over a candy bar. It brought a rush of satisfaction before she reminded herself:

Priorities.

"Give me the quick skim."

"I can tell you she did plenty of research on Lane and Fitzhugh over the last few weeks. Enough she nailed down their usual caterer, their cleaning service. She had the party on her fricking calendar."

"Adds weight."

"I did a search, just to save you time with it. Nothing on there that came up on poisons or cyanide."

"That would make it too easy."

"We love a challenge." He gulped coffee. "She's got a spreadsheet on there, names of people she hits up for money, the amounts, the dates. It looked to me like she has a kind of rotation. Ask Joe Soft Touch in May for two grand, whine to Jane Mark in September."

"That tracks. How about the 'link?"

He nodded toward it when Eve took it out. "Lots of tags, texts, v-mails. Got a pre-interview interview on there with the cleaning service. And texts going back and forth with a J. Z. Kramer setting up the references she gave the cleaning service. Phony websites, 'link contacts. Pretty slick, from my scan. Cost her three grand, and that's going to be a serious bargain, because it was prime work."

"Got a history together."

"Sounded like it from the communications. Like she called him Stud, and he called her Lovie."

"Isn't that just adorable? Where is this J. Z. Kramer?"

"I can find out."

"Do that." She pulled out two sealed bags of cash.

"The one—eighty-six dollars? That was in her handbag. The other, eighteen hundred and fifty, she had in a panty wallet she was wearing when you busted her."

"That's what she had left from the fifteen K she pulled in. She had to have more before she hit up her marks. Enough to get to New York, pay the first week at the hotel. Take out the payment to the Stud, the second week at the hotel. So where'd she spend something like nine thousand in under two weeks? There's a question for her."

She looked through the other contents. "Master swipe, burglar's tools, the award. Yeah, this should be enough for now. I'm going to turn the e's over to you. See if you can locate Kramer. If he's not in New York, I think we'll put the local heat on him wherever he is."

She looked back at her board. "If you find anything else that adds weight, pull Peabody out of Interview and pass it on."

"Got that."

She resealed the e's, signed them over to him, then heard the click of heels.

She looked over in time to see Nadine stop in her doorway.

"Whose ass do I need to kick in the bullpen?" Eve wondered.

"Now, now. McNab, I just had a whirlwind tour of the house and yard. Looking seriously fine."

"Check it. Did you catch the water feature?"

"It's going to be amazing. And Peabody's kitchen. I know it's yours, too, but it's so utterly her."

"Yeah, it is."

"Should I order up a cheese plate so you two can have some nibbles while you chat?"

Nadine only smiled, and again said, "Now, now," but McNab grabbed up the e's.

"I'll let you know what I find when I find it." And bounced straight out.

"I'm pressed, Nadine." Eve replaced the lid on the evidence box.

"I'm sure you are, as I happened to see Peabody taking Debra Bernstein into Interview A."

"Come on."

"I'm getting coffee. Would you like some?"

"Jesus."

"I'll take that as a yes." In her skinny peacock-colored heels and power suit, Nadine crossed to the AC. "I can also clearly see Bernstein holding a prominent position on your case board. Do you want to know how I so easily recognized her?"

"You're going to tell me anyway."

"I am." Nadine handed Eve fresh coffee. "A lot of media, including Seventy-Five, are doing compilations of Brant Fitzhugh's career, his personal life, and so on. I thought I'd take a different angle. Tragedy shadowed *Upstage* twenty-five years ago, and now with this silver anniversary revival, tragedy shadows it again."

"Why is it silver?"

"Nice attempt at deflection." She eased a well-toned hip on Eve's desk. "In order to create this circle—then to now—I, and my most excellent research team, had to go back to then. There was considerable coverage of that tragedy, but primarily in New York. Leah Rose was, after all, a Broadway ingenue. There's certainly been more coverage since, as Eliza Lane's career skyrocketed."

She paused to sip some coffee.

"One of the first pieces of interest we uncovered didn't rate any real press at the time, and that's Rose Bernstein, known as Leah Rose, had a younger stepsister acquired when Rose's mother—that's Debra on your board—and father divorced and the father married Alyson Crupke Novak. That stepsister, Minerva Novak, is the choreographer on the revival of *Upstage*."

Watching Eve over the rim, Nadine sipped coffee. "I'm sure you know Novak was at the party, or at the crime scene, however you want to put it. That's an odd little twist of fate, wouldn't you say?"

"Have you contacted her?"

"You were my first stop—well, after my house tour. And very brief sidestep. Mavis's kitchen. It shouldn't be, it really shouldn't be, but it's just freaking fabulous."

"Uh-huh. It would be best if you gave Novak a pass, at least for twenty-four hours."

Nadine sipped more coffee. "I'm going to point out I'm under no obligation, professionally, to share this information with you."

"You're not. And I'll point out I'm under no obligation, professionally, to share with you— Off the record, Nadine."

Nadine shrugged, sighed. "Off the record."

"That I know how to do my job, and made this connection, interviewed the subject and her husband. Neither she nor he is a suspect."

Lowering her coffee, Nadine frowned. "Because? Off the record, Dallas."

"First, no motive. If you've done your job, and I have no doubt, you know Rose Bernstein had a history of drug and alcohol abuse. As she was well aware of this, Novak has no motive to harm Lane or Fitzhugh. A thorough search—with their cooperation—of their residence, their work space, their electronics, their financials, turned up no evidence whatsoever. They've got a kid, Nadine, and another in the pot.

"I know my job," Eve repeated, "and they're clear. You know yours, and when you do interview them, you'll agree."

"All right, but it's part of the circle."

"It is."

"So is Debra Bernstein—someone my crack team was unable to locate. Since you did, brought her in, you already know her history."

Nadine gave the evidence box on Eve's desk a long look. Eve just said, "No."

"Well, back to history. A lot of petty crimes and cons in there, enough to earn Debra a little time served and fines and some outstanding warrants. Add . . ."

Nadine pushed up—tapped Debra's face on Eve's board. "I interview people, and if you're any good at it, which I am, you know how to read them, size them up. So add what strikes me, after digging up some of this one's old interviews after her daughter's death, as a grasping narcissist who'd have no issue crawling over her dead daughter's body to grab a gold ring. But nothing in the same universe as murder."

After easing her hip on the desk again, Nadine gestured with her mug. "Yet there she is, on your board and in Interview A. Maybe you figure she figured take Lane out, the show goes under, and she closes the circle. And," Nadine added, "maybe cashes in on the revived publicity."

"You'd have given her some of that," Eve pointed out. "And it's Fitzhugh in the morgue, not Lane."

"I see your board, I study the known facts, and conclude somebody shot an arrow and missed the bull's-eye. And yeah, I'd have given her some of that. But if what I figure you figure she figured is correct, it won't be the kind of publicity she'll enjoy or profit from."

"Well, this has been fun, but—"

"Dallas, we've both got a job to do. We both happen to be very skilled and smart at that job. Kyung says he doesn't have a time for the day's media briefing."

"And he won't until I conduct this interview."

"Give me something. 'A source from the NYPSD states.' Something, Dallas. I saw Debra Bernstein being escorted into Interview. I can go with that—nothing off the record when I saw it before we spoke—but I can hold that, if you ask me to, because I know you'd ask me to for good reasons. So, give me something else."

She would hold it, Eve acknowledged. If she asked, Nadine would hold that information until she cleared it.

"Hold it, and I've got those good reasons. Meanwhile . . . A source from the NYPSD states something of value was taken from the Lane/Fitzhugh residence on the night of the murder."

"This wasn't a botched burglary."

"That's not what I said. Something was taken, and taken Monday night." Eve hesitated, considered. Decided. "And has since been recovered."

Nadine's gaze shifted to the evidence box. "I see." After setting her mug aside, Nadine straightened. "I'll go do my job, let you do yours."

"Good idea."

She started out, stopped, looked back at Eve's board. "It does make a circle. Rose to Bernstein to Novak to Lane. Like a classic triple play."

"Jesus, Nadine, that actually gives me physical pain." And Eve rubbed at her heart. "A classic triple is Tinker to Evers to Chance." Eve shot up a finger for each name. "Three."

"Okay, well a quadruple play." She ignored Eve's wince. "Whatever. A circle, with the award-winning Broadway musical at the center. But circles have straight lines, too. Radius, diameter."

"If you say so."

"I do. A lot of names, a lot of history on those lines. But the circle goes round and round."

It did, Eve thought when Nadine left. It went round and round, but there were points along the way that made it go round and round.

Rose to Bernstein to Novak to Lane.

She needed to think about those points, and the lines that crossed the center to connect them.

But now, she had a suspect to grill.

Picking up the evidence box, she walked out to the bullpen.

Everyone got very busy all at once, but sharp cop's eyes noted a few stray crumbs.

"Betrayed for cookies? Et tu, fuckers."

"They were double chocolate chunk, Loo." Jenkinson didn't have the grace, or maybe the gall, to look ashamed as he brushed some of those stray crumbs off the tie of insanity. "You can't fight the double chocolate chunk."

"I didn't get any." Peabody rose, aiming a hard look at her brothers and sisters in arms. "Nothing left by the time I got back. She spotted me, Dallas, taking Bernstein to Interview, but I had to get her in there. And the cookies were history, Nadine was already in your office by the time I got here."

"With me," Eve said, and walked out.

"Honest to God," Peabody began when she caught up.

"It's not your fault. This time."

"Praise Jesus. I figured you'd deal with Nadine however you wanted, and I'd stay out of the way."

"She connected Minerva Novak—I called her off for a day there, gave some information off the record and enough on to satisfy her. She'd also connected Bernstein even before she saw you. She's working on a circle thing—*Upstage*, tragedy then, tragedy now."

"I can see that. But—"

"She'll hold off on us having Bernstein in Interview. I had to give her the award in exchange. Not specifically, just something had been taken that night, and we'd recovered it."

She paused outside Interview A. "Mira will come observe if she can make it. So will Reo. On the e's," she began, and filled in what McNab found.

"If he finds anything more we can use, he'll pull you out. Then we hit her with that. You set up the security feed, and we'll hit her with that. No lawyer yet?"

"She made noises about false arrest, physical assault, personal injury, mental cruelty, and suing. I'm a duck there. You know, it rolls off."

"Threats roll off ducks?"

"Water rolls off ducks, and her threats were like . . . You got that one. I can see it."

"Yeah, I got it." She opened the door. "Record on. Dallas, Lieutenant Eve, and Peabody, Detective Delia, entering Interview with Bernstein, Debra, on the matter of case file H-8546, and additional matters of possession of fraudulent identification, trespassing, theft, fraud, fleeing from police officers and assault on a police officer, resisting arrest."

"This is all nonsense."

No more flowy summer dress, but an orange jumpsuit. No more sassy black wig, but a short brown do liberally streaked with sunshine blond and currently disordered.

"I haven't yet contacted my attorney," she continued as Eve and Peabody sat. "Initially I was in shock due to your vicious and unprovoked attack on my person."

"Uh-huh," Eve said.

"Now I simply want to get this matter settled and be on my way."

"What way is that?"

"Back to my hotel, of course, where I intend to retrieve my things and leave this city and this horrible incident behind me. You've obviously mistaken me for someone else."

"Like who? Maybe Debbie Starr. Maybe Madame Rose." Eve stood, opened the evidence box, began to toss out the fake IDs. "Could be Rose Stein, Leah Starr."

"Those are various stage and professional names. I'm an entertainer."

"Are you entertained, Peabody?"

"Not yet."

"Me, either. You can have all the stage names you want, but you only get official identification in your legal name. That's Debra Bernstein, and not the identification or the name you used to register at the West End Hotel."

"I simply wished to be incognito." Debra pushed her shoulders back, did her best haughty stare. But the orange jumpsuit wasn't doing her any favors. "It's common practice for people in my art, my line of work."

"Yeah, it's common practice for frauds, cons, and grifters. What are you doing in New York?"

"That's certainly my business, but I came to do some shopping, to seek work."

"What kind of work?"

"I'm an entertainer. New York has countless venues for my talents. The stage, the screen, clubs, piano bars."

"Cleaning services?" Eve pulled out the maid's uniform, the blond wig.

Debra huffed out a breath. Her eyes, a tawny sort of hazel, radiated disdain. "Costumes, Lieutenant. An entertainer possesses costumes."

"Who were you entertaining when you wore this outfit, this wig to enter the Belmont Tower on Central Park West at around eight-thirty Monday morning? And shortly after, the penthouse apartment of Eliza Lane and Brant Fitzhugh?"

"I don't know what you're talking about."

"Peabody, cue up the security feed."

As the screen blipped on, Debra began to twist her fingers together.

"Now, before you say that's not you, I'll tell you that the rest of the cleaning team each, independently, picked you out of a series of photos. So did the owner of the company, who interviewed you for the job."

Instantly, like a tap turned, Debra's eyes filled. "All right, you're so determined to humiliate me. I needed the money, so I took a job cleaning. It's honest work. I wore the wig and used another name so as not to be recognized. I have a small but loyal following."

"It cost you three grand to get your pal J.Z. to set up the fake references so you could take the job. And it's just some wild coincidence that this cleaning job you took—needing money despite having recently come into fifteen thousand dollars—happened to be Eliza Lane's penthouse. Your deceased daughter's onetime understudy."

Now the tears fell, they fell like rain, like a torrent, gushing and sliding while Debra's shoulders shook. "My baby! My beautiful girl, lost, lost to me, to the world, even before the Rose had bloomed."

"For which you blamed, and continue to blame, Eliza Lane."

"Her and that monstrous boy. They pressured my darling girl, tempted her, played on her weaknesses. Imagine my shock when I realized where I was!"

"Debra, you were not only told who owned the property you'd work in that day, you signed—under your false name—a nondisclosure statement to ensure the clients'—Mr. Fitzhugh and Ms. Lane's—privacy."

"I simply didn't pay any attention at the time. I was so nervous." Eyes drenched, she crossed her hands over her heart. "Desperate. I had to pay for housing, such as it is, for salon services, some wardrobe. One must look one's best for auditions, after all. I didn't realize until I saw photos and the others were chattering about it all."

"Right. You had no clue. Are you saying you had no idea Lane was going into rehearsals for a revival of *Upstage*?"

"Of course I knew that! It broke my heart. A heart that has never, will never fully heal. May I have some water, some tissues? I'm very upset."

"I bet you are. Peabody?"

Peabody rose. "Peabody exiting Interview," she said, and went out.

"If you could give me a moment to compose myself. This is all very stressful."

"Sure, take your time. I've got plenty of it."

"I don't know how you can be so cavalier, so heartless. Rose was my world, and she was about to be on top of her world. It's all I wanted. I sacrificed everything for my bright, beautiful girl. My own career." She flicked a hand in the air. "What did it matter when I had Rose? I devoted myself to her, and hers. We devoted ourselves to each other."

"My information is she booted you the minute she turned eighteen."

A quick flash in those hazel eyes, then more tears. "Artistic temperament, nothing more. A tender bird who had to fledge, spread her wings before coming back to the nest."

"Why would she do that? Come back to the nest. I think she'd make her own."

"It's a figure of speech," Debra said stiffly. "I gave her the room to spread her wings because she needed it, and we'd completely and lovingly reconciled before her death. I can thank God for that at least."

"Huh. That's strange, as my information is she had you barred from the theater."

"Ridiculous. Lies. Lies perpetuated, no doubt, by that scheming, low-talent excuse for an actress who built her career on my daughter's tragic death."

"That would be Eliza Lane?"

"Who else? That grasping, conniving bitch drove my Rose to seek solace in pills and alcohol, aided and abetted by that sniveling bastard poor Rose fell for."

"That would be Gary Proctor?"

"They were sleeping together, you can be sure of that!"

"How do you know?"

Debra looked down her nose at Eve. "A mother knows."

"Peabody returning to Interview." Peabody set the water, a stack of tissues on the table.

"Okay, well, moving on," Eve began.

"Do you know what she did?" Fire came back, flamed from Debra's eyes, shot harsh color into her cheeks. "That whoring, heartless bitch played on Rose's giving nature, her kindness, and convinced Rose to agree to give her a matinee performance once a week, *and* an evening performance every month. Oh, to take some of the stress away, to give Rose time to rest her voice. Butter wouldn't melt."

She tossed her head, sniffed. "Well, I can tell you I put a stop to that as soon as I heard."

"Did you?"

"I certainly did. I had a heart-to-heart with my daughter, reminded her you never, ever give anything away. Reminded her the name of the play was *Upstage*, and that's just what that clawing understudy wanted to do. Upstage my Rose. I let that bitch know I was onto her, and Rose was, too."

Though they'd dried up in fury, Debra took a tissue, dabbed it under each eye as if wiping tears away.

"When was this?"

"Right before the final run-through, the friends and family performance. Oh, she was brilliant, my Rose. She had the entire house in the palm of her hand. And I let that conniver know she'd never step into Rose's shoes. As if she could! As if she could ever fill them. I let her know Rose knew what she was up to. Rose would make her mark on every performance, and bring down the house."

"What did Eliza say to that?"

"Oh, she tried to make excuses, tell more lies, but I wasn't having it! I'd have given her more pieces of my mind then and there, but . . ."

"But?"

Debra paused to sip some water. "Things got a bit heated, as you might imagine. I was protecting my daughter. She cried her fake tears to security and had me escorted out of the theater. I never saw my baby alive again. She saw to that."

"That must've been very painful."

Debra turned sorrowful eyes toward Peabody. "Beyond what you, or anyone, could imagine."

"Losing a child . . ." Peabody pressed a hand to her own heart, shook her head. "How could you ever forgive Eliza Lane? It had to be a stab in your heart every time you thought about her, your daughter, the play."

Well done, Peabody, Eve thought, and let her roll.

"Wounds that never heal." After snagging another tissue, Debra balled it in her fist. "How can the world be so cruel, so cruel? How can it be that woman has everything, everything Rose should have?"

"And now," Peabody continued, "bringing *Upstage* back to Broadway, to Crystal Gardens, the same theater, exploiting that, celebrating that, dredging up all that pain again. It's brutal, just brutal."

"It is, it is!" Debra actually reached across the table to grip one of Peabody's hands. "How could I bear it? What mother could?"

"You had to find a way to stop it, to stop her. What else could you do?" Peabody gave the hand gripping hers a squeeze, as if she understood. "She'd never paid for what she'd done."

"Profited, always."

"You found a way to get in, get close, right inside her big, beautiful home. A home she built on Rose's bones. You risked everything, what mother wouldn't, to avenge your beloved daughter."

"I wanted what was mine! What was Rose's," she corrected quickly.

"Risked everything," Peabody said again. "Lowered yourself to scrubbing, polishing what should have been Rose's so Eliza Lane could have her big celebration, one that should have been yours and Rose's, twenty-five years of a life that should've been yours."

"I'd worked so hard, gave so much." She laid the back of her free hand against her brow. "We were so close."

"You stayed behind when the others left, found a place to hide, to wait, to change so you could blend in with the party. Where?"

"A guest room on the third floor. Nobody was working. Assistants and assistants, as if that woman ever truly worked a day in her miserable life."

"You took the award. That was risky, too. Someone might have noticed."

"I took what was rightfully mine—Rose's. And she was much too busy primping and posing and ordering people around to go into her self-important office."

"Taking the award wasn't enough, of course. You had to finish it, pay Eliza back for Rose, for all the years, for daring to bring *Upstage* back to Broadway."

"I had a right! A mother's right."

"You styled the blond wig, put on the cocktail dress, fresh makeup." All understanding, Peabody exuded encouragement. "But you had to get downstairs without calling any attention to yourself."

"It's simply a matter of timing and playing a role." Debra brushed at her hair. "I'm a performer."

"But you had that bag, that big bag holding the maid's uniform, the award you'd taken."

Now Debra smiled. "The greeter at the door, one of the"—she used her fingers to make quotes in the air—"assistants. I simply walked up behind her. 'Oh, darling, would you mind tucking this into the closet here in the foyer?' Expect, don't explain." She shrugged. "She put it away, and I had some champagne, mingled, ate some lovely canapés. I even had a lovely bit of conversation with Brant Fitzhugh. A pity such a charming man wasted a decade on that creature."

"You talked to Brant?" Peabody said pleasantly.

"I made a point to. He couldn't have been more charming."

"I bet. Is that when you poisoned the champagne?"

"What?" Debra shot back in the chair. "What are you talking about? Have you lost your mind?"

"You didn't mean for him to drink it. It was for Eliza. How could you know?"

"That's insane!" The red wash came back to her face. "You're trying to trick me."

"You said it yourself," Peabody pointed out. "You had a right."

"To the Tony! To the party, the champagne, the caviar. To bask in what should've been mine. All of it. To poke around in her things, to see how she lived. I had a right!"

Eve stepped in. "You entered her home in disguise and under false pretenses. You laid in wait, for over five hours. You stole her property."

"Claimed. I claimed what was *mine*!"

"Call it what you like." Eve pushed up, leaned in. "You snuck downstairs to eat her food, drink her champagne. A woman you hate, a woman you believe took everything that matters to you, everything you want for yourself. And what, you want us to believe you just strolled out and less than twenty minutes later her husband's dead, dead after drinking the champagne meant for her?"

"I had nothing to do with that! I didn't even know about it until the next morning."

"Bullshit." Eve slapped her hands on the table and made Debra jump. "You didn't risk getting busted for a statue, one with her name on it."

"I—I'm going to have her name removed."

"I can buy that one. And have your name put in its place? Yours, because all of this is about you."

"That's insulting!"

"Murder's a lot more insulting. You were smart to get out before she drank it—or you thought she would. You've been around, you know how it goes. She drops, the cops show up. You can't be there to see that—what is it?—curtain call. But you had the ending written in your head. She pays, finally pays. She'll never stand in the spotlight again, in that play again."

"I left because I had what was mine. I left because . . . she saw me. I'd been careful, but she saw me, and I think—she might have recognized me. So I got my bag and I left."

"Where'd you get the cyanide?" Eve demanded.

"I didn't get any cyanide! I didn't kill anyone. She probably killed him herself. He probably finally saw through her and wanted a divorce. He was going to leave her, humiliate her. Everybody knows he was leaving for six months—it's all over the entertainment blogs. He was leaving her and never coming back, so she killed him."

She buried her face in her hands. "Like she killed my precious Rose."

"Where's all the money? You wheedled fifteen thousand. You sure didn't spend it on accommodations. Where did you drop over nine thousand in under two weeks, Debra? How much did the cyanide cost you?"

"I didn't buy any cyanide. I had expenses. I needed salon treatments and a new wardrobe. I had to pay for the résumés and the references and that horrible hotel. I had to eat! I had expenses!"

She lifted her head, and this time the tears seemed real enough.

"I have nothing more to say. She's probably paying you to do this to me. I want a lawyer. I want to contact a lawyer, now. I have nothing more to say until I get a lawyer."

"Your choice, Debra. You'll need a good one." Eve hefted the evidence box. "Dallas and Peabody exiting Interview. Suspect will be taken to holding and allowed to contact or request a lawyer, as she has invoked that right.

"Interview end."

18

"Have a couple of uniforms take her down," Eve said when they stood outside of Interview.

"I thought we had her."

Eve just shook her head. "Good job in there, the way you strung her along. Damn good job, and we've got a solid picture of what she did, when and how, in her own words, on record."

"Not a confession."

"Round one. Go ahead and take this back to Evidence." She passed the box to Peabody. "We'll see if McNab finds anything more interesting on her e's."

She started to walk back to the bullpen. She needed to think, to go over everything she'd learned in Interview. Time for quiet, she told herself, and time to ditch the frustration of dealing with a liar with a persecution complex.

Poor fucking me, she thought, then stopped when she saw Reo and Mira step out of Observation. Roarke followed them.

"I was only able to observe the last few minutes," Mira began.

"I can have the record copied to you if you want to evaluate the whole. Peabody softened her up, and McNab's going through her PPC and 'link now, thoroughly. We've got her on possession and use of false IDs, trespass, theft."

"But not the murder," Reo pointed out.

"No. She's only got about two thousand left out of the fifteen thousand she wheedled. We'll track her salon expenses, the wardrobe, any other purchases. At this point, she doesn't have enough left for a lawyer, and that means public defender. She may have more to say in a second round after she spends the night in a cell."

"I want to review the entire interview, but from what I observed, she didn't just feel entitled to the award, she considers it hers, through her daughter. That's a key point," Mira stressed. "Hers—for all her years of sacrifice. Rose was her conduit to fame, to fortune. And when that means to all she deserved was cut off, others were and are to blame. She bears no responsibility."

"She pointed the finger pretty hard at Lane," Reo commented. "Which, in turn, points a finger at motive. The timing's tight—her exit, and time of death—but it'll hold. She was on scene through false pretenses, and for several hours. Round two could break the rest.

"I'll see if I can get a line on who she pulls as PD."

"I'll send you my evaluation after I've reviewed the full interview," Mira added.

They split off, with Roarke falling into step with Eve. "I saw a bit more than Mira," he told her. "The woman's a player. A successful grifter needs to believe his own bollocks to make others believe. She's managed to stay out of the nick for the most part because she knows how to play the game."

"She fell for Peabody's tactic."

"She did, as Peabody reinforced her own beliefs, and very clev-
erly," he added. "Here, she likely thought, is someone who under-
stands, while also thinking, as a solid con requires, ah, here's a mark
I can use."

"Right." She walked into her office and straight to her board. "Fuck,
fuck, fuck!" The frustration she'd struggled to shove away shoved
back. Hard. "I have to go back to the beginning. Everything starts at
the damn beginning."

"True enough." He programmed them both coffee.

"She soaks a trio of idiots for fifteen K but spends close to two
weeks living in the next step up from a craphole. She spends hours
scrubbing up her mortal enemy's home, and all so she can drink some
champagne, eat some caviar, and walk out with a statue with someone
else's name on it?"

She whirled on Roarke. "That's not just crazy, it's stupid."

"It's difficult to disagree. Are you worried you won't break her?"

"She lies, that's how she lives. But there was truth in there. Peabody slid the truth right out of her." After rubbing at her eyes, Eve
stared at the board again. "Back to the damn beginning. Meanwhile
I have to give another time-waster of a media briefing because my
victim's name sells clicks and views."

Resentment for that bubbled up with frustration as she turned to
him again. "What are you doing here?"

"At the moment, listening to you vent."

"Here," she said, pointing to the floor between them. "Now."

"I had a meeting in the area."

"Yeah, you've been saying that a lot the last few weeks. What the
hell, Roarke?"

His eyebrows winged up, but he spoke calmly. "Is there a problem
with me observing a part of your interview in this case, Lieutenant?"

"If I say there is, after you put in your own time to contribute to the investigation, I'm an asshole. And that's not what I'm doing or saying anyway."

And wouldn't, she thought as she dragged a hand through her hair.

"I'm asking what the hell. You pop up in here at least once a week lately. Why aren't you furthering your plans for world domination or finding a way to buy Scandinavia?"

"Those might be considered one and the same."

"I mean it. It's a valid question, and I want a straight answer."

"All right then. I think you could use a boost."

"I don't need a damn booster."

"Not that kind of boost." He set his coffee aside. "I'll be back in a few minutes."

"What? Wait a minute. Where—"

But he just kept walking.

"Sometimes marriage is Crazytown." She dropped down in her desk chair, stared at the board. "Crazytown."

She closed her eyes a moment, tried her meditation mantra—*Fuck this, fuck this, fuck this*—to clear her mind. Sometimes it worked.

The beginning. And if Debra's reasons for getting into the penthouse, the party, taking an award—a trophy, a symbol—were to settle the score, a grudge against Lane, Rose Bernstein's death marked the beginning.

Or at least one point on the circle.

If Rose lives, maybe she wins the Tony—maybe not. Maybe she becomes a big celebrity, or burns out, or ODs at another time. But.

If she'd lived another day, another week, another month, everything that followed would follow from there. A different circle.

If Lane were the target, as the evidence, logic, and probability deemed, the choice of time and place for the murder put the play—the original and the revival—dead center of the circle.

Rose Bernstein connected to Lane, to Minerva Novak, to Gary Proctor, and to Debra Bernstein. And who on that short list was on scene? Take off Gary Proctor. Who on the shorter list had no legitimate business being there?

Only one. Debra Bernstein. A liar, a grifter, a thief.

Eve pushed up, paced as she went over the interview in her head, picked at details.

Annoyed with herself, she sat again, began to make fresh notes.

And Roarke walked back in carrying a large box.

"What's this?"

"Your anniversary gift."

"Jesus. It's not our anniversary yet, and I'm not looking for a present. I'm maybe going off on a tangent here," she added, shoving at her hair again. "I just need to lay it out and see."

"Open the bloody box, Eve."

"Damn it. Fine." She shoved up, yanked off the top. And stared inside. "What the hell? I'm wearing the magic lining." She held her jacket open to prove it. "It's not like somebody tries to stun or knife me every shift. Why a big-ass box of more?"

"These aren't for you to wear, Lieutenant. They're for your bullpen. This group at least."

"I don't—" She could only stare at him. "What?"

"We've been working with your commander and Tibble, and others, on this project for a while. The one you're wearing was the prototype, and once we had the tech, we've been able to begin production, which took a bit of time, as people will come in different sizes and shapes. It'll take a bit more time to produce enough to outfit the entire NYPSD. After some . . . negotiation, it was agreed to begin with Homicide, with your bullpen."

"Negotiation."

"It's a happier word than *ultimatum*. Roarke Industries will donate the Thin Shield—the brand name—to the NYPSD at no cost, with the agreement your division gets the first produced.

"Happy anniversary—a bit ahead of schedule."

She walked away from him; she had to. She walked away to rest her forehead on the glass of her skinny window.

"Every time I think I have you, have most of all this figured out, you throw in a curve. You flatten me. You just . . . flatten me."

"You wear that under your jacket for me. You wear it primarily so I'll worry less. You're in charge of everyone out there, people I've come to know and care for through you. This makes them a bit safer, and you'll worry less."

"They're cops. The job means—"

"I know what it means. To you, to those under your command, to others I know here. I can't and won't say it means to all with a badge what it does to you, to them. For some it's only about power and a license to wield it how they choose. I've known too many of that ilk to say otherwise."

He did. He did. And that part caught in her throat.

"But you'll outfit the entire department."

"I've neither the time nor the inclination to comb through and judge the deserving. I married a cop, and she works for the NYPSD. Whitney cleared you to distribute. They're labeled with name and rank."

She turned back to him, her eyes brimming with the emotion that flooded through her. "There's nothing, absolutely nothing, that could mean more to me than you knowing what this means to me."

She went to him then, pressed her face to his shoulder as his arms came around her.

"Absolutely nothing," she murmured. "I can't get the words out."

"The ones you did worked very well."

She lifted her head, framed his face in her hands. "Thank you."

When she kissed him, it was soft.

"Aww," Peabody said when she came to the doorway. "And oops."

"Peabody," Eve said, her eyes still on Roarke's. "I need everyone who's not in the field in the bullpen asap."

"Um, sure. Okay."

When Peabody hurried off, Roarke kissed Eve again. "Let me know if you manage another round with your suspect and will run late."

"Doubtful on the second round, but I have some things to work out in my head. What do you call the center of a circle?"

"The center."

"Really? No fancy word for it? How about the . . ." She drew a circle in the air.

"I think you're meaning circumference, the distance around it. Or you can think of it opened and straightened into line segments and—"

"That. That's what I'm trying to see."

"Then you could call it as the limit of the perimeters of—"

"Stop." She actually put her hands over her ears. "You're about to math stress me. It's the straight lines, point by point, and bent into the circle. I have to work on that."

"Good luck with it. I'm going to swing by Mavis's, since I'm this close. I'll let you get on with all of it."

"Oh, no you don't. Grab the box."

"I'd as soon—"

"I know what you'd as soon. You're not the only person who knows the person they married. So too bad. Consider this a part of the gift."

"That's a bit underhanded," he said, but picked up the box.

Thinking of circles, of beginnings, she walked out to the bullpen.

"Heads-up. This division is the first recipient of Thin Shield body armor." She opened her jacket. "If you have any questions about this new safety issue, you can ask the guy here who came up with it. I can tell you—from personal experience—it stops a sharp, a stun, and a bullet. It's lightweight and can—and will—go under your jacket just like your weapon, or your uniform top. Chief Tibble and Commander Whitney have accepted this donation to Homicide initially, and the whole of the NYPSD to follow, from Roarke Industries. I gratefully accept same as Lieutenant of this division.

"Detective Jenkinson, would you see these are distributed? They're labeled by name and rank. And see that those for any officers in the field go into the locker until such time as they can be distributed."

"Yes, sir." He pushed up from his desk. "I got something to say first on behalf of every cop in this bullpen, unless they're a stupid son of a bitch. There's a reason we pick up a badge and do the job, and it's right up there."

He pointed to the motto posted over the break-room door.

NO MATTER YOUR RACE, CREED,
SEXUAL ORIENTATION, OR POLITICAL AFFILIATION,
WE PROTECT AND SERVE,*
BECAUSE YOU COULD GET DEAD.

*EVEN IF YOU WERE AN ASSHOLE.

"Not everybody gets that. Not everybody with a badge gets it, either, and fuck every one of them. It means something when somebody not only gets it but gives a rat's ass."

He walked forward, took the box. Then passed it to Eve before holding out a hand for Roarke's.

"Thanks for getting it, for not being a stupid son of a bitch, and giving a lot more than a rat's ass."

"You're welcome on all counts."

Since it was closest, Jenkinson set the box on Peabody's desk, opened it, pulled out the first clear-wrapped vest. "Yo, Santiago, come get your prize."

"I'll just be on my way," Roarke began.

"Stand where you are, ace."

Santiago walked to Roarke first, held out a hand. "What Jenkinson said."

And so followed every cop in the room.

It took time, but Eve judged the time well worth it. Back at her desk, she looked at her notes—not really fresh, considering.

Did she see another pattern just because, or was it there? And where did you go if and when you thought you saw another pattern, but it made no damn sense?

You followed it, she told herself, and began to.

Circles, centers, the points that made a straight line before it evolved into the curve or arc or whatever the hell that brought it all together into that circle.

Had to follow it through, she decided. Or more accurately, backtrack.

Even as she rose, Reo hotfooted it into her office.

"Son of a bitch! Coffee. I've got approximately four minutes for coffee."

She didn't wait for Eve's go-ahead but hit the AC.

"Bernstein didn't pull a PD." Reo, the picture of irate in her rosy suit and fluffy blond hair, gulped coffee. "Damn. Hot. Shit! She hooked Carlton J. Greene."

Eve knew the name. Cops and prosecutors knew the name Carlton J. Greene, the diamond standard of criminal defense attorneys renowned for his dogged and dignified style, dealmaking, and record of acquittals.

"He retired. He retired like four, maybe five years ago."

"Well, he's come out of retirement for this." Reo gulped more coffee, more cautiously this time. "And he's pushed for a bail hearing now. Pretty much now. And whether it's our bad luck or he found a way to fix it, we've got Judge Pointer."

"Ah, fuck me."

"I'll fight it. Bernstein's got priors, a history, she was in possession of stolen property, false identification, and is, for good reasons, our primary suspect in Brant Fitzhugh's murder."

Reo let out a hiss, a sigh, finished the coffee. "But it's Pointer, and she loves to strap 'em, track 'em, and spring 'em. She'll set a high mark for bond, but—"

"If Bernstein found a way to get Greene—who doesn't do pro bono—out of retirement, she's got someone with deep pockets fronting her."

Eve turned to her board, decided she had a very good idea on who owned those pockets.

"I've got to get to court. I'll fight it," Reo repeated, "but I hate to say, I'm going to lose. I'll make it sting." Her eyes slitted. "I can make it sting, and ensure Bernstein reports here for further questioning tomorrow morning."

"I'll clear her hotel room, and I'll put a couple of men on the building. It's not a cell, but it's not paradise, either."

"Carlton J. Greene." Reo said the name like an oath and hotfooted it out again.

Eve snarled at Maeve Spindal's photo on her board. "It's going to be you. Just another way to stick it to Eliza Lane. One more way."

She hit the interoffice comm. "Peabody!"

Since she wouldn't make it back to the office, Eve copied her notes as Peabody hurried in.

"They're going to spring Bernstein on bail—"

"What the fuck?"

"Carlton J. Greene." Before Peabody's time, Eve realized. "High-dollar, high-acquittal-rate defense—and I'm putting my money on Spindal arranging it. And it's going before Judge Pointer."

"Oh hell, not Punt 'em Pointer."

"Have Bernstein's hotel room cleared, and assign two uniforms to sit on the building. Four-hour shifts—I want them sharp. She'll have a tracker, but I wouldn't bet on her not getting around it."

"And she's good with wigs and makeup."

"Fill them in, and get them over to the West End Hotel. I want them on it before she goes back."

"I'll put Carmichael and Shelby on the first shift. Why the hell would Spindal dump that kind of money into this?"

"Circles. She's got it in for Lane, this is a way to give Lane a nice slap. It's only money. I'm going to go inform her, work from home."

"Media briefing."

"Yeah, that's on you."

A measurement for the level of shock and horror on Peabody's face didn't exist. "Dallas!"

"You can handle it. Contact Kyung, tell him I'm in the field, notifying Lane the primary suspect is about to make bail. And pursuing a new angle."

"But—"

"Then read my notes on the new angle."

"There's a new angle?"

"Circles don't have angles, do they? A new . . . point of reference or whatever. Go."

Eve beat her out of the room, out of the bullpen, and hit the glides. She pulled out her 'link to start the ball rolling.

"Mr. Proctor," she said the minute his face came on-screen. "This is Lieutenant—"

"Dallas. I recognize you. I spoke with Detective Peabody before."

"Yes, and I'd like to follow up with you. Now, if you're available."

"Sure. Corrine! Turn down the music. Sorry—kids. How can I help?"

"I'd like to do this in person. I can come to you."

"Oh." Obviously distracted, he looked around. "Sure. I honestly don't know what else I can tell you, and I have to be at the theater in a couple hours."

"It won't take that long. I'm on my way now."

She banged down the steps to the garage.

And if this turned out to be a waste of time, she'd make it up later.

As she pushed through traffic, she tagged Roarke.

"I'm probably going to be late—said I'd let you know."

"All right. Round two?"

"No, it looks like Bernstein's going to make bail."

He said nothing for a moment. "What a strange system runs between law and order."

"It's the one we've got. I need to talk to some people, and notify Lane so she'll take precautions."

"Do you think Bernstein will try again?"

"I don't. She may try to rabbit, but I've got cops on her building. She's too fond of her own skin to try again at this point. Which is why . . ." She shook her head. "I don't know. I'm still working it out, probably chasing the wild duck."

"Goose. I'm just home myself. Can I help you?"

"No, no thanks. I just want to reel this out, I guess. I'll see you when I get there."

She worked her way up to Proctor's building, a nice faded brick on the north edge of Chelsea. Since parking looked hopeless, she considered doubling it, then pulled into a No Parking zone in front of a recycler.

With her On Duty light engaged, she stepped out onto the sidewalk and the river of people navigating it.

Restaurants and cafés with outdoor seating enjoyed a booming business, and it seemed to her people went into the shops as quickly as others came out with shopping bags.

What did they do with all the stuff? she wondered. Didn't they ever run out of room?

She walked by a trio of women sipping wine at a table under an awning. Each one had a rat-size dog sitting in her lap, and shopping bags tucked under the table.

Baskets of flowers hung from the posts that supported the awning, and the women's easy laughter flowed on the summer air.

A man strutted by wearing a panama hat and what she thought was a seersucker suit in pale blue. She judged him about fifty years senior to the woman on his arm in skyscraper heels, a white dress with a skirt about the size of a dinner napkin, a waist-length fall of glossy red hair—and a white rose tucked behind her ear.

Not an LC, Eve concluded, but from the shopping bags on his other arm, he was definitely paying for the companionship.

When she reached Proctor's building, she pressed the intercom.

"Four-oh-five."

"Lieutenant Dallas."

"Come right on up."

The door buzzed and she stepped into a small lobby that smelled like fake lemons. She might have preferred the stairs, but factored time and the fact the elevator looked reasonably safe.

It carried her up to four, where Gary Proctor stood outside the open door of his apartment holding the hand of a kid—the boy type—of about six. Both had springy brown curls and big, soulful brown eyes. Music spilled out of the doorway, but more muted than it had been over the 'link.

"Mr. Proctor."

"Yes." He offered a hand. "Come in."

When she did, the kid stared up at her. "You're a policeman?"

She looked down to where he stood in baggy red shorts, a striped tee, and sneakers.

"Yes."

"You get to arrest people?"

"When I need to."

"You need to arrest my sisters."

He sounded so earnest, she played along. "What's the charge?"

"Corrine plays her music too loud, and Flora said I had poop breath, and I didn't, either. And they're girls."

"Those offenses fall beyond my jurisdiction and under parental authority."

He stared at her with those soulful eyes. "Huh?"

"She said I'm in charge." Gary gave the boy's hair a ruffle. "If you go play in your room and don't cause any trouble, I'll talk Mom into pizza for dinner when she gets home from work."

"Yay!"

The boy ran off in the direction of the music. A door slammed. Gary sighed.

"When you're six and outnumbered, being a girl is a crime against humanity. Have a seat. Can I get you something?"

"No, I'm good, thanks. I appreciate you taking the time."

She sat on a chair, sky blue with a diamond pattern in cream in a comfortably disordered living area. The wide front window let light flood in. Family photos grouped with dust catchers on the open shelves that flanked it.

Gary sat on the couch, pushed a couple of fussy pillows out of his way. "What is it," he wondered, "about pillows? Travis and I are outnumbered—three to two—so pillows on the sofa, on the beds."

"I have no idea."

He smiled at her, an appealing, easy smile that showed a hint of dimple in his left cheek. He had an athletic body, a dancer's body, Eve supposed. And seemed very comfortable in his own skin.

"I don't want to keep you long, Mr. Proctor, but I'm hoping you can remember more details about Rose Bernstein's death."

"Leah." His smile lost its luster. "She made it clear that wasn't just her name, but who she was now. I don't understand why you'd want to know about all of that."

"Just making sure we tie up any loose ends. You and she were close."

"As close as you could get to Leah. She was—I'd say the word is *mercurial*. And at nineteen I found that fascinating. She was this amazing puzzle, this tough, talented girl with a soft middle. We wanted the same things—theater. And not just theater, Broadway. The attraction between us was quick and hot. We worked, we rehearsed, went to class, went to bed."

"You knew about her addictions."

"Not at first. She was pretty good at hiding them. She wanted that part. She wanted Marcie Bright, and she earned it. I found pills at her place one night. She was careless, left them out. Or maybe, when I've looked back, I think maybe she wanted me to find them. I was concerned. She called them Mother's Little Helpers. Her mother. Said no big deal if she needed a boost, needed to sleep. But it didn't take long, even through the sexual haze, for me to see it was a big deal. To realize she often took them with vodka."

He let out a long breath. "God, I've thought more about her, and all of that, in the last twenty-four hours than I have in nearly that many years. I wasn't a saint, Lieutenant. I was underage but I didn't say no to a brew. We worked hard, often twelve, fifteen hours a day. But I had a family member who was a recovering alcoholic, and I knew the signs."

"You spoke with her about it."

"I did. She even went to a couple of meetings—if I went with her."

"Did you speak to anyone else about her addictions?"

"Her mother. Her mother came to my place and went off on me, said I was putting pressure on Leah, making demands, cheating on her, specifically but not exclusively, with Eliza. Men were all animals and so on, and stay away from her girl.

"I pointed out Leah was eighteen, lived on her own, had a career, and could make her own choices. She'd cornered me before, offered to have sex with me if I talked Leah into firing her agent. I told Detective Peabody."

"Yes. Is there something more you didn't tell Detective Peabody?"

"Actually . . ." He flushed a little, shot a glance toward the music. "This time around, when she went off on me, she grabbed my crotch. She just . . . grabbed me and said she'd show me what sex was really all about. All I had to do was stay away from Leah when we weren't onstage.

"I went off." He blew out a breath. "Really went off. She grabbed me by the . . ." He glanced back toward the bedrooms again. "Anyway. My roommate came out because I was yelling. I said it was her fault Leah took pills, drank too much, stuck her fingers down her throat if she ate a real meal. So we're yelling ugly things at each other, and she slapped me, caught the corner of my eye with a fingernail. Hurt like hell."

"You didn't mention the assault to Detective Peabody."

"No, and I realized after . . . I should've. It's embarrassing even now. It's not something I like to remember, to be honest. Because . . . I almost hit her back. I've never hit anyone, but I almost—I would have. I would have hit her if my roommate hadn't stepped in, told her to get the hell out or he'd throw her out."

"Did you tell Leah?"

"I didn't. Maybe I should have, but I thought it would make things worse for her."

"Anyone else?"

"Eliza. Eliza and Leah spent a lot of time together. The three of us did, on and off. They rehearsed together, hung out sometimes. Her mom just wouldn't leave her alone. Some days, Leah would tell them to keep her mother out, others it was fine, let her in so she can watch. Mercurial," he murmured. "Things got a little strained between us, and that would be the reason. From my end, I guess. Her mother was toxic, but Leah couldn't let her go, not all the way. Like another addiction."

He lifted his hands. "When I think about how young we were, how self-involved and naive—well, me on the naive anyway. So much I didn't know. If I'd known more, maybe I could've helped her more. Maybe I pushed too hard. Anyway, the heat was dying out between us. Then we're doing final dress—a friends and family night. She told me she'd had her mother barred, but I saw her mother walk right into her dressing room before curtain. It pissed me off. One thing, the performance, but another? I thought fine, she brought it on herself."

He glanced back once again. "And I didn't tell the detective this, either. Trying to shove it away again, I guess, but my wife, when I told her about talking to the detective, said how you shouldn't leave things out when talking to the police. And she's right."

"What did you leave out?"

"It probably doesn't mean anything, not after all this time. That night, between scenes—I honestly can't remember at what point now—I saw her again, this time going after Eliza. She actually slapped Eliza like she had me. I couldn't do anything about it. Eliza was stage right, I was stage left. Security got Mrs. Bernstein out, and I could see Eliza was shaken up."

"Did you speak with her about it?"

"I did. I asked her what she'd said—Mrs. Bernstein—and as I remember, Eliza just said, like, the usual or something along those lines. I was going to have it out with Leah after the performance because you can't come in and upset the players that way, you just can't. She needed to be banned. But when I went to Leah after—we were all going over to this club to hang out, unwind, celebrate because we really brought it down."

He blew out a breath, rubbed at his eyes. "Hell. When I went to her dressing room, she was drinking, the pills were out, and I'd had enough. Just enough. I told her if she wouldn't help herself, I was done. She said: 'Bye.' Just like that. Eliza and I walked over together, whined to each other some then—hell with it."

"Were you and Eliza ever intimate?"

"Eliza and me? No. No." He laughed. "One thing, I was burned. Another, she was seeing someone. Not serious, I don't think, but still. Most of us hung out until closing, about two, I guess."

"You, Eliza, and most of the cast?"

"Yeah, and some of the crew. Some of us walked around awhile after—it felt like we owned the city—and we dropped off Eliza and ah . . . Shelly, yeah, Shelly, she was in a swing. They lived in the same building. My roommate—Elliot, he's directing the play I'm in now—we peeled off and went home. We didn't hear about Leah until the next day.

"It didn't seem real," he murmured. "I said, the last thing: 'Enough. I'm out.' She said: 'Bye.' The last things we said to each other."

19

The interview gave her plenty to chew over, and a couple more names to check if she kept running along this line.

Toxic, he'd called Debra. And poison was poison whether it killed you emotionally, mentally, or physically.

She continued uptown, hugging the West Side until she got to Eliza's building. The doorman greeted her like an old friend.

"Hey, Lieutenant, how's it going? Don't you worry about your ride. I've got my eye on it."

"Appreciate it. Do you know if Ms. Lane's in the building?"

"She hasn't come out. Haven't seen her since that night. We sent up a card—the whole staff signed it. We're going to send flowers when we know where."

"I'm sure she appreciates it. Do you know if anyone's with her?"

"Well, Mr. Jacoby came in a couple hours ago, and I heard how Dolby and Ms. Ricardo went up this morning. Haven't seen them come out."

"Thanks." She went in and to the desk.

"Lieutenant, how can I help you?"

"Would you let Ms. Lane know I'm here to speak with her?"

"Of course, just one moment." He tapped his earpiece. "Ms. Ricardo, this is Robert at the desk. Lieutenant Dallas is here for Ms. Lane. Yes, thank you. You can go right up."

"Has she had any visitors today?"

"Her staff, and Mr. Jacoby. I believe all are with her now. We have had a few . . . adventurous journalists attempt entry. One offered me five thousand for entry to her private elevator."

"That's pretty adventurous."

He smiled. "I agree. My integrity is worth a great deal more than that."

"Who else can clear that elevator?"

"The desk, the head of security, and Ms. Lane or her staff from the penthouse. I can assure you no one with that authority would violate her privacy or security."

"Good to know."

No one had used it the day or evening of the murder—they'd already checked. But good to know.

She rode up, smooth as silk, and came out in the foyer, where Dolby Kessler waited for her.

He'd been crying recently, she noted, but offered her a smile.

"Thanks for coming. We've got Eliza out on the terrace—some vitamin D and fresh air." He glanced that way. "We've been working on plans for Brant's memorials. She needed a break. Guess we all did."

"I'm sorry I have to bring his loss back to the front of the line."

"No, no, anything you can tell her—us—helps. Um, Cela's up in her office making some of the arrangements. Do you need her?"

"I'd like to speak with everyone at once, at least briefly."

"I'll go get her. You can go right out."

"Mr. Kessler—"

"Dolby. I just don't go with the 'mister' thing."

"Dolby, on the day of the party, you were here when the cleaning crew arrived."

"I think so. Cela, Lin, and I were all upstairs that morning, dealing with stuff until, I guess, about maybe eleven? I'm not real sure."

"They were here when you left your office space."

"I know that for sure. I saw Aileen working on the second floor. She sort of heads things up."

"Alone?"

"She was working with somebody—I just don't remember the name right off. They had extra help because of the party. Eliza's fierce about everything being just so. I know Wayne fixed them all some lunch because I grabbed some myself. Eliza, Cela, and I ate in the dining room. Cela had a salon appointment, so she left right after lunch. Lin and Brant had lunch out and hit the gym for a bit. I guess I zipped out about five, maybe, to change for the party, but I was back before seven."

Since she'd already checked the security feed, she knew he had the times close enough.

"Did you go up to your office again, the third floor?"

"Not after lunch. Plenty to do, and we worked on tablets. And the cleaners had to get to that."

"All right. I'd appreciate it if you got Ms. Ricardo for me."

At a table under the shade of an umbrella, Eliza sat with Lin Jacoby. She'd twisted her hair into a stylishly careless knot and done some careful makeup.

Still, the signs of sleepless nights and strain showed through.

Lin, showing strain of his own, rose when Eve stepped out.

"Lieutenant. We've been so anxious to hear from you. Sorry," he said immediately. "Please sit. We've got some of Wayne's amazing raspberry lemonade, fruit, cheese."

As he poured her a glass, Eve sat. Eliza shifted her hands to her lap, gripped them together.

"You have news? Anything?"

"The investigation into your husband's death has been, and will be, our focus. We've made an arrest on related charges."

"An arrest?" Her hands flew to her face; her eyes filled. "Who? Who did this?"

"Related charges?" Lin said. "What does that mean?"

"It means this individual committed illegal acts that pertain to Mr. Fitzhugh's death. We're compiling evidence, and if and when we have evidence, we'll charge her with his murder."

"Her?" Eliza reached out to grab Lin's hand. "Who is she? Who is this woman who killed Brant?"

"She's not charged with his murder at this time. We can, however, prove she was on the premises, and stole your award for the original production of *Upstage*."

"My Tony?" Her face went blank. "I don't understand."

"You had your awards displayed in your office space. Have you been in there since the night of the party?"

"No. I . . . I've been at Sylvie's until this morning. She had a table reading, and it was time for me to come home, to start making arrangements. I haven't been upstairs at all yet. I just can't face it. Lin."

"I'll go check."

"There's no need. We have the item in evidence, and the individual admitted to the theft. It'll be returned to you as soon as possible."

"As if I care about that now! It's Brant. Why would this person steal my Tony and kill Brant? Who *is* she?"

"She's not charged with your husband's murder," Eve repeated. "Debra Bernstein."

"Debra . . . Do you mean Leah Rose's *mother*? But that's impossible.

She wasn't here. She'd never have been invited. I'd have seen her, surely, and recognized her."

Eve glanced over as Dolby and Cela stepped out.

"I think Dolby saw her. Dolby, can you describe the woman you saw cleaning with Aileen on the day of the party?"

"Um . . . I didn't pay much attention, just said hi to Aileen, and she said hi back, and this is . . . I don't know. She had blond hair, I think. Maybe a blond white woman."

"Debra Bernstein entered your apartment as a new hire for the cleaning company."

"Their screening is exceptional," Eliza interrupted.

"And Bernstein paid a considerable sum to have her references created and verified to pass that screening. She stayed back on a pretext when the rest of the cleaning crew left, then hid on the third floor."

"We never went back up there," Cela murmured. "After the lunch break, we didn't go back up there. No need. But I saw her, too, at the lunch break, in the kitchen with the others. Blond—a long blond braid. She wasn't at the party. I'd have seen her. I'm sure I would have."

"She changed her hair, her wardrobe, her appearance. You did see her. She asked you to put a large bag in the foyer closet."

Eyes huge, Cela covered her mouth with her hand. "Oh God. Oh, Eliza! I—"

"It's not your fault. Whatever happened, it's not your fault."

"She had a glass of wine, came up behind me. Blond, but sort of flowing and wavy. In a black dress." She shut her eyes. "Yes, yes, a black dress. A large summer bag—more a tote. I don't remember getting it back out for her, and I would! I never thought of it again. I'm so sorry."

"It's not your fault," Eliza said again. Her face was set now, her eyes hard. "She had my Tony in that bag, didn't she?"

"She did."

"And whatever held the poison that killed Brant."

"We haven't verified that yet."

"You're telling me this woman came into my house, stole my property, ate my food, drank my wine, swanned around my party, but you can't verify she poisoned my husband? Does two and two still make four in your world?"

"Eliza," Dolby murmured, and rubbed her shoulders.

"I . . ." The stone-cold fury on her face ebbed as she reached back to cover Dolby's hand. "I'm sorry. I apologize. Forgive me, I—"

"No need," Eve told her.

"Every need. You're working so hard, and I . . . I'm sorry," she repeated. "Dolby, would you get me a real drink? My nerves are shot. Not a champagne cocktail. I'll never drink one again. A Bellini."

"You bet." He bent down, kissed the top of her head. "You hang on now. We're all here for you."

"Dolby, would you mind? A gin and tonic."

Dolby gave Lin a nod. "Lieutenant?"

"On duty."

"Right. Cela?"

She just shook her head. "I was as close to her in the foyer as I am to you now. I should've recognized her. I should have. She's on the No Contact list."

"Has she tried to contact you, Ms. Lane?"

"Eliza, and not in several years. But I don't take chances with her type. When she could get press, she never failed to take a swipe at me. I can ignore that. Just as I ignored it when she tried to extort money out of me."

"When?"

"Oh God, it was right after Brant and I got together. She contacted me—I'll never know how she got my number—and threatened to go to Brant, to the press with how I plotted and cheated with Gary—Gary Proctor, who played Charlie—to drive Leah—or Rose as she insists on calling her—to overdose, to get the part of Marcie."

Eliza leaned her head back, shut her eyes. "I told her to fuck right off. I said exactly that. I never had that kind of relationship with Gary. We were friends, the way you are in a company. He cared about Leah. So did I. So did everyone. If anyone drove her to her death, it was her mother."

"Did she follow through?"

"Not that I know of, and I'm sure I would have. She'd ridden that story or some version of it before. That horse was tired."

She straightened again. "But she must believe it. How could she do this if she didn't actually believe it? She must be extremely unwell. If anything, I tried to help Leah. God knows Gary did. And yet she . . . all these years."

She rubbed at her throat with a hand that trembled lightly.

"I've never had children, but I've played mothers. A good actor has to be, know, feel, believe, so I understand to a point. But to blame me after all these years, to do all this. The Tony? She'd see it as Leah's—or more likely hers. Killing Brant . . . It was supposed to be me. He died because she wanted to kill me."

When Dolby came out with the drinks, she took it, stared at it. "At least she's been arrested, she's locked up while you prove the rest."

"She made bail."

Eliza lowered her glass. Her fingers went so white on the stem Eve braced for the snap.

"How could that happen? She killed my husband! You know that. You know she did."

"I know she used fake identification and references to gain entry to your home. I know she stole your property and remained hidden in your home for a number of hours. I know, by her own admission, she harbors a serious grudge against you, and I know she has a history of fraud and confidence games. The rest, I'm working on."

"But they just let her go?"

"She'll be required to wear a tracker. And to appear with her attorney at Cop Central tomorrow morning for a continuation of Interview. She ended the interview today by claiming her right to an attorney. And she pulled Carlton J. Greene out of retirement to represent her."

"I don't know who that is."

"He's a high-dollar criminal defense attorney. Very."

"And she could afford him?"

"Somebody could. Just as somebody could afford to pay her bail, one set at a million. That's a hundred thousand on the line, and Bernstein doesn't have anything like that."

"So she's whined and wheedled enough for all this, and can sleep in luxury tonight instead of in a cell."

"I can promise you her hotel isn't luxurious, but yeah, she gets a night out. I need you to go back to that first production of *Upstage*."

"Why?"

"Because that's when it started. This is where it ends. You had at least one altercation with Bernstein, on the night before the official opening."

"Oh, more than one, but that was a doozy, so I remember it very well. Friends and family night—it's a full dress with an audience of friendlies, some critics and reviewers, of course. Leah had banned Debra—except when she didn't. They had, at least to my eye, a strange, codependent relationship. I know she slithered her way into Leah's dressing room before curtain. Gary told me, and I could see Leah was upset. We didn't have time to talk about it then, but I could see it. I was in the wings, waiting for my cue into act two, when she— Debra—went at me. She said Leah was going to have me fired, which was a terrible lie, but it rattled me. She went off about me scheming to replace Leah, about Gary and me cheating and plotting together to ruin Leah.

"I fired back. Usually I just tried to avoid or ignore her, but I'm minutes from going out onstage and she's attacking me. And she slapped me. She actually hit me, and that was it. I had her tossed. I didn't say anything to Leah about everything her crazy mother said, but I— God, I was hard on her. I said she had to control her mother, keep her the hell away, not just from me but from the theater. And if she didn't, I was going to press charges. Others saw Debra hit me."

She drank deep. "Maybe I am partially to blame for her reaching for the pills and vodka. I said all that, stalked out, so maybe Debra's not altogether wrong."

"She is wrong." Lin reached across to her. "And you weren't. Aren't. You stood up for yourself. You had to."

"I was so angry. I was shaking. I still remember how I was shaking when the curtain went up for the second act. And I really let Leah have it. I've never told that story, not all of it. And not just because I took it out on Leah, but I didn't see any point in adding to it all. I told the police Debra and I argued, I couldn't lie about it, and that I told Leah about the argument. I . . . softened it all, I guess. A little."

She picked up her drink again. "I went to take off my stage makeup, my costume. I was toying with just going home—Debra had just ruined the night for me. But I ran into Gary, and he was upset. He told me Leah was at the vodka, and he'd had enough. Misery and company, I guess, so we walked over to the club together.

"It helped," she murmured. "I mean, we didn't know Leah was . . . We didn't know, and it had been such a good performance despite everything. Just being with everyone, reliving it all, it was such a lift."

"Have you kept in touch with Gary?"

"Yes, off and on. I went to his wedding. I know he was invited to the party. Why didn't he come, Cela?"

"His daughter's thirteenth birthday party."

"Oh, right." Eliza looked vaguely out toward the river. "That night changed everything. But we moved on. We had to. But not Debra. She hasn't, has she? She wanted me dead, and instead, it was Brant, who never harmed a soul, who never even knew Leah. And now Debra's facing prison. She'll never be able to move on now."

"Mr. Jacoby, did you notice the woman, the blonde in the black dress? She spoke with Mr. Fitzhugh at some point during the party."

"There were so many people, and Brant probably had at least a few words with most of them. I honestly don't know for certain."

"Eliza, she claims you looked at her, and she thought you may have recognized her. That's why she left at the time she did. You were near the foyer with Ms. Bowen."

"If I'd recognized her, she'd have been out on her ass." Eliza all but snarled it out. "I hate to admit it, but most of that night, it's hard to bring it into focus now. And while I may have seen a blonde in a black dress—she wouldn't have been the only one—I didn't recognize her. Not consciously anyway.

"What's going to happen now?" Eliza demanded. Tears swirled in her eyes but didn't fall. "Please tell me this lawyer someone bought for her won't help her get away with it. It can't end that way. It can't. We've spent nearly all day planning memorials for the man I loved with every bit of my heart."

"We're going to continue to work the case. We'll interview Bernstein again in the morning, with her lawyer. She can't deny she was here—we have her on the security feed, we have her fake ID, and she confessed to that during Interview. We know she blames you for her daughter's death, as she's said so, plainly, on record."

"Why now?" Cela murmured it, then shook her head. "I'm sorry, but it's so hard to understand why, after twenty-five years, this woman would go through all this to try to kill Eliza."

"The revival." Eliza answered before Eve spoke. "I can add two and two well enough. The revival and the buzz about it set her off. She saw herself, back then, in the part of the mother. Leah told me, and she laughed about it. It's how Debra got so tight with Maeve. Maeve wined and dined Debra to pick her brain about the character type."

Her eyes narrowed; her mouth tightened. "Maeve Spindal, of course. She had a real soft spot for Debra and a serious hard-on for me. She'd help Debra now, no question about it. She'd pay for an important lawyer and for bail. She absolutely would find it entertaining."

"I'm not able to access that kind of information."

"Two and two," Eliza repeated with a sharp, angry shrug. "And Debra took the Tony because killing me wouldn't be enough for her. She had to have that, that tangible thing, but it wouldn't be enough."

She covered her eyes with a hand for a moment. "I'd have given her the damn Tony. I'd have given her all my awards, if only I could have Brant."

She dropped her hand, stared out at the city.

"Now I'm alive, and she won't have the tangible thing, either, but a long time in prison. It all fell apart for her. And Brant's dead. He's gone."

She set the drink down, rose. "Excuse me a moment."

"She's trying so hard to hold up." Lin looked after her. "She's tough, but this is all too much. She's determined to go into rehearsals tomorrow. I thought, mistake. Take another few days first. But now I think maybe it'll help."

"I know it's difficult." Eve got to her feet. "Please let her know I'll be in contact with any developments."

"I'll show you out." Cela walked her to the elevator.

"She was standing right here, and I put the bag in the closet."

"Do you remember the time?"

"People were still arriving. I think around eight-thirty, or not long after. I hadn't left the door or done my first sweep of the upper floors."

"Eliza's office is included in that sweep?"

"Yes. I didn't notice the award was missing. Eliza has so many awards. If I had . . . He was so kind, Lieutenant. He was such a kind man. She has to pay for this. She has to."

Eve took the smooth ride down, thinking everything she'd heard here lined up neatly with what she'd heard in Interview.

And still.

She checked in with Officer Carmichael. Debra had just arrived at her hotel by cab. Her tracker verified her location.

On a whim as she drove home, she contacted Maeve Spindal.

"Ah, Lieutenant Dallas."

Eve decided the woman rode in a plush car or limo, a glass of champagne in her hand.

"How'd you talk Greene out of retirement?"

Maeve smiled and sipped. "We're old friends. Good friends. At one time, long ago, more than friends."

"You'd pay his freight for someone like Debra Bernstein?"

"Why not? The woman's down and out while the Icove cop and Eliza Lane team up to railroad her for murder."

"I'm NYPSD's cop, and Eliza Lane isn't on my team. You shelled out for her bail, too. Hell of an investment. Did she tell you she faked her way into the victim's home, laid in wait, stole property—the award Lane won for *Upstage*—and crashed the party?"

Maeve shrugged. "None of those transgressions add up to murder. Now, I've just come off a stellar performance. I'd like to enjoy my champagne."

"Go right ahead. You might not feel so smug when you find out you backed the wrong horse."

"I've lost bets before. Good night, Lieutenant."

She cut Eve off as Eve drove through the gates.

"Smug bitch. Love, just love to find a way to tie you into the murder."

But shook her head because she just didn't see it.

When she parked, she sat a moment. Too much in her head, she admitted. Circles, lines, connections, gaps.

Lies and truths. And sometimes, she thought, truths had a way of hiding lies.

Summerset and Galahad waited when she walked in.

Eve gave him a narrow look. "Smug goes for smug," she decided. "So I bet you think Maeve Spindal is just terrific."

"The actress?" He lifted a—smug to her mind—eyebrow. "I saw her once with my wife—before she was my wife, long ago, in the world that was before. Young, so young, all of us then. She was quite good. Years later, during the Urbans, after I lost my wife, we worked to put on a sort of benefit for the wounded and the lost. We had a number of performers donate their time and their talents. She wouldn't. She named a fee well beyond reach and sent word through her representative she was a professional, and professionals were paid.

"I haven't thought much of her since. Art without heart is hollow, after all."

"Smug bitch then, smug bitch now."

She thought about it as she walked upstairs, the cat at her heels.

Some people—mainly most people—just didn't change. Some did, sure. Some because they wanted to, some because something shifted in their lives. But smug bitch then and now? Not unusual. Not at all.

When she walked into her office, she heard Roarke in his so she peeked in.

Work mode, she saw as he sat swiping and scrolling at some air holo with symbols, numbers, drawings that meant absolutely nothing to her. Hair tied back, jacket and tie gone, sleeves rolled.

And more, not just concentration on his face, but frustration.

She started to back out, but he saw her.

"You're busy."

"I am, bugger it. I have to deal with this fuckup."

She started—knee-jerk—to offer her help. Then thought about the symbols and numbers and admitted she wouldn't know where to begin.

"I'll get out of your way."

"Another thirty, I'm thinking. I nearly have it. Nearly. Bloody hell, there's the thing. And when I'm done, I want a very big drink."

She stepped out, actually set the timer on her wrist unit. She opened her terrace doors, drew in some summer air while she heard Roarke's thickening Irish cursing those weird symbols.

After programming coffee, she updated board and book, then sat, feet up, and thought about a new circle.

20

When Roarke came out, Eve stood at her board, hands in pockets. "How bad was it?" she asked.

"It could've been entirely worse."

Because he needed it after the last hour of work, he walked to her, kissed her.

"What was it?"

"Hmm? Ah, bollocksed programming, misread code, fecking the system right up across a particular network. Fixed now, and I'm after that drink."

"Wine's on the table."

He glanced over, saw the two domed plates, the wine bottle, glasses, the basket of bread.

"Well now, look at this."

His pleased and obvious surprise had her rolling her eyes before he took her hand to walk to the table by the open balcony doors.

Lifting a dome, he found fish and chips.

"And not pizza."

"Yeah, well, pizza was the default choice, but I resisted. Fish and chips is kind of your comfort food, so I get points for that."

"You do indeed." He poured wine generously into the glasses. "Thanks for this."

"You'd do the same for me. You do the same for me pretty much always."

"We've both had a day, haven't we? And though you no doubt have more work, here's to the end of it." He tapped his glass to hers. "And before I ask about yours, there's some news you'd have interest in."

"I know! Peabody chose the paint color for her craft room. Don't keep me in suspense. Is it Passion Pink or Blissful Blue? Or maybe, just maybe, she went wild with Orangutan Orange. I can't wait to hear!"

Laughing, he nudged her into a chair, then took his own. "I believe she's nearly there, but this is regarding another piece of property, Lower West."

"Don't you already own the Lower West? Wait. Is this Mary Kate Covino's ex-asshole, that fucker Teegan Stone? The bar with his apartment above?"

"It is, yes. Negotiations with the building's owner finalized shortly ago." He toasted her again, drank, then sampled the fish while she rained a monsoon of salt on everything on her plate.

"Then you get to kick him the hell out. See how he likes it."

"That would be up to you. You bought it."

Her jaw dropped. "I did not."

"Once the papers are drawn up and you sign, you will have. It's a good investment," he continued as she goggled at him. "Solid bones there and an excellent location. I'd advise investing, oh, another two-fifty, three hundred into it. Give it a good polish and upgrade."

"You don't mean hundred. It's thousand, three hundred thousand."

"If a thing's worth doing." He offered her half a slice of buttered brown bread. "There are other tenants, of course, but the inconvenience to them could be minimized—and the benefit to them worth that inconvenience—if you decided to concentrate that work primarily on the commercial area, and the unit directly above."

"Stoner's and his I-Bang-and-Discard-Women apartment."

Roarke sampled a chip. "His unit does have that vibe, doesn't it? Well, in point of fact, the commercial area needs some work on the infrastructure, which is why negotiations took a bit of time."

Enjoying himself, he drank some wine before he continued.

"Of course, with that kind of investment, and the time it takes for the polish and upgrade, the current bar owner may need to find another venue for his business. Up to you," he said again.

"It's kind of mean, but all I have to do is think of Covino locked in that basement for days. That's on Dawber, but Stone sure as hell added to it by not giving a rat's ass. But I don't know what to do with a damn building, how to polish and upgrade. I can't go around owning a building."

"Aren't you lucky to have someone who not only knows but enjoys it? Your find, after all, and a bloody good one at that. Now, your day?"

She stabbed a chip and decided not to think about owning a building. "Ups and downs. Nearly had Bernstein nailed—nearly. Then she lawyers—and that smug snot Spindal buys her a BFD lawyer just for spite. Even Summerset doesn't like that smug snot."

He smiled at that. "Is that so?"

"Not important. She made bail, Bernstein—and Spindal's responsible there, too. Bernstein's wearing a bracelet, and I've got men on the building, but."

More than annoyance here, he thought. Something more under that.

"Are you worried she'll manage to undermine the tracker and try for Eliza Lane again?"

"No." She stabbed another chip. "Maybe she'd work on the tracker, but if she managed that, she'd rabbit. Or try to."

"Cut her losses."

"Yeah, so cops on the building, and if she tries, there goes the bail money the smug snot put up, and it weighs heavy on Bernstein's: 'Okay, I did all of that, but I didn't kill anybody,' when we have her back in the box tomorrow."

"Big-deal lawyer or not, you'll break her down."

"Peabody played her like . . ." Eve mimed drawing a bow over strings.

"A violin?"

"Yes, but no. The person doing the playing."

"Violinist, Eve."

"No. Bigger." She spread her arms up to demonstrate. "Big deal like the lawyer."

"Virtuoso?"

"That's it! She played her like that. Virtuoso—good word. But."

She scowled at the fish, ate some.

"You're not worried about pulling a confession out of Bernstein," Roarke realized. "You're worried she didn't do the murder after all."

"She was there, and she shouldn't have been. And she spent a hell of a lot of other people's money to get there. I checked with the salon she used, and she spent over four thousand, fucking thousand, on treatments and services."

Scowling over that alone, she reached for her wine.

"Then the party dress and shoes—close to another four on that. That's over half the fifteen she had right there. Her fee to get the references and the verification to get the cleaning job. I'd say she got the friends and colleagues discount there, but it's another three. So the problem is, when you factor in the food and lodging, what she had left, what she had in her damn shopping bags when we busted her, it adds up."

She drank some wine while he watched her.

"She could've had more," Eve continued. "Could've had more in cash, or she brought the poison before she hit New York and wheedled the fifteen."

"But," Roarke said.

"Yeah, but, but, fucking but. Peabody's playing her like the virtuoso deal, and Bernstein's singing the tune. It's all, 'She did this to me, and all I wanted was that.' We've got her, it's all right there. But we hit her with the murder, and . . ."

"An and instead of a but," Roarke commented as Eve stared at the board.

"I saw her face. Is she that good? She likes to pump herself up as a performer. Is she that good? Maybe it's like you said, a good con artist has to believe the con. Maybe it's that. And maybe she's that stupid under it all. She admits everything—not that she had much choice, because we had her. She more than admits it, though, going off on how she hates Lane, how Lane's responsible for her dead daughter. She hands up motive on a platter."

"The smart thing would be to play up how she only wanted the memento, the award. A mother in perpetual mourning. You could pick that apart, of course."

"Sure, if that was all, why didn't she steal the damn thing and leave with the rest of the crew? Then poof. But she didn't, because she did want more. They'll play it that way tomorrow, on her lawyer's advice, and he'll get shrinks in there and all that."

Brooding over it, she ate some of the mushy peas on her plate. "And we'll pick it apart, and they'll move to she wanted to stand in for her dead daughter at the party, the celebration of this landmark revival, blah blah. Harmless, really, just a chance to play dress-up and hob with the nob."

Rolling it, rolling it, rolling it, she ate more fish. "It's sick, it's twisted, it's stupid, it's obsessive. But what if it's true?"

He considered it as he topped off his wine. "You're fond of saying coincidence is bollocks."

"Because it is. But isn't there this thing about you need one to prove that out?"

"Ah. The exception proves the rule."

"This could be that. Coincidence, yeah, but it's also, from another angle, just another point on the circle when you start the circle with Rose Bernstein's death."

She sat back with her wine while the evening breeze floated in the open doors.

"Why don't I top off your glass there, and you and I take a walk out to the pond while you tell me what's running round in that cop brain of yours?"

She started to object, then considered that laying it out, and doing so away from the board, the book, the notes, might open it up. Or shut it down. Either way was a kind of progress.

"Let's do that."

"I'll deal with the dishes so the cat doesn't end up on the table lapping at the plates."

She wandered back to the board, studied the players. That's what most of them were, weren't they? she thought. Players of one kind or another. Being someone else for long periods of time, and like a successful grifter, they had to believe the pretense while they lived it.

They walked out, leaving Galahad sprawled on her sleep chair, his belly content with the cat treats Roarke offered in lieu of fish and chips.

"So, I talked to Rose's—or Leah's, depending on who you're talking to—boyfriend from back in the day. Married, father of three, still working pretty steady on the stage."

"And how did he strike you?"

"Like he's put it behind him, like most people would. He remembers it, and remembers some details."

She filled him in as they walked through the summer evening, around flowers scenting the air, under a sky slowly deepening its blue toward twilight.

"The summary," Roarke commented. "Debra pushed herself into, interfered with, and did her best to run her daughter's life. Rose pushed back, but often caved. Debra, in temper, struck both Proctor and Eliza in separate incidents, accused them of having an affair behind Rose's back and colluding to pressure Rose so she'd fall back on the pills and alcohol."

"That's the upshot."

"Do you believe Eliza and Proctor were involved and/or conspired to push Rose deeper into her addictions?"

"It'd be handy, but no. And what would Proctor get out of it? If he'd wanted Lane and vice versa, what's to stop them? And there's nothing to indicate that. Peabody dug up the gossip crap from back then, and I rechecked. Nothing linking those two except as members of the cast. And he said Lane was seeing somebody back then, and she was. That came out after she hit. Didn't last more than a few months, but there's no indication she was involved with Proctor."

"And you believed him."

"And I believed him," she confirmed. "I believed him when he said he wanted to save her, he cared about her, and I believed him when he said he'd finally had enough. And I believe he still feels that little stab when he thinks about how he left it that night. He feels that and, if he goes back to it, wonders if ending it that way helped her along to the OD."

"Eighteen years old." Roarke ran a hand over Eve's hair as they walked through the grove of peach trees. "So troubled, and under such pressure."

"All that, but she knew what she wanted, she worked to get it. All the reviews from back then for the out-of-town performances, the VIP ones, the one that night, full of kudos for her. Not only her, but always her, right? And she drinks and drugs herself to death right after a zillion curtain calls?"

"Let me follow you here." They came out of the trees, walked toward the pond with its floating lilies, its tender young tree. "You're questioning that it was an accidental overdose. But not a suicide."

"She was an addict," Eve began, "with a mother who absolutely contributed to that addiction. And she'd overdosed before, but . . . She's coming off a really big night. The next night, opening night, that's the dream she's worked for all her life. So yeah, maybe she falls back on the bottle and pills to take the edge off. But she just holes up in the dressing room, alone, drinking, hitting more pills while the rest of the cast and crew are celebrating?

"Why?"

"Lost herself in them, in that bottle, in those pills."

"Yeah, that's how it looked with her history, with those circumstances. But when you really start scraping off how it looked, you could see something else."

"Such as?"

The breeze fluttered sweet, carried the scents of summer as the light softened.

And Eve looked back, to another time, another place.

"Say you start at that night, that point, those circumstances, those results. You've got death by poisoning. That's what it is. Twenty-five years later, pull in a couple of the same players, the same play, and you've got a death by poisoning."

They sat on the bench by the water, in the quiet evening.

"You're considering murder for both," he concluded. "And you're not looking at Debra Bernstein."

Eve shrugged, drank. "You always look at the spouse."

"What would possibly be her motive for killing Brant?"

She shifted toward him. This, she realized, was exactly what she needed. To play it out, lay it out.

"I'll get to that, but stick with me on the first. Who benefitted when Leah Rose died? Eliza Lane. Who knew about the addiction besides her mother and her boyfriend? Lane. Others may have, but we know Lane did, as she's said as much."

"For a part, Eve? For a part she'd certainly have played at least a handful of times as understudy?"

"You wouldn't think so, but she had to settle for second place. In Interview, Debra claimed Lane had talked Rose into letting her perform a matinee every week, and a night performance monthly. Take some pressure off, rest her voice and all that. But that night, before the performance, Debra pushes into her daughter's dressing room and goes off about just that. Both Proctor and Lane claim Rose was upset, but she didn't let it affect her performance. Between acts, Debra goes after Lane, tells her to forget about standing in for Rose the way they'd agreed. She'd fixed that, and she'd see to it Rose made every performance."

"That would be next to impossible."

"Yeah, but you're eighteen, you have this shot to show how damn good you are, and now it's shut down. You want that shot, you deserve that shot. Not only has this old bitch taken that away, she slugs you right before your cue. You get her booted, but you're a—what is it?— trouper. And you hit the stage, do the job."

Eve let it play through her mind because she could see it. "You have a chance to confront Rose backstage. Maybe Rose brushes it off, or tells you to back off, whatever, it's not what you want to hear. Or maybe you're pissed enough not to care what the hell she says because you've already taken care of things. You know where the bottle is, where the pills are. It wouldn't be hard to drop some pills into the bottle. Maybe you're thinking she'd just get sick—not your fault she popped more pills—just get sick enough to take her out for opening night."

Thoughtfully, she drank more wine. "The investigation didn't miss anything back then. It all added up. Yeah, Debra made accusations, but she's a lunatic, somebody who attacked her dead kid's little sister at the funeral. Somebody most of the company had complaints about. And both Lane and Proctor were at that bar, dozens of wits. It added up to accidental OD, but what if it wasn't all the way accidental?"

"A lot of supposition, Lieutenant. But I never bet against your instincts. Still, how do you tie this to Brant Fitzhugh's murder?"

Eve drew a circle in the air. "They call it an encore, right? When somebody comes out and does another song or whatever. A kind of repeat. Big party, big plans, same play, same theater. Twenty-five years older, so the mother role—which is, actually, the starring role. Your money as well as your time and talent's invested this time. It's a big one, and again, a kind of encore.

"For the next six months your husband's going to be on the other side of the planet, focused on his own career. You're not happy about that. Nobody interviewed spoke of real conflict, any real fights, just being unhappy about it. Never been separated for that long before. Who'll rub my feet?"

"Hard to swallow murder due to lack of foot rub."

"Attention," Eve said. "Being there. It's *her* big deal, and now he's decided to have his own big deal, and not be there for her. Even when she's wiping away tears, she mentions it. It's in there, it matters."

"All right."

Knowing she hadn't convinced him, Eve pressed on. "She handed the glass back. She never took a sip. Not one—she said so herself. And he routinely brings her that drink, her signature drink. Nadine even mentioned he did when she met them at some Oscar deal."

Eve lifted her own glass. "All she had to do was wait. She said something stupid and hurtful to her friend, and I'm saying that was scripted in her head. I'm saying if Sylvie Bowen hadn't suggested she do a song, she'd have said it herself. And handed the untouched glass to her husband. After she added the cyanide."

"They'd been married nearly a decade. I've seen them together. They were devoted."

"That's right. And how's he going to be devoted to her when he's in New Zealand and she's in New York? That night, I believed her. She's shocked, she's shattered, she's struggling. I believed it because she was, all of that. I believe she loved him, and he loved her. But nobody knows what goes on tight inside a marriage but the people in it."

"Well, true enough that."

"They had words about this, Roarke. She demands perfection, loyalty, and like . . . center stage. He wasn't giving that, as she sees it. He broke a bargain, like Rose had. They had plenty of words about it, but he didn't give up this vid, this part, for her."

"You found no trace of the cyanide in the penthouse."

"She flushed whatever she had it in. I did a quick follow-up with the doctor. When they took her upstairs, she went into the bathroom. Insisted she needed a moment of privacy. Flushed it, done. No trace. I believed her that night," Eve repeated, "but not today.

"She lied today when I talked to her. I could see the lie when I brought up Rose Bernstein. How she didn't tell Leah about the broken bargain. You can bet your ass she did, and lying there is cover. It's cover so she presents the image of a young, naive girl, a loving friend, a supportive colleague who'd just reacted, justifiably, to being slapped.

I could see the lies because she said that bargain mattered a hell of a lot more than the slap."

Eve shook her head. "It wasn't in the file."

"The slap?"

"No, what she spun for me today about confronting Leah about it, about telling her to keep her mother out of the theater. She didn't tell the investigators that, and neither did anyone else."

Sipping wine, she studied the pond and the purity of the floating white lilies. Tangled roots down there, she bet; you just had to look under the surface.

"I have to conclude if she did have that conversation, she kept it low-key, so it was strictly one-on-one. She lied about what she said, did, because it changes the whole story line if she confronted Rose about keeping the deal. She has to look like a kind of victim in all of that. Like she is now, playing the strong but grieving widow."

Eve shook her head. "They weren't mistakes in memories, a slipup in details after twenty-five years—I'd have bought that. She lied. No reason to lie unless you're covering up something. She's going back into rehearsal tomorrow."

"I'll give you that's fast. I'd have thought she'd take a few days at the least."

"Can't. She can't. That's the thing. This play—whatever she's done between the first time and this? This makes her circle. It's her triumph again. The first, only more so as she stepped into the part of a dead friend. And this?"

"She continued on," Roarke finished. "And the show must go on, as the brave widow."

"Yeah. She didn't take a single sip of that drink. That bothered me, had a bell ringing. But everything else pushed away from that. Until you start at the beginning and start connecting the points."

"Could she have lured Debra Bernstein here as a patsy?"

"Played with that, but I don't see it. She was really pissed when she found out Bernstein had been in her home, even more about the Tony. And there she lied again when she said, with tears—she'd have given her the award, given all her awards if she had Brant. Trust me, she wouldn't. She loved him, but she gives up nothing."

"Well now, you've convinced me, and I wasn't expecting to be convinced. How do you intend to prove any of this?"

"Working on it. I think the next round with Bernstein may give me more play. And she got the poison somewhere. Does she know a film photographer who does his or her own darkroom work? Did she commission something from a textile artist who uses cyanide in his or her work? And so on. Maybe she managed to get it off the street, but that's more doubtful."

Fascinating, he thought, how, with her points and circles, she'd made this leap. It shouldn't have been altogether logical, he considered. And yet it was.

"Where do you begin there?"

"Assistants, staff, friends, and any connection there to possible access. I believed her that night—always look at the spouse, but I believed her. Then Debra. All that's put me behind on this, so that's a pisser."

"I suppose we'd best walk back and catch up."

"Yeah." They rose. "You don't travel nearly as much as you used to."

"I don't, and have more reason to stay home than I once did."

"I just want to reassure you that if you did, I wouldn't poison you for it."

He took her hand, kissed it. "What man could ask for more?"

She worked on two fronts. That the most logical and obvious equaled Debra Bernstein. And the more convoluted solution pointed to Eliza Lane.

Either way, she needed to prep for the next phase of the interview and find ways to work around the lawyer. At the same time, she laid out her theory on Eliza as concisely as possible, revised it, replayed it, ran the probability.

She got under eighty percent on Rose Bernstein's death, but closer to ninety on Fitzhugh.

The computer agreed, she thought. Always look at the spouse.

After one more pass, she sent it to Mira for an opinion.

Considered coffee—again—as Roarke came in.

"You'll be interested to know that, after an extensive search, I've found Cara Rowan, Eliza's housekeeper, has a nephew who's a metal artist. Fairly unsung at this point, but he's had a couple of small shows, has his own studio in Brooklyn, and does electroplating in his work."

And there it was, Eve thought.

"They use cyanide for that. That's not coincidence, that's connection. If Lane didn't commission something, visit his studio, something, I'll kiss Summerset on the mouth. With tongue."

"As much as I'd enjoy seeing that—and his reaction to it—I can't see how you're wrong. It's too bloody convenient."

"Give me the name, the contact, and we'll find out."

"I'll do that, of course, but, Eve, it's gone midnight."

"It can't be. Shit!" She banged the heels of her hands on the sides of her head. "Why does that happen?"

"There's that pesky rotation of the Earth again. Shut it down now, Lieutenant, and you can sleep well knowing you're likely to close this tomorrow."

"Fine, good, yeah. Let me text Peabody, let her know I'll pick her up. We can get to Brooklyn and back, check this guy out, before we put Debra back in the box. Or put that off until the afternoon and pull in Lane instead."

She sent the text and pushed to the next step as they walked to the bedroom.

"No payments from Lane to this guy?"

"None from her accounts."

"Cash, maybe. That's smart, and she's not stupid. If she ordered something, commissioned a piece—'Oh, how does this work?'—and gave him a cash deposit, what are the odds of us finding out, putting it together?"

"Exceptional, I'd say, as you've done just that."

"Maybe. I've still got it laid out pointing at Debra. The thing is . . ."

In the bedroom she took off her weapon, emptied her pockets.

"She's not stupid, either, but not as smart as Lane. And she sure as hell isn't as good an actor. I don't buy that shock from her when we hit her with killing Fitzhugh was faked. She never went there—which is how she's not as smart as Eliza. She never went there because she didn't do it. It was the award, the payback, the basking in the celebrity light at that party. She admitted to talking to Fitzhugh. Hell, bragged about it."

She dragged on a sleep shirt.

"You had it from the beginning."

"I had it at the beginning," she corrected as she slipped into bed with him. "Then I lost it, now I've got it again."

He drew her against him, and the cat curled against her back.

"All's well that ends with the killer unmasked and justice done."

"The victim's still dead, but yeah, it's the best you can do. Except there's one more benefit to this one." She smiled as she closed her eyes. "That smug snot currently in London ends up paying a crapload for a hotshot, high-priced lawyer to do not much of anything."

The signal from her communicator woke her barely two hours later.

"Hell. Lights on, ten percent. Block video. Dallas."

"Lieutenant, Officer Manning. A nine-one-one came in from the hotel we're sitting on, for the individual we're sitting on. We took it. On scene now. We've got a DB, sir."

"Bernstein?"

"Yes, sir. We've secured the scene."

"Keep it that way. I'll be there in twenty. Fuck it," she said, and shoved out of bed.

"I'll go with you."

"No, no. I'll drag Peabody out of bed. How the hell did this happen?"

"I'd like to know myself."

In her closet, she dragged on clothes. "I'll let you know. If Lane got to her . . . How would she get to her? How would she know where to get to her?"

She came out, black jeans and boots, black shirt. With no comment, Roarke handed her a go-cup of coffee.

"Thanks." She gulped some, then strapped on her weapon. As she grabbed her 'link and the rest, Roarke came out of her closet with a black vest.

"You might as well go all the way. The lining's in."

"I have vest linings?"

"You do."

"Huh. Get some sleep," she said, and kissed him.

"Take care of my cop."

When she rushed out, already talking to Peabody, Roarke looked back at the cat. "And here we are, mate."

21

Eve avoided the endless party around Times Square and sped through mostly empty streets.

She was pissed.

Pissed some stupid, smug snot of a bitch in London had tossed her money away on a thieving grifter out of spite, pissed a judge had granted the thieving grifter—with priors!—bail. Pissed she herself hadn't found some way, somehow, to keep the thieving grifter alive in a cell for one damn night.

One damn night.

She breezed past street-level LCs hoping to rack up one more date before calling it a night. Ignored the junkies and dealers who slipped in and out of shadows to make a score.

A group of three teenage types popped up from subway stairs laughing like loons, and a sidewalk sleeper curled up like a cat in the doorway of a souvenir shop.

She pulled up in front of the hotel. The lights blared in the excuse for a lobby. Inside, a man in a dingy white tee, cotton shorts, and flip-flops shoved up from behind the counter.

He headed her way, pushing his hands in the air.

"No vacancies!"

She held up her badge. "Funny, I heard you just got one."

"Man. Man." He dragged his hands through orange-streaked black hair, then dragged them down a face sporting a nose ring and an along-the-jawline scruffy beard.

"I'm just the night man, right? Just the night man. I sleep in the back so somebody's here if something happens. Jesus, something happened. Water starts flooding through the ceiling of 201, right, and the guy's ringing the bell and waking me up. Like it's my fault, right? I go up, bang on 301. I can hear music, right, I can hear it so she's in there, but she don't answer."

"Being dead and all."

"Yeah, well, I don't know that, right? So I say how I'm coming in because 201's breathing down my neck, and now the lady across the hall comes out bitching at me. So I use my passkey and all that, and she's lying there dead. Just dead. Lying there."

He scrubbed his face again. "Now the lady's screaming in my ear, and the guy, he's making noises like maybe he's going to puke. He didn't, so that's something. So I shut the door and called the cops, because jeez, she's lying there dead."

He sucked in some air. "And you know what? They were here like pow. I mean pow! And they take one look and say I gotta shut off the water. I gotta tag the boss, right, because how the hell do I know how to shut off the water in this shithole? He tells me how, and he's pissed, and the cops say I can't let anybody in but more cops, and I've got to move 201 to another room because the ceiling's leaking."

"Rough night," Eve decided.

"Fucking A, lady!"

"Lieutenant." Eve tapped her badge. "Did anyone visit 301 tonight?"

"I don't know. Man. Jesus. I'm asleep in the back."

"What time did you come on duty?"

"I come on at ten. I go back, watch some screen, whatever, turn in. Manager comes on at eight, and I go have some breakfast."

"Did you give the officers your name and contact information?"

"Yeah, sure, but I was asleep in the back, right?"

"Right. My partner's on her way. Send her up."

"Do I just gotta, like, sit out here?"

"Looks that way."

"This night blows."

"I bet 301 agrees."

She took the stairs.

On three an officer stood on the door. Her partner stood down the hall talking to a mostly naked couple.

"Sir. Officer Fenton. We took over from Officers Carmichael and Shelby." She opened the door.

Eve stood in the doorway. And yes, as advertised, Debra Bernstein lay dead on the floor. She lay faceup, wearing a peacock-colored robe, with a lowball glass a few inches from the fingers of her right hand.

She'd used a thick blue band, one Eve had seen in her traveling case, to bundle up her hair. Red patches marred her face; her fingernails, painted cheerful pink, showed a dark blue undertone.

Eve pulled a can of Seal-It from her field kit. "Round it up, Officer."

"We came on at ten, Lieutenant. As reported by the previous officers, the light was on in this unit. Privacy screen engaged, but it's old and a little patchy. We could see her moving around if she got close enough to the window. Or standing at it. The nine-one-one came in at zero-one-forty-eight. The night man, Joe E. Clark—that's Joe, middle initial *E*—reported the DB, and we responded immediately.

"We came up, verified. Water had leaked into the unit below, Clark came up to check. The lights were on, music playing on the screen. We could see water leaking from the bottom of the closed bathroom door, so told Clark to shut the water down, secured the scene. My partner contacted you and is now getting statements."

"Did anyone come into the building while you were on duty?"

"Yes, sir. Clark just after twenty-two hundred, a man and woman together, about twenty-three hundred. A woman shortly after midnight; the same woman left about thirty minutes later."

And there we go, Eve thought.

"Describe her."

"Caucasian or possibly mixed-race female. About five-five, a buck and a quarter, brunette, shoulder-length with a thick fringe. Dark pants and T-shirt." Fenton narrowed her eyes a moment. "Sneaks, dark sneaks. Carrying a black or dark gray handbag."

Fenton looked back in the room, looked at the body. And said, "Shit."

"Yeah, it's likely. Did you get a look at her face?"

"No, sir. She was . . . rummaging around in her bag when she came out, so head down. Walked north. She was easily three inches shorter and at least fifteen, maybe twenty pounds lighter than the subject, so we just noted her going in, then out again."

"Not on you, Officer." On me, Eve thought, on me being a step behind. "Use that description, see if anybody saw the woman."

Sealed up, she stepped into the room and stood over the body of Debra Bernstein.

A bottle of vodka stood on a rickety table. She'd seen the bottle—fuller—when she and Peabody had searched. There'd been two short glasses in the room, she recalled. Now she saw only one.

A 'link sat beside the bottle. No passcode, Eve noted when she picked it up. Cheap, prepaid job, probably provided by her lawyer for contact. She swiped it open, and the notation app came up.

I can't take it. I can't go to prison.

I failed. I lost. The bitch won again.

I'm going to my Rose.

"Make it look like suicide? Why the flood? What's the point of that?"

She crossed the room, felt the sponginess of the cheap carpet. Inside the bathroom, water and a skim of fading bubbles filled the tub. A couple of candles in tins sat on the narrow rim. Two more had fallen to the floor, likely washed off by the overfilled tub. A tube of face gunk—the pricy kind like Trina used—sat on the rim of the sink.

She'd seen the candles in the room, seen the face gunk in Debra's kits.

No second glass in sight.

"Okay, I see how it played."

She went back to the body, knelt, opened her kit again.

"Victim is identified as Debra Bernstein, age sixty-six."

She took out her gauges as she read the salient into the record. "TOD, one hundred hours. Yeah, that fits. Scent of almonds present, red patches on victim's face, undertone of blue on the fingernails. COD, cyanide poisoning, to be verified by the ME."

Bending down, she sniffed at the glass. "Cyanide mixed with vodka. A bottle of Popi's Vodka on the table, about a quarter full. During the search of the victim's possessions yesterday, my partner and I found a bottle of the same brand, nearly half-full, in the cooler.

"But no cyanide then, no second glass now. Should've left it alone, Eliza. Should've let it ride. No evidence of violence or defensive wounds. A note on a prepaid 'link was left on the table with the vodka."

She recorded as well as read the note into the record.

As she finished her examination of the body, Peabody opened the door.

"Oh, hell."

"Seal up, and tell one of the uniforms to have the night man turn the water back on. It'll probably take him a few minutes."

Eve stood up, scanned the room. Not a big space, but the bed sat opposite the bathroom in that space, and the sitting area—such as it was—beyond that. Closer to the screen, where the music played—not loud, background. And the window where street noises rose up. The climate control hummed and rattled.

Peabody came in.

"Apparent suicide note on that 'link by the vodka."

Reading it, Peabody scowled. "Where the hell did she get the cyanide? It sure as hell wasn't in this room, and she couldn't have had it on her."

"There's question one."

"No way she was suicidal, Dallas. No way there. And what's with the tub full of water?"

"We'll get to that. The door to the bathroom was closed when the night man opened the unit door."

"Well, I don't . . ." She looked around. "Where's the second glass? There were two glasses before."

"This is a proud moment for me."

"She's in a robe, bathtub's going. Maybe she's going to take a soak. Yeah, look here, hydrating facial mask—she had this in her kit. Going to hydrate her skin, soak awhile with the candles. De-stress herself. If the door was closed . . . would you hear the water running with the music on, with the street noises?"

"A very proud moment. I believe you've earned another five minutes of blathering about your house project, at a later date."

"Also she didn't write that suicide note."

"Because?"

"Well, no cyanide in her possession, no second glass, but the note alone? She'd have had a lot more to say. A mother this, my years of sacrifice that. I don't see her using her last words to give Lane the win, either."

"I don't know if my heart can hold any more pride. I may have to just rip it out of my chest before it explodes."

"Do I get ten minutes of blathering?"

"No, and pull the plug on the tub. No point adding to the flood below when he gets the water on. Make sure you get it on record."

"She let the killer in," Peabody said as she opened the drain.

"That's how I see it. She probably had a shot or two of vodka beforehand. No communications on that 'link—likely provided after she got sprung by the lawyer. Nobody to tag. She's stuck in here, wandering around, maybe checking the media, whatever."

"Water's on. Not full force—if this place runs to full."

"Leave it running, close the door."

She could hear it, barely, and if she focused on it. But otherwise, no. Just like ambient sound, quieter by far than the annoying hum of the climate control.

She opened the door. "Switch with me."

When Peabody went out, she stood watching the tub.

"If I didn't know it was running," Peabody said when she opened the door again, "I wouldn't know it was running. You've got the music, the AC, the street."

"Without the overflow, we wouldn't have known she was dead until morning. Gives us a jump. Call in the sweepers, then we start going over this place."

"What are we looking for?"

"There goes a proud point. We assert she didn't have the cyanide. We add to that by proving she didn't have a container thereof."

"Damn it. I should've thought of that."

"I'm waking Morris up. I want him to get to her asap. Cab and car services, Peabody. Let's find out if a female passenger was picked up within three, make it four blocks of this address, dropped off within the same of Lane's. Between the hours of midnight and two."

"You really think she did all this. I can see how you ran it that way in the notes you sent me, but—"

"I damn well know she did. She killed her husband, she killed Bernstein, and twenty-five years ago she killed—or contributed to the death of—Rose Bernstein. And we're going to wrap her lying, murderous, Tony-winning ass up."

Twenty minutes later, Peabody all but danced into the hall where Eve ran through her needs with the head sweeper.

"What are the odds? I ask, what are they? We hit with the cab. A female matching the description given by the officers on stakeout flagged one down two blocks north. He dropped her a block from Lane's building. She paid cash."

"More arrogant than smart."

"But I'm smart, and I want those proud points back. A woman matching that description hailed a cab two blocks south of Lane's building at twenty-three-fifty-three on the cabbie's log, and the drop-off was a block north of this hotel. Cash payment."

"Good work."

"Pride point."

"Half a point. Let's go to Brooklyn."

"The artist?" Peabody scrambled to catch up. "It's still shy of five in the morning."

"So we beat the traffic. She started planning this while I was talking to her on that terrace today. She got hot thinking they'd let Bernstein out on bail, pissed, seriously pissed—Bernstein had her hands on that Tony—and she not only gets to punish her for that, she gets her patsy."

In the lobby, Joe E. Clark had his head on the counter, snoring softly. Eve left him to it.

"And now she gets to play the grieving widow—that's not that hard a stretch—and the horrified, guilt-ridden intended victim. Plus, the trouper thing. 'I won't let the company down, despite my grief. I won't let my adoring public down, despite my loss.'"

Eve got behind the wheel. "She gets the hat trick. Plug in the Brooklyn address."

"Then coffee?"

"Oh Christ, yes."

"She must've already had the cyanide. I mean enough for this, too. Where the hell did she stash it? No way Baxter, Trueheart, and McNab—plus us—missed that."

"She had another place."

"Not a bank box. Banks were closed by the time you talked to her today. A locker maybe, but—"

"In the building. Somewhere she could go in and out easy."

"They've got a fitness center, a pool. So locker."

"Too risky, too public. Plus, she didn't have one. Fitzhugh and Jacoby did. I had Trueheart check that when they searched the penthouse. I'm betting on Bowen's place."

Peabody's eyes popped wide. "You think Sylvie Bowen's in with her on this?"

"No. Lane wouldn't trust anybody that much. But they're close friends, spend time together. If Lane's writing this script, she knows she's going to stay at Bowen's after the murder. She knows she can drop in—before the murder—anytime she wants. Just hide the bottle away somewhere, somewhere she can retrieve it after we've searched her place. Or just leave it there, take more when she decided she wanted more."

"Should I get a warrant and a search team for Bowen's place?"

"Not yet." No, Eve thought, not quite yet. "Let's make sure Lane thinks she's in the clear. Let's let her get to the theater, to rehearsal.

We do this, see what we find, go by the morgue, see what Morris can tell us, then we talk to Bowen. We get a warrant if she doesn't cooperate."

"Okay. How do you feel about a bacon and egg pocket to go with this coffee?"

"Bacon is never wrong."

Peabody programmed two. "Did I do okay on the media briefing?"

"Crap, Peabody." A tug of guilt pulled along with frustration. "I couldn't take the time to watch."

"No problem, I get that. Kyung said I handled it fine, and after, Nadine texted me a thumbs-up emoji."

"Nadine," Eve muttered.

"It's still shy of five A.M.," Peabody said when Eve engaged the in-dash 'link.

"If Jake's with her, you may get a glimpse of his naked ass."

"Let's wake her up!"

When she did, Nadine didn't bother to block video, and muttered her lights on to five percent. "I have another two hours coming." She closed her eyes, moaned. "Tell me you're doing this because you're about to give me the scoop of the century and ensure my entry into the Pulitzer Hall of Fame."

"You'll be several steps ahead if you go back a quarter of a century and start working on an in-depth piece on Leah Rose—née Rose Bernstein. A bright, rising star snuffed out by the tragedy of an accidental overdose. Or was it accidental?"

Nadine's sharp green eyes popped open. "Suicide or murder?"

"You be the judge."

"You're not waking me up at—Jesus, I don't want to think about those numbers—over a suicide. Are you tapping Debra Bernstein with her own daughter's murder on top of Brant Fitzhugh?"

"Here's an interesting tidbit, and one I bet eager-type reporters who man the graveyard shift might be nibbling on now. I sent Bernstein's body to the morgue about an hour ago."

Nadine shot up in bed. Eve heard Peabody sigh when the screen showed her as the only occupant.

"Cause of death?"

"The ME determines."

"Dallas."

"Cyanide's popular these days. That's all you get for now. Gotta go."

"Avenue A's in Chicago," Peabody told Eve. "I just checked."

Eve cruised into Brooklyn and wound her way to Tyler Vance's building. He had his studio on the ground floor, his apartment above in a post-Urban box with a short gravel yard.

The sign above the studio read METALWORKS STUDIO AND SHOWROOM.

Eve mastered into the apartment entrance, currently quiet as a tomb.

On the second level they buzzed at Tyler's door.

It took a second buzz before she heard a sleepy voice through the intercom.

"Yeah, what?"

"Mr. Vance, this is the NYPSD. Please open the door."

"It's the what?"

Eve held up her badge to a security scan—a good one.

She heard locks click before the door eased open. Tyler had a lot of brown hair tousled to his shoulders and around a smooth, pretty face with sleep-heavy blue eyes and a night's scruff of beard.

He wore black boxers and blinked at them.

"I was sleeping. I don't—" Those sleepy eyes went wide awake. "Shit, a break-in? I need—"

"No break-in. We'd like to speak with you. You may be able to answer some questions pertaining to an investigation."

"Investigating what?" He started to yawn, then his eyes popped wide again. "Jesus, I'm not dressed. I'm sorry!" He actually angled a hand over his crotch. "I beg your pardon. Just—just come in. I need to put some pants on."

"He's pretty adorable," Peabody commented when he dashed across the apartment with its living space open to the dining and kitchen. "Oh! Look at that lamp. It's like it grew there. So organic."

She moved over to a pole lamp made up of metal leaves and vines and some birds.

"This would look great in our place. I probably can't afford it, but it would look great."

"You said that about that other lamp."

"I can have more than one lamp."

He came out again wearing ragged painter's pants and a faded blue T-shirt.

"I'm really sorry about answering the door like that. I was mostly asleep."

"No problem. And we apologize for disturbing you so early."

"I guess I get a jump on the day. I don't drink coffee, but I've got cold caffeine. I need a hit if I'm going to keep putting words into actual sentences. You want?"

"You go ahead."

"Did you make this lamp?"

He glanced back at Peabody as he opened his friggie. "Yeah."

"It's wonderful."

He lit up—very much like a lamp. "Thanks."

"And the wall sculpture, and the other pieces you have in here. I really like your work."

"I don't often get compliments on it at five-whatever in the morning. It's nice. Can we sit down?"

He cracked a tube of Dr Pepper and gestured to a couple floppy cushioned chairs.

"You do electroplating in your work," Eve began.

"Sure." He gestured to the wall sculpture. "Like that."

"And you use cyanide in that process."

"Yeah. I'm registered for it and keep all the records."

"Where do you keep it?"

"In my studio downstairs. Secured in a cabinet with other chemicals. Is there a problem?"

Eve took out her 'link. "Do you know this woman?"

He angled his head. "Sure. That's Eliza Lane, the actress. My aunt and uncle work for her. She— Oh my God. Her husband—they said maybe cyanide." His adorable face went dead white. "I'm a suspect? I'm a suspect? I never—"

"You're not. Has Ms. Lane ever been in your studio?"

"She—she—" He broke off, drank deep, closed his eyes, breathed deep. "She commissioned a piece—a garden sculpture—for her friend Sylvie's birthday in September. She came in to talk about it, approve the design two weeks ago. About. I don't—"

"Did you explain the electroplating process?"

"She was interested—the piece is going to be mixed metals."

"You explained about the use of cyanide. Maybe you showed her."

Dead white edged toward sickly gray. "She—she . . . She was interested. And my aunt works for her. They just love her. It's a major commission for me."

"So you gave her a tour of your studio." Peabody nodded. "Explained things."

"Yeah, yeah, but—"

"Was she ever alone in the studio?" Eve asked.

"No, but . . ." He swallowed hard. "No."

"But?"

"I have a little kitchen down there. It's closed off because of the work. I went in for a minute or two to get her some water."

"She asked you for water?"

"I guess, yeah. It only took a couple minutes. I feel a little sick."

"Just breathe, Tyler," Peabody advised. "Slow breaths. Have you used the cyanide in your work since?"

"No, actually. She decided against the electroplating, and I haven't had any work that called for it. I've been working on her piece—the design, and now the work."

"You know the amount you had at that time?"

He bobbed his head at Eve. "To the milliliter, I swear."

He actually crossed a finger over his heart.

"Would you take us down to your studio?" Eve rose. "Tyler, I need to tell you not to contact anyone about this. Not your aunt, not a friend, not anyone. I'd like your word. We could take you into custody as a material witness if necessary."

"My aunt would never—"

"No, she would never. Let's keep her safe."

Now his eyes went huge, and color flooded back into his face. "I swear to God, I won't talk to anyone."

He was missing more than a milliliter.

"That poor guy," Peabody said as they started the drive back. "She used the crap out of him. I wish I could buy that garden sculpture, because Lane never will now. Mavis would freak over it. The fairies and the flowers. He wants to tag his aunt, but he won't. You scared him enough on that."

"Once we have Lane, you can let him know he can talk to her. It'll be awhile yet," she said. "Because we're sure as hell not missing the traffic now."

Still they arrived at the morgue before most people began their work-day. If the people weren't cops or doctors—the dead or alive types.

Morris, with his protective cape over a pair of jeans and a bold red shirt, his hair twisted back in a tail, stood over Debra Bernstein. Her chest still lay open.

And Peabody stared at a point well above the slab.

"You said you wanted fast, so it's casual day. Cut music volume by half," he ordered. "How about a cold one, Peabody?"

"I bet she's cold."

"Drink."

"Oh, sure. I'll get them."

Morris smiled at Eve as he gave Peabody an excuse not to look too closely at the open chest. "A healthy woman, robust. Some decent work here and there, face and body. Death by cyanide, to confirm your on-scene. She also consumed six ounces of vodka before twenty-three hundred, and another four, along with fifteen milliliters of cyanide, minutes before TOD."

"She had the vodka in her room. I'd say about six ounces were gone from when we initially found it yesterday."

"I don't have the report yet. What brand?"

"Popi's."

"Ah. She came up in the world with her second round. The vodka she drank with the cyanide wasn't Popi's."

"How come?"

"Popi's, and others in that price range, have additives. Rye, in this case. The type she drank later and last? No additives, made with distilled water, filtered several times for purity. I'd look for a top-drawer brand. But the lab should be able to narrow the field on that. Myself, I prefer Comistar, iced, if I'm drinking vodka."

"The mistakes just keep coming." Eve paced away, paced back. "She brought a bottle with her, the good stuff. Peace offering? A way in anyway. She couldn't know if Bernstein had any, but she knew she liked her vodka. Like mother, like daughter. It's fucking poetic.

"Bring your own. Let's have a drink. Easy enough to distract her for the instant you add the poison to her glass. Take the bottle and the glass you used with you after she drops."

"Walk out," Peabody said when she passed out the soft drinks. "Walk a couple blocks, catch a cab, and go home. They have damn good security at her building."

"She's got a private elevator. No cams in it. Use it, go down to the garage. Yeah, a cam's going to catch you somewhere in the garage, but why would we check—that's how she figures it. Bernstein killed herself. She killed Fitzhugh and we caught her, so she decides to end it. Case closed."

"Well." Morris patted Bernstein gently on the shoulder. "She has something to say about that."

"Damn right. Thanks for the quick work. We'll go check out Bowen, then, Peabody, let's go to the theater."

22

Sylvie opened the door herself when Eve buzzed her apartment. Despite the relatively early hour, she was fully dressed—casual black leggings with a flowing white overshirt.

"Lieutenant, Detective, come in, please. You must have news."

"We're sorry to disturb you so early."

"Not early when I've got wardrobe and photography in an hour. I was just having another cup of coffee. Why don't we all have one while you tell me why you're here?"

Eve noted she took a discreet glance at her wrist unit as she started across the living area.

"My housekeeper's on vacation. I've got a backup droid, but . . . I guess I find them a little, well, creepy. And it's nice to do for myself for a few weeks anyway."

She led the way to the kitchen with its banquette tucked against a wide window.

"I wasn't able to spend much time with Eliza yesterday, but when

I checked in with her last evening, she told me she'd spoken with you. She told me about Debra Bernstein. I just can't get a handle on it. How anyone could harbor that much hate for so long."

She shook her head. "How do you take your coffee?"

"Black for me. Peabody's coffee regular."

"I'm a coffee regular girl myself," Sylvie said with a smile. "Have a seat, please. As horrible as all this is," she continued as she stepped to the AutoChef, "it's a relief to know what happened, and why."

"What do you think happened, and why?"

She glanced back, obviously puzzled. "From what Eliza said, you arrested Debra Bernstein when you learned she'd, well, basically, broken into Eliza's home, stolen the Tony for *Upstage*, killed Brant. Mistakenly killed him, which only makes it more horrible."

She brought Eve and Peabody their coffee, went back for her own.

"And all of this rooted in her own daughter's tragedy. Blaming Eliza for all of that, hating her because she did exactly what an understudy is meant to do. Go on."

"Did you know Eliza back then?"

"Oh, no." She laughed, idly stirred her coffee. "We go back, but not that far. We played sisters in *Body of the Crime*."

"I love that vid."

Sylvie flashed a smile at Peabody. "Thanks. I have a special place for it, as that's where Eliza and I met, bonded. Fifteen, sixteen years ago."

"Did you know Debra Bernstein?" Eve asked.

"Not personally. We never met, but I knew of her, certainly. From Eliza, and she—Debra—would occasionally crop up on some gossip blog taking shots at Eliza. Infuriating, but better ignored. Or so I thought. Now, when I look back . . . I would never have imagined it would come to this. She's obviously sick, but I can't make myself care. Brant's dead."

"So's Debra Bernstein."

"What?" Jolting back, she pressed a hand to her chest. "My God. What happened?"

"Cyanide poisoning. Around one this morning."

"I don't understand."

"Can you tell us where you were last night, between midnight and two?"

"Good God." Sylvie pressed a hand to her mouth, then dropped it. "In bed, alone. In bed before eleven, as I have another full day. I got home about . . . eight, I think. I never left the apartment afterward."

"You visited Eliza?"

"No. I tagged her after I got home, and we talked. I offered to go up, but she said she and the others—Lin, Dolby, Cela—had an early dinner in. She'd sent them home because she wanted the quiet. She'd spent most of the day making arrangements for Brant's memorial. She was worn out."

"What time did Eliza leave here? She'd been staying with you," Eve said. "What time did she go back to her apartment yesterday?"

"I'm not sure. I left about nine. I had a table read. Then interviews and other promotional business. I had dinner with my daughter, son-in-law, granddaughter. On the early side, as Clara's just three."

"She was still here when you left in the morning?"

"Yes. She didn't want me to put off my work, and frankly neither did I. And Dolby and the others would all be with her most of the day. I did check in on her a couple of times.

"You can't possibly think Eliza and I somehow conspired to get our hands on poison and use it on that woman. I don't know where she was, though she should have been behind bars. Eliza said she'd been released on bail, which is a travesty, and she was upset. But—"

"No, I don't think you conspired, Ms. Bowen. Would you show us the room where Eliza stayed when she was here?"

Her face hardened. Eve could all but hear her shoulders stiffen. "Why?"

"We can get a warrant, but I'd rather do this simply. Just clear things up."

"They're pretty damn clear to me! Whoever Debra Bernstein was working with in her botched attempt to kill Eliza killed her."

"Maybe. If we could see the room."

"For— Fine." She shoved up. "I'm going to cooperate because I don't want Eliza to deal with any more of this. She's grieving. I have three bedrooms," she continued as she sailed out of the kitchen. "My own, one I use as an office or study, and the guest room. My granddaughter has monthly overnights with me."

Clearly annoyed, she led the way through the apartment to a pretty bedroom done in roses and creams. "It has a small en suite." She gestured. "And more than enough room in the closet for the toys we keep here."

"It's very pretty," Peabody commented.

"Clara calls it her Big Girl Room. Eliza used this little suite."

"I imagine the two of you visit often. You go up there, she comes down here. Just to hang out."

"Of course."

"In the days before the party, did she spend any time down here?"

"Yes, I suppose. Yes. She helped me clear out Mikhail's things. I didn't want my housekeeper doing it. It's why I sent her on vacation. Eliza helped me, and we drank a lot of wine."

"We'd like to search this room."

"Lieutenant, you have a fine reputation, and I respect that. But this is insulting."

"I don't want to get a warrant, Ms. Bowen, and I'd like you to allow us to pursue this line of inquiry voluntarily. Two people are dead. One was a good friend of yours. Our job is to find who took his life."

"And you think you're going to find that in Clara's Big Girl Room?" Temper seared across her face. "You go ahead, you go right ahead. Then I want you to leave. I'm not going to speak to Eliza about this because I don't think she can take much more. But I will speak to your superiors."

"Understood. Peabody."

Peabody took the mini can of sealant from her pocket, used it, passed it to Eve.

"We have our recorders on, but you're welcome to watch us search."

"You better believe I will." Folding her arms, Sylvie leaned against the doorjamb.

"Take the bathroom, Peabody. I'll start in the closet."

A good-size closet, Eve thought, with a shelving system mostly occupied by dolls with their dead, staring eyes, stuffed animals in weird unnatural colors with their sly smiles.

Naturally, the kid had a big stuffed cow. Naturally.

Cubbies held crayons, markers, thick paper in a rainbow of colors, boxes of odd, chunky beads.

"We make jewelry," Sylvie said from behind Eve. "You can fit the beads together in different ways—make a necklace, a tiara, a bracelet, then keep it, or take it apart again. We make jewelry, wear it, then have a tea party with her dolls."

Eve noted the tea set—she'd seen similar at Mavis's. A bright pot, cups, plates, other pots for cream or sugar grouped on a tray on a higher shelf.

"Bathroom's clear, Dallas."

"Of course it's clear," Sylvie began. "Now, would you please leave? I have work."

Eve reached for the teapot, took off the lid.

She looked at Peabody, then turned to Sylvie, tipped the pot so she could see the bottle inside.

"What is that?"

"It's going to be cyanide, Ms. Bowen. The lab will confirm, but that's what it is." Eve took the bottle out. "Not much left. Maybe enough for one more round."

"I don't understand. I didn't put that in there. Didn't I tell you my granddaughter sleeps in here? She plays with that tea set. I would never . . ."

Eve saw when it struck. As if something inside her died, Sylvie went gray. She shook her head and backed away.

"No, no. Eliza knows this is Clara's room. She couldn't . . . My grandbaby plays here. She could have . . . My grandbaby!"

"Let's go sit down, Ms. Bowen." Peabody put an arm around her waist. "I'm going to get you some water."

Eve pulled the evidence bag out of her pocket, sealed the bottle.

"There has to be a mistake," Sylvie was insisting to Peabody. "It's not possible."

"It's more than possible. Go ahead and get Ms. Bowen some water, Peabody. Who else has been in that room since the night Brant was killed?"

"No one, but—"

"And how about the week before his death?"

Sylvie pressed her fingers to her eyes. "No one. Clara stayed over two weeks ago—nearly three weeks ago now. I sent the housekeeper on vacation right after that. She's due back the end of the week."

"And Eliza came up, helped you pack up your ex's things?"

"Yes." She rubbed at her temple. "A couple weeks ago."

"Could she have gone into that room without you noticing?"

"Of course, of course she could, but . . ." She took the water Peabody brought her. "Why would she? You're trying to say she killed Brant, or she conspired with Debra to kill him, then killed Debra. It's insane."

"Tell me about the state of their marriage."

"They *adored* each other. They loved, Lieutenant. They were a team in every sense."

"Never a cross word?"

Sylvia waved a hand in the air. "Everyone has cross words from time to time, disagreements, annoyances. That doesn't lessen love. In ten years they've rarely been apart more than a handful of days at a time because they wanted to be together."

"He was leaving for six months," Eve pointed out.

"Yes, and that was difficult, for both of them. The two opportunities—very big opportunities—just hit at the same time. I know Brant planned to fly back, even if just for a day or two, when he could. I know she'd do the same if she could manage it."

"She wasn't happy he took the job."

"It wasn't the job, it was the separation. And especially with her going into rehearsal for the revival."

"She complained to you about it."

"If you can't complain to your best friend, who?"

"Did she ask him to turn down the job?"

Sylvie opened her mouth, shut it, then looked away before she answered. "Yes. He'd done so before—and so had she—turned down a solid project, a really good part because of the scheduling conflicts."

"But this time?"

"It's his company, and a brilliant part. Just as this is Eliza's show, and a part she will absolutely own. She could win a Tony for playing both generations. It's a triumph ready for her to take."

"And he wouldn't give up this job for her, to be here with her. She was angry."

"I wouldn't say angry. She complained to me, yes, and I know she asked him, more than once, to stay in New York. She got emotional when she told me he'd insisted he needed to go, how he put a part in a vid before her. When I pointed out that if you reversed it, she wasn't going with him to New Zealand because she put the part in the play before him. And I didn't see it either way."

"How'd she take that?"

"She got sulky, weepy, snippy—then came around."

"And decided to throw a big party."

"Yes." Sylvie sipped at the water. "Yes, the party was her idea. It surprised me because she held it the night before Brant was to leave. I thought she'd want him all to herself. But I didn't think that much about it, as I was dealing with my own stupidity and Mikhail and lawyers."

She set the water down, looked into Eve's eyes. "I love my daughter, my son beyond measure. My son-in-law is an absolute treasure to me. But that child, my Clara? She is everything."

Sylvie took a shaky breath. "Everything to me. Eliza knows that. She knows Clara plays in that room, with that tea set. A three-year-old child, Lieutenant. A child finds something in the teapot? She's going to drink it, isn't she? How could Eliza do that, risk that sweet child?"

"We'll ask her." Eve rose. "If you contact her—"

"Oh, you can trust me there. If you're wrong and this is a horrible mistake, I'll grovel to her. But if she did this? If she killed—maybe, maybe I could forgive that somehow. Fifteen years of friendship, like sisters. More than sisters. But if she put that bottle where my grand-baby could get to it? If she dared? There's no forgiveness."

Tears ran down her face. "And you're not wrong, are you?"

"No. I'm not wrong."

When they left, Eve tagged Reo. "Get me a warrant to search Lane's place again. Just so what we're going to find doesn't slip through any legal loopholes. Then get me one for her arrest. Two counts, murder in the first."

"You're damn sure?"

"Absolutely damn sure. My info is she's at the theater rehearsing, so if she's not home, we'll do the search, then go arrest her. Peabody will give you a heads-up. She hid the cyanide bottle—the one she used to tap the metal artist's cyanide—in Sylvie Bowen's grandkid's play teapot."

"You're fucking kidding me."

"I'm not. I want to find what I'm going to find, then we'll send the bottle to the lab for confirmation. Get me the warrants."

"Stand by."

"The kid could've done a drop-by," Peabody said as they took the elevator up. "'Hey, let's go see Grandma.' Kid goes in to play, decides tea party. She just has to stand on that lower shelf to reach the set. That's what Sylvie Bowen's thinking."

"And that's why she won't send up a warning flare. Contact Dick-head at the lab. Tell him what we're dropping off and why. It gets immediate priority."

"What's the bribe?"

Eve shook her head. "Tell him where we found it—the kid. It's a kid, he won't need the bribe."

She paced the hallway in front of the penthouse as Peabody talked to the lab chief and she thought through the next steps.

"Not only giving it priority, he's sending someone to pick it up."

"Good. Saves us the time and the trip."

Reo signaled. "Search coming through. Working on the arrest."

"Work fast." She buzzed at the door.

Cara Rowan answered. "Lieutenant Dallas. I'm sorry, Ms. Lane's gone to rehearsal."

"We have a warrant. Just a formality. We need to check a couple things again."

"Of course. Mr. Jacoby's in his office upstairs if you want him."

"We may, thanks."

"Ms. Lane doesn't like to be interrupted at rehearsal unless it's an emergency, but—"

"No need to disturb her. We shouldn't be long."

She went straight to the butler's pantry, opened the liquor cabinet. No top-shelf vodka, she noted, but a space between the top-shelf tequila and top-shelf whiskey where it had been.

She checked the inventory panel, found a fifth of Morris's brand listed as in stock.

"Didn't put it back yet. Little mistakes, Eliza. They get you every time."

From there she headed up to the master, and into Eliza's dressing area.

"Black sneaks," Peabody called out. "Got some trace fibers in the treads."

"Bag them. A lot of black pants and tees, but only one of each in the laundry hamper." Eve bagged those.

"Here's the wig. It matches the description."

While Peabody labeled the evidence bags, Eve muttered her way through purses.

"Black bags, black bags. Why does anyone need so many black bags?" Then she drew something out of one. "But only one with one of these."

Peabody stepped over to study it. "It looks almost like a refill for a purse atomizer."

Eve tugged off the cap. "No sprayer deal." She sniffed inside. "Sure doesn't smell like perfume. And here's what else."

She pulled out a fifth of vodka, unsealed, half-full. "I bet what's in there matches what was in Bernstein's stomach contents."

"Jesus, we've got her." Peabody grinned. "It's curtains for her."

"Have Berenski send the pickup to the theater, and they can take in what else we've got." She started out. "You know, the curtain goes up when things start, not only down when it's over. How come people don't say 'it's curtains' when something starts?"

"It would be confusing, so I guess somebody, somewhere, sometime decided which it would be."

It didn't seem like a solid answer, but Eve couldn't think of better.

She pointed to the private elevator. "Let's have EDD take a look, verify its use for Lane's goings and comings re Bernstein."

"Our day may have started last night, but it's cruising now, baby."

Eve side-eyed her as they took the main elevator down to the lobby. "Are you going to need a booster?"

"Right now, this is my booster. But when I crash, I'll crash hard. I really liked her, Dallas, so I'm feeling a little pissed. Her work, yeah, I liked watching her perform. But I liked her."

"If you're a little pissed, think about how Sylvie Bowen feels. You liked the murdering bitch for a couple days. She's loved her like a sister for fifteen years."

"Yeah." She waited until they'd crossed the lobby, then the sidewalk to the car. "And Brant Fitzhugh. She freaking killed him, and he loved her. Had to like her, too. You may love somebody for a decade, but you sure as hell couldn't live with them happily if you didn't like them."

Eve pulled into traffic. "She's smooth as long as everything's going her way. Screw up or cross her, say no to something she really wants—one way or another, she'll make you pay."

"Now she'll be the one to pay for murdering two people."

"Three. I want her for Rose Bernstein. We won't get Murder One for it. That was more impulse, more heat of the moment. Maybe when she put those pills in the vodka—and I know damn well she did—she just meant to take Leah Rose offstage for a few nights. Add some bad press. But it sure didn't hurt her career, did it, when Leah Rose died? Got what she wanted, and then some. Never going to settle for understudy again."

"Arrest warrant's coming through."

"Let Reo know we're picking Lane up, bringing her in. And what we found in her bedroom."

Eve tapped her own wrist unit. When Mira's admin answered, she just said, "This is still about your hall pass."

"One moment."

She suffered through nearly two of holding blue.

"Eve."

"I have an arrest warrant for and a shitpile of evidence on Eliza Lane."

Mira's eyes held steady. "For both murders. I have your on-scene on Debra Bernstein."

"For both, and I intend to wrap her up for Rose Bernstein's. And you don't seem in any way surprised by that."

"If she did the two current murders, and I trust you have the proof of that, I'd be more surprised if she played no part in the death of Rose Bernstein. I'm going to rearrange a couple of things and observe. She won't call for a lawyer right away. And you don't seem surprised by that opinion."

"She won't think we can make it stick. She's wrong about that. Peabody will send you and the commander what we've compiled this morning. We'll get back to you."

She went to the back of the theater, into a loading area, pleased to find a pair of uniforms waiting.

Eve gave them the evidence bags, and specific instructions.

Then she made them repeat the instructions.

"Good," she said. "Get to it."

"I don't know why I'm looking forward to this one so much," Peabody said as the uniforms drove away.

Eve glanced over as they approached the stage door. "Because you admired her, then she made you like her, feel sorry for her."

"Did you? Feel sorry for her?"

"I did."

She banged on the steel door. When the man with a shock of silver hair answered, he scowled at them. "Theater's closed."

Eve held up her badge. "We've got tickets."

He gave the badge a long, hard look. "This about Brant?"

"It is."

"I'll take you up. Brant Fitzhugh was the genuine article. He'd sit backstage sometimes, play pinochle with some of the crew. He heard how it was my birthday, and he brings me a bottle of scotch. The genuine article. Brant and the scotch."

They wound through, past dressing rooms, storage rooms, equipment, by a passageway that ran under the stage.

Up some sturdy iron steps where Eve heard voices raised in song.

"Just keep going—don't be touching anything—and this'll bring you stage right."

"Thanks.

The way was dim, a little twisty—but Eliza Lane's dressing room— bold white door, her name in gold—showed clearly enough. They'd go through that, too, very soon. But for now . . .

A dozen people stood onstage, most of them sweating in dancewear. Samantha stood doing a one-legged quad stretch. Eliza huddled on the other side of the stage with the choreographer and director.

The director crossed over. "Okay, let's take it from the top. And let me see some energy. The number's 'I'm the Talent,' so prove it. Places."

Eve stepped out. "Sorry to interrupt."

Every eye turned to her. She wondered how they all felt when they knew every eye in the theater—hundreds of eyes—all focused on them.

She supposed that's why they got up onstage to begin with.

"Take ten, everybody," the director called. "Lieutenant, do you need Eliza?"

"I do."

"Please tell me you have something." Eliza strode across the stage. "Something real, something definite, something worth stopping rehearsal."

"I do," Eve said again. "Eliza Lane, you're under arrest for the murder of Brant Fitzhugh, a human being."

Gasps and cries of shock erupted around them, but Eliza only stared at Eve.

"You've lost your mind."

"No, and I can warn you, that defense won't work for you. You have the right to remain silent," she began, and cuffed Eliza's hands behind her back as she read off the Revised Miranda.

Dolby had all but flown out from his seat in the audience and leapt onstage.

"You can't do this to her! That crazy woman killed Brant."

Desperate to get to Eliza, he shoved at Peabody.

"Mr. Kessler, step back now." Peabody blocked him. "It won't help if we have to arrest you for interfering with police officers."

"But you can't do this! Don't worry, Eliza. I'm going to get your lawyer right now."

"Don't, don't bother. This is insane. I'll straighten it out."

"I'm going with you!"

"No," Eve told him. "You're not. You're welcome to get yourself down to Cop Central and wait."

"Then you can just arrest me, too, because—"

"Go back to the penthouse, Dolby." Eliza gave the order, deadly calm. "Go straight there, and don't talk to any reporters."

"But, Eliza!"

"You do that for me, Dolby. That's what I need you to do. I'll be there soon."

"Don't count on it," Eve told her.

Eliza kept her head high. "Please, everyone, keep this horrible, desperate act inside our family. Not for me, no, not for me, but for Brant."

Don't count on it, Eve thought again.

They led her out the way they'd come in. Eliza didn't speak until they were outside.

"You'll pay for this." She said it quietly, coldly, bitterly. "You can't imagine how much you'll pay for this."

"I *get* paid for this." When Peabody opened the back door, Eve put a hand on Eliza head, nudged her in and down. "But this is one of those times I'd do it for free."

23

Before they got in the car, Eve turned to Peabody. "You're going to take her straight into Interview."

"You don't want to book her?"

"Not yet. Take her in, uncuff her, offer to get her something to drink."

Peabody gave Eve the puppy dog eyes. "I'm going to play nice with her."

"You know how you played Debra? They're the same, Peabody. Under the polish and money, the fame, they're the same. Eliza here? She's probably got more brains, and she's a cold-blooded killer, but they run on the same fuel. You play her the same way."

"Yeah. All right. I see that."

With a nod, Eve pulled out her 'link and tagged Reo. "I'm bringing Lane in. You're going to want to be there."

She got behind the wheel. "Text Mira, Peabody. Give her an ETA."

"I'll bury you for this."

Eve flicked a glance in the rearview. There's the face, Eve thought, the true face under the mask. Stone-cold.

"You humiliated me, onstage, in front of the cast and crew. You wanted to."

"You happened to be onstage with the cast and crew at the time of your arrest. But yeah, that was an added perk."

"You think you're important. You think because some marginally talented actor played you on-screen you're somebody? You're nothing."

"I think I'm a cop and you're a murderer cuffed in the back of my ride. Maybe I'm nothing, but I've got one up on you, Eliza."

"You really don't understand who I am."

Once again, Eve flicked a glance in the rearview. "That's where you're wrong. I understand exactly who you are."

"I'm Eliza fucking Lane." Anger, deep and dark, brought hot color to her cheeks, and turned those icy eyes colder yet.

"If I were to get out of this car right now, dozens of people would flock around me for a photo, for an autograph, for even three seconds of my time."

"If you were to get out of this car right now, I'd stun you. That would make a hell of a photo, wouldn't it, Peabody? Eliza fucking Lane, sprawled on the sidewalk after being arrested for her husband's murder."

"Jeez, Dallas." Peabody hunched her shoulders.

"Just saying." Eve looked in the rearview a third time. Smiled broadly. "Want to test me?"

"You married a rich, important man, so you think that makes you something."

"Uh-huh. Oh hey, Peabody, remember that building, the one where that asshole Teegan Stone has his club, lives over it?"

"Sure."

"Looks like I bought it."

Sincerely stunned, Peabody twisted in her seat. "You did what!"

"Well, my rich, important husband bought it for me. Now I have to figure out—or he will, because what the hell do I know?—how to beef it up. Of course, that means Stone has to find another place to house his business and himself."

"Okay, wow. This is beyond the mag. Oh, oh, you could ditch the slick and rock it out extreme. I bet Avenue A would play there, and you know Mavis would."

"There's a thought. I have these rich, important friends," Eve said casually to Eliza. "Funny how that works."

She pulled into Central's garage.

"Mavis Freestone is a flash in the pan, riding the wave on questionable style and no substance."

Eve got out, came around to pull Eliza out of the back. "I think that's what they call mixing metaphors. Here's today's news for you, Eliza. Mavis will keep right on flashing while you're sitting in a concrete off-planet cage wondering why nobody gives a flying fuck about your autograph."

In the elevator, Eve and Peabody flanked her.

She decided to ride it all the way up to Homicide, no matter how often it stopped to let on more cops. Cops who did a quick double take at Eliza or shot Eve a what-the-hell glance.

"Make a hole," Eve ordered when they reached her level.

After they escorted Eliza out, Eve stepped back. "Take her to Interview."

Eve veered off, went straight to her office, and tagged Berenski at the lab.

"Christ's sake, Dallas, it's been five fucking minutes."

She stared into the beady eyes in his egg-shaped head. "Kid who could've found that bottle, downed it like soda pop? Her name's Clara."

"Shit. I hate getting my heartstrings plucked. Yeah, it's cyanide. It's the same as what took out Fitzhugh and Bernstein."

"Why didn't you just say so?"

"You pluck my heartstrings to get me to push everything aside and do this, I yank your chain. Vodka in the bottle is the vodka Bernstein drank with the cyanide."

"I'm feeling very fond of you at this moment, Berenski. I'm grateful the feeling will pass, but at this moment, fond."

"Ah, kiss my ass."

"Not that fond," she said, and made him snicker.

"You're gonna be fonder when I tell you what Harvo got for you."

Eve had counted on Harvo, the Queen of Hair and Fiber. "It's the shoes."

"She ain't finished with the rest, but you had it right on the shoes. Cheap-ass carpet, good treads on the shoes picked up some cheap-ass fiber that matches what the sweepers brought in from the crime scene."

"Maybe I'll kiss Harvo's ass. Those uniforms standing by?"

"Yeah, yeah."

"I need everything back here—Interview A—as soon as you can process it. She knew that kid played and slept in that room. She knew it and didn't give it a thought."

"We'll get them to you."

She clicked off and turned. She'd heard Reo coming down the short hallway.

She'd smoothed her hair, sort of rolled it up at the back of her neck. A new look that showed off a pair of short, dangling earrings. Instead of a suit, she'd gone with a body-skimming dress in a color that wasn't quite blue, wasn't quite gray.

And shoes with those needle heels that were absolutely blue and bold with it.

"What's this?" Eve wondered, and flipped a finger up and down.

"You noticed."

"I'm a cop. I notice everything."

"Eliza Lane. I thought, Cher honey, it's not every day you get to take on a multiple murderer, multiple Tony and Grammy winner, an Oscar winner. How about a sleek new look for this opportunity? You can't tell me you didn't think about that when you went with 'I'll kick every square inch of your ass before I hand it back to you' black."

"It was two in the morning. I grabbed the handy. But now that you mention it. Let me catch you up and tell you how I want to play it."

Reo pointed to the AC; Eve held up two fingers.

And with coffee, they got to work.

Toward the end of it, Peabody came in carrying an evidence box. "From the lab. Uniforms said Dickhead sent the reports."

"He did." Eve patted a file on her desk.

"I settled her in, got her fizzy water—fizzy spring water. I'm playing nice," Peabody told Reo.

"You do it so well. You lull them the way Dallas couldn't pull off."

"I told her I was sorry for the inconvenience, then went on about how I loved her in *Beyond the Grave*—that's her Oscar winner—and which I really did. Now won't ever be able to watch again. You look way uptown, Reo."

"Thanks. Well, ladies, shall we?"

"We damn well shall."

They headed out with Reo going to Observation for the first act.

Eliza sat, slowly sipping her water as they entered, as Eve started the record, read in the data.

"You'll verify you were read your rights?"

"Read to me for the express purpose of embarrassing me in front of my people, yes."

"Actually, the express purpose is to inform you of your rights and obligations. You do understand your rights and obligations?"

"I understand everything."

"Great." Eve sat, put her file on the table beside the evidence box. "So, first question. Why the hell did you kill your husband?"

"That's a horrible, vicious, ugly thing to say." Tears swirled, and a single one slid slowly, gracefully down her left cheek.

"It's a horrible, vicious, ugly thing to do. Like you told me, you're a really important woman. So let's not waste your important time. Why'd you do it?"

"You know very well that monster Debra Bernstein killed my Brant. She took him away from me. She came into my home, stole my award, killed my husband."

"Here's what I noticed, he came last on that list of offenses. Anyway—"

"Don't you *dare* demean my love for Brant! Don't you dare."

Peabody, who'd anticipated, set a stack of tissues on the table, nudged them over.

Eliza grabbed one, wiped at tears. "You told me she killed him."

"Did I?"

"You came to my house, told me. Of course, at first you thought that crazy man, that stalker, did it. Now you're going after me."

"It's like they say—whoever the hell they are—third time rings the bell."

"The charm," Peabody corrected.

"Rings the charm?"

"No. Is the charm. Never mind. Ms. Lane, there are some, well, discrepancies we have to clear up before—"

"So you attack me?" She grabbed another tissue. "I lost the love of my life in such a horrible way. He's gone because that vicious woman tried to kill *me*! I've tried to be strong, tried to think of what Brant would want me to do."

"Bet he'd say he wouldn't want you to kill him."

"I see what you are," Eliza tossed back. "Second-rate at best, over-hyped because you got lucky here and there, because you married lucky on top of it. You want another notch in your belt, that's what I am to you. Get your name and face splashed all over again, strut around like you're a big deal."

"I don't strut. Do I strut?"

Peabody hunched her shoulders again. "You've been known to, on occasion."

"You just want the power," Eliza went on. "The control. You just want to be on top, whatever it takes. Believe me, I'm going to see you crushed at the bottom when I'm done."

"Because you're not half-bad at pretending to be somebody else? Because you can break into a song and dance on cue, like a puppet?"

Fury full-blown, Eliza shoved to her feet. "Because I'm Eliza Lane. I can snap my fingers and thousands, millions of people will come for you. I've spent twenty-five years in the spotlight because nobody does it better. I'm admired. I'm beloved. My fans, my colleagues will swarm you like wasps. And when that's done, I'll sue you for every penny Roarke has."

"That's a lot of pennies. Sit your ass down."

"You will speak to me with respect."

Eve got to her feet. "In this room, I *am* the power and the control. You'll sit your ass down, or you'll be sitting it down in a holding cell, where you can get acquainted with some of the unlicensed LCs, some of the junkies and other residents of that area. Some may be fans."

"Please, Ms. Lane. Take a seat. I asked the lieutenant to let me bring you straight in here so you avoid holding."

"Very well." She sat. "But whether I stand or sit changes nothing.

I'm innocent, and you know it. You're doing this for your own advancement, your own press. My husband's dead, taken away from the world in my place. Debra Bernstein came into my home, disguised, hid in my home, then snuck into my party. She poisoned my drink, and Brant . . ."

She looked away, dabbing at tears. "He died in my place."

"Funny you didn't even take a sip of that drink."

"I'm sure you'd be happier if I were lying in the morgue instead of Brant. Perhaps he'd be sitting here now, being accused and insulted by you. And I know why. You embarrassed yourself trying to pin this on that stalker. You couldn't get your publicity-generating arrest there. You were all set to get that with Debra, and now you can't because she's dead."

Eve sat back, smiled, and said, "Oops."

Peabody winced. "Yeah, major oops."

Eve leaned forward. "How do you know Bernstein's dead?"

Eliza looked blank, but only for an instant. "Someone on the crew was talking about it."

"Who?"

"I don't know! Someone. I overheard. She committed suicide, poisoned herself. Clearly, she killed Brant, but you want the splash so you're torturing me."

"First, nobody in the crew talked about it so you could overhear because at the time of your arrest her death hadn't been made public."

"Don't be ridiculous. Things like this leak all the time."

"Here's what leaked, the ceiling in the unit below hers because she'd left the water running in the tub when you came to call. Didn't know that, did you, Eliza? Changes things. We found her hours before you'd planned."

"It changes nothing. Crew gossip, that's all. I could hardly have killed her when I had no idea where she was."

"You found out. It didn't just piss you off—and boy did it—that she made bail, but opened an opportunity." She nodded at Peabody, who took a 'link out of the evidence box.

"Right after we left the theater, EDD went in," Peabody explained. "This is Lin Jacoby's 'link. The one you used to contact Maeve Spindal in London, where you pretended to be L. W. Jacoby, Carlton J. Greene's admin's assistant."

"I did no such thing."

"Ms. Spindal was more than happy to confirm the contact by Greene's office, about ten minutes after I left you yesterday. Of course," Eve added, "Greene also confirmed he has no one by that name working for him, and no one contacted Spindal for his client's address for the files."

"If Lin did such a thing—"

"It was a female on the contact."

"I made no such contact, I had no idea where that woman was staying."

"You never went to the West End Hotel," Eve asked, "to room 301?"

"I certainly did not."

"Next," Eve said to Peabody.

"These are your shoes." Peabody pulled them out. "Taken from your closet this morning."

"You had no right to—"

"We had a warrant, Ms. Lane. Fibers taken from the treads of these shoes are from the carpet in Ms. Bernstein's hotel room. Room 301."

"Then she planted them there." Eliza pointed an accusing finger at Eve.

"It's all on the record, Eliza. We're careful about things like that. Then there's this." This time Eve stood to take the vodka bottle out of the box. "You took this to her room, knowing she'd drink. She liked her vodka. And this is the good stuff—not like the swill she had in the room. We recovered this from the bag you carried it in. And this." She took out the small vial. "With traces of cyanide inside."

"None of that is mine. I don't drink vodka."

"She did, and you knew that very well. Her daughter picked up the habit. Thing is, you like everything just so. And this very bottle is missing from your home bar. You just didn't put it back. I'm sure you would have, but you were tired, you had rehearsal today. And guess what! It has your fingerprints on it.

"And there's more," Eve said before Eliza could recover. "You were observed entering the West End Hotel twenty minutes before Bernstein's time of death."

"Who observed me?"

"The two cops I had watching the hotel. Black shirt," she said as she took it out, "black pants, black sneakers, long black wig with a fringe."

She laid all of them out on the table.

"I was home all night. I never left my apartment."

"You're a damn good liar. I'm going to give you that, but you're off script now, no rehearsal time. You don't have the words in front of you, so the lies don't come across the same."

Eve took the EDD report out of the file.

"Your private elevator was in use last night, leaving the second floor of your penthouse and going down to the garage, street level. No cams, but we have a superior EDD and they can pinpoint the time of use, and have."

"Then they're either mistaken or colluding with you, or my domestics used it."

"Nope, they need a swipe. You only need your voice to activate it. And the garage does have cams. EDD has the garage feed, which shows a woman in this shirt, this wig, these pants, these shoes, with this bag crossing the garage to the exit. It also shows this same woman entering the same way. Didn't take you a full hour to get there, kill her, get home again.

"The private elevator going up to your second floor also shows no use of swipe and the time of use. Between that we have the two cabs you used, your pickup and drop-off location coming and going.

"Care to explain any of that?"

Eliza fell to weeping. "She killed Brant, she killed my husband. I lost my mind. You said they just let her go free. I only wanted to talk to her, to confront her. I did take the vodka, I did. But after she told me she wanted me dead, wanted to finally make me pay for Leah, she poured something from that vial into her glass and drank it. She killed herself right in front of me."

"That must've been horrible," Peabody put in.

"It was! It was. I was so shocked. I didn't know what to do. I should've called the police, but I panicked, and I ran."

"Took the vodka, the glass you used, and the vial with you," Eve pointed out. "That doesn't sound like panic."

"That might explain the glass, even the vodka, but why the vial, Eliza?"

"I don't know." She sent a beseeching look at Peabody. "How could I think straight after that?"

"Straight enough to walk three blocks before hailing a cab," Eve commented. "Walking time, not running time. Then there's the water in the tub, bubbles, too. Why take a nice bubble bath if you're going to drink poison?"

"How am I to know? Maybe she wanted to kill herself in the tub. I shouldn't have gone there, but I needed to look her in the eye. I needed that."

"You needed the cyanide when you decided to kill your husband. And you got it. Tyler Vance, metal artist, nephew of your housekeeper. Talented guy, and one who keeps very good records. You could even say meticulous. He hasn't done any electroplating since your visit, so he has records showing the precise amount he had in his cabinet. We've got it to the milliliter, Eliza."

Eve shuffled out that report.

"I can see you're wondering how the hell we found out about him, about your visit, about the commission for a sculpture for your good friend Sylvie. A visit two weeks before the party, your husband's death."

"Of course I commissioned the sculpture. I certainly didn't take any poison. I know nothing about that sort of thing. How could I know it was used in his work?"

"I've got EDD checking the Internet cafés—easiest way to find out what you needed to know. They'll get there. We're really good at what we do here. And then there's this."

Eve took out the bottle. "Not much left, but enough to kill a three-year-old kid if she came across it, since it was in her fucking toy tea-pot."

"That—that's cyanide? You—you found it in Clara's . . . Sylvie had it! Sylvie tried to kill me?"

Eliza shoved a hand in the air as if warding off an attack.

"I can't—no, I can't believe that."

So much for friendship, Eve thought.

"Yeah, me neither. Trust me, nobody will. You're good, Eliza, but not that good. You killed Brant because he didn't bend, this time any-way, to your wants and will. He was looking out for his own career, put that ahead of you and yours. How could he do that to you?"

Eve smacked her fist on the table. "How could he leave you for six months, go so far away when you needed him here, with you?"

"It was selfish," Peabody murmured it. "It must've made you feel so unloved. You'd given him so much. I've read about you turning down parts so you could be with him, could stay with him in some location. To be there for him. But he wasn't going to be there for you."

"I was always there for him."

"Of course you were, of course." Peabody reached over, laid a hand over Eliza's. "You knew he was the one the first instant you saw him. He was your soul mate. And now, the revival—a highlight of your career—the rehearsals, the pressure, the demands, the need to be at the very top of your game, he was going to desert you."

"I won't be second. I won't settle for second place."

Peabody nodded sympathetically. "Why would you? You're Eliza Lane. You're the best there is. He broke your heart, and your trust."

"He crushed it! I told him and told him, I asked and I asked. He put himself first. Once that happens, it's done! So easy after that happens to do it again, to look at another woman and think, why not? She's younger, she wants me. I will not be humiliated by another man, by anyone. I will not have my needs brushed aside."

Falling apart now, Eve thought. Couldn't hold the mask up any longer.

"You'd be better off with him dead than risk that humiliation," Eve said.

"This is a pinnacle of my career, of my *life*, and he chose to leave me."

"So you chose to have him leave permanently. And why not get some benefit out of it? The outpouring of sympathy for you. Clutching your dying and dead husband to your breast, weeping. A hell of a performance."

"I wasn't! I loved him. I loved him, more, I realized, than he did me. I did what I had to do for myself."

"When he brought you the drink, as you knew he would because it's what he did for you, you slipped the vial out of your pocket, tipped it in. Maybe during a hug, a kiss. Then you handed it back to him."

"I couldn't be sure he'd drink it."

"But sure enough. Then it would look as if someone tried to kill you. More benefit for you. All you had to do was slip into the bathroom when Sylvie and the doctor took you upstairs. Flush the container. The rest of it was already down in that toy teapot where you put it when you, the good friend, helped Sylvie pack up her ex's things."

"I am a good friend to Sylvie. I've always been a good friend. I warned her about Mikhail, and I was right. I wasn't going to let Brant do the same to me."

"A good friend who put her friend's granddaughter's life in danger."

"Don't be ridiculous." She waved that away. "Clara isn't due to come back for nearly a week. I'd have dealt with it by then."

"Unless they just popped in one day," Peabody pointed out. "And the little girl wanted a tea party."

"It wouldn't be my fault."

"Yeah, that's how you'd see it. Not my fault if the kid drinks the poison I left in her room. Not my fault Brant's so selfish. Not my fault Debra decided to offer me the perfect patsy."

Eve waited a beat. "Not your fault if Leah Rose popped more pills than you slipped into her vodka."

There was shock, Eve thought, and shock. Shock that said: What the hell are you talking about? And shock that said: How the hell do you know that?

Eliza's face registered the second.

"That's insane. Leah's death was ruled an accidental overdose twenty-five years ago."

"It was, and I can't really blame the investigators at that time for not seeing through you. The victim was an addict with a history. It was her bottle, they were her pills. You were blocks away, surrounded by witnesses, when she died. She was under so much pressure. Her mother was driving her crazy. I figure, in your way, so were you."

"I was a friend to her. I tried to help her."

"Easy to say now. You were jealous of her. Understudy? Second place? Oh no, not Eliza Lane. But you convinced her to let you have some performances. A matinee a week, an evening show a month."

"That was her idea."

"Again, easy to say. Might even be true. And it was what you needed. A chance to outshine her, to grab that big break. I bet you asked her not to tell anyone, at least not until you'd shown the director you could handle it. But she told her mother."

Eve rose, walked around the table, leaned down. "She just wouldn't kick her mother all the way out of her life. I bet you encouraged her to do that, but she just couldn't. Not all the way."

"Her mother kept her an addict because it kept her dependent."

"You're probably right about that. Debra was a crap mother. But Leah told her anyway. And just like you? Debra's not going to settle, not going to risk being outshined. So she pushed and pushed, demanded, harangued, and got Leah to kill that agreement. And made sure you knew it, right before your cue. Made sure you knew her Rose would make every performance and never give you the chance to shine. And she slapped you."

"That's low," Peabody commented. "Right before you went on."

"That burned and churned. You played your part, hit your mark, but it burned and churned. And it burned more when Leah verified. Deal's off."

"'Give it the first month to get her off my back,' she said. And I could smell the vodka on her," Eliza added in disgust. "She was weak. She'd made a deal but was too weak to keep it. Even after her mother assaulted me. I knew she'd keep going back to her. She was too weak to stay away from the pills, the vodka, her mother. All addictions, all weaknesses."

"And you knew that, so you went in her dressing room, put a few pills in the bottle."

"If I did, and you'll never prove it, it would have been to make her sick." She shrugged. "If I did, it would have been to make her just sick enough to miss opening night, maybe a couple more performances."

"And you'd replace her, not just as understudy. As one of the head-liners, because you'd show everyone you were better than she was."

"I *was* better. I am better. It's not my fault she kept taking pills, kept drinking. I wasn't even there," she reminded Eve.

"It's your fault for adding what you did to the bottle. And we will prove it. I've seen the backstage at that theater. Do you really believe no one saw you go into her dressing room when she wasn't in there? Nobody'd think anything of it at the time. You were friends, on- and offstage, you were her understudy. But now? With all we have?"

"It was an accident."

"Right." Eve paused as Reo came in. "Reo, APA Cher, entering Interview."

"Ms. Lane." Reo sat. "As the lieutenant stated for the record, I'm Assistant Prosecuting Attorney Cher Reo. You have, on the record, confessed to the premeditated murder of Brant Fitzhugh, to the pre-meditated murder of Debra Bernstein, and are hereby charged with that second murder. You also confessed to child endangerment, and are hereby so charged. You're also charged in the matter of Rose Bern-stein's death. We'll go with Man Two on that one."

"I won't serve a day. I'll take the stand, and no one will believe any of this when I'm done."

"May I?"

Reo opened Eve's files, took out the photos of the dead, forensic reports, the child's teapot holding the bottle of poison.

"Seeing's believing," Reo said. "The State of New York will ask for and get two consecutive terms of life, off-planet. And I believe another ten for the heinous risk to a three-year-old child. You may get the Man Two tossed—and I stress *may* because we're going to dig up every scrap of evidence there. But you'll spend the rest of your life in prison."

Now Eliza leaned over. "I'm going to get a lawyer, the best there is, and the expert psychiatrists that come with that lawyer. I won't serve a day."

"Bring it on. You killed an icon, a man—I'll use your word—beloved. You killed him because he wouldn't give you what you wanted when you wanted it. And you were just narcissistic enough to admit it. No deals," she said to Eve. "She'll do life."

"That's what I wanted to hear." Eve rose. "I'll leave her to you, Reo."

"Lawyer," Eliza said. "Now."

"Peabody, take Ms. Lane down, book her on all charges, then allow her to contact her lawyer. Your play just closed, Eliza. Interview end."

Epilogue

She wrote it up herself—for the satisfaction. She did the damn media briefing, which was a separate kind of hell.

Eliza would get plenty of media attention, but Eve doubted she'd appreciate the tone of it.

After she sent Peabody home, Eve found Reo and Mira talking outside the bullpen.

"Well done on the briefing," Mira told her. "Or what I saw of it."

"Does she realize the wolves are drooling at the door?" Eve wondered. "'Eliza Lane, charged with two counts of murder.' 'Eliza Lane poisons Brant Fitzhugh.' 'Eliza Lane allegedly complicit in the death of Leah Rose.' Hell, the tabloids will scream it. 'Eliza Lane launched her career with murder.'"

"Take one of these." Mira held out a blocker. "The headache shows, and Roarke will push one on you when you get home. Take it now."

"Fine." She popped it. "Lawyer?"

"She actually tried for Greene." On that, Reo's voice was nearly giddy. "Major conflict of interest there, since she murdered his client. She got a good one, and one smart enough after reviewing some of her interview statements to ignore her pleas of being framed, of you wanting a career boost by arresting her, to ask for a deal. Twenty for each count of murder, served on-planet and concurrently. Drop the other charges."

"Fuck that."

Reo smoothed a hand over her smooth do. "I said that, but in much more legal and ladylike terms. So her lawyer went over my head to my boss." Reo smiled. "Which pissed my boss off. They will have her evaluated by their expert shrinks, try for diminished capacity, insanity, whatever."

"She's legally sane," Mira put in. "She's a malignant narcissist with borderline personality and well able to convince herself nothing she did was her fault, but the fault of the victims. But she knew right from wrong, knew what she was doing every step."

"They're going to rip her to shreds in the media. I could see it. I gave Nadine a heads-up because she won't do it for the juice, and she'll do it right. She'll get off on Leah Rose."

"Maybe—likely," Reo admitted. "Legally anyway, but not in the court of public opinion."

"That'll have to do. I'm going home."

"Good job, Dallas," Reo told her. "You and Peabody, good job."

"Good job all around."

The job, the case, played through her head on the way home, but the headache went into retreat.

And when she drove through the gates, every muscle in her body relaxed. She'd done the job, and the job was done. Once out of the car, she realized she'd started to feel the barely two hours of sleep, but she didn't want sleep.

She just wanted home.

Summerset waited, of course, along with the cat.

"It appears you've closed a case without any major injuries or blood loss."

"Day's not over," she said, and kept going.

The cat beat her to her office, headed straight for her sleep chair. She heard Roarke in his, let him be.

She wanted to take down her board, close her book.

But she simply stood a moment, studying it, and Roarke came out.

"Welcome home." He went to her, wrapped his arms around her from behind. "I caught a good portion of your briefing."

"They'll eat her alive—mostly because she's Eliza Lane. I'm not sorry for it."

"Why should you be?"

"If she didn't outright kill Rose Bernstein, she was responsible. She not only lived with that, she thrived on it. Debra? Offered herself as a patsy. A selfish, stupid, sick woman who wanted what Eliza had, and didn't have the talent. Didn't deserve to die for it, and hell, she got a lot of it right. Her kid was dead because Eliza wanted the part, simple as that."

Roarke kissed the top of her head.

"Brant Fitzhugh. She loved him, as much as she was capable of loving anyone but herself. She lived with him, slept with him, ate with him, talked with him in the time between her taking that poison from the artist to dumping it in the champagne she counted on him drinking. All he had to do, in her mind, was say: 'I'm not going. I won't leave you. You come first.' And he'd still be alive. That's how she sees it. His fault."

"Love, when it's real, doesn't hang on conditions."

"You gave things up for me."

"I gave up things—and was already heading that way before I met you—for us." He turned her to face him. "We compromised, and still do, though that doesn't always come easy for us. Love doesn't hang on conditions, but marriage bloody well hangs on compromise."

"I would never poison you if you had to take an extended trip without me."

"I'm very relieved to hear you reconfirm that."

"I love you." She framed his face with her hands. "There's not a single condition attached. I want to take down this board, then I want to eat outside, in the air. And I really want it to be pizza."

He ran a finger down the dent in her chin. "I'll help you take down your board, and I'd love to eat outside. I could use a slice myself."

"Good, that's all good. Let's just hang on here another minute."

She laid her head on his shoulder, breathed in his scent, felt his arms around her. Hanging on to each other, she thought, at the end of a long, hard, difficult day?

That was love. And more than enough.

NORA ROBERTS

For the latest news, exclusive extracts and unmissable competitions, visit

f/NoraRobertsJDRobb
www.fallintothestory.com